Touba

and the Meaning of Night

WOMEN WRITING THE MIDDLE EAST

Baghdad Burning: Girl Blog from Iraq
by Riverbend

Children of the New World
by Assia Djebar

Naphtalene
by Alia Mamdouh

On Shifting Ground: Muslim Women in the Global Era
Edited by Fereshteh Nouraie-Simone

Women Without Men
Shahrnush Parsipur

Touba
and the Meaning of Night

SHAHRNUSH PARSIPUR

TRANSLATED FROM THE PERSIAN BY
HAVVA HOUSHMAND AND KAMRAN TALATTOF

TRANSLATING WOMEN'S EXPERIENCE
BY KAMRAN TALATTOF

AFTERWORD BY HOURA YAVARI

BIOGRAPHY BY PERSIS M. KARIM

THE FEMINIST PRESS
AT THE CITY UNIVERSITY OF NEW YORK
NEW YORK

Published in 2006 by the Feminist Press at the City University of New York
The Graduate Center
365 Fifth Avenue, Suite 5406
New York, NY 10016
www.feministpress.org

First published in original Persian as *Tuba va ma'na-yi shab* in 1987.

Library of Congress Cataloging-in-Publication Data

Parsipur, Shahrnush.
  [Tuba va ma'na-yi shab. English]
  Touba and the meaning of night / by Shahrnush Parsipur ; afterword by Houra Yavari ;
[translation by Havva Houshmand and Kamran Talattof].-- 1st Feminist Press ed.
     p. cm.
  ISBN 1-55861-519-9 (hard cover : alk. paper)
  I. Houshmand, Havva. II. Talattof, Kamran. III. Title.
  PK6561.P247T8413 2006
  891'.5533--dc22

                                                        2004014752

This publication was made possible, in part, by public funds from the New York State
Council on the Arts, a state agency, the National Endowment for the Arts, and a grant from
the Open Society Institute.

Text and cover design by Lisa Force
Printed on acid-free paper in Canada by Transcontinental

12 11 10 09 08 07 06   5 4 3 2 1

Contents

Translating Women's Experience: A Note on Rendering the Novel

Touba and the Meaning of Night[1] is the second of Shahrnush Parsipur's novels to be translated into English. The first, her brilliant short novel *Women Without Men*,[2] was published in English in 1998, and both books, along with a few of her other novels, have been translated into other European languages. The English-language publication of *Touba and the Meaning of Night*, often considered Parsipur's masterpiece, must be considered as a major literary event, allowing a whole new readership access to the finest work of a unique and important Persian writer.

Touba and the Meaning of Night resembles *Women Without Men* in terms of its themes, its popularity with Persian-language readers, and the controversy that it created at the time of its publication in Iran. Both books, along with many of Shahrnush Parsipur's other novels, also represent a break with the literary norms of Socialist Realism that generally prevailed in Iran in the years before the Islamic Revolution of 1979. The story of Touba does not have a conventional realistic ending, and its frequent shifts between reality and imagination transgress the rules of the dominant prerevolutionary literary trends. Time is not confined to the period of the story, but rather travels to the distant past through the narrative's inclusion of historical and mythical stories—smoothly integrating, for example, a bloody tale of medieval Iran into the present. *Touba and the Meaning of Night* is also different from prerevolutionary works in that it portrays the upper class and royalty neither as entirely negative nor as simple foils in a larger class conflict. Indeed, as in many postrevolutionary writings by women, cultural, intellectual, and spiritual issues eclipse class issues.

Without claiming that Parsipur's works belong to a new genre hitherto unknown, it must be said that her texts do frequently blur the boundaries not only between reality and fantasy, but also between novel and history. She often seems to be eager to tell the history behind her stories, and the stories of her people's history—both at the same time, and often in the same breath, fast and infuriated, as if she is about to run out of time, as if she will soon be prevented from writing. And indeed, Parsipur did a lot of her writing in her available time between prison terms in those post-1979 violent revolutionary days.

In any case, the importance of history to Parsipur's fiction presents special challenges for readers outside Iran who lack an intimate familiarity with the history of ancient and medieval Persia and of modern Iran. During her journeys into the distant past, especially through the stories related by Prince Gil, Parsipur describes the thirteenth-century invasion of Persia by the Mongols under the leadership of Genghis Khan, a brutal campaign that by some accounts killed millions, reduced major cities to rubble, and marked the end of what many consider a golden age in Persian culture.

Touba's own long life begins in a largely pre-modern Iran under the Qajar dynasty, during the reign of Naser O-Din Shah (1848–1896). As a child she experiences the effects of modernization, including the encroachment of European powers—especially of the British and Russian empires, which were embroiled in their strategic "Great Game" for control of Central Asia. When Naser O-Din Shah is assassinated, power passes to a chain of other Qajar monarchs—Mozafar O-Din Shah (1896–1907), Mohammad Ali Shah (1907–1909), and Ahmed Shah (1909–1925). These changes take their place in the background of the narrative, along with such events as the Constitutional Revolution of 1906: Touba's mentor, real life leader of the constitutionalist movement Mohammad Khiabani, is called Mr. Khiabani in this story. In addition to being a spiritual leader, Mr. Khiabani is a member of Iran's first parliament and represents the elusive promise of Persian democracy. Likewise, Touba's life is dramatically affected by the 1909 coup against Mohammed Ali Shah. Touba's husband, a Qajar prince, is forced to flee to Russia, leaving Touba to raise their four children alone. Another important shift in Touba's life occurs when Reza Khan, soon to be crowned Reza Shah Pahlavi (1925–1941) overthrows the government in 1921. Along with all Iranians, Touba experiences the rapid industrialization and secularization that characterized the reign of the dictatorial Reza Shah. Parsipur takes her narrative through World War II, when many Iranians sided with Hitler in opposition to the hated British and Russians—who retaliated by occupying the country and forcing Reza Shah into exile, to be succeeded by his son, Mohammad Reza Pahlavi (1941–1979). Through the story of the next generation, and especially Ismael, Parsipur also alludes to more recent events in Iranian history, including the 1953 coup against the nationalist, left-leaning Prime Minister Mohammad Mosaddeq, engineered by British intelligence and the U.S. Central Intelligence Agency. Parsipur's novel thus traverses nearly a century of turbulent Iranian history, ending—with Touba's life—some time shortly before the 1979 Islamic Revolution.[3]

It was with careful consideration, therefore, that we made the decision not to create a glossary or insert footnotes, even though at every turn of the page the translation called for explanations. In addition to its complex historical backdrop, Parsipur's novel is replete with religious, literary, and other cultural references. Some readers may not fully appreciate how central to the narrative is Sufism, the Islamic mystical tradition whose followers pursue spiritual truth and direct perception of God.[4] The religious masters in the novel are Sufi masters, who guide the dervishes, or initiates, in their quests for spiritual truth. Many readers will understand references to Rumi, the famous Persian Sufi poet and teacher;[5] fewer are likely to grasp Parsipur's references to the ethereal girl in *Blind Owl*[6] by Sadeq Hedayat, an early-twentieth-century modernist author, when she writes about the killing of a woman in the past or during the Mongol invasion. They also might easily overlook the subversion of the symbol of the pomegranate, an image that has symbolized the feminine in classical works such as those of Nezami Ganjavi, the twelfth-century Persian poet.[7] In Parsipur's work, it is a tree that stands tall and fruitful on female corpses. Such footnotes would have been indeed necessary every time the text referred to or portrayed something from the medieval period, or some complex aspect of a society in a state of transformation from a traditional time to a peculiar mode of modernity.

In the end, we decided that the narrative would have been interrupted too often if we succumbed to the expediency of footnotes. Instead, to the extent that was possible, we incorporated the necessary information into the text.

To explain further how Parsipur has stretched the genre, we note that even with their historical tendencies, her narratives are always told from several angles, from multiple perspectives, from the points of view of ordinary people. They are also often concerned with ordinary, quotidian things—things that a formal historiography naturally overlooks. Her texts are often replete with the names of people, places, and items; with signs, symbols, and references that bring the cultures of the past to the fore and the narratives of previous authors to mind; and with a plethora of titles and personal pronouns that make the rendering of the novel even more challenging.[8] Native speakers of a gender-free language like Persian might very well be able to weave through such names, titles, and ambiguous pronouns, freely relying upon cultural assumptions and insinuations; for even the most attentive English reader, however, a literal translation would have been too mystifying. Thus, we frequently replaced personal pronouns with names.

Another temptation in the first rounds of rendering the work into English was to leave out some of the sharp digressions that we thought would be confusing to English-language readers, or even slightly disagreeable to some. These included some tangential political discussions that some critics may argue do not further the course of the novel. However, in our final draft we included those sections, leaving it up to the reader to judge. Here, more than anywhere else in the text, we played the role of mere transmitters.

The act of translation is a very engaged form of reading. It entails research, cultural deliberation, editing, criticism, and interpretation. These elements are necessary to produce a useful, credible, and precise translation of any selected text. However, a successful translation may involve a few additional elements. These elements include the translator's creative abilities, the translator's level of interest in the guest language, and the availability of a friendly discursive paradigm into which the rendered work can be placed, something like the universal discourse of women's rights.

Moreover, the interpretational efforts regarding this particular text were not always about understanding the text or the context, or about the cultural experience, or about the discursive paradigm into which it might fit. The efforts were about getting the work done well. Simply said, sometimes the meaning could have changed by assigning a different rendering to a single word that could have been selected by the author either carelessly or quite deliberately. In these instances, we did not want to embark on a truth-finding journey; we simply did our best to be practical.

In all this, we have been hoping that with a practical rendering of all the signs, symbols, and references, the appreciation of this novel in the guest language will also be enhanced by the similarity of women's experiences worldwide. Touba's aspirations, agonies, failures, suppression, hopes, and life story are too universal to be lost between languages. Concerns about the condition of women, long-lasting sexual oppression, the challenges in accepting one's sexuality, complexities in the concept of chastity, and resistance to male-dominated culture—all themes that call for a harsh reaction from the advocates of the state ideology in Iran—can also easily find an audience in other parts of the world and in other languages. The translators' hope in rendering this work is that, despite the language and cultural differences, readers elsewhere, like those in the author's native land, can embark on the main character's journey—a journey through which Touba gradually realizes the reality of women's historical oppression as she endures social, cultural, and personal hardships.

In the course of the novel, through shifts between surrealism and bitter realistic portrayal of historical events, Touba realizes that her difficulties emanate from the fact that she is a woman. Seeking answers to the causes of women's misfortunes, resisting her victimization by all possible means, venturing into orthodox religion, Sufism, nationalism, and other forms of thought to find only them all unfulfilling, Touba at the conclusion of her search for truth realizes that women have suffered throughout history mainly because they live in a world that does not belong to them, in a world where they do not even have a chance to "look for a while at a butterfly, or gaze at the beautiful wings of a cricket." She realizes that women suffer from social upheaval, religion, tradition, marriage, and a lack of power over their own destiny. All this is revealed to her inside a house with symbolically tall but crumbling walls. The walls indeed make palpable that very state of confinement between tradition and attempted modernity. Until the walls collapse, modernity cannot be achieved. And no one can do anything about this excruciating situation, not even the armed radical revolutionaries who are ready to sacrifice their lives for the sake of society.

At the end of the work, we, too, felt that, no matter how repetitive the message about the conflicts and contradictions of modernity might be, sharing the process and the nuances of the translation, as well as providing another glimpse into the work of a pioneering author, made the rendering more than worthwhile. Parsipur's works cast a stark, bold light on a rich, troubling, and complex culture, revealing aspects of that culture that we might only be able to perceive through just such fictional accounts of women's historical experiences.

For the publication of this novel in English, many thanks go to Florence Howe for her great care and interest in the project and to Anjoli Roy for her constant care in seeing the work through. Jean Casella must be acknowledged for her superb editorial work and for her intellectual contribution to the creation of this final version. Finally, thanks are due to Christine Dykgraaf for her valuable comments and suggestions.

Kamran Talattof
Tucson, Arizona
January 2006

NOTES

1. Shahrnush Parsipur, *Touba va mana-ye shab* (Touba and the Meaning of the Night) (Tehran: Esperak, 1989).

2. Shahrnush Parsipur, *Zanan Beduni Mardan* (Women Without Men) (Tehran: Noqreh, 1989).

3. For more information see, Ervand Abrahamian, *Iran Between Two Revolutions* (Princeton, N.J.: Princeton University Press, 1982) and W. B. Fisher (ed.), *The Cambridge History of Iran* (Cambridge: Cambridge University Press, 1968–1991).

4. For more information see, John Spencer Trimingham, *The Sufi Orders in Islam* (New York: Oxford University Press, 1998); Seyyed Hossein Nasr, *Islam: Religion, History, and Civilization* (San Francisco: Harper, 2003); Martin Lings, *What Is Sufism?* (Berkeley: University of California Press, 1975); Michael Sells (ed.), *Early Islamic Mysticism* (New York: Paulist Press, 1996); and Steven T. Katz (ed.), *Mysticism and Religious Traditions* (New York: Oxford University Press, 1983).

5. Many great translations of Rumi's poetry in book and even tape and CD formats have been produced over the years. Some have been bestsellers over the last several years.

6. Seadiq Hideayat, *The Blind Owl*, translated by D. P. Costello (New York: Grove Press, 1957).

7. The poet Nizami Ganjavi (1140–1202) is one of the giants of the Persian literary tradition. For a translation of some of his poetry into English see Nizami Ganjavi, *The Haft Paykar: A Medieval Persian Romance*, translated with an Introduction and Notes by Julie Scott Meisami. See also G. E. Wilson's translation of *The Haft Paykar* (The Seven Beauties), (London: Late Probsthain and Company, 1924).

8. These titles were in vogue during the late Qajar period. Mirza referred to someone whose generation from the mother side went back to the Prophet Muhammad. Anything with the word *saltaneh* referred to the crown. Defining every single one of them would have been taxing on the text. We thought that their frequent occurrence alone could convey the intended meanings.

List of Characters
(in order of appearance)

Touba, the main character, also referred to as Shams Ol-Moluk
Haji Mostafa, Touba's tenant
Haji Mostafa's two wives (**Narges** and **Fatemeh**), tenants
Zahra, Touba's maid
Haji Mahmud, Touba's first husband
Haji Adib, Touba's Father
Touba's mother
The Englishman, a European diplomat in Iran
Moshir O-Doleh, a Government functionary
Morvarid, Haji Adib's family's maid
Kazem, servant and Zahra's husband
Mr. Khiabani, a Muslim cleric and member of the parliament
Auntie Monavar, Touba's father's second cousin
Mirza Kazem, Monavar's son
Madam Esmat, an acquaintance of the other woman from the bathhouse
Madam Efat, the woman from the bathhouse
Turan O-Saltaneh, the sister of Prince Feraydun Mirza and Prince
  Kamal O-Doleh
Morteza, Prince Feraydun Mirza's friend, attendant, Touba's brother
Abdolah Khan, Touba's stepfather, a military cadet
Prince Feraydun Mirza Kamal O-Doleh, a noble at the Qajar court,
  Touba's second husband, Turan O-Saltaneh's brother
Prince Mansur Mirza, Princess Turan O-Saltaneh's husband
Shams Ol-Moluk, another name for Touba
Mostafa, Prince Feraydun's servant

Mirza Abuzar, Prince's accountant in charge of the estate in Azerbaijan
Yaghut, servant
Prince Gil, a friend of Prince Feraydun Mirza
Layla, Prince Gil's wife
Geda Alishah, the master of the spiritual Sufi orders
Manzar O-Saltaneh, Touba's daughter
Habibolah Mirza, Touba's son
Almas Khatoun, Prince's maid
Aqdas Ol-Moluk, Touba's daughter
Moones O-Doleh, Touba's daughter
Mr. Biyuck and his family, Touba's later tenants
Monsieur Boghosian, an Armenian emigrant
Dervish Hasan, a wise ragged man
Ivan, a Russian
Amin, a shepherd
Madam Amineh, Touba's father's cousin
Madam Saltanat, of Tehran
Prince Manouchehr Mirza, Touba's brother-in-law
Davoud Khan, the owner of teahouse
Abol Hasan Mirza, Turan O-Saltaneh's son, Aqdas Ol-Moluk's husband
Madam Alavieh, Mirza Abuzar's sister
Setareh, daughter of Madam Alavieh
Ismael Kazemi, son of Madam Alavieh
Prince Hesam O-Din Mirza, Manzar O-Saltaneh's husband
Mr. Khansari, Moones's husband
Mansour Mirza, Turan O-Saltaneh's husband
Tabandeh, Habibolah Mirza's wife
Abdullah, close friend of Ismael
Taymour, close friend of Ismael
Monsieur Ardavez, bar owner
Mahmood, mason
Karim, Mahmood's son
Maryam, Mahmood's daughter
Kamal, Mahmood's son
Ghadir, Kamal's friend in the slum
Akbar, Kamal's friend in the slum
Mohammad Hasan Mirza, Hesam O-Din Mirza's uncle
Abdullah, Maryam's guide

1

The sky was crazy. Rain had been falling for three days, bringing an end to the seven years of drought that had caused the pool in the middle of the front yard to be covered with dried scum. Touba took the opportunity to scrub away the old scum with a broom. So that she could continue her work, she emptied the water bucket by bucket onto the ground beside the pool. The earth no longer had to remain a slave to its dream for water.

Haji Mostafa's two wives were staring out of the window toward the pool at the eighteen-year-old divorcée, who was so engrossed in her task that had it not been pouring rain, she would have poured with sweat instead. The younger wife, naïve and childlike, was tempted to join Touba in washing out the pool. The older woman, more shrewd and cunning, was gripped by the fearful thought of what would happen should Haji Mostafa suddenly arrive home and see the half-naked woman in the courtyard pool. She opened wide the window and called out to Touba. Touba stopped her work and turned to face her. The older woman told her that it wasn't right to be washing out the pool like this, half-naked. What if a man showed up—if Haji himself arrived, or even someone else.

Touba pursed her lips and went back to work. But she had lost interest. She paused and looked around. The pool had been cleaned as well as it could be. Nothing else could be done. With a bowl, she collected the remainder of the pool water into her bucket. With broom, bucket, and bowl in hand, she lifted herself out of the pool and stood on the edge to let the rain wash her feet. Walking toward her room, she was aware that the women were still gaping at her.

She shut the door and pulled the curtain to escape the curious gaze of Haji Mostafa's wives. She took off her underwear and realized that her body was covered with mud and scum. She prepared her bathhouse supplies and dressed herself, putting on her long black chador and face cover. With her bundle under her arm, she locked the door to her room and headed toward the house gate. Haji Mostafa's two wives rushed to the window again, and the older woman asked Touba where she was going. Touba replied that she was headed for the bathhouse and that when Zahra returned she was to follow Touba there. Haji's older wife wanted to say something, because she had orders from her husband—but she did not dare. As she left the house, Touba thought that she would no doubt have to ask these tiresome tenants to leave.

The rain pattered on, light but persistent. By the time Touba reached the bathhouse, it was dripping from the edges of her black chador. Touba was neither saddened nor disappointed by the rain. From the first day it appeared, the rain had brought happiness, just as, during the four arduous years of her unhappy married life, each dry day had brought the continuing accusation that she was responsible for the drought. Her husband, Haji Mahmud, had received a vision telling him that there was a connection between the drought and her presence in his house. In the beginning, Touba could not comprehend the significance of this accusation. She was not used to thinking of herself as a damned being.

When Touba was nine, her father, Haji Adib, had returned from Mecca and told his daughter that he had stood under the golden waterspout of God's house and prayed for her life to be as long as Noah's. Her father was a tall man with penetrating, pensive eyes, a man as great as the world, and the memory of him was dear to her. In addition to the title of Haji, which he acquired because of his pilgrimage to Mecca, he was also titled Adib because of his knowledge. Touba knew this from the day that she had first been able to distinguish her right hand from her left. Touba's mother, who was an illiterate woman, had often told her and others that their benefactor "is an Adib, and that means a greatly educated person."

She was no more than six or seven years old when the Englishman came to their home. Never had anyone seen an Englishman, never had an Englishman come to anyone's home. But he came to Adib's home. Only much later did she realize the significance of the event.

Earlier, the Englishman had been galloping his horse down the dusty street when her father had begun to cross. The English horse had shied, and Adib had fallen down right in front of it. The Englishman struck Adib on the face with his whip and in broken Persian cried, "Stupid fool!" and galloped away. Asdolah the butcher had been chopping meat on a tree stump in front of his shop. Ten steps behind, he tried to catch up to the Englishman, his chopping knife still in hand, cursing the man as loudly as he could. Unsuccessful, he returned to help the other shopkeepers lift Adib from the dust and the mud, and to stare in amazement at the reddened whip mark on his face. This incident was to become a torment to Adib, a memory that would not leave him for the rest of his life. The shopkeepers surrounding Haji Adib stared at him expectantly. If Haji had given the order, they undoubtedly would have gone on a rampage. Haji Adib never gave the order, and he never gave an explanation either. At the time of the accident, Haji Adib had been lost in thought, solving one of Mullah Sadra's great philosophical propositions of Transcendent Theosophy. Because he was thinking about sitting in discussion with his friends that night, he had not noticed the horse.

Now that his thoughts had returned to the street, he noticed the people gazing at him. He also felt the burning of his left eye, reddened by the Englishman's whip. He wanted to cover his eye with a handkerchief to stop the cold wind from causing him pain, but he could not do so in front of the people. In a loud voice he said that he would show the Englishman such retaliation that it would be written down in the stories. Filled with determination, he started walking. The shopkeepers followed him silently, but also with determination. After five or six steps, he turned around and assured everyone that the Englishman would be whipped there and in front of

3

them, but now it was best that they return to their work. He walked away quickly, and his anger grew deeper within him with every step.

By the time he arrived at Moshir O-Doleh's home he was flushed with rage. Moshir O-Doleh's servant was shocked by the unannounced arrival of the guest, and in such an extraordinary state. The servant directed Adib to the parlor. There, Adib's anger gradually turned to a confused agony over the whole situation.

The room in which Adib sat was furnished in European style. All around the room were various easy chairs and other fringed furniture. Paintings depicting scenes of Swiss mountains and European cities hung on the walls. The house had electricity, and it glowed with the light of immense crystal chandeliers. It truly belonged to someone with the name Doleh, which was a title given to those affiliated with the government. Haji seated himself on the edge of one of the upholstered chairs. Numbness and exhaustion overcame him as he waited.

His host finally arrived, apologized for his delay, and the two men drank tea and ate some pastries. Adib was beside himself. Though he searched for words to describe the event, he did not feel he could demean himself by complaining as the peasants did. But neither was he a warrior who could go out and claim what was his right. He explained to his host that their country and the fundamental and constitutional rights of the people were in the hands of the great men, a segment of whom were educated. If these men did not exist, then the wheels would stop turning, the peasants would grow impatient, and chaos would reign.

Moshir O-Doleh listened to him with great interest and agreed with everything he said. With a sense of degradation and humiliation, Adib continued by recounting the story of the Englishman. It was with great difficulty that he overcame the trembling in his hands and his voice. He was trying to say that he considered himself neither great nor important, but if he could be whipped by an Englishman, in front of enemies and friends alike—he, who carried the robe and turban of an educated man—then what would the people think? What could happen?

Moshir O-Doleh must have realized the significance of the problem, for his anger was now as deep as Haji Adib's. He spoke with resounding rhetoric, and in the end he promised to bring the incident to the attention of His Majesty Mozafar O-Din Shah, and to pursue the English culprit through the British ambassador and give him his due. He added that things like this should not happen at the threshold of the twentieth century.

On his way back home, Haji Adib recounted his visit with Moshir O-Doleh to the shopkeepers in the street, emphasizing that they would soon see the results. He had calmed down by the time he arrived home at sunset.

The Englishman came the following week. The day before his arrival, European furniture was delivered to Haji Adib's home, with no prior notice. Moshir O-Doleh's secretary apologetically explained that Europeans were not used to sitting on the floor. And it would not be appropriate for the Haji Adib to sit on the floor with the Englishman's head higher than his own.

He also reported that, while His Excellency Moshir O-Doleh sent his regards, he wanted to mention respectfully that the culprit was not an Englishman but a Frenchman. His Excellency had been very diligent in trying to find the Englishman through the British Embassy, but to no avail. Then another Englishman told him that a Frenchman had been heard reciting the story of the incident. His Excellency pursued the matter through the French Embassy, and the culprit was found. Nevertheless, the European culprit continued to be called the Englishman, even by the secretary himself.

The Englishman was coming to apologize personally to Haji Adib. In expectation of his arrival, twenty-four hours of absolute frenzy reigned in the old-fashioned house. To make things a little easier, Moshir O-Doleh sent his personal servant, who was familiar with serving Westerners, in order to make sure that no mistake would occur.

Haji Adib's wife, Touba, and the younger children, together with the maid, Morvarid, were all seated behind the curtain that separated the living room from the salon so that they could view the Englishman. As Haji walked back and forth in the living room, he heard a knocking at the front gate. Moshir O-Doleh's servant opened the door and directed the Englishman to the salon.

The man wore a riding suit, and the spurs on his boots made loud metallic sounds. He had blue eyes and colorless skin, and his hair was blond. Haji's wife turned instinctively to look at Touba. She wanted to know if her daughter's hair was lighter than the Englishman's. Touba had been born with blond hair and was different in this respect from all her brothers and sisters. The Englishman's hair was lighter. In fact, his hair was golden, while hers was more of a strawberry blond. The child paid no attention to these matters. She was totally absorbed in the Englishman.

The servant poured tea, then signaled for Haji to enter. Haji drew aside the curtain between the two rooms, and the Englishman stood up and bent his head slightly. He smiled and stretched his hand toward Haji. Haji shook his hand in a Western manner. Then the two men sat facing each other.

The Englishman gave a brief speech in his own language—not one word of which was comprehensible to Haji Adib, who had no alternative but to listen through to the end with a smile. The absence of a translator was deeply felt. Haji Adib assumed that the Englishman was asking his forgiveness. In response, Haji Adib uttered a few distracted sentences of understanding and forgiveness while staring at the man's riding boots, which somehow defiled the carpet. At the same time, he looked at his own bare feet. He had not thought of putting on shoes for the Englishman. He considered the Englishman's act bold, though he had, in this very brief time, come to learn a few of their customs. He was wavering between viewing this act as a new insult or disregarding it, when suddenly the Englishman rose, took a small box out of his pocket, and stepped toward Haji to put the box in his hands. Haji Adib stared at the box with amazement and turned questioning eyes toward the Englishman. The man spoke, gesturing to Haji Adib that he should open the box. Haji Adib removed the cover and found a ring with a large diamond in it. The Englishman apparently had said that the ring was a gift for the lady of the house, but Haji Adib, not comprehending a word, looked at it in bewilderment. The sparkling glow of the diamond caught the eyes of Haji's wife, and she involuntarily pinched her daughter's back.

Haji Adib wanted to return the present. He uttered some words refusing the gift. The Englishman could not understand and merely smiled. Finally, Haji Adib also had to gesture. He put the ring to his lips and kissed it, then touched it to his forehead. In his mind, this was the way to show his gratitude. Then he stood up and put the box on the Englishman's knees, and repeated, "No, no! Never! It is impossible!" The Westerner seemed to understand some of the words. He tried to return the present to Haji Adib, but Haji Adib again adamantly refused. The man put the box in his pocket and shrugged his shoulders. It was time to go. He stood up, spoke a few words, bent his head slightly. They shook hands again, and the Englishman departed.

The shopkeepers had gathered around the arched entry where the Englishman had tethered his horse. They watched him bend his head to avoid hitting the door frame as he exited, and their eyes followed him as he calmly led the horse away from Haji's undistinguished house. The people whispered among themselves as the Englishman calmly mounted his horse and rode away at a walk, disappearing at the end of the alley.

The next couple of hours at Haji Adib's home were spent entertaining the neighborhood and recounting details of the visit. The part about the diamond and Haji Adib's rejection of it was very well received. However, that night Haji Adib's wife nagged at him. She could not forget the glow of the diamond. Haji Adib, who never shouted, now screamed. How could he possibly accept a gift from someone who had lashed him with a riding whip? But the woman sulked, and a week passed before husband and wife spoke to each other again.

For a few months after this incident, there was a great deal of coming and going. Haji Adib was invited many times to the homes of Moshir O-Doleh and other important people. It seemed that elite society wished to spread its protective umbrella over the head of a man who was a distinguished retainer of the old sciences. At the same time, through these gatherings, Haji Adib came into contact with the new sciences. He had known, of course, that the earth was round, but when he saw the large globe at Moshir O-Doleh's home for the first time, he was shaken. Haji Adib was introduced to the story of Christopher Columbus and other discoverers. Moshir O-Doleh explained to him how everything had been turned upside down and the state of things was growing worse, proclaiming it was now a fact that one needed to adapt to Western ways, or else become subservient to Westerners.

Soon the excitement of all the socializing died down. Haji was not cut out for these comings and goings, and his limited income was also a consideration. Once more, he returned to the privacy of his own home and to the chests that contained his books. Gradually the episode of the Englishman settled into the deeper parts of his being. His ever-present thirst for learning about the mystic Mullah Sadra had abated. In fact, it had been a long time since he had thought of him. In the afternoons, dressed in his cape, he walked back and forth in his courtyard and thought instead of the roundness of the earth. What most excited him was not Columbus's voyage, but the idea that because of the earth's roundness, there would suddenly appear an Englishman at his house and he would have to furnish his home in Western furniture and hang Western-style paintings on the walls. All of this because the earth was round. At Moshir O-Doleh's home he had also met Western-oriented Iranian gentlemen. Though he could deny neither their existence nor the fact that they were growing in number every day, he did not like them.

The question about the shape of the earth continued to weigh on his mind. Everyone now knew that the earth was round. But the sky—well, perhaps it was four-cornered? No. It couldn't be four-cornered; the sky was also round, as every schoolchild knew. The sky was round, so below the earth there was also blue sky, as blue as the sky above. But if that were true, the sewer wells dug on this side of the earth could open up on the other side facing the sky. And the bodies of the dead were not actually buried in the earth, but only suspended in a heap of dust and stone. And the whole planet, the earth, turned under a motionless sky. Who knows? Perhaps it was not motionless after all.

During his years at the seminary school, as a teenager, Haji Adib had believed that the sky was the husband of the earth. Haji loved the sleeping lady earth, especially in autumn and winter. In the winter, when snow covered everything, he thought of the sleeping lady earth who cradled wakefulness in her sinews until the sudden tremble of thunder and rain in the spring. In autumn—which was the spring of the mystics, according to his father—he would go on long walks to hold communion with the clean, quiet, and motionless lady. Without knowing it, he was in love with the earth. He had a feeling of support for her, even though he knew that in the end it would be this same earth's job to take him into her, to disintegrate and to digest him. Still, in his mind Haji supported the earth. His hidden excitement would reach its peak when, in his games of fantasy, he imagined himself higher and grander than the lady earth. There could be no doubt that the eternally motionless lady, half asleep and half awake, needed infinite protection. And yet, how could the lady who was so large, so very large that she was perhaps infinite—how could she have a protector? A grander thing could not be conceived. The bittersweet sadness that filled him at the discovery of his own smallness seemed odd even to him. In those days there had been a vague rumor about the roundness and finiteness of the earth, but his loving feelings for her prevented the young man from believing it. Perhaps this was the reason he had not learned the new sciences. And since he did not discuss these matters with anyone, he was naturally categorized among the scholars of the old school. Coming home from school every day and passing the cellar rooms of his parental home, he could hear the women of the family talking, continuously and relentlessly, as they wove their carpets. The sound of their shuttle combs on the looms created a delicate rhythm that accorded with the laws of spring, summer, autumn, and winter. Haji was also the protector of these women. There was no grandeur here to frighten him. He thought, "We have our own four walls." And even in the near-infinite grandeur of the lady earth, he felt that his four walls had a place of their own. His parental courtyard had rectangular garden patches and an octagonal pool in the middle. Deep in his mind, he felt that he stood at the center, where the pivot held the wheel, turning the sky dome unceasingly.

He remembered the chaos of war in the city of Herat, and the flood of deserters, the hunger, and the inflated food prices. He remembered how he had thought that if only he could spread his body on the earth so it would cover these four walls, if only he could for one second take her with love and aggression, then all wars would end. People would become calm. They would look after their own business, and there would never be famine. And after that loving domination, he would have only to give orders, and the lady would submit. She might give birth, she might not; she might bear fruit, she might not. Whether the sky poured rain or not, everything would be at his command.

When his father died after a long illness, he was left with the responsibility for the many women in the family, those who did their weaving in the cellar of the house. They were from the city of Kashan, where weaving was a tradition. His brothers were all in the carpet business, but he had turned to the sciences. Every time he entered the house and announced his arrival by invoking the name of God, the women would run to different corners to cover their hair. Haji enjoyed their imposed silence when he was there. And without knowing how or why, he cared for their affairs. He would arrange for the girls' marriages and find wives for their sons. In order to take care of everyone's needs he spent his own youth without a wife. Unknowingly, he had married the lady earth. And though he did not confess it, he feared her. He was afraid of her chaotic laws and her famines. At the age of fifty, when he finally married his illiterate wife, he actually enjoyed her ignorance and simplicity. A single sharp glance was enough to put the woman in her place, and the turning wheel of life's activity continued.

After the incident of the Englishman, having paced the yard of his home for many long days, Haji Adib finally came to the conclusion that women do eventually lose their innocence. In fact, the lady was never asleep, nor even half asleep. Rather, she was always awake and spinning frantically. It was just this turning that caused the seasons to follow one another, floods to occur, and droughts to descend.

The rhythmic sound of the shuttle comb on the loom now implied something different. Haji Adib thought about the women,

"They can think." Something had been shaken in him again, just as it had the first time he had seen the globe. Haji Adib thought, "Very well, you know that the earth is round, you knew it very well. But then why so much anxiety?" This knowledge threw him rapidly into depths of thought. In his studies he had read that some of the Greek philosophers had hypothesized the roundness of the earth. He knew that the scientists of the East also had knowledge of this fact. At least, a few of them knew it. Then Galileo had come and proven it. Haji Adib knew all of this, yet he wanted to continue believing in the squareness of the earth.

He sat on the edge of the octagonal pool and leaned his head on his left arm. He needed to understand why he wanted the earth to remain square. Impatiently, he wanted to throw aside any thought of the sleeping lady earth. But the thought would not leave him, spinning in the sphere of his mind. Who was it who had said that servants were merely tools that spoke? Haji Adib had at last found a thought to keep him from dwelling on the sleeping lady of the earth. Who had said it? Perhaps it was a Roman. He raised his eyebrows, but it would not come to him. He could not remember.

Who was it who had said, "Let us shut the books and return to the school of nature"? Again, his memory failed him. What had been the use of all his reading? he thought.

On the ground, ants were coming and going in a straight line. Haji Adib placed his index finger in the way of one of the ants. The ant stopped, shook its antennae, then climbed up his finger. Now that the earth was round, everything took on a different meaning. The ant walked aimlessly up and down Haji Adib's finger. Without a doubt, Rumi had been right: Nature progressed, ascended, and was always becoming. But did an ant think? Perhaps it had some kind of thought process. Not everything could be Haji Adib's sole possession, particularly not thought.

He put his finger back on the ground and the ant climbed down and joined the line of its friends. It seemed as though the ant was telling them something. Every once in a while it would stop in front of one of the other ants and move its antennae in response to the other one's, and then they parted quickly. Haji smiled. Possibly they were informing each other about a pink moving wall. The ant did not have an image of Haji Adib, even if it could think. But somehow, fearfully, it understood him.

Haji Adib went to look at the small hill the ants had made. He thought, "What about dust? Does dust think?" For the earth turned, and everything on it turned with it. And each individual, minute item was capable of thought, and also rotated, just as the larger principle did, the earth itself. Even a tree was therefore a whole, and would have its own kind of treelike thought process. And its parts, perhaps each in its own wholeness, would think separately, so that the parts that formed the roots and descended into the depths of the earth had the tendency to grow downward, and the parts that were branches had the desire to ascend; they were parts and whole alike.

Haji Adib knew he did not have to worry about the thought process of dust particles. Some of the laws of this rotating living being were clear. If at the end of February one planted the proper seeds, by mid-spring one would have a garden full of colored pansies. Pansies also had their own thought process, and so did water and dust. All together, they created an exhilarating combination. To possess this much knowledge, he thought, was enough for now.

Then Haji Adib thought, "I am old." His heart sank. There was not much time left to spend on the subject of becoming and metamorphosis, or the spirit of dust in part and whole, or to contemplate the trees as a whole or the minute parts making up the whole. He thought that probably each, in its own minute society, had a few Haji Adibs and Moshir O-Dolehs and Englishmen who fought each other. He laughed and imagined that probably Asdolah, their local butcher, chopped their meat for them. And then he laughed loudly again.

Suddenly the rhythmic sound of the shuttle comb stopped in the cellar. Haji Adib could no longer hear the soft conversations of the women. The sun had not yet reached the middle of the sky. Haji Adib still sat on the edge of the octagonal pool, his fist under his chin. He turned his head around and, through the sharp angle that formed between his head and his arm, looked in the direction of the cellar. The women had gathered by the cellar window, staring in his direction, and they were whispering. He had the feeling that they were talking about him. He remembered that just a few seconds ago he had laughed, loud and without inhibition, in a manner that was not appropriate to his position, and that the women had never seen such behavior in him. As he slowly tapped his foot on the ground, he thought, "They think. Unfortunately, they think. Not like the ants nor like the minute parts of the tree, nor like the particles of dust, but more or less as I do." He was certain, however, that they would never have thoughts about Mullah Sadra.

Suddenly he was shaken again, for of course they could think about Mullah Sadra as well. Had that not been the case with that rebellious and audacious woman who had lived in their town when he was a child, who had created all that uproar and sensation? People said that she was a prostitute, but they also said that she was learned. How much talking there was about her! He remembered someone telling his father that she was the messiah.

The women were laughing behind the cellar window. Haji thought disparagingly that they were behaving with typical women's foolishness. One pushed and the others burst out laughing; one tick-led while the other tried to get away. If there had not been a man in the house, their laughter would probably have been heard all over. Undoubtedly some of them were going crazy for not having a hus-band, but it was not possible to find husbands for them. They were dependent on Haji Adib, and there was not a man available at the moment who was rich enough to take one of them. Besides, if they did get married, who would then weave the carpets? For that, he couldn't bring strange women into the house. They might then par-ticipate in some perverse activities with one another.

Haji Adib pressed his lips together in anger. He decided, "Yes, the earth is round. Women think. And soon they shall have no shame." A small cloud covered the sun, a gust picked some dust and twigs off the ground. "That is the way it is. As soon as they discover they are able to think, they shall raise dust. The poet Hafez of Shiraz was right, 'This witch was the bride of a thousand grooms.'" He suddenly realized why the earth had to be square, why it had been considered unmoving, and why every man had the right to build a fence around his land. If they left this prostitute to her own devices, she would constantly spin around and throw everyone off balance. Everything would then be chaos.

With a sharp, aggressive gesture, Haji Adib turned toward the cellar. The women's murmuring suddenly stopped. He heard their footsteps as they returned to their weaving looms. The clouds had moved away from the sun. Haji felt angry and humiliated. Most of all, he felt afraid. He felt the day would soon come when the Englishman would appear and tell his own version of the story, just as he had shamelessly brought a diamond ring for the lady of the house, his wife. How dare he?

Suddenly, Haji Adib stopped his pacing. He turned and looked at his daughter, who had sat down by the side of the pool and was attracting the fish by splashing the water with her fingers. Her curly golden hair, uncombed and disheveled, glowed in the sun. It shone like a rainbow. It was necessary that Haji Adib tell his daughter everything before the Englishmen did. His wife could no longer be educated, but it was not too late for his daughter. Then, even if the Englishmen did tell her their own version, it would not have the same effect. His daughter, with all her intelligence and her clever questions, needed to know.

Haji Adib called Touba to him. The little girl ran toward her father. In the room, they sat across from each other and Haji Adib explained to her that from this very day forward she must begin her education. They would begin with the Qur'an and the alphabet and read Sadi's *Rose Garden*. The first sentence that the girl learned remained in her memory forever: "Touba is a tree in paradise."

The child learned that the earth is round. She had never thought what kind of a thing the earth was. Her father brought her a globe upon his return from a pilgrimage to the holy sites in Syria. A disturbing week passed before she was able to work out how all those large objects could fit on such a small globe. It was particularly necessary that she learn where Russia and Prussia were located, and that England was only a small island at the end of the world. Though its people had golden hair like hers, they were not used to washing their bottoms, and if one were to sit too close to them they would emit a bad odor. The Russians also smelled, but God had created the Prussians with a good smell. The French had neither a bad smell nor a good smell. Haji Adib explained his political views to the girl through associations of smell. Though the child paid careful attention to her father, she nevertheless had her doubts—which of course she never revealed to him. Without her knowing, however, her delicate lips would press together just like her father's, as though she were continuously working on a grave problem. Her eyes stored the glow of her father's eyes. Her head often leaned forward as she gazed on the angles and corners of the room. By the age of twelve, at the time of her father's death, she had stopped laughing altogether.

In this world, there were men who received revelations. These men grew in the wombs of women who were as pure and innocent as the Holy Mary. Haji Adib had chosen Holy Mary as the preeminent model among holy women. It was she whose pregnancy had occurred in absolute virginity, just as the earth had been the unblemished wife of the sky; in fact, this belief filled his mind. God had impregnated her by the Holy Ghost in the bathhouse. The angel had appeared to her in the body of a man. The girl, who had always swept God's mosques and watered the gardens in servility, had covered her nakedness at the appearance of the stranger. God's angel, bearing His gift, had placed the divine seed in her womb.

Haji Adib went on to explain that the birth of this child had created a distance between Mary and God. Prior to this event, she ate of the fruit of paradise. Now that the child had been born under a tree, Mary had to shake the tree to eat its dates. There came no more fruit from paradise, and the angel told her, "Your love for your son has reduced your devotion to God." Haji Adib read the chapter of Mary in the Qur'an to his daughter five times so that she could decipher the words and understand their meaning. Haji promised that if she memorized the chapter, he would give her five golden coins to hang on the chain she wore around her neck. Touba promised her father she would memorize it, and she spent a week doing so. She told her father that she would allow nothing, not even her child's love, to replace her love for God.

Touba's education was interrupted by her father's death. They had read the Qur'an in its entirety a few times. She knew the meaning of some of the shorter chapters. She had read both of Sadi's books, *The Rose Garden* and *The Orchard*, and she was able to recite ten or twelve of Hafez's sonnets, but that was all. From the time of her father's death until she turned fourteen, she busied herself with two things: She wove a carpet for her dowry. And, whenever she had the time, she lay on her back and stretched her arms open so the angel of God could appear to her and plant the divine seed in her.

As the oldest child, she had to grow up very quickly. Because she was the only educated member of the family, she took over the leadership of the household in the absence of her father. Her mother had no opinions of her own; and a sister, who was born with the mark of holiness upon her, as well as her brothers, all followed her orders. Touba's younger sister, when she was still just seven years old, performed her prayers regularly, and she was fasting like an adult by the age of nine.

Touba had come to understand that if she swept the house every day and kept at her weaving, with God's love she would be able to receive His child. She said her prayers and fasted, but nothing happened.

Every week on Thursday afternoon, Haji Mahmud, her father's nephew, would come and sit behind the fly screen of the room, and the boys, who had just started going to school, would stand in front of him politely and report their various activities to him. Haji Mahmud would ask after the well-being of the ladies, and then he would slide over a purse full of money for the week's expenses. In this way, he oversaw their affairs from outside the house.

A suitor was now interested in marrying Touba's mother. Two years had passed since her husband's death, and her relatives had sought this man out for her. But every time she tried to discuss the matter with Haji Mahmud she became tongue-tied and anxious. The girl noticed that every time the suitor, accompanied by the relatives, came to their house, her mother made herself up and used eyeliner. Although the man never saw the woman, she nevertheless put on her best dress and changed her veil, used blush on her cheeks and made herself more beautiful.

The suitor sat in the guest salon, and Touba's mother, with her relatives and her family, sat in the other room. The suitor spoke from behind a curtain. He was a sergeant, and he talked about military life. He would tell them of that week's riding parade and of next week's military maneuvers. He reported important events, and the women sat listening with their mouths open. In fact, the man transformed her mother's feelings like a cool summer breeze. Although she was sitting behind the curtain, she covered her face and laughed into her hands. She felt embarrassed in front of her children and her relatives. She would bend down to pick a bit of dust or a thread from the carpet, though often there was nothing there. Touba decided to help make things more comfortable for her mother.

One Thursday afternoon, two years after her father's death, the girl sat behind the curtain in order to assist her mother in her predicament. But she suddenly realized that the problem was more complicated than she had imagined. It was very difficult to engage in this type of intimate conversation with Haji Mahmud, who was a very serious man, and on this day he spent a longer time than usual discussing matters with the boys. At last, just as the girl had gathered her nerves and was about to open her mouth, Haji Mahmud cleared his throat and began speaking. He said there was an important matter he must discuss with the lady of the house.

The woman, sitting across from Touba, turned white and looked at Touba in desperation. Touba nodded, and her mother could only say, "I beg of you," before listening in silence. Haji Mahmud explained that it had been three years since his wife passed away, and his house was now managed by his old and faithful maid, Zahra. His commuting so often to Haji Adib's home did not leave the right impression. Therefore, if the lady cared to, she could become his wife so they could have a relationship that was proper in the eyes of the public—so that he would be *mahram*, the way a husband or someone related by blood is to a woman. He could then manage the affairs of their household better as well.

The woman began to tremble and scratch her cheeks, holding her breath in silence. Touba suddenly decided to speak in place of her mother. She explained that the lady, her mother, already had a suitor asking for her hand and that the suitor was related to her. If they were to refuse him, bad feelings would develop among the rela-

17

tives. But if Haji Mahmud were interested, she herself was willing to marry him and thus solve the problem of the public's probing eyes.

Haji Mahmud, who was about fifty-two or fifty-three years old, thought of his own daughters and sons, all older than Touba. The long moments were filled with a heavy silence. When Haji finally spoke, his voice had changed from its usual dry and unfriendly tone. Trembling, Haji said that he believed the respectful daughter of Haji Adib was much too young for a man of his age, who had seen fifty-two years. The girl answered with simplicity that she saw no problem in the matter, considering the primary issue was to legitimize his visits.

And so Touba endured a very quiet and colorless wedding, marrying Haji Mahmud only to spend four cold, lifeless years with him.

The first problem arose in bed on the wedding night with the discovery of Touba's golden hair. An outspoken fourteen-year-old girl who personally proposed marriage to a man—for her also to be beautiful and, above all, have golden hair was just too much! If these matters were discovered, she would have thousands of devoted lovers. A hundred times before the wedding night Haji Mahmud had said to himself, "She probably has a defect." Then he discovered that the girl had no defects whatsoever. So it was that he acquired his habit of harshness, as a protection against her beauty and youth. He would never use a kindly word or express loving feelings toward her. In a single unguarded moment he had said, "Your hair is golden"— and then, immediately, in order to cover up his mistake, he had added, "just like a brass teapot."

Peace in the country was disturbed by demonstrations demanding a constitutional monarchy. Haji Mahmud was constantly thinking of the British and the Russians. There was famine everywhere. Like a good merchant, he filled all his storage spaces so there would be plenty of flour in the house. But the anxiety of being unable to predict the future drove him crazy. Rainfall was scarce. People were dying in multitudes from the plague, typhoid fever, and hunger. And it was all Touba's fault. Why? Not even he himself understood this entirely. He did know that women who are blessed bring happiness and plenitude. With this woman had come famine and devastation. Haji Mahmud detested three people: the British, the Russians, and Touba. At times he would reveal these thoughts to Touba, particularly her connection to the absence of rain.

Touba had no responsibilities at her husband's home. Every household chore was seen to by Zahra, Haji Mahmud's old and trusted maid. Haji Mahmud himself had presided over her wedding vows when Zahra married his personal servant, Kazem. Zahra managed the household affairs with careful precision, while Haji Mahmud's young bride would sit cross-legged day after day in her own room and stare into space.

Contrary to the custom in the homes of all families from Kashan, in the cellar of this house there was no carpet-weaving in progress. The young bride did not even dare to visit the stored goods in the cellar. She was afraid of her husband's questions. And Zahra, who was well acquainted with her master's moods, did not encourage the girl either.

Touba's first attempt at cooking was met with such adamant disapproval by Haji Mahmud that the girl never again made the effort. Her only activity was to walk back and forth across the room and take quick, secret glances at the sky, longing for rain. The childhood dream of bearing the divine seed was now wasting into humiliation and depression. She was not even worth enough that God would make rain for her at least once.

Friday nights were a great torment for Touba, but for Zahra they were a great feast. On those nights her husband, Kazem, who spent weeknights as a security guard at Haji Mahmud's shop, would come home. Zahra had made it clear that on Friday nights even the dead were free, and on these nights, in accordance with a custom that Haji Mahmud had long since established, they cooked a more elaborate dinner. Zahra and Kazem were permitted to spread their food-cloth in the lower part of Haji and Touba's room, near the door, to eat their dinner there. Neither of them cared much for these formalities; they preferred to eat in the privacy of their own little room or in the kitchen. The women usually put on some makeup and clean

19

clothes. There were two food-cloths spread with food, one at the top
of the room for Haji Mahmud and Touba, and the other one for
Zahra and Kazem at the lower part of the room. Dinner was often
eaten in silence, or sometimes Haji Mahmud preached a moral tale
or told the story of some great person's life. Once in a while, Zahra
or Kazem cracked a joke about the merchants in the bazaar or the
neighborhood shopkeepers, and on such occasions Haji Mahmud
would clear his throat and pretend he did not hear them. After dinner Zahra prepared her masters' bed, and after saying good night
would leave the two of them for her husband's bed. Shortly after the
usual exchange of intimacies, Haji Mahmud would say his prayers,
turn his back to his wife, and go to sleep.

At midnight the house was awake again. Their bathing equipment had been prepared ahead of time. Kazem carried his master's
bathing bundle and, with oil lamp in hand, led the way to the bathhouse. Behind him walked Haji Mahmud, then Touba, and last of
all Zahra, carrying her mistress's washing paraphernalia. With their
bathing finished, they would return home for the dawn prayers.

Friday was also the day when Haji's children, together with their
spouses and their offspring, came to his home. Haji Mahmud and
his wife visited one of the children every third Friday of the month
in turn. These visits were tiring and burdensome for Touba. She
could hardly bear them.

The habitually serious way of life that she had inherited from her
father reached its peak with the presence of Haji Mahmud in her
life. Her face was always grim and austere. She had not yet grown
old enough for everyone to be afraid of her, but a chilly atmosphere
surrounded her. She spent long periods of time kneeling in the corner of her room, gradually going into a trance. She had not yet
brought a child into the world. She did not know that Haji Mahmud was purposely preventing her pregnancy, for the man did not
desire to have a child by her. The thought of such a young and beautiful woman caring for his little ones after his death frightened him.
Many nights he would come to the door of young Touba's bedroom,
only to find that the very thought of her becoming pregnant—or
too sure of herself, or arrogant—would force him to return to his

own quarters. Touba, who once aspired to carry the divine seed, was now frightened about the possibility of her own infertility.

Outside, famine and cholera were devastating the city, but Touba knew nothing of these matters. She went regularly to the bathhouse at midnight on Friday nights. One afternoon each month she was allowed to visit her family. She was not permitted to eat there or stay too long. Haji did not want his family to be indebted to a strange man, and as far as he was concerned, the husband of Touba's mother was an outsider.

Their marriage was beginning to feel the burden of economic problems as well. At times Haji would say, "If only you had brought better luck with you . . ." and then he would be silent. Sometimes Touba would think of killing herself so that her cursed existence would not burden this benevolent man. Sometimes she would be indifferent to his comments. And sometimes, when he stood above her and stared at her, she wished the ground would open up and swallow her.

There came a day when Haji Mahmud gave her a task to complete, perhaps for the first time in the four years of their married life. Dough had been prepared for the weekly bread and had to be taken to the bakery. This job could not be done without supervision, and Zahra had gone to prepare one of Haji Mahmud's daughters for childbirth. Haji Mahmud himself was busy and also felt it below his dignity to attend to such affairs, so he assigned Touba to follow Kazem to the bakery. Kazem carried on his head a large, round wooden tray piled up with mounds of dough covered with a cotton cloth. He walked ahead and Touba followed.

Touba was not used to walking in the streets and witnessing its sights and sounds, and now and then she would be distracted from Kazem. And Kazem paid her little heed. The tall, able-bodied man was in no need of the protection of a delicate seventeen- or eighteen-year-old woman. The eleven o'clock dust of commuters lingered in the morning spring air. In the bazaar, people had crowded around the pushcart filled with bowls of cooked rice. Each person who stood in line held an empty bowl, and constantly accused the person ahead of stealing his place. It seemed as though they would soon be killing one another. At the end of the small bazaar, near the copper-smith's shop, a young boy of five or six sat cross-legged, his head hanging down, rocking his upper body back and forth like the pendulum of a clock. At each swing he repeated, "Hungry! Hungry!" His childish voice was dry, and its echo resonated in his surroundings. Touba paused in front of the child for a moment, but then had to hurry in order to catch up with Kazem, who moved on rapidly. She would certainly never find her way home if she lost Kazem, since she knew nothing of the city.

The two of them reached a small narrow alley with a bakery on the corner. People had lined up here also, and there was a great deal of commotion as everyone complained about something. Kazem passed the front entrance and turned into the alley. He took yet another turn into a blind alley, and after a few steps, he stopped in front of a door and knocked. A woman with her chador wrapped about her waist and her scarf tied around her head in the manner of a washer woman opened the door and stepped aside silently. They entered. It was the baker's backyard, with an oven in the ground. Kazem explained that Haji's wife would stay, but he was leaving and would return in a couple of hours. The shy woman shook her head in acquiescence.

Touba sat by the little round pool in the middle of the yard and watched the woman work. There were some ten more trays of dough waiting to be baked. With the help of her daughter, the woman spread each mound of dough on a round pad, whereupon the young girl would bend down and slap the dough onto the wall of the hot oven. The two of them worked steadily and without conversation as Touba watched. She was bored, but there was nothing she could do except wait and watch. The work lasted longer than expected, and when he returned, Kazem joined the women in waiting. On his way back to the baker's, he had procured a few bites of bread and cheese in order to partially calm Touba's gnawing hunger.

By late afternoon the job was finished. The bread loaves were placed back on the round wooden tray, covered with the same cotton cloth and tied with a string. The bread was visibly poking out from under the cloth, and as they headed away from the house the baker's wife told them in one short sentence to watch out for the hungry crowd and the ruffians.

There was still a great deal of commotion in front of the bakery. People were swearing, cursing, and pushing. They seemed angrier than in the morning. Touba followed Kazem with quick steps. They reached the bazaar corner where the same boy was sitting by the coppersmith's shop. The child no longer rocked himself or said a word. Touba stopped in front of the child and stared at him. The child's head was hanging down low, and he was staring at his hands, which lay on his knees. Touba leaned forward to see his face better. The child remained motionless. Kazem lingered briefly. Touba asked him to place the bread board down, and with great difficulty she pulled one loaf from under the wrapped cloth and placed it in the child's hand.

Just then, the growing noise and commotion drew her attention back, and her eyes searched for Kazem. An angry crowd had gathered around, toppling the bread tray and spilling loaves all over. Kazem was shouting, kicking and being kicked. There was hardly any bread left on the tray. Kazem ran in all directions, trying to recover the disappearing loaves.

Dazed, Touba turned away from the scene and back to the child, who had made no attempt to eat the bread. She knelt down and lowered her head to see his face. His eyes were open, staring at his hands upon his knees. A man's voice said, "He is dead." Touba kept her gaze on the child. The man said that the child had been dead for an hour or two, and they were waiting for the undertaker's coach. His voice actually blended with the sound of the wheels of the coach.

Touba raised her head and saw the coach coming to a stop by the side of the street, an older man standing at one end, a younger man at the other. In the coach lay some bodies. A human leg protruded. The younger man approached the child, picked him up in his arms, and turned back to the coach. The bread loaf was still in the child's hand. The young man tried unsuccessfully to lay the child on his back, but the child's body would not yield to his strong arms. Finally the old man told him to leave the body as it was, and the young man did so.

Touba followed the coach to the cemetery, where a mass grave had been prepared for the dead. The men lowered the bodies down one by one. It was a time of famine, and nobody worried about routine burial rites. They tried to straighten the child's body once more, but he would not flex and remained in a seated position. Anxious, the young undertaker kept looking at Touba. He was unsure of what to do with the stiffened child. Getting no response from the woman, he tried to straighten the child again. But the piercing voice of a man suddenly filled the air around the mass grave: "Leave him alone!" Touba and the two undertakers looked in the direction of the voice and realized that it came from a cleric standing on the opposite side of the grave. The young undertaker stopped his vain attempt and lowered the child, still seated, into the grave.

They poured soil on the bodies, making the child, still holding the bread, disappear under the waves of earth. Touba and the cleric watched all of this from opposite sides of the grave. The yellow spring sunshine was fading and the grave appeared even smoother, indistinguishable from the earth around it. The undertakers had left in their coach, but Touba remained there, deep in contemplation of the actual image of death. She had a hazy impression that she had just buried her own child. The cleric was saying prayers for the dead as he crouched by the grave, one hand on the fresh-turned soil.

He looked up for a moment at Touba, and then told her to pray with him. He told her not to mourn the dead, for they are the blessed. Touba knelt involuntarily, but did not know any prayers. She was trying hard to remember something when the cleric said that hunger can kill people, and that it is an abomination. He continued, saying that for thousands of years people had turned gray trying to solve this predicament. They referred to predestination to explain hunger, not knowing or not wanting to know that there exists a system behind it, the law of hunger. It is a faulty system, conquered by human beings thousands of years ago. Now, at the beginning of the twentieth century, it was killing them again, because they failed to understand the law. This lack of knowledge, this very ignorance, the cleric said, was the cause of hunger. Poverty was not. As Touba listened to the man, dusk spread its wings on the cemetery.

In the darkening silence, Touba felt anxious to leave, and without saying a word to the cleric, she headed in the direction she thought would take her home. Uncertain of her way, she stepped on rough rocks, became confused among the graves, and suddenly came across two men blocking her way. Their breath smelled of alcohol, and one of them walked unevenly. Stumbling, the more drunken man grabbed Touba's arms and tried to pull away her face cover. The other man pulled her long, veiling chador from behind. As her chador fell to the dusty ground of the cemetery, the man again pulled at the face cover. He pulled her hair along with it, and Touba felt a sharp pain through her whole body. She knelt down, trying to free herself. Suddenly, she heard the same voice she had heard by the graveside, but this time he was screaming forcefully, "You bastards!" Then she heard the loud sound of a face being slapped. The two men had stopped harassing her. She heard the shaky voice of one of the drunken men say, "Oh, Mr. Khiabani!" as he was shuffling, tripping over everything, and trying to disappear into the darkening cemetery. The other man, nervous and fumbling, picked up Touba's veil from the ground and placed it on her head. The drunkard felt Mr. Khiabani's heavy fist on his back and heard his loud cry, "Get lost!" The second man disappeared rapidly into the darkness as quickly as the first. Mr. Khiabani looking away, asked Touba to cover herself. In distress and confusion, she pulled her veil over her head and began to search in vain for her face cover. Thinking that she was ready, Mr. Khiabani told her to walk ahead of him at a close distance so that he could escort her home. He realized that she did not know her way, and the only words they exchanged on the journey back were about the directions.

Kazem was standing at the entrance to their alley, holding a lantern in his hand. When he saw Touba he began to strike his head with his left fist, and whispered in panic that his master Haji Mahmud was waiting for her, angrily pacing in the house. He showed her his bruised lip from the severe beating he had endured. Walking next to Touba, he continued telling her that she did not do a good thing coming home so late. Midway down the alley, Zahra appeared, flushed and thumping her head with her fist. When she saw her mistress's uncovered face, she said, "Oh, God let me die." At the end of the alley, at the threshold of the house, stood Haji Mahmud, furious and holding a stick. His anger grew as his piercing eyes fell upon his uncovered wife, wrapped in dust and filth, approaching by the dim light of the lantern. However, before he could take any action, he saw the cleric coming in his direction as well.

In a glance, Touba saw her husband's rage suddenly shift to utter amazement as he said, "Your Excellency, Mr. Khiabani!" in the same tone the attacker in the graveyard had used. His anger dissipated instantly. Haji Mahmud showed great respect by bowing and greeting the distinguished guest. Mr. Khiabani then told Haji Mahmud, "Do not worry; the lady was visiting the cemetery, and because of the darkness I decided to escort her home." In the meantime, Zahra took advantage of the moment to push her mistress into the house.

Although she had already slipped into the house, Touba could hear Haji Mahmud anxiously ordering Kazem to prepare the guest hall for the arrival of the patron. Mr. Khiabani apparently accepted the invitation and came into the house. Breathing a sigh of relief, she thought she now had some time to herself to scheme before having to face her husband.

Away from the men, Zahra scratched her face when she noticed that Touba was wearing her chador inside out. She thought what a shame Touba had caused. But Touba was sitting in the corner of the room with her dusty chador on, unmindful of Zahra's grieving. She was contemplating a death similar to that of the boy who died of hunger. She decided to fast to death, a decision that quickly provided her with a new personality. In that state of mind, she stared at Zahra until she stopped complaining.

Zahra roamed around the room a little longer, looking for a chance to unleash her anger at Touba. When finally she opened her mouth to complain again, she found her tone of voice was sorrowful and friendly. With a swelling knot in her throat, almost crying, she explained that Kazem searched the streets for her four times, and each time he had been beaten and punished by the master upon his return. She further explained that it was not fair for Kazem to be punished for someone else's faults. She asked Touba why she had gone to the cemetery in the first place. Kazem had provided her with some explanations about a dead child, and now, in Zahra's mind and in face of the crushing silence of the eighteen-year-old girl sitting in front of her, the seed of a story began to take shape.

Zahra had heard of Mr. Khiabani before. What she did not understand was how her mistress had gone to visit a great man, but had returned with a messy chador and uncovered face. Zahra looked at Touba with suspicion as she found herself unable to come up with an explanation about the inside-out chador. She did not dare to ask for an explanation from her mistress, whose lips were tightly sealed. She left to bring Touba a bowl of stew. When she returned, she placed the warm food in front of Touba and stood by, waiting for some words. The appetizing aroma of the stew delighted Touba's sense of smell. She felt a passing desire to break her pledge to fast. Nevertheless, despite her noisy, empty stomach, she resisted the urge to indulge. Zahra implored her several times to eat, but each time she was met with Touba's deafening silence. She began to realize that despite four years of pampering and caring for Touba, the girl was still a stranger to her. This caused Zahra to give up and finally submit to her overwhelming need for sleep.

Touba heard Zahra making the bed. Soon, she was relieved to hear her snoring. From the guest hall, a faint light spread to the courtyard and penetrated through the window of Touba's room. The stew had chilled, fat forming a thin film on the top of the bowl. Touba slid the tray away and kneeled on the floor as if she were praying. In a semiconscious state, she dreamed of the experiences of the day that had just passed, thinking constantly of the dead child, holding a piece of bread with open large eyes. The child was determined to stay in Touba's mind, to continue to exist in this world. Apparently, the child's short life was to be entwined with Touba's forever.

Mr. Khiabani stayed at Haji Mahmud's home until late in the evening. He first apologized for mistaking his wife for his daughter, an apology that once again pierced the depressed man's heart like a dagger. Mr. Khiabani censored the events that had taken place in the graveyard and did not say anything about the drunken men. He had correctly ascertained that Haji Mahmud was the kind of person who would blame Touba for the men's sin. He gradually changed the subject of the conversation to the country's current political situation.

Haji Mahmud found the views of Mr. Khiabani, who was a member of parliament, most interesting. He knew him to be an unequalled leader of the anti-despotic movement that had grown since 1907. They were in agreement about the country's critical condition. They knew that Mohammad Ali Shah was about to return, and that the newly established constitutionalism was in danger. Although the host was less worried over this latter issue, he did not deem it appropriate to explain his opinion to this radical-minded member of parliament. Indeed, they differed in their aspirations. Haji Mahmud hoped to see peace and order instead of the chaos and disorder that currently threatened the country. The revolutionary cleric wanted liberty and modernization. Nevertheless, the guest's powerful personality and his sweet rhetoric gave Haji Mahmud an opportunity to know a dissenting activist, and to evaluate differing ideas in an intimate way. Moreover, the presence of a member of parliament in the house of an average merchant might serve a higher cause. He had quickly calculated that the neighbors knew of his wife's temporary disappearance, and would probably gossip about it in the community and at the bazaar the next day. The presence of Mr. Khiabani in his house would quiet many wagging tongues.

Late that evening, as Haji Mahmud escorted his guest to the end of the neighborhood, he made sure that at least twenty people saw them together. Only then did he return home. The light in Touba's room was off. For a while he stood indecisively in the middle of the courtyard; then he decided to postpone the talk with his wife until the following day.

Touba awoke at dawn freed from her nightmares. An uncanny sensation, derived perhaps from hunger and anxiety, suddenly brought her to some sense of self-realization, with an overwhelming desire to return to the cemetery and to speak with Mr. Khiabani. She believed that if only she could find the mass grave, she would also find him. Suddenly, she felt that there was much to tell him. She needed to tell him how throughout the years of her life she had dreamed of someday giving birth to a messiah. She wanted to explain to him the reasons she had married Haji Mahmud, and how, in doing so, she had deliberately denied herself the possibly of giving birth to a Jesus-like messiah. She wanted to throw herself at his feet and tell him everything. The man was undeniably holy, a reflection of the infinite, vast universe. She wanted to ask him if the boy who starved to death might not have been her Jesus. She wanted to ask the agonizing question: Was this child's mother a fourteen-year-old girl who, just like Mary, had experienced an immaculate conception? Weren't these people the same ones who unmercifully abandoned God's gift of the boy to the claws of hunger in the marketplace? Was it possible that God punished this land with famine and drought for this sin? Was it her fault that rain did not fall, as her husband had always accused her? Did she, by coming to this world and by troubling Haji Mahmud, arouse God's rage? Should she have waited for God to appoint her a husband? Had she not sinned by demanding this man for a husband?

Suddenly, all of the vague, perplexing questions that had eaten her up for the four years of her marriage became clear to her. She rose and walked to her storage chest and opened its lid with care. She dug through the contents to find a face cover. She put it on, pulled the curtain aside, and walked silently past Zahra, who was still asleep. She put her shoes on and started walking quickly through the courtyard. Haji was doing the ablution for the morning prayer by the washstand in the cellar. He heard the steps and at first thought it was Zahra moving around as she prepared the samovar for the morning tea. He soon realized, however, that the footsteps did not sound like hers. But by the time he climbed up the steps and reached the courtyard, Touba had unlocked the door and was already walking into the alley. By the time he reached the door she had already rounded the last bend in the alley. Immediately, anger began to consume his body like leprosy.

In the fresh air of early morning, Touba walked through the silent street as though she was walking in her sleep. Nothing was in its proper place. Though hungry, she pushed forward, partly filled with fear and partly delighting in flight. In the early dawn, every supernatural and miraculous thing seemed real. As she moved on, the sky turned from indigo blue to turquoise, and the red rays of the sun spread from the east onto the face of the sky, covering it in a glowing halo. A great man was placing a glowing jeweled crown, infinitely large, on his head. Beams of light shot from the diamonds and blended with the ruby rays. Amid all this sparkle, Venus had begun to lose her glow, as if she were her own sacrificial offering. And Touba, who had only seen the sky from the four corners of her own house, absorbed with her whole being every instant of this infinite spectrum of light.

A little girl was crying out from the depths of her being, "Sir, please love me!" It was the voice of her childhood, and she was awakening to the fact that it was receding, going far away. Perhaps it was going to that great man.

She stopped suddenly in the middle of the street. She could see her childhood in front of her, fading away. Softly, to herself, she said, "I have grown up." And her heart sank. Being grown-up, she would now have to make her decisions accordingly. Suddenly she let out a cry, and her tears poured out.

A waterman stopped and asked timidly if "sister needed something." The man was shy, but Touba could see his desire deep in his eyes: They penetrated her veil, attempting to grasp what kind of creature lived behind it.

Touba came back to herself from her dreams of oneness with the being and nonbeing of her childhood. She remembered her experience with the men who had accosted her at the cemetery. Unaware of the weary tone in her voice, she asked the man if he knew the way to the cemetery. At the same time, she too looked into his eyes and saw his expression change from one of desire to a simpler feeling.

He pointed out the way to her, and she departed immediately. A moment later, she looked back and saw him staring after her. She knew that her look had not been prudent and that it might tempt the waterman. She hastened her steps.

She had to stop and ask the way many times before reaching her destination. The streets and alleys and the bazaar gradually formed a distinct pattern in her mind. Hallucinating from hunger, but also aware of her sudden maturity, she was at the same time discovering the city.

Finally she reached the barren, humble cemetery, where she faced a sea of graves. Relying on her memory from the night before, she tried to reach the communal grave. The cemetery beggars were all around her. She looked wealthy to them, despite her dusty chador. But she had brought no money, and in time they stopped following her, for they could tell by her manner that she had no alms to give.

With the help of the gravediggers, Touba found the communal grave. The earth on it was still fresh and uneven. It looked, from the mound that covered it, as though the boy's body had grown larger. That was how she accounted for the roundness of the earth. She sat under the protective shade of a nearby tree and looked around in wonder. She now felt apprehensive and wondered if the cleric would indeed come.

Groups of mourners were scattered here and there. The cholera had been devastating. Touba herself longed for the disease, to free her from the gnawing hunger. She had no fear of the newly arriving bodies as they were brought in one after another. The hunger, the increasing heat of the day, and the buzzing of the flies gradually made her listless. At times the child's face would fade from her memory. She had flashbacks to her own childhood. At times she felt like laughing. She saw herself as a laughable creature. What if people were to suddenly abandon the dead and begin dancing? What if the dead arose, went into the city, and began to exterminate everyone? And then she would be filled with fear and anxiety. Each passing moment she vacillated from laughter to sorrow, and from sorrow to fear.

The cleric did not come. She was now certain that he would never come there again. He had come one evening at sunset to observe the communal grave and feel the impact of the cholera from close up, and he would never return again. There was no use in waiting.

She rose unsteadily, feeling listless and confused, came out of the cemetery and, relying once again on her instincts, searched for the road home. The memory of her feverish meandering through the city brought an overall map into her mind. Gradually she found the more recognizable streets. She came to the small bazaar with its cooked-rice stand and crowd of beggars standing around. The rice was issued by the government, and its smell now turned her stomach. Heedless of her hunger, she passed the food and turned into the alley that led to her house. She stopped by the closed door and raised the knocker.

Zahra opened the door, her face ashen. Touba entered without a word, passed through the portal, and stepped down into the courtyard. Haji Mahmud stood by the round pool, holding some switches in his hand. It was his habit to keep a few of them there, to use "on the asses that needed correcting in this world!" The woman turned her eyes to look at the pomegranate tree nearby. The tree was covered with young green leaves and freshly swelling buds. She turned her eyes to the man again, unaware of the appearance of frozen death in them. Her will to die had become like a mountain of ice in the midst of a storm-tossed ocean; from it poured nothing but denigration. The man, the husband, could not bear her look.

Before today, he had always been the one to look at her in just such a manner: those early mornings when he turned to his wife and looked at her as if she were a pile of scum or the place where he would relieve his bowels; or when he entered the room and looked at the golden hair of the woman who sat in the corner. And she had wanted to sink into the earth, so deep that only her hair remained visible; to become stalks of wheat blowing in the wind. Then perhaps the old man would take pity on her.

Now, filled with four years of experience and no longer self-conscious, he angrily hit himself on the shins with his own switches.

Touba had prepared herself for the beating and now needed, in her fear, to experience it in actuality. She also wanted to atone for the pain Kazem had endured. She came forward resolutely and stood directly behind her husband. She stared at his shoulders and suddenly, without knowing the reason, felt a rush of joy. The morning's elation had returned to her, the feeling of flight and of growing up. It seemed that if she only willed it, she could grow larger than life-size, even larger than the yard. What pleasure if her husband were to beat her in this state. She imagined that her skin was callused, as hard as the bricks of the walls around her, and that Haji Mahmud went on beating and beating until his fingers lost control, kicking until his legs broke. And all this made her very happy. She continued to stand and stare at his shoulders. She believed that his shoulders would burn under her stare.

Haji Mahmud hesitated over whether or not to turn and face the woman. He knew that if he did turn he must beat her, but if he were to commit such an act he himself would be the one beaten. Without turning, he stepped to his left and walked toward the guest quarters of the house. He was still holding the switches, though they seemed a heavy burden and he wished he could dispose of them.

Touba headed toward her own room, took her shoes off, threw her veil to one side, and stood in the middle of the room. Zahra had followed her on tiptoe. She picked up the veil from the floor and whispered that she would wash it. She had a great desire to kiss Touba's hands. An old hatred for Haji Mahmud, whose face was always so angry and disapproving, had suddenly opened in Zahra's heart like an old wound. She had often had to experience the distress of Kazem being beaten by the master, while she herself escaped to hide in a corner so that she would not witness the scene and thereby add more pain to her husband's sense of humiliation.

Touba asked for a sacred earthen prayer stone to perform her prayers. She wanted to offer the experience of that dawn as the dowry of her prayers, praying in a manner unlike any she had known before. She felt uncomfortable performing her prayers without ablution. Yet she was afraid of coming face-to-face with her husband if she went down to wash. And so, facing south, her head still uncovered, she stood and announced the call to prayer. She cried and laughed to herself, both at the same time. Her body trembled from all she had endured, and nothing could stop the trembling. She began to pray, repeating the words carefully with mixed pleasure and pain, then knelt for the appropriate supplication. As she recited the morning prayer, she framed clearly in her consciousness everything that had been so memorable about this particular morning. Her head remained bowed in supplication for a long time, and Zahra, who stood in the corner of the room, was filled with awe at the holiness of the scene.

Touba wished to be alone. She did not actually know what that meant—perhaps it was that she wanted to feel free. She had always felt spiritually alone, but growing up communally and being constantly among others, she had not had the chance to experience true solitude. Even though she had performed her prayers in total surrender to God, she had also been in the presence of Zahra and consequently did not see herself as completely free. She crawled to the corner of the room and sat in her usual position. Zahra brought food and placed it in front of her, and again Touba refused to eat.

That night Zahra felt it necessary to mention to Haji Mahmud that her mistress was refusing food. But the man had such a frown on his face that Zahra slipped out of his room as quickly as possible. She was concerned not only for Touba, but for herself and Kazem as well. She felt that an important event was taking place, one that stood out in her long, calm life. She went to the woman's room to try to persuade her to eat something, then headed for the kitchen where she aimlessly moved objects from one place to another. She wished Kazem would come so she could talk with him, so they could confide in one another. After a while she returned to her mistress's room and persuaded Touba, by now nauseated and dizzy, to drink some water.

Early the next morning she felt braver, and reported to Haji Mahmud on Touba's case. The man listened in silence, then left the house without breakfast. Touba lay in bed and had no desire or will to move. It occurred to Zahra to go to Touba's family and ask them to come and save the girl, but she feared her master's reaction and could decide on nothing.

Haji Mahmud returned home late that night with Kazem and another man. Kazem managed to tell Zahra briefly, in the kitchen, that Haji Mahmud meant to undertake some transaction. Accompanying them was a moneylender with several sacks of cash. He stayed late and ate his dinner there.

Touba continued her hunger strike, and now it was beginning to show in her appearance. She had no color in her face and was growing thin. Once more, Zahra spread her bed in Touba's bedroom and,

crying, begged Touba at least to say something so she could understand the reason for her behavior.

Zahra was awakened suddenly the next morning by Haji Mahmud's harsh voice calling for breakfast. She rushed to the kitchen in
a panic to start the samovar and get some bread and cheese together.
Her master instructed her to spread the breakfast cloth in Touba's
room. Zahra had not yet finished setting the tea in front of Touba
when the man walked in and ordered Zahra to leave.

He sat by Touba's bed silently. Touba was oblivious to everything
around her. He placed a few sacks of money in front of her, cleared
his throat, and told Touba to cover her hair because from that
moment on she was no longer his wife. The woman quickly sat up
in bed and searched for her headscarf. Haji Mahmud reached
behind where he was seated to pick it up and, looking away, handed
it to her. She pulled the veil over her hair and tried to steady herself
in bed, propping her body against the wall. She would have liked to
gather her legs up and be more collected in front of the man, but her
body did not obey her will.

Haji Mahmud, eyes downcast, sensed her movements. After she
was more composed, he ordered her to eat. Touba followed his
orders unconsciously. But in her confused and dizzy state she had
heard a voice tell her she was no longer *mahram* to this man, and her
desire to die abated with the first bite. She took a bit of bread and
cheese and sipped the tea that Zahra had prepared. The second bite
stuck in her throat as she tried to control her quivering stomach. She
had to wait a moment for the food to work its way painfully down.
Then she could eat no more.

It seemed that Haji Mahmud understood her situation, and for
the first time a sense of compassion and sympathy awoke in him.
Though the woman's behavior during the last few days had disturbed his peace, it had also activated his brain. Without realizing it,
he felt a sense of respect for her.

When Touba stopped eating, Haji Mahmud began to speak. He
explained that he had divorced her ethically, morally, and legally,
that her stepfather had witnessed the process, and that everything
had been done justly. The house they presently occupied had been

appraised at a market value of 1120 tomans by three honest men, and he had purchased it from himself at that price for Touba. He had added a few shops adjacent to the house, as well as their upstairs apartments. Haji subtracted this total from what Touba had inherited from her father's estate, and assumed control over the rest until she married again. Haji had paid her dowry of twenty-five tomans in five silver coins, pushing the sack of coins toward her. Management and rental of the shops and upstairs apartments would remain his responsibility. Each month Kazem would bring her the earnings. Haji had also rented the guesthouse to a trustworthy man named Haji Mostafa and his two wives. The three of them were to live there and help supervise matters in the house.

Zahra was to remain with Touba during the three months and ten days of abstinence that must follow their divorce. Touba was allowed to go to the public bathhouse once a month. She was not permitted to visit or to receive visitors from her family during this time. Zahra had been appointed to oversee these rules, and the two wives of Haji Mostafa were to stop Touba from leaving the house if she attempted to do so. After three months and ten days, she would be free to go wherever she wished and see whomever she desired. But Haji Mahmud told her that even after this mandated period, she would be best advised to stay at home in order to keep her good name in the neighborhood and to uphold the honor of her father, who had lived respectably. It was also her duty to be respectful to her divorced husband and not to cause him embarrassment or disgrace.

Haji Mahmud looked at Touba, waiting for her response. Her head bowed low, she murmured her acceptance of all the conditions.

Sunlight streamed down through the window and onto the flowered pattern of the carpet, where it seemed to dance for joy. Though her head was lowered, she was aware of the brilliance of the room, and when Haji pulled the curtains to disappear from her life forever she could hardly refrain from shouting out loud in glee.

She slid into her bed and drew the covers up to her neck, her veil still on her head. Then she thought of her hunger for the first time. When Zahra came back, Touba asked if they had any vegetable soup, and Zahra ran happily to the kitchen to begin preparing some for her. Then Touba closed her eyes and fell into a deep sleep, unable to imagine the boredom and loneliness of the three months and ten days ahead, and the hot summer with which they would coincide.

The dry and tiresome summer arrived, along with Haji Mostafa and his two busybody wives. Through the long days, Touba endured their long-winded talk and inquisitiveness. Haji Mahmud's appointment of these women as spies had extended their sphere of freedom into the deepest corners of Touba's private life. They entered her room whenever they wished and, on a whim, would order her not to come into the yard because a man was present. Touba remained in the corner of her room, as she had for the past four years, and received no news of her family. She did not yet even dare to go to her own kitchen, or see to the affairs of her own household.

But gradually the ice melted between Touba and Zahra, and in Haji Mahmud's absence, Zahra gave Touba new spirit. At times Zahra spoke of her childhood and her father's love for her. Touba had also eventually managed to make contact with her own family through Kazem.

In these last days of preserving Haji Mahmud's reputation, she walked up and down her room, and whenever she heard the footsteps of Haji Mostafa's wives she rushed to her bed, pretending to be asleep. Then she could either think about her dead son or picture Mr. Khiabani on the other side of the grave. She remembered how sad and sorrow-ridden he looked with his head resting on his chest, deep in thought about the deaths from cholera and famine. Remembering him like this, she felt as if a bullet was passing through her, and she trembled. How grand and magnanimous this man was. Such was his spiritual bearing that he seemed to emanate rays of light. He was woven of the sun's rays, as though to spread his light and warmth over the earth. At such moments, even if Haji Mostafa's wives were in the room, Touba would go into a trance and disregard everyone.

On one of the last days of August, Touba's period of abstinence was over, and she no longer had to hide or be under anyone's control. She longed to go to the bathhouse and to dress in new clothes. Anxious not to lose a single day of her newly gained freedom, she actually began her preparations a day early. She told Zahra nothing, fearing that she might prevent her from carrying out her plans. She chose all her clothing, shoes, and other necessary items and laid them out.

Touba waited impatiently, counting the moments until the morning of her freedom. The night before, she dreamed that the days were moving backward—that instead of her three months and ten days wait becoming shorter, it increased in length. In her night-mare, she had seen the image of a moat, dug by the two wives of Haji Mostafa, between her and the door of the house. The trench held dark, stagnant water, from which leeches and worms emerged to crawl up the walls. She woke up sweating to witness the first rays of early dawn on the walls of her room.

The nightmare subsided as she rapidly put her bedding in order, wrapped it in its spread, and leaned it against the wall. Then she dressed herself in the clothes she had prepared for the celebration. She could hear Zahra moving about and grumbling to herself in the adjacent room. Touba pulled the curtain aside and greeted her. Zahra was stunned. Paying no attention to her look of amazement and surprise, Touba quickly explained that yesterday was the end of her three months and ten days. Today was the day of freedom.

The two women went to the kitchen to prepare their breakfast. Touba asked Zahra to dress for an outing. Zahra hesitated for fear of what Haji Mahmud might say or do, but Touba reminded her that from this day forward he no longer had any hold on her, and Zahra had no ethical or moral commitment to report to him. Zahra pre-pared the tea, feeling anxious but also joyful. Then the two women, in their veils and face covers, left the house in the early hours of the morning, before the two wives of Haji Mostafa had a chance to question them.

In the street, Touba hailed a carriage and they climbed aboard. When she told the driver their destination, the Old Locomotive Sta-tion, Zahra was beside herself with excitement. They were going to the holy tomb of Shahabdol Azim south of Tehran. Zahra had always dreamed of visiting there and had confided as much to Touba long ago. They climbed onto the crowded train. On arrival they jumped off the platform and, amid tourists and pilgrims, ran almost the entire distance to the tomb. They made ritual circles around it, and then adjourned to the side court of the holy grounds to sit among the other tired women and exchange trivialities. Contrary to her past silence, Touba was unusually talkative. She related a few legends and religious conundrums for the women and, as Zahra looked at her in absolute amazement, expounded in response to their questions on Islamic dogma, further increasing her stature in Zahra's eyes as a wise and educated woman. They then walked together the whole length of the bazaar, purchased bracelets, earrings, and a few knick-knacks. With Zahra's approval, Touba bought a pair of moccasins for Kazem. They had lunch at a restaurant serving rice and kebab, and afterward Touba rested in the shade beneath the trees in the garden near a grave, while Zahra cried a little, grieving over Saint Shahabdol Azim's exile. She and Kazem were both strangers in this city, and she identified with others in exile. Even Touba cried a little. On their return, before boarding the train, Touba purchased a secondhand copy of the book *The Forty Parrots* and also a copy of *Hossein Kurd of Shabestar*. They arrived home an hour after dark, tired but happy.

Haji Mostafa and his wives, Narges and Fatemeh, were all standing in the courtyard. The man was silent, but he signaled with a finger to Narges, the older wife, to speak. Nervous and angry, the woman touched her face with a slapping motion and demanded to know where they had been until this late hour of the night. Touba said only, "Holy Shahabdol Azim" and walked toward her room. Zahra felt it best to remain behind and explain to the others, who by this time appeared calm, that her mistress's waiting period was now over, and that she had had some almsgiving duties to attend to. Zahra, who had learned the necessary tricks and politics of keeping secrets, put on an innocent expression and explained away whatever seemed suspicious or questionable to Haji Mahmud's informers. It seemed that the explanations were acceptable. Haji Mahmud's specific orders applied only to the period of abstinence. Nevertheless,

Touba's actions had shown some disrespect and lack of consideration for the efforts that Haji Mostafa and his family had made during those months. The man was thinking that if the event were to repeat itself, he would need to report the matter to Haji Mahmud. And indeed, it did repeat itself.

On the very next morning, Touba and Zahra dressed and veiled again and headed for the Cemetery of the Fourteen Innocents. Touba asked for directions and found the communal grave where the boy was buried. Zahra cried continuously while Touba retold the sorrowful story of the child's death. They tied a green wishing knot on a branch overhanging the grave so that the boy would intercede for them on the day of resurrection. They tidied up the grave, decorated it with leaves, and left. On the way back, they bought some cheese, bread, and sweet sesame paste, then sat next to the muddy stream near the shop and ate greedily. As they returned home, clouds began to gather and cover the sun. The sky slowly darkened and turned black. It began to rain lightly, then suddenly it turned thunderous and poured heavily. People ran joyously in the rain and expressed their gratitude to God. The younger ones, in their joy, danced and snapped their fingers and pushed each other in merriment. Touba stopped and lifted her head to let the rain hit her face. It seemed to her that the boy had seen the green wishing knot and taken it to God, saying, "I died of famine and hunger. Have mercy on my young mother and let the skies rain." And it seemed that God, who surely had love and benevolence for Touba and had given her the vision of the old man webbed with strands of light, now bestowed his grace through the drops of rain that fell on her and on the city. Touba felt proud and held her head up. She told Zahra, "Surely he loves us." In answer to Zahra's "Who?" she said, "He, he," and pointed to the sky. She let Zahra run to the house, as she herself walked slowly through the rain to let the wetness soak into her clothes and touch her body. She felt that by doing this she was expressing her infinite gratitude to the Almighty.

Unhurried, Touba shut the gate behind her and walked up and down the yard, allowing Haji Mostafa's wives to sneak a few glances at her through their windows, to ask her questions and receive no answers. When the older wife finally appeared in front of her with a headband and asked her why she walked up and down in the rain like a crazy person, Touba looked at her pensively, put her finger on the tip of her nose, and told her in a whisper not to make noise, for if she talked nonsense God's wrath would be awakened once more and the rain would disappear from the land forever. The woman, who thrived on gossip and small talk, grew silent at Touba's wise warning. She merely raised her eyebrows. The mocking side of her, which had been about to surface, subsided unconsciously. Touba was certainly not of any type she had come across before. Touba was approaching victory in the silent battle with these women. Resolutely, step-by-step.

On the second day of rain, Touba sat by the window and read from the book *Hossein Kurd of Shabestar*, and as she progressed page-by-page, she raised her head to observe the falling rain. For the first time she wished she could talk with Haji Mahmud and ask him if he had any knowledge of God's degree of love for her. The man was right; the wrathful drought had descended on the world because she had chosen, without God's permission, a husband who was perhaps the target of God's anger. Now that the man was gone and her days of abstinence were over, God was removing the veil of anger. After that night's prayers, Touba lay on the floor on her back, deep in meditation, and begged God to bestow on her, in any manner he saw fit, a messianic child. She could hear the sound of the rain on the adobe roof of her room, and of the water pouring continuously from the gutters and into the yard. Touba felt the cold penetrate her body and shivered; she wrapped her veil around herself and walked around the room. She wanted to walk in the rain, but knew that if she tried it again the two busybodies would reappear in the yard, even if she tiptoed on bare feet.

On the third day of rain, Touba felt an urge to clean the small pool. It was half filled with rain, and the dried scum that had accumulated through years of drought was now soaked and peeling. The peelings fell into the clean rainwater, making it impure. Touba attacked the walls of the small pool with a stiff broom and dustpan. She scraped the walls with all her strength. She poured the rainwater and scrapings out of the pool while the two imbecilic women, forever on guard duty, watched.

Later, at the public bathhouse, to the surprised woman manager's question as to how Haji Mahmud's wife had come to the bathhouse alone, Touba merely responded that she was now divorced and Zahra would follow. She wrapped her bath cloth around her and, carrying her own basin and tray, headed for the inner bathing and washing area. She placed the tray upside-down by the hot water pool and sat on it to soak her body. Here, too, she could smell the same stink of old mud. She thought what a pity it was that the bath water was still stale; she did not feel content with this cleaning. She tried unsuccessfully to escape the stares of a middle-aged woman who was appraising her. News of her divorce had spread. Deep in her own thoughts, she played with the water, provoking further rumors about herself.

Touba had not yet finished washing her hair when Zahra arrived. The woman had gathered her bathing paraphernalia and rushed to the bathhouse as soon as she had heard the news from the two wives. Along the way, running and panting, she cursed her bad luck. Her mistress's exhilarated state made Zahra joyous. But every event that was out of the ordinary frightened her. What would people say if she and Touba were to frequent the bathhouse too often? The woman did not have a husband, to need to come to the bath weekly. Last week they had already come here together. And now, today, they were here again, in the light of day, rather than at dawn on Friday morning. People would think of sinful activities and would drag the woman's honor into the mud—the honor that now needed to be protected and defended most devotedly by Zahra. No one knew that her mistress was able to expound on religious issues and read for hours by the window, activities that Zahra had never seen any woman, ever, partake in. She could not even imagine that a woman would be able to perform these acts. She went quickly into the bathhouse, gave her clothes to the woman attendant at the dressing room, and entered the inner rooms. She stared carefully at everyone until she recognized her mistress from her golden hair, fluffed with foam. She sat next to Touba and in a hushed voice began to reprove her. She helped her to wash her hair, pouring water on her head until a smiling, happy face appeared through the dissolving foam. The woman said, "Zahra, dear, the water still stinks of mud."

Then Zahra's eyes met the appraising eyes of the middle-aged woman. For an instant she thought, "What a disaster! The woman must be the typical busybody of the neighborhood. Oh, what misery." The woman, who had been trying in vain to attract Touba's attention, thought that Zahra was an easy catch. They smiled and greeted each other from afar. Their lips continued to speak words that neither one could hear clearly or understand. They were moving closer, and suddenly the middle-aged woman began to talk loudly. She expressed her amazement and surprise at Touba's beautiful long, golden hair and her Venus-like body. Zahra explained proudly that her mistress was quite a person. She mentioned that she was the daughter of an educated man who was an advisor to the royal court and was offered great gifts from many lands, but of course did not accept them because he was a seeker of knowledge and lover of wisdom, and the daughter was the very image of her honorable father. She was able to solve problems and interpret the canons of Islam, and the whole world was amazed at her knowledge and education. Then Zahra's eyes met with Touba's, who was staring dumbfounded at her. Zahra smiled lovingly at her mistress and turned to the middle-aged woman to continue her talk. Touba felt angry. She did not care for lies. She did not remember her father ever having been offered great gifts from many lands, nor did she remember telling any such stories to Zahra. Pretending to be occupied, she got up from her place to walk away from them, unknowingly showing off her tall and beautifully strong body. She stopped at a distance. The women had their heads together and were exchanging intimate secrets. By now, Touba was truly angry. She sped up her washing and headed for the rinsing pool. As she was leaving the inner room of the bathhouse, she murmured to Zahra that she should not worry about her; she was walking home alone, and Zahra should kindly bring her bathing towel and clothing.

In the dressing room, the women were talking of the rain. The bath attendant was happy and was planning to change the water in the bath reservoir as soon as the streams were filled. Others were anxious. The rain had been pouring down for three days straight. Thank God the epidemics had subsided. The weather had turned cool, and a heavy winter was expected. But then, what about the leaking roofs? Many were beginning to show signs of damage. It was possible that some roofs would collapse and people could be hurt. Broken legs and arms or even some deaths might result. As Touba dried herself with the large towel she could hear other women's conversations, but she was slowly fading away from their world. Without knowing why, she thought of Mr. Khiabani and wondered what he would say about this blessed rain. Would he be worried that it was too much? And the boy—If only he had lasted a few months longer, until the arrival of the rain, would he still have died of hunger?

She paid the bathing fees for Zahra and herself and headed out to walk once more under the unrelenting rain. She wished that the rain would wash away the muddy smell of the bath water left on her body. Out in the street it was quiet. Occasionally, someone would run through the street, holding an old cloth or piece of cardboard over his head. Touba turned into the long, narrow alley. She had not gone far when she suddenly stood still. She felt a pang in her heart as though struck by a bullet. Mr. Khiabani was leaning by the wall at the turn of the alley, staring ahead, his turban and cloak soaking wet. It seemed as if his eyes were glued on Touba. He has recognized me, she thought. He must have known that I would pass through here. The man, woven of light, continued looking straight ahead. Touba approached him, her steps shaky. She noticed his eyes went past her. Unconsciously she turned and looked in the direction of his gaze. The alley was empty behind her. Touba, trembling excitedly, passed Mr. Khiabani. At the end of the alley, she turned and looked back. The man was standing in the same position, deep in thought. She went on down the street, feeling drunk, as far as Malek Crossing, then she turned into the dead-end alley that led to her own house. She knocked and Haji Mostafa's younger wife opened the door, complaining about the rain. Without responding to her greeting, Touba went back to her own room.

When she opened the door to her room, the air was disturbed, and the little tea glasses and saucers, sitting upside-down on a tray

on the alcove shelf, shook. Touba's heart told her, "This is a sign."
There were powers trying to contact her, powers of great significance
related to the presence of that man, lightning and the songs of King
Solomon's hoopoe bird, the spirits of ancestors and prophets, the
innocent souls of dead children, women without husbands, and
orphans. These spirits were calling on her. She was certain that Mr.
Khiabani was a messenger of the prophets. He was now invoking her
by his divine power.

She turned around at the doorstep, stopped herself from tripping, and ran back to the gate. She pulled the old door latch,
stepped into the alley, and ran on. Her veil dragged in the mud.
From their room, Haji Mostafa's wives stared at her back in total
horror. Touba ran past Malek Crossing, and into the street to reach
the alley and to tell Mr. Khiabani, "Sir, take me, take me with you,
wherever you wish!"

It was silent in the alley, wet with rain, and its adobe walls awaited the coming of autumn. Touba leaned against the wall, exhausted,
breathing heavily. But she still felt feverish. The man must be here.
Every leaf on the tree knew, and knew eternally, that he was here.
She could not return home. The prying women would come and ask
her questions. Then she would have to touch those tea glasses. To
process and receive the breath of that holy man, the presence of God
in the moment of miracle—it would all be too much to endure in
front of Zahra and those two women. Touba ran toward her mother's home. Her mind worked automatically. She was going there to
pull out her father's books from the hope chests in the cellar and take
them with her. There must be some information in the books that
would clarify all these secrets for her.

At her father's house, she was greeted with amazement. It had
been nearly four months since she had seen her family. She sat
among them for about half an hour, feeling nervous. She had missed
all of them, but she was not in the mood to visit at this time. She sat
across from Auntie Monavar, her father's second cousin. The woman
held Touba's shoulders, talking incessantly, and Touba could not
understand any of it. She was finally able to tell them that she actually had come to take her father's books. She invited everyone to

lunch on the following Friday, to celebrate her coming out of her waiting period. She asked her brother to fetch a horse and carriage, and with the family's help she loaded the red, green, and blue velvet chests full of books onto the carriage, and she huddled next to them. The books were covered by the carriage's top while Touba herself was exposed. She reached home soaking wet. She and the driver agreed that he would get a coin if he delivered the chests to the covered entry of the house, where she once more had to confront, face-to-face, the two wives of Haji Mostafa and a flabbergasted Zahra. She explained with a smile that these were her father's books and asked them to help carry them to her room. Touba had to bear their curiosity for the next two hours and refused to open the chests with them in the room.

She waited until the next morning, and on the fourth day of continuous rain, after breakfast, she opened her chests. The globe, wrapped up in a black handkerchief, was placed carefully among the books. She removed the globe with care and respect, as if touching a holy object. The names of Russia and Prussia came to her mind, but she could not place them on the globe. She noticed the shadow of Narges, the older wife, on the curtain behind her. In a loud voice, Touba said, "Good morning, Madam Narges!" The woman hurriedly opened the curtain and entered. She explained that they were running short of sugar and forgot to explain that her night's sleep was all lost in her anxiety to discover the content of the chests. Touba let the woman come and sit next to her to inspect inside the chests and see the books. Then she held the globe in front of Narges and explained to her that the whole world had lived on this small globe since the beginning of time. Haji Mostafa's wife would not touch the globe. She just sat staring at it. For the first instant she felt shocked, and spent a few minutes looking at the round object. Then Touba noticed the usual look of ridicule appearing in the woman's eyes. Narges said, "God forbid," arched her eyebrows, and turned her head away from the globe. She let her chador slide down her shoulder, then turned toward Touba. It was as if she had heard the worst possible profanities. Her face tense and sour, she murmured that she would go to the kitchen and ask Zahra for some sugar, and headed for the door. Touba thought to herself, Now the second one will appear. Narges moved toward the door slowly, but as soon as she was in the yard she could be heard running.

Touba decided to count up to twenty, and then in a loud voice she said, "Salaam, Madam Fatemeh!" The second woman, like a genie, appeared from behind the curtain by the door. This one wanted an egg for her omelet. She was round and plump, with a common-looking face. Without dwelling too much on the egg question, she looked around innocently. Touba still held the globe in her hand. Fatemeh took a step forward so she could see it better. She sat across from Touba and put her hands carefully forward, and Touba placed the globe in them. The woman looked with awe at the globe, slowly opening her lips. Touba explained again that the whole world is placed on this small globe. Without taking her eyes from the globe to look at Touba, as if mesmerized by a magic object, Fatemeh asked, "How?" She received the answer, "Just like that." She asked again, "How?" Touba, feeling her inability to fully answer, lowered her head so that Fatemeh would not continue her persistent inquiry. But gradually her father's words came back to her. She explained that the world is much larger than what was in front of them, but its form truly is like this object. Touba moved her hands a great deal to fill in for the shortage of words she felt. The woman listened politely and docilely and believed everything she heard.

At night, when Zahra was placing buckets and bowls under the drips from of the leaking roof, the two wives sat in their own room next to their husband and whispered. Undoubtedly, an ominous event was to take place. Since the end of her abstinence, the divorcée seemed to have gone crazy, and soon she would bring disgrace upon everyone. The women retold the story of the chests for Haji Mostafa. The man first listened to the older woman, who was wiser and dearer. Narges believed that the divorcée had begun to practice black magic and was aiming to capture the devil. Then Haji Mostafa listened to Fatemeh, who was simpler and could easily be deceived, but who relied on instinct. She believed that the divorcée had turned to learning and education, that she was following in her father's footsteps and was already a wise person. Haji Mostafa fell deep in thought and finally decided that he must take the issue to Haji Mahmud. But the man had gone on a trip to the city of Qazvin, not too far west of Tehran, and would not be back for several days.

Touba spent the fifth and sixth day of rain with the books. She placed them in order on the alcove shelf, dusted them, opened them one-by-one and read a few pages of each. Vague and confusing thoughts took form in her mind. By the seventh night of rain, as she lay in bed, she arrived at the conclusion that the most honest people are those who seek God, who turn away from false love and set their heart on true love, as did the Holy Mary, or the Prophet's great daughter, Fatemeh. Touba decided to go in search of God. As a child, she had heard that in order to discover the treasure one needs seven sets of armor, and discovering God was undoubtedly a far more difficult job than treasure hunting. She remembered the glass teacups shaking in their tray, and her heart sank once more. She wondered what this strange sensation was, that always kept her next to Mr. Khiabani without necessarily seeing him. She firmly believed that he knew about every moment of her life. He knew right now that she had turned to her father's books, and if he knew that, then he is also aware of her desire to seek God, and knows that she, Touba, must do all this in absolute, genuine honesty. The man was spun of rays of light and could recognize dishonesty. He probably knew of Touba's love for him, and therefore someday he would come, lift her up, and ascend with her. Touba, in the midst of hearing Zahra's complaints about the leaking roofs all over the house, had submitted herself to the love of this man, and without any real attempt, she beckoned him to come to her. She did not need to do anything. On the third day of rain, if she had not run out in search of him, the man would have come to her door, because he was supposed to do that. But once more, she had messed things up. Perhaps she had aroused God's wrath by running out into the streets like a crazy person. Perhaps, this continuous rain was an indication of God's anger. In her heart she constantly begged forgiveness; she had been demanding, had not been submissive enough, had not obeyed God's commands, and thus she kept making a mess of everything.

There was a knock at the door. It was her father's cousin, Monavar, crying, wailing and full of anguish. It seemed that the rain of fruitfulness and bliss was turning to the rain of God's wrath. Auntie Monavar's chador was covered up to her middle in mud. She had tried to catch a covered buggy, had covered her head with another cloth, but to no avail. No one was in the street and she had walked the whole way. She was very worried about the possibility that her roof would collapse and felt she was in imminent danger. The roof of a house on her street had already come down, and a child had died beneath it. The streets were covered with water, and garbage was accumulating, clogging the sewers. Floods were washing the southern part of the city away.

Auntie Monavar talked and complained continuously, and Touba grew more and more nervous. She suddenly opened the window and shouted, "God, please don't let it rain anymore." Then she closed the window, sat across from the old woman, and tried to help her untie the chador from her skirt. With Zahra's help they wrapped her in a blanket to warm her. Still sneezing, old Auntie Monavar explained that her son, Mirza Kazem, had recently arrived from Kashan and was seeking cousin Touba, that he was well trained in the carpet-weaving industry and could recognize good quality wool from miles away, and was famous in Kashan for this. Out of the corner of her eye she watched the young divorcée, who was not paying attention to her. Yet she continued, saying that he could read and write and had good handwriting. He had not married so that he could raise his brothers and sisters. But if he were to continue alone, what was the use? He would only be bad-tempered, old, and lonely.

The talk of carpet weaving attracted Touba's attention. For some time now she had been thinking of setting up looms, just like those in her father's home, and weaving some carpets. This meant income, and the house would become active again. Old Auntie Monavar took the words out of Touba's mouth when she told her that she would send Mirza Kazem to help her set up the looms and start the business. The old woman was happy, and said, "We must keep the blood clean in the family." She looked at Touba meaningfully to see if she understood the intention of her statement.

As these words passed between them, the clouds were slowly

breaking up, and the sun began to shine through them. On this seventh day of rain, the blue noon sky reappeared from behind the gray clouds. A pleasant sense of warmth filled the house, and steam began to rise from the brick walls. Touba's heart once more began to beat tremulously. She wondered if her father's old cousin had heard her when she shouted to the heavens to stop the rain. Whatever she desired would happen, and whatever she wished would come true. The rain stopped, and old Auntie Monaver felt better spirited after smoking her water pipe. They ate delicious meat stew and fixed a bed for the old woman. Then they all lay down for a nap. But just then, another knock was heard at the gate.

One of Haji Mostafa's wives opened the door. The voices of many women could be heard at the entrance. Zahra put on her veil and went into the inner courtyard. Soon she ran back into the room, excited and flushed. With short and hushed breaths, she explained that the older woman they had met in the bathhouse was there, along with a prominent lady, to visit Touba.

She said this and quickly began to clear the room. She straightened the large cushions and with her fingers picked up any bits of crumbs she could see on the carpet. She then quickly ran out of the room to the courtyard, which the two women had by then reached, to direct them to the room. Old Auntie Monavar sat up straight. She was not happy about this turn of events. She was aware of the role this type of old woman played in bathhouses. There was a shuffle at the entrance, and Zahra humbly showed the two ladies into the room.

Touba covered herself with a light blue house veil patterned with small flowers, then stood to show her respect for the ladies. The two women were of approximately the same age, but the strange one looked like a mountain of fat. She introduced herself personally as Madam Esmat, an acquaintance of the other woman from the bathhouse, Madam Efat. She began taking in her surroundings and examining the decor of the room. One could notice a slight sense of disapproval in her eyes. She focused on Monavar and did not stop staring at her until she had clearly understood her relationship to Touba. Monavar merely turned her head, threw her eyebrows up,

and quickly sat down. She did not feel it necessary to stand on ceremony any longer for these women. Madam Esmat was now measuring up Touba, examing her from head to toe, and vice-versa. She had
her head cocked and one eyebrow raised. She explained that last year
she had been fortunate enough to go on a pilgrimage to Mecca in
the company of Princess Turan O-Saltaneh. Since she was an intimate of the princess's court, she had the obligation to make the pilgrimage as well. She pronounced the word *saltaneh*, referring to the
monarchy, very emphatically.

Madam Esmat sat down on a cushion at the head of the room,
leaving the other cushion empty for Touba. Although the older
woman put on the air of a dignitary, it seemed that she did not really believe herself to be one. Touba sat in an even more prominent
place at the head of the room, not herself knowing why. Madam
Esmat was practical, and in order to break through the formalities
she insisted on talking. She complemented Madam Efat on her dis-
cerning choice. Zahra placed a tray of pastries and fruits along with
tea in front of the guests, which made Monavar even more upset,
and Touba continued listening dumbfoundedly as the woman
talked.

Madam Esmat recounted how the princess had become curious
and interested in the Adib family after she heard Madam Efat's
report of their meeting in the bathhouse. The princess's father,
Prince Moezel Sultan, the half-brother to Naser O-Din Shah, knew
Mr. Adib personally, and Touba's father had attended many court
gatherings. Madam Esmat continued that Princess Turan O-
Saltaneh's brother, Prince Kamal O-Doleh, who was a noble member of the Qajar court and a pride of the country, was currently in
search of a wife from a proper family, perhaps a widow. Touba suddenly blushed and her pulse quickened. Finally becoming aware of
the intent of the women's visit, she turned unconsciously and looked
at Monavar. Monavar, thinking that Touba was not interested in this
wedding, began to explain to the two women that Touba had only
recently gone through a divorce and was yet committed to her period of abstinence. Zahra cut Monavar short and explained that her
mistress's period of abstinence was well over, and she was free. Mean-

while, Touba's eyes moved from one woman to the other. Madam Esmat turned to the young divorcée and told her that a week from today the princess would like to come and visit Touba. She commented that the princess did not usually leave the house since there were enough servants and attendants to take care of all of her needs. But only for Adib's daughter, who was a pride and joy to humanity, the princess was willing to step out and visit this lady of knowledge in person. But then, every divorcée rules her own life.

She continued, saying that the divorced lady's father had passed away, she had no marital commitment and, from what Madam Efat had explained, there did not seem to be an older brother. Therefore, one would have to consult with her directly for all matters concerned. She kept her quizzical stare on Touba. Touba, feeling the pressure of the stare from this mountain of meat and fat, lowered her head and gazed at the carpet patterns. Just this very day she had communed with God; she had asked God to stop the rain, and it had stopped raining. That holy man should be coming, as well, but he had not yet arrived. She murmured that she was not interested in marrying again and intended to go on a pilgrimage.

The fat woman sniggered and raised her eyebrows. In her opinion there was no conflict between having a husband and going on a pilgrimage, particularly when the woman could go with her husband and achieve greater reward from that pilgrimage. The divorcée responded that she was searching for God and intended to spend her life in pursuit of God. From one holy place to the other and one saint's tomb to the next, she would finally, somewhere, find God. The fat woman, feeling playful, asked Touba by what means she intended to cover these distances. Touba stated simply that she could achieve her purpose by walking. The woman fell into hysterical laughter that went on and on, wearing on Monavar's nerves just as an untuned musical instrument assaults the ears. Finally Monavar could bear it no longer and spoke up. She said that since Touba's mind was made up, no one could interfere. After all, she was a woman who answered only to herself, and could live as she wished.

Madam Esmat pulled herself together, silenced the whirlwind of her laughter, and addressed Monavar directly for the first time. She asked Monavar how an eighteen-year-old divorcée, with her golden hair and voluptuous white body, could go from one holy place to another. She turned suddenly toward Touba and said, "My dear lady, a woman is only a pendant that is inevitably chained." She then fidgeted in her place and said that if Touba were old perhaps she could, like the old woman of the fairy tales, hide in a pumpkin and ride down the dangerous roads to go on a pilgrimage. But in her youth, even if she were to hide in a pumpkin, it would not be possible to achieve her intent. She looked at Touba tenderly. She was feeling attached to the woman in spite of herself. In Touba's personality was a simplicity and lack of wit that caressed her whole rounded body. During her lifetime in the household of Princess Turan O-Saltaneh, she had never come across such a personality. For an instant the two women's eyes met. Touba wished to tell her about her dreams of Mr. Khiabani, but something stopped her. She said, "I seriously want to seek God."

Madam Esmat turned her attention to her tea and pastry. The conversation shifted to the rain and the flood in the southern part of the city. They exchanged some news, and when the two women were leaving, Madam Esmat emphasized that Princess Turan O-Saltaneh would pay a visit on this same day, Tuesday, a week hence, in the afternoon. They pulled the curtain aside to depart, and saw Narges, the older wife of Haji Mostafa, running away from the door, hoping no one would notice that she had been eavesdropping.

Monavar was standing in the middle of the room when Touba returned from accompanying her guests to the gate. As soon as Touba pulled the curtain aside, Monavar warned her that she should be very careful. Members of the royal family were not to be trusted. They piled wives and concubines into their harems, gave them six and half pounds of bread a day, and expected their women to be grateful, even if they performed their husbandly duties once in a blue moon. In the harems of Naser O-Din Shah, she said, there were herds of deprived wives waiting for their daily food rations. The wives were expected to be content living in the shah's harem, even though they were living a dog's life. Under these conditions, a wife might never bear a child. Or she might become the target of the other wives' jealousies. She might end up crying blood. In the end she is neither loved by the shah nor respected by the people. It was impossible to find a family in the city willing to marry a daughter off to the royal family, and thereby bring ruin upon the family and the girl. Touba said that she had no such plans; those women had come of their own accord, and she had no obligation or intention of marrying royalty.

Touba stood by the window to look at the beautiful blue, clear sky that had appeared after the rain. It seemed to hold so much promise. Monavar whispered to her that tomorrow she would send Mirza Kazem to talk about setting up the carpet looms. She said that family and relatives should protect each other. As they say, blood is thicker than water. Relatives ought to support one another, and must not allow strangers to come among them and cause disunity. She reminded Touba of the fact that her first husband, Haji Mahmud, had he been a stranger, would have inflicted great grievances upon her. But in commitment to being a relative, he had divorced her respectfully and considerately. He had provided her with the house and cared for her and the rest of her family.

Monavar headed for her large cushion to lie down for the afternoon nap she had missed, while mumbling something under her breath. Touba was still staring at the sky and said to herself, Oh God, please send Mr. Khiabani to me before next Tuesday. Please help me.

Mirza Kazem seemed about twenty-five or twenty-six years old. He was dressed in a new long jacket, white moccasins, and a pressed wool hat. He was standing in the yard uncomfortably. When he had knocked at the gate, Haji Mostafa's two wives had told him to wait, gone to put on their chadors, and come back to open the door, only to then stare at him. Zahra came and brought him to the middle of the yard. She had him stand there so that when her mistress covered herself in her chador and came out to talk with him, everyone could observe them and know that nothing immoral was happening and that he was a relative and not a stranger.

Now, the two second cousins were talking face-to-face, and Touba felt as if she had an older brother on whom she could rely.

Zahra had put a chair by the pool, and Mirza Kazem was sitting on it with a hunched back, his feet pulled together, feeling nervous and sheepish. Touba sat on the edge of the pool. The early fall cold was bothering her. She exchanged cordialities, meanwhile looking up and noticing Haji Mostafa's two wives standing on guard by the window. She raised her voice so they could hear her as she asked her second cousin about setting up the weaving looms. The man, suddenly released of all anxiety and tension, reported quickly that he had come to check the cellar and allocate the appropriate space for the looms. He had only drunk half his tea, but he headed for the cellar, accompanied by Zahra and Touba, to inspect the room. In the cellar all three felt relaxed until they noticed the shadow of one of the wives again. Mirza Kazem found the right spot for the looms and said that tomorrow he would bring the carpenter, who was also from Kashan and very skilled.

Touba noticed some papers rolled up under Mirza Kazem's elbow and asked what they were. Mirza Kazem said, "a newspaper." He then opened the folded pages for her to see. He explained that the news of the day was reported in a newspaper.

Touba's eyes focused on the large print of the newspaper headline, on the word *Khiabani*. Mirza Kazem, noticing the direction of her gaze, explained that Mr. Khiabani's speech at the parliament that day was printed in this newspaper. He lowered his voice and told her that they did not sell this newspaper everywhere because Mr. Khiabani had many enemies. By now he was whispering. The basic essence of constitutionalism was in danger, he said, and Mr. Khiabani would defend it to his grave. Touba was all ears. She invited Mirza Kazem to come to her room. Her desire for learning overpowered her fear of being slandered by the two wives of Haji Mostafa. There, in the constant presence of Zahra, the young and enthusiastic Mirza Kazem spoke to her about Mr. Khiabani and the other constitutionalists.

Touba heard things she had never heard before. Her ex-husband, Haji Mahmud, was anti-constitution, and also would never discuss such issues with the women. Touba was suddenly entering the everyday life of society. She listened so intently that it made the young man feel like a genius, and he tried his best to make a good impression. The aristocracy had united, he said, opposing the constitutionalists. In addition, many groups were not pleased with the constitutionalists. But Mr. Khiabani was very steadfast in his beliefs. The young man was warming up. He drank many cups of tea and once in a while received a sweet shy comment from Touba. What was not clear in the woman's mind were the two different personalities of Mr. Khiabani. To her, the great man was a spirited being who originated from light. But Mirza Kazem portrayed a noble, ethical man who was politically radical. Mirza Kazem expressed the idea that Mr. Khiabani was too revolutionary, and Touba lost a couple of chances to ask about the term *revolutionary*, which she had difficulty understanding. Mirza Kazem said that such people are good and great, but they endanger the country. We must be careful these days, he said. Russia and England are watching Iran like hawks, and we have to be careful not to give them a chance to fish in this muddy water. From Mirza Kazem's point of view, Mr. Khiabani was very respectable, but not immune to criticism. The woman listened timidly. She wondered if Mirza Kazem really knew how grand Mr. Khiabani was, how he spent his nights in graveyards, weeping for the poor people. She knew Mirza Kazem was someone she could confide in. Nevertheless, he was a man and probably knew more than she did.

Touba asked Mirza Kazem to buy her the newspaper. He promised to do it and told her not to worry about the money. Suddenly she remembered the globe. She asked Mirza Kazem if he knew anything about globes. He said that he knew some things, so she got it out. Standing two yards away from it, he tried to explain the colors and areas, though he could hardly read the printed Latin words. He explained that every color stood for a country, and the lines in-between were the boundaries. Mirza Kazem pointed out Russia to her. It was bright green. Then he pointed out Iran, right below Russia. It was yellow, and he called her attention to its catlike shape. The woman immediately grew fond of the yellow cat. Undoubtedly, in this color and shape were hidden secrets that she was not yet aware of. God wanted it this way. On the other side of Iran was India, in dark green, and Mirza Kazem told her that India was very green,

green and luxuriant as paradise. Beyond all of these was the far-off land that had been discovered by a man by the name of Christopher Columbus, but it was named America, after another man. This country had many different colors, and it was surrounded by large waters, separating it from the rest of the world. Mirza Kazem showed her England and Japan and many other places. So much time passed that he had to stay for lunch. Touba left him to eat alone and went to the inner room where she usually slept, where she had her lunch with Zahra. That night Haji Mostafa's two wives reported to him about all of these disgraceful episodes, and he decided to confront Touba on these shameful matters in the morning. However, by the morning he realized he did not have the courage to face the woman. The way she often looked at the world about her without acknowledging him, and gave open and direct answers, made it difficult for him to have discussions with her.

He had not yet left the house when Mirza Kazem arrived with workers and carpenters. They unloaded the boards, beams, and tools for their loom-making in the middle of the yard, and Haji Mostafa's two wives became prisoners in their rooms. By evening the loom was set up. Mirza Kazem and the carpenters had eaten their lunch, the usual stew, right there. Mirza Kazem had also remembered to bring a newspaper for Touba. That night, after the long, noisy, and busy day, Touba began reading the newspaper. She sat next to the oil lamp and opened it almost reverently. A wave of events from the outside world rushed in. After she was finished reading, she folded the newspaper respectfully and placed it on the alcove shelf.

On Friday her whole family came over for lunch. This included Touba's mother and her stepfather, Abdolah Khan, the military officer; her younger sister; and her two brothers. Zahra told them in detail the story of Madam Esmat's visit on behalf of the princess's brother. The news created great excitement in the family. From Abdolah Khan's point of view, the marriage with royalty was of great importance and would bring great respectability to the family. Their status would increase in society, and Touba's brothers, who were in school, would benefit greatly in the future. Abdolah Khan decided to take over the arrangements. He said that he would send velvet and gold-tasseled cushions from the house. He advised Zahra on where to buy the appropriate fruits and pastries, and it was decided that all members of the family would return on Tuesday to ensure that the pre-wedding visitation had all the necessary aplomb and grandeur. They agreed that they should have a few chairs and a coffee table so that Abdolah Khan would not have to sit on the floor in the presence of strange women. This would also increase Touba's worth in the eyes of her suitor's family.

The divorcée dealt with all of this in a half-asleep, half-awake stupor. On Monday, on Zahra's advice and along with her, she went to the bathhouse. When they returned home, Zahra braided Touba's hair into forty braids, put gold earrings on her, and dressed her in her new clothes. On Tuesday morning Zahra cleaned the house. Many times she wondered anxiously if she would be able to serve a princess. Mirza Kazem again brought the newspaper, and also wool. The wool had just arrived from Kashan, and it was of the highest quality. The young man was not aware of the changes going on, so he simply handed the wool and the paper to Touba and left for his work.

Late on Tuesday afternoon, the family arrived. The children were to stay in Touba's room and keep quiet. Abdolah Khan sat on the chair. The table and the chairs were arranged near the door so that Abdolah Khan could sit there without removing his shining boots and thus look more impressive. All around the room were cushions of velvet with gold tassels, replacing the older velvet cushions from Touba's room. After a while Abdolah Khan decided to go for a walk around the neighborhood and to return after the ladies had arrived. This way, he would not have to stand up upon the women's arrival.

At five in the afternoon, there was a knock at the gate. Haji Mostafa's wives ran to the gate, but Zahra was there far enough ahead to push them aside and open the gate for the princess herself. The princess, in a formal black chador, was standing there, her face cover pulled up, revealing only her beautiful, hazel eyes. The carriage driver and Madam Esmat were standing behind her, and further back stood Madam Efat, the bathhouse woman. Zahra bowed down to her knees. The princess ordered the carriage driver to stay by the carriage, and he respectfully agreed. The lady entered, brought her hand out of her chador, pointed to the two women of Haji Mostafa and asked who they were. Her hand was white and chubby, and adorned with two rings with huge diamond and ruby settings. The two women automatically recoiled. Zahra said quietly, "Your maids, the wives of Haji Mostafa." Touba's uneducated and clumsy mother was standing by the entrance to the building, bowing and greeting continuously. When the princess found out who this woman was, she merely nodded her head out of courtesy and headed to the room. Madam Esmat followed. Madam Efat was not sure what to do. She followed, keeping a few steps behind, anxious about whether she would be invited into the room. But she heard Madam Esmat telling her to stay behind in the yard and ended up sitting contentedly by the edge of the pool.

Touba stood at the door to her outer room, covered in her blue chador. Zahra attended to the princess's chador and face cover and offered her a lounging dress of greenish tone. The princess pulled the dress on gracefully and walked to the head of the room. Touba and her mother sat halfway up the cushioned wall, and Madam Esmat parked herself closer to the room's entrance. Zahra, anxious about proper manners of attendance, left the room. The princess looked at the samovar in the corner of the room, then looked straight at Touba and asked, "Don't you feel cold?" It was direct and sudden. Touba explained that they usually began using their charcoal heaters in the month of Azar. Zahra brought in a heater and placed it next to the princess, who quickly held her hands close to it. She said, "It seems that this year is going to grow colder sooner, and there will be lots of snow." Abdolah Khan's voice was heard from behind the door. The princess covered herself without haste. He entered and all the women, even the princess, stood up. He invited them to sit down and seated himself on the chair. He tried to avoid dirtying the carpet with his boots, which prevented his showing off his spurs to the princess. He had even thought of crossing one leg over the other, just as he had seen in a picture of Kaiser Wilhelm of Prussia. But somehow—he did not know why—it made him uncomfortable to consider it.

The introductions were now over.

The princess was thinking that the family was not provincial, and they seemed to be reasonably well off. Abruptly she began to speak of her brother, Prince Feraydun Mirza Kamal O-Doleh. She said God had not created a more pleasant and jovial person than he. She wanted to find him a good wife who would help him become somewhat more serious. She laughed, and Abdolah Khan thought to himself that it was not proper for a woman to laugh in the presence of a man. But perhaps there was a reason for everything. The princess had laughed, and one was probably supposed to laugh too. He therefore laughed dryly in response to the princess's laughter. He was feeling more and more uncomfortable every minute. The woman was showing her naked arm with no inhibition or shame. A heavily jeweled bracelet glowed on her right arm, and as she moved her arm the bracelet moved up and down. Her dress sleeve came down to her wrist, but it was loose, full of folds, and edged with lace. Every time she lifted her arm, the sleeve moved down, revealing her delicate wrist.

The princess asked Touba whether it was true that she wanted to go in search of God. Touba simply responded in the affirmative. A sweet smile covered the princess's lips, and she said that being the daughter of an educated man provided such wisdom and completion in a being, and that Touba was definitely permeated with innocence. And then, suddenly, she asked her why she had separated from her husband. Abdolah Khan entered into the conversation to explain about the significant age difference between husband and wife and their lack of compatibility. He knew about the graveyard episode, but wanted to keep things in check. The princess told them that her brother was forty-six years old. But, he was not really a forty-six-year-old, more like an eighteen-year-old, who can bewilder everyone. Regarding the question of whether he had another wife, she revealed that he also had just divorced his last wife. He had a few children from some other wives whom he had divorced, but those children lived with their mothers. Touba did not have to be concerned with her future husband's previous children. The princess explained that the prince was against polygamy, that he believed in one God and one wife. Even as she talked, her eyes focused on

Touba's gold earrings and she decided that for the wedding she would give her a pair of diamond earrings.

Everything moved along easily. It was decided that the wedding should be held as soon as possible, before the commencement of the fasting month of Ramadan, perhaps in fifteen days.

The princess told them that tomorrow she would send the mirror, the candelabra, and the silk cloth. She went on to say that it was not really necessary to see the groom. The prince was well known, and Abdolah Khan could meet with him at his government office if he thought he must. She stated that if she had approved of the girl it was as though her brother had approved of her, and when she got up to leave, she had even set the date for the wedding; Tuesday, in two weeks. In the courtyard the princess nodded to Madam Esmat and placed a gold coin in Madam Efat's hand, which led that woman to bow almost to the ground.

The princess, indifferent to her surroundings, walked abreast of Touba, her mother, and Abdolah Khan to the gate, where once more the two wives of Haji Mostafa stood, amazed at seeing a princess for the first time in their lives. The carriage driver opened the door, Abdolah Khan accompanied the princess to her carriage, and the other women returned to their rooms. Just one month after her period of abstinence had ended, Touba was to be married again.

The news traveled like electricity among the relatives, and when Mirza Kazem heard, it was like an arrow to his heart. Since that first meeting with Touba he had planned on having her as his own wife. They had been so intimate on that day when they spoke about the globe, Mr. Khiabani, and carpet-weaving. He planned to have a simple wedding; only one cleric would conduct the marriage. After all, his second cousin was a divorcée, and therefore one avoided all the complications that came with marrying a virgin. On the other hand, she was beautiful, and she could weave carpets and manage her house well. But now, this bastard prince had appeared from some God-forsaken place. Even if they did not actually get married, Touba could always flaunt this fact in later years as an advantage over him.

Mirza Kazem's first act was to stop taking newspapers to her.

Thus Touba's contact with the outside world was cut off. Without knowing why this had happened, her wondering mind began to go wild again. It seemed to her as though some power from beyond had a hand in stopping her newspaper reading. It just did not make sense to her that her second cousin would disappear from her life of his own accord.

Mirza Kazem's second act was to pursue his own studies. He needed to go to night school, study science, and show this stupid prince, whom he already hated even without meeting him, who was on top.

The third action he took was to change his attire. He had friends who dressed in Western styles and he decided overnight to do this as well. The process was so sudden that it caused his mother great surprise. But Monavar had learned to accept sudden changes since her son had arrived from Kashan; the pace of life in Tehran was so different from what it had been back home.

Mirza Kazem next struggled to get a job as a civil servant. He wanted to be inside the system in order, someday, to fight against it. He talked to someone about learning French. He also needed to be able to read the Latin script on the globe, so that these insignificant women would get their questions answered and would not go looking for husbands among princes. He also increased his contact with the groups that associated with Mr. Khiabani. This member of parliament was not against modernization. Among his followers there were many wearing Western suits and ties. In just ten days, Mirza Kazem made all of these changes, and then he decided to go and speak with Touba. Though he hated to do it, he needed to get the accounts settled with her for his expenses on lumber, wool, workmen, and so on. He also needed to somehow get even with her.

He went to the house. Although Zahra invited him in, he would not enter. He asked if Touba would kindly come to the gate. Touba covered herself in her house chador and went to the door. She was astounded at what appeared to be a transformation in her second cousin. She repeatedly invited him to come in, and each time he refused. In the end, he gave in and entered, but his manners were very formal. Touba sat in the inner quarter near the door while

Mirza Kazem sat on the chair in the outer guest room, which had been left there since Abdolah Khan had used it. They had decided to leave the furniture as it was until the wedding was over. There was a long silence between the two, then Touba asked, in a soft voice, if the newspapers were not published anymore. Mirza Kazem said that the newspaper was published every day, but finding it was more and more difficult each day. He told her of having seen Mr. Khiabani, and of the man's announcement that he would leave Tehran as a protest against injustice and discrimination. Her heart filled with sorrow, and there was heavy silence again. She then asked if they could settle accounts, so she could pay him all she owed him. He suddenly decided not to accept any money from her and leave her with a heavy conscience forever. Each persisted on their point, and it finally ended as Mirza Kazem wished.

He told her that he was looking for a civil service position at the Department of Land Management. He wanted to become a government employee. After ten years, he would have improved his administrative position so as to become an important minister. He then hated himself for having said all this. He would have preferred if there had been someone else to explain all this to her.

Touba listened to this, not yet able to distinguish the difference between a merchant and a civil administrator. She could not understand the meaning of it all, except that Mirza Kazem reminded her of the Englishman of her childhood.

Mirza Kazem wanted to ask questions about the prince. He was torn between asking and not asking. Finally he said, "Is it true that my second cousin is marrying a Qajar prince?" If anyone had been there, they would have seen that his face turned as red as a beet. Touba said yes, it was true. Mirza Kazem asked her if she knew about the Qajar dynasty's coming demise. This question was bold. Though Mirza Kazem had been reading the pamphlets of the constitutionalists, he had never permitted himself to speculate on the fall of the existing regime. Now, suddenly, in the presence of his second cousin, the thought revealed itself from the depth of his consciousness. The woman thought he must be mistaken. Kings never lose their thrones. As long as there had been a world, there had been kings and kingdoms. She thought, This is not right. If she was not supposed to marry the prince, then Mr. Khiabani must somehow inform her. But the great man had been silent. He had not sent her any messages, except on that rainy day when the tea glasses and saucers had trembled on their shelf. Touba had not yet been able to discover the secret meaning of this event, and the shortage of news and her distance from him was disturbing her more and more. "Mirza Kazem could not understand her state of mind. He thought, Perhaps marrying a prince has caused her this trepidation. Now she believes she will be the jewel of the harem, will dress in gold and damask clothing, and her servants will follow her. She will no longer weave carpets. She will not be her simple self. Tomorrow she will become the witch who will put poison in someone's tea glass and push a needle into the brain of her competitor's children. Poor second cousin. Mirza Kazem was in a desperate state of mind, with mixed feelings of respect, contempt, and resignation."

There was a knocking at the gate. Madam Esmat and Touba's mother had arrived. They were to go shopping for the wedding with the bride-to-be. Zahra had come into the room well in advance of them so that Mirza Kazem's presence there would be excused. Madam Esmat would not leave the matter alone until she found out everything about Mirza Kazem. Touba gave Zahra a pouch full of money to give to Mirza Kazem, to cover what she figured to be the cost of the newspapers and wool. Mirza Kazem accepted the sack of money being offered to him so as not to arouse any suspicions in the mind of the princess's go-between and attendant. He counted the money and returned some of it to Zahra. Although he said his farewell politely, he left the house committed to attending a revolutionary meeting against the Qajars that very evening. Mirza Kazem had made up his mind to overthrow this decadent dynasty.

In the bazaar, while the women were bargaining over the purchase of brocaded silks and velveteen, Touba made an abrupt decision. She decided to go and see Mr. Khiabani in person. She had to think of an excuse so the women would leave her alone. She said her legs were weak and she was getting tired, therefore she needed to return home. The women offered to accompany her, but she dissuaded them, and before they could make any further plans she had disappeared around one of the bazaar corners. She quickly tried to reach the entrance of the bazaar. She was not familiar with her way, so she hailed a carriage and almost shouted, "The parliament." She thought that she would now reach a palace in the clouds, the appropriate place for Mr. Khiabani. The carriage stopped before her thoughts could ascend any higher. They had arrived.

Touba descended from the carriage and observed her surroundings in amazement. She was in a large, clean, well swept, square; horses, carriages, and donkeys were passing by, but there was no dust. She turned to the iron gate. It took her a while before she lifted her head and looked at the clouds above the gate. Atop the two sides of the gate were statues of two lions with suns on their backs, holding swords. Across the top of the gate was written: "Mozafar's Justice." She then noticed there were guards at the gate, and wondered if she could ask them the whereabouts of Mr. Khiabani. The guards appeared serious and tough, and were ignoring her. She walked up and down the street, trying to summon up her courage. She definitely could not ask them about Mr. Khiabani. She walked around the square helplessly, only to return to the gate of the Parliament again. She was now certain that she would not ask them anything at all. She was afraid they would shoo her away or ridicule her. A veiled woman at the Parliament? What would they say?

She walked around the square again. On the corner of the street was a small kebab shop. She stopped and looked at the meat, presented with eggs halves displayed on top. It made her hungry. Every time someone went through the door of the shop a nice-sounding bell chimed. Touba stared at the display for a long time. Could she go in and ask for kebab? The shopkeeper himself stepped out finally and asked what the sister would like. Touba said, "Kebab." The man asked, "Money?" She offered him a ten-rial coin. The man returned to his shop. He wrapped two skewers of kebab in thin bread and returned with her change in his hand. He told her there was an alcove in the alley where she could eat her food and to hurry before the kebab went cold. Touba ran quickly to the alley, hiding her food under her veil. It was a narrow, isolated alley. She sat in the corner of an alcove and, pulling her face covering up enough to be able to eat, she began to devour the food. She was swallowing without chewing, and it was getting stuck in her throat. A few times she had to stop to allow the food that was stuck in her throat to pass down. The fat in the meat had coagulated into cold grease, and the bread felt stale. When she had finished eating and was getting up to leave, she noticed a man standing a few steps behind, watching her. She ran faster than she had ever run before. She reached the gates of the parliament again where she stopped to catch her breath. This time she was not so awed by the parliament, and looked at it with no great love.

If Mr. Khiabani wanted to, he could come out here and visit with her. The blessed man was capable of anything he wished to do. Waiting around was useless. She called a carriage and on the way home she thought of the taste of the kebab in her mouth, and of how food had never before tasted so good. It was only the second time in her whole life that she had eaten a meal of her own choice. The other women arrived later. Because Zahra had gone with them to the bazaar, there was nothing to eat. Zahra took a tray and went to the kebab shop near the house to fetch some kebab, and Touba smiled to herself.

The wedding took place at Princess Turan O-Saltaneh's home. The princess went all out for her brother's wedding. She had vowed to herself to get her brother settled down so that she could save her own husband. Since Prince Feraydun Mirza had divorced his last wife, he had become a burden to her. And worst of all, he was taking her husband, Prince Mansur Mirza, out drinking every night. News of their activity would reach her from other ladies, arousing the princess's jealousies. She knew that her husband was like a pliable metal in the hands of Feraydun Mirza. A few times she faked fainting spells to the point that the physician was called in, but it did not put an end to their evening outings.

Unconsciously—or at times consciously—Mansur Mirza followed the avant-garde tendencies and unquenchable desires of Feraydun Mirza. There was always some way to excuse their behavior. They followed the motto that life is short and one must make the best of it.

Turan O-Saltaneh personally supervised the design of Touba's wedding dress. It was soft blue silk mixed with white satin, and covered with gold embroidery, especially around the edges of the sleeve and the skirt. Madam Orus picked the designs from the Russian costumes, and the princess made the necessary changes.

On the morning of the wedding, Touba was given the bridal bath, and her hair was plaited into forty braids. On each row of braid hung a pearl with a golden ring. She was made up and primped to the point that she could no longer recognize herself in the mirror. An extremely beautiful woman looked back at her. Her clumsy mother, in a self-made, poorly fitting green velvet dress, fidgeted around Touba, and her younger sister, wrapped in her prayer chador, sat in a corner staring at her sister's transformation in total amazement. Turan O-Saltaneh ordered a dress for Touba's mother from her personal wardrobe. It was arranged that the bride would dress up after lunch, and at two o'clock, because it had been foreseen as the lucky hour under the astrological signs, the wedding vows would be exchanged.

At lunch, while the women all were gathered around the large, decorated food-cloth, eating and watching Morvarid, the Jewish singer and tambourine player, the men were eating their lunch in the men's quarters, drinking red wine while Morteza, the ever-present servant and attendant to the prince, played his tar for them. He was skilled with this traditional musical instrument.

Prince Feraydun Mirza had the mustache of a dervish, and Mansur Mirza, the companion of his bachelor nights, also had a similar mustache. Morteza wore the dervish mustache as the third in their trio. All three were attracted to the world of the Sufis. But Morteza was considering officially undergoing the initiations on the "path of the dervishes." He was thinking that after the wedding of the prince, if his full-time tar playing were to not make enough money, he would ask the prince's help to obtain a job in an office and try to earn a conventional living for himself and his family, and then definitely pursue the mystic path.

Morteza had clear visions about his spiritual experiences, which at times he told to the prince and his friend. These visions at times transported the other two men from the material world to the world beyond. These three men were inseparable, and as this third one was poor and of lower status, he had accepted his position humbly. He accompanied the prince and his friend to all their debauchery but never touched the many women whom the prince visited. He loved his wife and was devoted to her, and he bore his poverty patiently.

Feraydun Mirza anxiously waited to see his new bride. He had heard so much about her in the last few weeks, and he had formed an angel-like image of her in his mind. He had made arrangements with Madam Esmat so that at an appropriate time he would be able to sneak a look at Touba through one of the windows. Well experienced, Madam Esmat had managed to delay the moment of visitation until she had squeezed the promise of a golden coin, as her payoff, from the prince. Now, after lunch, with her chador on, she came to the men's quarters to tempt him further.

She told him that his bride looked like a cherub in paradise. Her beauty was over and above the beauty of the moon. Madam Esmat sat at an angle that would show her cleavage at the opening of the veil as her body swayed. This woman knew that everything is dependent on the flesh; and the more flesh, the better. She had the advantage over the bride of being fat. Very fat! This advantage must not be overlooked, and she knew that Mansur Mirza, contrary to the prince, preferred fat women.

Of course she was devoted to her mistress, Turan O-Saltaneh, and knew that she must not compromise her situation and source of income. But then, the house had many corners and she knew how to be discreet. And she was not necessarily committing a sacrilegious act. The option of temporary marriage, to become an official part of the family, was available. Nothing could go wrong, and therefore she took advantage of the privilege. She had lived long enough to know how to protect herself against the princess's entourage. But not so long as to lose her youthful appearance. The prince listened carefully to the woman describing Touba. Everything was described in detail, but with tact and coyness.

The prince had no scruples about hearing his future wife described in the presence of his friends. The woman was his, and he knew how to keep her under control. Besides, he had heard much about the woman's chastity, and he liked this. Considering his own wild behavior, it would not do for her to be wild.

At last he lost patience. He was determined to see the woman in any way possible before the marriage vows took place. Madam Esmat requested her reward. She placed the golden coin in her bosom, then instructed the prince to follow the back steps of the building, go through the passageway, and hide in the pantry. She intended to lure the bride, under a pretense, to the family room that was adjacent to the pantry. And she succeeded in her plan. She told Touba that there, in the room, she could take a good look at herself dressed in the bridal gown. Touba stood in the middle of the room looking at herself in the mirror. Thoughts concerning the pursuit of God, the dead boy by the sidewalk, and giving birth to another messiah undulated through her mind like a cloudy dream. She firmly believed that what was in progress was God's will, unfolding as fate demanded. Her father's books and the looms were objects of a forgotten dream in a far corner, already in storage. What had happened during these last two weeks had been rapid and rushed. She had not thought of her second cousin, Mirza Kazem. And Mr. Khiabani . . . he had occasionally appeared and disappeared in her thoughts like a ray of sunshine hidden behind the clouds. She had even reflected, for an instant, that the man was not as illuminatingly holy as she had imagined. But she immediately pushed those thoughts away.

At present, Touba was alone with the mirror. Apparently Madam Esmat had left her, to attend to a chore. Touba, enjoying her solitude, turned around a few times, looking at her whole figure in the mirror. She had to admit that she was beautiful, and smiled approvingly. Meanwhile, the prince was taking in his vision the woman hungrily. His forehead and nose were flattened against the glass window. In mid-twirl, Touba saw the face and screamed involuntarily. Suddenly Madam Esmat appeared out of nowhere and stood by the curtain in front of the door. The prince pulled his face away, laughing out loud joyfully before he disappeared.

Madam Esmat explained that the observer was Touba's future husband and that one look was not immoral. And the first memory of their common life formed in Touba's mind.

Upon his return to the men's quarters, elated and smiling, the prince noticed Mansur Mirza's unhappiness. Mansur Mirza was worried that after the marriage the prince would inevitably leave their circle and join the domesticity of hens and chickens. On the glory of Imam Ali, whom he considered the great master of Sufism, Prince Feraydun swore that he would never abandon his group of friends. Women were the object of pleasure, but men must go only as far in their relationships with women as would not interfere with the mystic path.

The prince further declared that if he reached fifty, which he did not think he would, he planned to join the circle of dervishes and devote himself completely to the pursuit of spiritual truth. Morteza did not believe any of this, but he did not say so to either man. Mansur Mirza wanted proof from his friend. It was agreed that after consummating his marriage with his wife that evening, the prince should sleep with the black woman who worked at the house, in order to prove his disregard for the companionship of women. The men locked their thumbs and middle fingers of their right hands together, a customary sign between them, to seal their promise.

Some of the guests had come early in the morning to join in the bridal lunch festivities. Others were arriving in the afternoon to participate in the wedding ceremony and enjoy the night's wedding feast. A silken veil was placed on Touba's head and she was seated by the spread damask wedding cloth. The cleric performed the wedding vows, and women's jubilant voices filled the air.

Turan O-Saltaneh ordered the women to be silent and announced that Madam Touba, who was now considered the bride of the royal court, would from now on be addressed as Shams Ol-Moluk, by the order of his majesty Mohammad Ali Shah. The proxy to the marriage was the influential wife of the late Mozafar O-Din Shah. This particularly important wife was now occupying the new harem allocated for the former shah's wives. After Turan O-Saltaneh's announcement of Touba's title, the women ululated again and the festivities began.

The bride was escorted by the women to the top of the salon, where a curtain separated them from the men. They could hear the murmur and hum of men beyond the curtain. Feraydun Mirza, laughing himself, was telling a story that had the other men doubled over with laughter. Morvarid, the dancer, played her tambourine again. Another dancer appeared from behind the curtain and recited a couple of sentences in praise of the bride and the bridegroom. A woman playing the fiddle followed the dancer. Then the all-female orchestra sat in their appointed place, and music and dance filled the room. The dancer began twirling, and it was obvious that she was a professional. Still twirling, she made her way to the curtain, pulled it open, and continued on. Some men turned to look at the women. Touba's little sister, covered her face and turned away from them. The dancer remained among the men for a long time. She whirled and received tokens from her audience; the men now tipped her more generously. Morvarid, following the dancer, kept playing her tambourine and sang on while the guests ululated. The dancer returned to the women's section once more. She twirled and circled on her knees, bent backward, in front of the wife of the late Mozafar O-Din Shah. The grand lady placed a gold coin on the dancer's forehead. Morvarid let out a sustained yodel and the dancer continued her circling and backbends by every important woman guest and received a token from each until she reached the mother of the bride, where she once again, following the music, knelt and bent backward. But the simple-minded woman hid her head behind her daughter Touba. Some women laughed and some smiled demeaningly. Touba, embarrassed and surprised, did not know what to do. But Turan O-Saltaneh intervened and placed a coin on the dancer's forehead. Touba's little sister, whispered, "How shameless."

At seven in the evening the bride was escorted to the nuptial room. Turan O-Saltaneh had arranged for the bride and the groom to eat their dinner privately. In the main room, the women attacked the platters of food, while Touba was left alone in the middle of the nuptial chamber. Platters of colorful food were set on the elaborately woven tapestry that surrounded a heater in the middle of the room. A black object in the corner of the room made a strange burning sound. Touba was looking at a coal-fed stove for the first time in her life. Mirrors hung around the room, reflecting opposing images into eternity. The light of the grand chandeliers was increased in intensity because of the mirroring. Touba heard the sound of a door opening, and the ululating of the women grew louder, and Touba's

71

heart palpitated faster. The women pushed the groom into the room and shut the door behind him. The prince turned the latch to lock the door before moving toward the bride. Touba noticed the long black jacket embroidered in gold tassels and the black shining shoes. Just like the Englishman, the prince moved into the center of the room with his shoes on. He stopped in front of the bride and looked at her intensely. Touba stood in the middle of the room with a pale face and lowered head. She closed her eyes to avoid looking at her future husband. The young woman did not look like a divorcée. She looked more like a virgin, like a girl. The prince tenderly touched her cheeks and lifted her head up slowly. Then she heard a soft voice, resembling a little creek, saying, "Are you scared of me Shams Ol-Moluk?" She came back to herself with these words and opened her eyes. She saw a pair of hazel eyes framed in an attractive manly face gazing at her. Feraydun Mirza was handsome, and he knew it. He asked, "Are husbands frightening?" And then he kissed her cheek. Touba blushed and her heart raced. Prince Feraydun Mirza took his hat, which had the golden emblem of the lion and sun shining on it, and placed it on the chair. He turned toward Touba, held her shoulder, and turned her to face the mirror. Now they could see themselves together in the mirror. He looked much younger than his age of forty-six years, and he smiled. He said, "People don't consider me the kind of man to settle down. They are mistaken. I am in love with women and there is nothing more valuable to me than women. Of course, you are a jewel among women." Skillfully, he slid the silk chador off her body and snatched it up before it hit the ground. He then placed it on the chair over his hat. Pointing to the chair, he said, "This arrangement indicates the superiority of Shams Ol-Moluk over the prince. That is, it is you who will rule the world. No man would ever dare to insult you since you are the ruler of Feraydun Mirza's heart." He said all of this in a very kind and delicate voice, a voice Touba had never known before.

The prince took off his military jacket and the satin white shirt beneath it. He turned toward Touba in a friendly manner and held her hand to his lips and kissed it. Touba's fear slowly melted away. He took her toward the heater and there they sat down beside one another. As he fed her food, bite-by-bite, he explained to her that his previous divorces, one and all, were the fault of the wives. A woman must be patient. Men are naughty. And sometimes they are in a bad mood. If a woman is patient, a man will eventually come back home.

Then they talked about Touba's father. He had heard the story of the Englishman from his sister and he had liked it. The late Haji Adib was an exemplary devout and learned man. And he had taken care of the Englishman in the best possible way. Basically, people with roots were different from these peasants. A noble may lose all he has, but he will always retain his dignity. People of noble birth must of course always remain humble. A tree that has more fruit bows more under its weight.

The prince told his bride that all members of his family were obliged from now on to call her Shams Ol-Moluk, the Sun of the Land. Now married to a prince, Touba no longer existed. She was now a highly regarded person whom all others must respect. She was above everyone.

Touba looked at her surroundings. The room looked small to her, yet she wondered how she could ever go back to her old house, which compared to this one looked like a dilapidated hut. All the time they were talking to each other, the sound of a tar could be heard from beyond the door. Morteza's playing was perfect and added pageantry to the prince's wedding night. Touba was taken away by the sound of the music. She sometimes was so drowned in the floating notes that she could not hear the prince's words. He said, "This is the sound of Morteza's tar." He promised to arrange for Morteza to teach her how to play. After all, a prince's wife must be familiar with music theory and performance.

In the middle of the night, imagining the luxurious life her husband had just laid out for her, Touba fell into a sound and satisfying slumber. Morteza's tar was silent. The prince rose from his place. His heart's desire was to lay down next to a woman he had just discovered to be a girl rather than a divorcée, but he had promised to fulfill his gang's rituals. He dressed silently and carefully opened the door and left the room. Behind the door, Morteza had fallen asleep with his tar in his arms. The prince kicked him gently in the ribs.

Morteza jumped up and immediately remembered the promises they had made to one another that morning in the men's quarters. They both tiptoed toward Turan O-Saltaneh's room. They had decided that the prince should knock at the door lightly and wait. Mansur Mirza apparently had been waiting in ambush behind the door because in the same instant he came out, already dressed.

Mansur Mirza felt pleased that he had succeeded in getting the prince to go out on his wedding night and in annoying his own wife, who was pretty, but for whom he felt no love. The three of them set out toward a lady friend's house.

She spent the first week in Turan O-Saltaneh's house. On the morning after the wedding night, there was vague whispering throughout the house. The disappearance of the prince and the man of the house along with Morteza had provided the servants with rumors to tell one another in the cellar and back rooms. Turan O-Saltaneh, who did not know where her husband and brother had gone, was on the brink of a nervous breakdown. She ordered servants to warm up the in-house bath. Indeed, knowing her brother's nature, she had the servants heat up the bath every day. She went to the bath with Touba, her mother and sister, and several other women guests. The young bride was not aware of the secret events in the house, and thus far no one had reported to her on her husband's behavior on the first night of their marriage. She considered his sudden disappearance as one of the house's normal customs. Before noon, the prince and his companions returned and they too went to take a bath. In the afternoon they went to the men's quarters to take a nap.

In this way, Touba passed a memorable week. She went to the bath as was necessary after conjugal contact. Every day she also wore a new dress and different jewelry, which she had received from her new and famous relatives. Each evening she participated in a different party for every type of occasion.

The prince told her that he had rented a house on Armenian Street from a woman who was known as "Madam Pump" and that the servants were preparing it for them. Touba's belongings and the furniture from her previous husband's house were transferred to the new house under the supervision of her new father-in-law. When she finally moved, she realized that she would be living in a house less sophisticated than that of Turan O-Saltaneh. The prince was not too wealthy after all, and he wasted whatever he earned. Nevertheless, the level of her lifestyle was significantly higher than it had been before. She had a personal maid named Almas, who moved to the new house along with her husband Yaghut and their two little, naughty boys. These were all gifts from Turan O-Saltaneh. In addition to this, they had a servant by the name of Mostafa, who would take care of the prince's personal affairs. And there was also Mirza Abuzar, who was in charge of the prince's estates in Azerbaijan. He would visit on occasion. Touba's attempts to keep Zahra were in vain because Haji Mahmud reclaimed her as soon as he received the news of Touba's marriage. She returned to Haji Mahmud's house and to her husband with one eye filled with tears, the other filled with blood. From the bottom of her heart she cursed Haji Mahmud and his bad temper.

The advantage of Madam Pump's house was the same as the reason behind her name: Its pool had a hand pump, which could bring water from the reservoir into the pool. Touba joyfully filled the pool by herself to make sure it actually worked. She had always wished to have one of these pumps in her own house, which she now had rented out to one of Haji Mostafa's son-in-laws. Her mother's husband was taking care of her affairs associated with that house and her other properties. Her time was now completely consumed by her husband's evening parties. She oversaw the work of the kitchen and watched her husband's guests from behind the curtain. Sometimes some ladies would also come. Turan O-Saltaneh tried to visit her brother's house once a week. But the two women maintained a chilly relationship at best. They did not have much to talk about. It seemed that the princess's main objective was to change the nature of the friendship between her husband and her brother. She told little secrets to Touba to invoke resentment in her. And then Touba would repeat these things to her husband. Gradually it became clear that Mansur Mirza was not keeping the prince's secrets. They did, then, begin to drift away from one another. Turan O-Saltaneh's plan had worked marvelously.

Touba learned from Morteza how to play the tar. The prince himself had pronounced them sister and brother so they could spend the time together and Touba had come to believe in such ceremony. Nevertheless, she wore her chador in her teacher's presence. She was a smart student. She learned how to play rather quickly, not knowing how she was able to recognize such previously unknown melodies. It seemed as if she had heard them somewhere before. Morteza told her that everyone has to seek out his or her past, especially since everyone is born several times until he or she becomes the perfect being, just like a thousand-year-old wine. Touba felt that there were things in her life that did perhaps belong to a previous life, just like this music. She had to wipe aside the dust in order to reach the spring that every soul possessed and touch its clean, crystal water. All of this was just the beginning. Eventually, the spring water would flow unhindered through the prairies, mountains, deserts, and pick up worldly soils on its way to the sea.

They sang Rumi's poetry, accompanied by the tar. Touba gradually memorized some lyrics. In this way six months passed like a dream, like a sweet dream. She did not in all that time become aware of the prince's adventures, nor she did not want to. The prince was too clever. Nevertheless, the secret of his going to the black female servant on their wedding night was eventually revealed to her. But the prince had tried to convince her, through Morteza, that all of that was in a way a demonstration of his detachment from the material world. His going from the bed of his beautiful wife to that of a black maid in the same evening, he said, represented his rejection of the material world's charms. He indeed had come to believe this interpretation, forgetting that most women with whom he had made love had been black. He did not know why he was so charmed with women of that color. He had not dwelled on it.

One day an automobile came to pick up the prince. Touba wore her chador to go out and sneak a peek at the car. It was strange, this thing that had now appeared on the streets. People also talked about airplanes. When she returned to the room, she saw the prince rapidly getting dressed. He said, "Something important has happened and I will not be home for a few days." It was obvious that he was involved in something of great consequence. In the kitchen his servant Yaghut told Touba that there was a disagreement between the shah and the constitutionalists and that the streets were now filled with Cossack troops. Shouting could be heard from the streets and this worried Touba. She remembered Mr. Khiabani and she wondered what had become of him.

Mirza Abuzar, the estate manager who had just arrived from Azerbaijan, went to a room on the far side of the house, and was served tea. Touba went to receive him and to see if he knew Mr. Khiabani. As soon as he heard the name his face opened up, and his eyes shone. He did know the gentleman. He stood up and bowed in respect to Touba and explained that the prince did not like the cleric, but he himself believed that the man was above normal human existence. He said all of this in an Azeri accent, which had a positive effect on Touba. She invited him to go outside to the veranda and she stayed there with him, at a respectable distance. Mirza Abuzar offered to tell her all he knew about Mr. Khiabani. He had heard him speak a few times in the city of Tabriz. "What rhetoric, what insight," he said. "There is no man greater than he." Touba's heart filled with joy. Her love for Mr. Khiabani was different from her feelings for her husband. It was something else. It was the kind of love that caused a person to become mad, to run wildly into the street—not to find the beloved, but to be annihilated in him. He said, "It is a pity that the cleric is not a mystic like yourself, otherwise I would have become one of his followers."

The two became instant friends. They agreed that the estate manager should stay there for the night, and when Touba sent a plate of rice to his room, she put a chunk of butter on top of it. She then returned to the storage room in her bedroom to dance to Rumi's lyrics, the same dance that she had once seen, from behind the curtain, at one of her husband's parties. At the party they had danced the dance of the dervishes to Rumi's poetry and to Morteza's own lyrics. She was heading full force toward Sufism, even though Mr. Khiabani was not of that world.

Touba spent the three days in the absence of the prince conversing with the estate manager. She also sent him to her own house to oversee its renovation. He worked for her honestly. His mistress's interest in Mr. Khiabani had excited him. They both worried about what was happening with the constitutionalists. They were both constitutionalists because Mr. Khiabani was one. And yet they were both attached to the prince, who certainly was not a constitutionalist. They prayed for peace between the two groups.

On the third day the prince arrived, dusty and tired. Mostafa had arrived before him to convey the prince's order to prepare the in-house bath. The prince went to the bath directly and took his wife with him. As they were bathing, the prince said, "The constitutionalists were taken care of. Group by group they were executed in the Garden of the Shah." Touba trembled, "Mr. Khiabani?" The prince, rising out of the bath, ignoring his wife's state of mind, said, "He has escaped, but he will be trapped soon, for all of his nonsense." Touba involuntarily replied, "God forbid." The prince paid close attention to her for the first time. He asked if the estate manager had poisoned her brain, or if her brain had already been poisoned of its own accord. She said that she knew the cleric from before, and told the prince the story of the graveyard. She also told him the story of the boy, which was the reason she separated from her ex-husband. The prince was standing there naked and she was too shy to look at him directly. She remained in the water up to her neck. Suddenly the prince wanted her again, and returned to the water. She really did not know what to do with this man whose presence always made her happy and nervous at the same time.

They washed again and returned to the room. The prince said, "Mr. Khiabani is a real troublemaker." He repeated the sentence ten times to implant it in Touba's head. Then he said, "Women should avoid politics because they are too easily ensnared in ruffians' traps, like so many domesticated pigeons." He asked if Touba knew what disaster the English wanted to inflict upon the Iranian territories. The bastards had gone as far as trying to direct Tehran's water into pipes, on the pretext that they did not want it to be dirty. But then they could close the pipes off any time they desired to turn the city into a battlefield. They wanted to cover the streets with gravel and asphalt so that people could no longer clean their water canals. They provoked the peasants to rise up against their landlords, and in this case Mr. Khiabani was these foreigners' agent. So were the rest of the constitutionalists. And now she, the Sun of the Land, the heart of the prince, has fallen into their trap even while sheltered in the house of Madam Pump.

There was a knock at the door. It was a horseman with a message from Prince Gil. "The prince conveys his greetings and invites Feraydun Mirza and his young wife to dinner in his garden on Lalehzar Street." Glee spread across Feraydun Mirza's face and he asked the messenger, "When did Prince Gil return from his journey?" The horseman replied, "It has been a while, but he returned under a veil of secrecy."

Prince Feraydun Mirza told his wife to prepare quickly. He explained that Prince Gil was the prince of all the princes and the Sufi master of all Sufi masters. He was a wonder among men. The prince shouted for the carriage to be brought from the stable.

On the way to the garden Touba realized that the face of the city had changed. The Cossack troops stopped the carriage at every other street corner to ask the password of the night, which Mostafa, their driver, uttered quietly each time. The city was deserted. The closer they got to the garden, the scarier the town looked. To Touba it seemed like a dream in which she was riding a chariot with a man she did not know well. She turned her head toward the prince to make sure it was her husband who had sunk into the depths of the seat in the darkness of the dawn. Touba's body moved in harmony with the swaying of the carriage. She was no longer looking around, feeling as if she was walking in the clouds. She wished she could close her eyes and rest like her husband.

When they arrived, she was not sure if she had indeed fallen asleep or if she had daydreamed. The carriage stopped in front of a painted green wooden door. They stepped out of the carriage and began to follow the gravel path that stretched around to the front of the building. The pine and cypress trees touched heads over the road, creating a green tunnel that now, in the darkness, looked black. They were directed to a building that was at the end of the garden. The gravel path passed an oval basin with a fountain at its center before it divided to reach a pair of staircases on the eastern and western sides of the building. From a distance they could hear the sound of the fountain, and see the dance of a small ball on top of its waters. The scent of blossoms hung thick in the air, filling the space with a lovely aroma. Prince Gil, standing on the top of the staircase with his arms locked across his chest, watched the guests approach. A light from behind his head kept Touba from seeing his face. His thick hair hung loose on his back and looked a bit disheveled. Touba thought she was looking at a living lion in the darkness of a jungle.

Prince Gil took two steps down. Prince Feraydun Mirza shouted in an excited voice, "Prince!" The answer came in a kind and humorous tone, "Prince!" The two hugged one another, and Touba had a chance to look at this being whom in her husband's view was so marvelous. Then Touba and Prince Gil locked eyes. His eyes were as black as charcoal and as piercing as fire. She could not take his gaze, and so bowed her head. Prince Gil took a satisfying breath and said with a smile, "Is this your wife?"

"Yes, your majesty."

"Shams Ol-Moluk?"

"Yes, that is her."

"The one who wanted to go on pilgrimage, to see God?"

Prince Feraydun confirmed this by laughing. Prince Gil asked his guests to enter the parlor. This was the biggest hall that Touba had ever seen. European furniture had been placed on one side, and traditional pillowed lounges on the other. In every direction she looked there seemed to be a different room with different decor. Prince Gil led them to the Iranian side. A black woman took Touba's chador and gave her instead a blue flowered praying chador. She did not feel comfortable changing her clothing in front of a stranger, but Feraydun Mirza pointed out that they were like brothers. He did not seem to be acting like a prince anymore.

Prince Gil began, just like that, to tell stories of his travels and to explain why no one had heard from him during his trip. "I did not want anyone to have any news of me." Then he offered a chalice filled with red wine to Feraydun and asked if Touba would drink. Touba shook her head resolutely, but the prince extended a chalice toward her anyway and said carelessly, "Drink." Touba involuntarily stretched her hand out and took it. With a smile on his lips, Prince Gil said, "It makes no sense for the husband to drink and for the wife to be sober." Feraydun Mirza shrugged his shoulders with indifference. Touba had not yet put her chalice down when a curtain opened, and a velveteen creature, light as a feather, entered the room. She stopped at the curtains, one arm holding them open. She was a woman whose appearance brought to mind the sensation of softness. She was dressed in a black or dark navy blue velvet, it was difficult to discern the exact color in the dark. Her hair hung down to her waist, dark as coal, and ringlets covered part of her face. Her large black eyes stared tenderly and caressingly at the guests. Feraydun Mirza half stood up, automatically. Touba stood up fully, and Prince Gil said, "You can see I have also taken a wife."

Feraydun Mirza, still shocked from seeing the woman, said, "It is improbable of you." "But you can see that I have done so. What is your name, Layla?" asked Prince Gil. The woman coyly turned her head and said, "Velvet." She had verbalized exactly what they had all had been thinking. Prince Gil asked, "Layla, how old are you?" The woman, who had stepped toward Touba and was pressing on her shoulder to invite her to sit down, replied, "One year." The prince insisted, "No, no, I mean your other age." She laughed, "Ten thousand years!" and threw her shoulders up. "No, no, that is too much, you were never so old." "Seven thousand years," she retorted. Prince Gil said, "No, this is too little," provoking the reply, "I am not yet born," to which he responded, "This is far too much."

The woman turned coquettishly, "Is this the Shams Ol-Moluk who wishes to go in search of God?" The prince said, "It is she, indeed." The woman said emphatically, "Touba, yes?" and everyone agreed. She then asked, "Do you know that Touba is a tree in Paradise?" Touba responded, "Yes! No! Of course, it is a tree in paradise, and the branches extend into the house of the Prophet." The woman nodded, "That is so, in the Prophet's home and in every home. But where are the roots?"

Prince Gil said, "I prefer Shams Ol-Moluk. She is the sun, the ruler, and her hair is golden, too, I just saw it." Layla pulled Touba's veil off and Touba did not resist. For reasons not very clear to herself, she felt closely related to the prince. Touba's golden hair spread around her. She had not had the time to braid it after her bath. Layla said, "You are right, her hair is golden, but I prefer the name Touba." Prince Gil commented, "But Shams Ol-Moluk is more becoming." The woman persisted, "Touba!" The prince shot back, "Shams Ol-Moluk!" The woman whispered, "Touba." The significance of this argument was not clear.

The sound of the tuning of a tar could be heard from somewhere in the distance. An unveiled black servant woman brought them juices, sherbet, and sweets. Indeed, it seemed that all the women in this house went unveiled. Prince Gil said, "I heard you massacred just about all of the constitutionalists?" Feraydun Mirza, in defense of himself, said that they had not been massacred, but executed by His Majesty's orders. Prince Gil said, "You did wrong. I tell you today, you will see it tomorrow, you have done wrong." Feraydun Mirza experienced a trembling sensation in the region of his spine. Prince Gil, as though fortune-telling, said, "No use in trembling!" Feraydun Mirza explained that a sudden breeze had caused his trembling. Prince Gil threw his shoulders back and said, "You do not understand the spirit of the day. Time has its own laws—laws that have absolute clarity and are changeless. What you have done has been a return to yesterday. It is fantasy. You are caught in an illusion." Feraydun Mirza explained that he followed two leaders in life. First, His Majesty the Shah, then His Holiness Geda Alishah, the master of the spiritual Sufi orders to whom he would soon devote his life, and who had at times permitted this poor follower to be in His Holiness's presence.

Prince Gil looked intensely at Feraydun Mirza. He said, "And your mustache is slowly getting whiter and droopier. It seems as though there is a halo around your head!" Feraydun Mirza explained that he was worth less than the dog of this royal prince's court, let alone in possession of a halo, but he hoped that he would always be in the presence of Almighty God the exalted. Prince Gil said, "But you are always in his presence," pointing with his hand, "here, there, everywhere." Layla turned to Touba and asked, "Touba, in your opinion, what does God look like and where is he?" Touba, who had inherited the serious personality of her father, said, "Heaven forbid, he has no shape or form. God exists everywhere as light." Layla kissed Touba's cheeks kindly. Music had begun. The woman got up and circled the room, dancing in rhythm to the music. She picked up two wooden castanets from an alcove and placed them on her fingers. Now she moved through the room playing the castanets. She had begun a soft dance that resembled the delicate breeze on a wheat field, or the breath of wind through silken curtains. This dance did not resemble Morvarid's type of dancing, or even the dance of the dervishes that had so powerfully absorbed Touba. It was as though the moon came up in the sky slowly from the east—which was, in fact, happening at the time. Moonlight filled the room, and the magic of the woman's dance created a tantalizing electrical sensation in those who watched her. The woman finished the dance and left the room, but the place still shimmered with the aura of her movements.

The sounds coming from outside brought them to themselves. Now they could hear the woman's laughter. Prince Gil warned them, "She is going to perform a play for you. You have to see what an incredible creature she is." Layla pulled the curtain aside again and glided in. She held one end of a string with a cloth hanging from it, and moved lightly to the window. The cloth separated the room into two sections. The other end of the string was held by a man dressed as a shah. Touba thought she needed to get up and pay tribute to His Majesty. Spontaneously, she stood up. Feraydun Mirza explained that this was theater, and the shah was only a character playing a part. It was not His Majesty in actuality. Touba sat down. Prince Gil smiled kindly once more. It was obvious he had no intention of ridiculing them, and therefore Feraydun Mirza did not feel embarrassed by his wife's simplicity and ignorance. Layla, however, just stood by the window, where she had hung the string, and looked at Touba in pity. Perplexed, she shook her head regretfully. Touba was trying to calm her heartbeat, which was pounding from the shock of seeing the shah. She had never seen a play in her life. Without thinking, she picked up her wine chalice and put it to her lips. Prince Gil watched her. Since he had offered the woman the chalice, he had been waiting for this moment.

From a corner of the room, players and musicians moved behind the curtain. Touba no longer looked at them, although she was curious about what went on back there. She considered those creatures superior to the people around her, as though they were from another world. The orchestra suddenly began to play. A lively and exhuberant music filled the room. After a few minutes of drums, horns, and cymbals, suddenly all went quiet. Layla appeared before the curtain. She said, "Ladies and gentlemen, this play takes place in our town." Two players lifted the curtain from either side and held it up. The shah was sitting on a bejeweled, throne-like chair. In the middle of the stage, a man dressed as a laborer stood next to him. Layla explained, "This man is a sculptor." The sculptor bowed to his audience. Then he turned to the shah, pretending to work on his face and body. When he moved away, the shah looked like Naser O-Din Shah, grandfather of the current ruler in the Qajar dynasty. Touba had seen photographs of the shah here and there, and, particularly after her marriage, she had seen them in the homes of her husband's relatives. She unconsciously pulled herself together, became serious, and sat kneeling upright. Even though she had come to understand that this was a play, since she had no understanding of theatrical logic, she continued to genuinely respect the shah. The sculptor continued, "This is His Majesty Naser O-Din Shah, king of kings, center of the world." The music accompanied him as he spoke. A few women danced and circled around the shah, then respectfully bowed in front of him. The music suddenly stopped, and someone looking like Mirza Reza Kermani holding a revolver appeared on stage. Layla said, "This is Mirza Reza Kermani. He has been burning to assassinate the shah for many years." Mirza Reza Kermani approached the shah, brought the revolver near his head and fired. A red dust spread over the shah's face and his body went limp as a corpse. Layla was about to speak, but Touba's scream drowned out her voice. The woman screamed, "No, no, don't kill the shah! It is evil! It is evil! You will go to hell," and she fell to sobbing and trembling. Whether it was the effect of the wine or her discomfort in Prince Gil's home, the woman was no longer really herself.

Layla quickly ran to the middle of the stage and said, "Do not cry, do not cry, everything will work out all right in a moment." She signaled to the sculptor with her head. The sculptor placed a tube under the shah's foot and with his hands he mimed pumping. The shah slowly raised his body and leaned back on the chair again. This time he looked exactly like Mozafar O-Din Shah, son of Naser O-Din, and there was no red powder visible on his face. Touba, in the middle of her crying, stopped in dumbfounded amazement and began to laugh uncontrollably. Affected by her laugher, Prince Gil and Feraydun Mirza also began to laugh. Joyful music filled the room and the women dancers appeared again dancing around the shah. But the shah seemed ill and tired. He kept himself on the throne only with great effort, and once in while he burped, which caused further laughter. Amidst all this, Layla brought out a long scroll and unraveled it in front of him. One end remained in her hand, the other end dropped onto the shah's lap. The woman said, "My life to Your Majesty, this is the constitution. If you do not sign it, the peasants will consider shah killing again." A thought emerged deep in Touba's mind. She now connected the issues of constitution-alism, Mr. Khiabani, and the assassination of Naser O-Din Shah. For the first time in her life, she understood the relationship between the two events. The shah wanted to lift his hand to take the scroll, but he was too weak. Each time he used energy to lift his hand, the horn blew, accentuating his motions. Finally, the sculptor intervened. He handed a pen to the shah, lifted his hand, and held the scroll. Thus the shah, in the midst of cries and applause from the dancers and Layla, signed the constitution.

Everyone was joyous. But as soon as the sculptor let go of his hands, the shah bent over like a lump of meat. Layla said, "Oh, poor shah, how soon you died." She rolled the scroll and threw it to Touba. The woman spontaneously caught the scroll in mid-air and held it as a precious object. Layla smiled at her.

Musicians continued playing and the dancers, out of the dead shah's view in the back of the room, glided in dancelike motions. Suddenly the sculptor made a decisive move, placed a tube under the shah's feet and began to pump. The shah straightened up, and instead of sitting up on the throne, stood up, looking very much like the living monarch Mohammad Ali Shah. When he reached full standing position, Touba wanted to run out of the room. She threw the constitution scroll at the shah's feet. The shah, whose attention was focused on Touba, cast his gaze upon her with fearsome eyes. She was trembling. She had become paralyzed and could not escape as she wished. Feraydun Mirza, carried away by the actions of the shah was entirely unaware of Touba's state, whereas Prince Gil and Layla were watching her instead of the stage. The shah lifted his right foot and trampled on the scroll, laughing and looking at Touba. His large white teeth gleamed out, and Touba's heart beat rapidly. A strip of blood flowed out from between the shah's clenched teeth onto his chin. Touba was shaking again and her teeth were chattering. Feraydun Mirza, now noticing Touba's condition for the first time, reminded her, "This is theater, it is only a play!"

For the woman's sake, the players stopped their performance suddenly. Prince Gil said, "That is enough, let the rest of the play be. Shams Ol-Moluk does not like plays." Layla clapped her hands, moved toward the shah and flipped the hat off his head with a single stroke. The shah laughed. The white painted face and normal skin color under the hat were clearly visible. Layla said, "Everybody wash your face and come so that Touba can see from close-up that you are not scary." The actors bowed to the audience, and Feraydun Mirza put his arm around his wife's shoulder. She no longer trembled. She was only tired and wished to sleep. Now that the play had stopped, she also felt hungry. The wine had gone to her head. The party atmosphere suddenly changed. Feraydun Mirza told Prince Gil that this kind of theater was not good to perform, for it stirred up the peasants. The prince answered that there were no peasants present and he should not worry, this was a private performance.

A short-legged table was placed among the guests and was covered with appetizing food. Layla sat next to Touba and the actors came out one-by-one. The shah was a thin young man with a shy face. Layla explained that he had to dress in many layers of clothing to acquire the shah's imposing appearance. The actor smiled at Touba modestly. They all sat around the table as equals to the prince and as his guests. Feraydun Mirza tried hard to ignore the tempting presence of Layla as he ate his dinner, but to no avail. The woman attracted his attention to herself unwittingly. He felt like a lamb cornered by a tiger. He wished to ask Prince Gil where he had found this woman, but the prince, reading his mind, said, "Where do you think I found this woman?" Feraydun Mirza joyfully shrugged and remained silent so the prince could go on and explain. Prince Gil said, "In one of Ray City's slums, would you believe it?" Feraydun Mirza could not believe it. It was not possible for a woman with such sophistication and artistry to live in one of Ray City's slums without the big city of Tehran knowing of it. Layla had now turned her attention from Touba and was making the rounds of the actors at the table, joking and laughing with them. The party continued until late into the night, until the moon was directly overhead in the sky.

The guests were directed to an opulently decorated room. Magnificent bedding was spread out for them to sleep upon. Even after the candles and the chandeliers were put out, the sound of music and women's laughter could be heard from the far reaches of the house. Feraydun Mirza's arm was under Touba's head, but his ears were in search of the other woman's voice. If that night he slept with his wife, it was only in longing for oneness with the distant voice of the woman of his dreams, that night made manifest before him.

2

Suddenly, the noise of children playing ceased. Touba's maternal instincts prompted her to leave the loom to investigate the cause. Her older daughter, Manzar O-Saltaneh, who was about eight or nine years old, had been weaving next to her mother. She followed behind, hoping for relief from the tedious work. Touba approached the cellar window and saw her aunt crouched by the small pond in the courtyard. The woman's bare bottom was clearly visible. Touba's three other children, Habibolah Mirza, Aqdas Ol-Moluk and Moones O-Doleh gathered around the woman, stared inquisitively at her nakedness. Touba, filled with anger, called for Almas Khatoun.

Prince Feraydun Mirza's escape to Russia, accompanying Mohammad Ali Shah, had altered the quality of Touba's life. The bitterness of reality clung to her like the stale odor of rancid, muddy water. She ran to the poolside with an uncovered head and the children scattered immediately. In the absence of the man of the house, she had to perform double-duty as both parents, but the children did not show her much respect. She had performed a prayer between Yaghut, her servant's husband, and her own daughters, making them *mahram* to one another. She had instructed the servant to go ahead and scold the children, and even, if necessary, give them a beating. But the man could not find it in his heart to beat his master's children, although he beat his own mercilessly. Whenever it was necessary to discipline Touba's children, Yaghut would thrash his own instead. In his mind, this was the right approach. When his master's children saw how severe a beating was possible, and saw the effects of crying to the point of fainting, they would certainly pull themselves together and curb their wild behavior.

Almas Khatoun herself would not even beat her own children. She would rather beat herself. Pulling her hair and scratching her face, she would sit in the middle of the courtyard with legs outstretched and damn the day that some men stole her from her village. She claimed that she could still remember the day when strangers came to her country and snatched her from her mother's bosom. She insisted that she had lived where there were many trees and people of black skin, and her name had not been Almas Khatoun but Hatou, then later changed to Hadjar and finally Almas Khatoun. Where she grew up they had spoken a different language. She said she had been transported by ship from her homeland. The children used to gather around her to listen to her incredible tales, while she interspersed her sagas with bouts of weeping. Gradually, her crying would subside, and she would become more and more lost in her reminiscences. She swore she had seen a man with a tiger's face. The tiger man had killed her father with an ax and her mother had grabbed her and fled and hid among the trees until, one day, some men had come from the sea and taken the child from her mother by force. Then Touba would call her to get on with her work in the kitchen, and the woman would go. When she stood by the pots mixing the food, she would laugh continuously to herself, and the children were afraid.

Yaghut was born in Turan O-Saltaneh's home and did not take his wife's tales seriously. He told the children she was crazy, and sometimes, when the woman could not see him, he would stand behind her and imitate her. This would amuse all the children, but if the hilarity passed beyond the limit, Yaghut would scold his own children, and sometimes ended up beating them. One day, because Touba felt she could no longer afford to feed so many mouths, she told Yaghut to send the children to live at Turan O-Saltaneh's home. Yaghut only accompanied the children to the end of the street and then told them to get lost; to go begging, or to go to Turan O-Saltaneh's house.

Yaghut's older boy eventually became Turan O-Saltaneh's chauffeur, and the younger son became the cook at the master's country estate. The parents never asked after their children any more.

Touba had to play the role of the patriarch. Although the children would run away from her, she usually managed to hit them a few strokes in the process. Moones, the four-year-old, who was the least guilty and the slowest, received the most beating. Touba finally warned her children that if they were seen just once more around her crazy aunt, she would hang them upside-down from the tree and beat them until they forget not only their parents' names, but also their own names. Then she turned to her aunt, who would always pick up her excrement with her right hand, dump it on the poolside, and then take a handful of water from the pool in her left hand and pour it over her right, repeating, "Purity becomes infelicitous in Satan." Touba could stop neither her amazement nor her laughter. The aunt's shapeless and worn body, squatting by the pool to relieve herself, was actually more pitiful than amusing. Manzar O-Saltaneh, who had inherited her mother's golden hair, explained to the old lady, with her head held high, that the pool water was now polluted and it was no longer possible to wash the dishes there. Touba approached her aunt with a small tree branch in hand. She struck the ground with the branch and told the aunt that if she defecated once more by the poolside, Touba would cut the rope so that she could not go to heaven. The old woman felt afraid. She pulled up her pants over her still dirty behind, and immersed her filth-covered hands in the pool water. At this, Touba burst out in anger, dropped the branch, and hit her own head with her fist. Now she would have to change the pool water. There was currently a water shortage and the reservoir was low. The hand pump, whose installation was inspired by the one at Madam Pump's house, did not have sufficient power and could hardly fill the pool. To make matters worse, they were permitted only the equivalent of three hours use of water per month.

Almas Khatoun, holding a spatula, emerged from the kitchen and was infuriated when she learned that she would have to wash the aunt at the washbasin and clean up her filth. Imitating her mistress, she spanked the crazy old woman with her spatula. The latter howled like a wounded dog and, swearing by the exalted glory of God that she would climb the rope of light there and then, she frantically tried to grab the invisible rope and climb it. Now they had to purify the spatula, too, but with what water? Touba held the spatula under the pump and Manzar O-Saltaneh, with her weak child's hands, worked the pump handle. Almas Khatoun directed the old aunt to the washbasin in the cellar to wash her with soap and water. The mother and daughter started changing the pool water by emptying buckets into the gutter.

The aunt had come to Touba's home in the first year of the prince's escape to Russia, when Manzar O-Saltaneh was still a baby and Habibolah Mirza was yet in his mother's womb. The old lady was not so far gone in those days. She had explained, "Where else can a poor old woman with nothing to her name go?" Obviously, she would turn to her relatives. Touba's economic situation was not yet so bad, and she had welcomed her aunt. This particular aunt had given birth to seven children, all of whom had died, one-by-one, a few months after their birth. The eighth child, a daughter who was born after her father's death, had miraculously survived. The old woman had raised her to the age of seventeen, when a small merchant of good reputation had come to ask for the daughter's hand in marriage to his son, and the aunt had agreed. On the wedding night, it was discovered for the first time that the groom was sixty years old. Tears, cries, and regrets had no effect. The girl had been married to Satan, and on the birth of her first child, who was stillborn, she too took her last breath. Grief-stricken, Touba's aunt spent some time wandering the streets of Isfahan, where they lived at the time. When she finally returned home, she was carrying a small infant. She had found it wrapped in papers, and it seemed to her that it was God's gift to a woman who had lost all her children. She loved the child with all her heart. One night, when the boy had reached two years of age, he asked for some water. Half asleep, the woman had sent him to a large bowl of water in the corner of the room. The child had crawled on all fours to drink, and in the morning his adoptive mother woke up to find him drowned. His head had lodged in the water bowl and he had suffocated. The woman was shattered after this event. Dazed and stupefied for a long time, she took to wandering the streets again. It was then that she walked the whole 270 miles from Isfahan to Tehran and by asking around found her niece, who was well known because of her marriage to the prince. In the beginning she was comparatively well, although one had to endure her constant rocking back and forth. Touba, however, was a patient woman.

When the prince returned from Russia, feeling belittled and demeaned by the fact that he was housebound, he considered the aunt's presence a reflection of God's wrath. He recalled all of the abuse and oppression that he had inflicted on the peasant classes. Now it was being handed back to him by those same peasants.

The prince considered anyone who was involved in the revolt against the short-lived monarchy either a peasant or of the peasant category. They had now moved back to his wife's house in order to save on rent and expenses, and Touba was back at the loom weaving carpets to provide partial income for the family. She had sent for Mirza Kazem again to obtain wool and to find out about Mr. Khiabani. Mirza Kazem by now had become a civil servant and worked in the department of Arts and Crafts. He wore a bow tie, spoke a little French, and was trying to translate a book about European art from French into Persian. He told all of this to Touba with a sense of pride. He was now married, had two children, was in charge of a whole section in the department, and had a lot going on in his life.

Once he had dispensed with these formalities, however, he returned to being the same old Mirza Kazem and the devotee of his knowledge-loving second cousin. The woman had found no time to organize her father's books, which were in storage boxes in the cellar. Mirza Kazem brought them all out and arranged them on shelves in the room. He regularly brought wool for her from Kashan. When the rugs were completed, he would make all of the arrangements for their sale and took a small percentage for himself after subtracting the cost of the wool. Touba also made some profit from this. Almas Khatoun sat and worked at the loom, and so did the aunt, whenever she was healthy enough. Until the night that she mistook moonlight for sunrise. She rose to go to the bathhouse, picked up her bath bundle, and headed out the gate. Of course the bathhouse was closed at that hour, so she returned. Afraid of causing alarm in the house by knocking at the door she went to the mosque and sat by the alcove at the gate, rocking back and forth in her customary fashion. As she described later, a sayed wrapped in a green turban appeared to her and asked, "Dear mother, why don't you enter the mosque?" The woman turned around and noticed that the mosque gate was open. The sayed directed her into the mosque, and there, at the pavilion, was a body in a coffin prepared for the next morning's burial. The woman put her head next to the coffin and cried her heart out, and all the while she could hear the sayed reciting the Qur'an. She cried until dawn, when the voice stopped the recitation and the woman lifted her head. She saw a rope made of light rays hanging down to the floor from the dome's central ventilation opening. The aunt got up to take hold of the end of the rope in order to climb it. But as soon as she touched it the voice of the proprietor of the mosque woke her and the rope disappeared. The proprietor pressed her with questions as to why she had hidden in the mosque for the night, and the aunt swore that she had been let in by a luminous sayed who had opened the gate for her. After all, as his name and title suggested, he was a descendant of the family of the Prophet Muhammad.

Early that morning, when Touba came to the pool to do the ablution for the morning prayer, she heard a knock at the door and found her aunt standing there. The aunt recounted all of the previous night's events for Touba. Touba ran to the mosque, after performing her prayers, to get the truth of the matter from the proprietor. He swore to Touba that he had locked everything quite well and was certain that there was nothing left overnight in the mosque except the corpse. In Touba's eyes the aunt's respect and worth increased—but to what end? As soon as Touba returned home, she saw the aunt dancing around the yard, snapping her fingers and trying to grab a hold of an invisible rope to climb. And she could not weave any longer either, since Touba would have to constantly watch her to prevent errors.

Yet another famine struck. Every day there was less in the cooking pot. Touba prayed for rain, but the skies were uncooperative. Almas

Khatoun would line up the children and have them all pray together. She would hold the Qur'an on their heads and wail, but to no avail. Touba became more and more sour each day. She was now certain that she had committed a sin that she had to answer for, but she had no idea what it was. She scrutinized every detail of her life. She could not remember having committed a sin—until, perhaps, when she was fourteen. She must have committed the first sin by courting Haji Mahmud. She returned to her past again and again. She had also committed other sins. She had once viewed her father's naked body while he was bathing, and also she had observed her own body a few times. She remembered the childish games of the little girls and sometimes the little boys. She had always tried to see their naked bodies one way or another. She thought, "The world is built on sin. It was not without reason that God expelled the sinful couple from Eden." Whenever she lined up the children and Almas Khatoun for rain prayers, she would also lecture them on the subject of sin for a good half hour. Heaven help the one who commits a sin in childhood. Such a one will be cut off from innocence and God's wrath will prevail upon everyone. Drought will come and the rain's blessing will be cut off. What did they really think? That rain would just fall randomly, by chance? Touba would stop her sermon and withdraw into herself only after Manzar O-Saltaneh began to cry out of fear, Habibolah stared at her with his mouth agape, and Yaghut's children crawled into each other's arms like two scared rabbits.

Through those years that she had to live without her runaway husband, Touba endured additional worries. On top of everything else, a world war had started and it was in the first year of that war the prince returned. For the first six months he sat around the house and would not appear in society. The pressure of his idleness and his repeated praises of Kaiser Wilhelm of Prussia drove Touba crazy. He believed that Kaiser Wilhelm was the king of deliverance, that after defeating Russia and England he would come to Persia and save the Iranian people. The prince clung to this dream with abnormal persistence; and gradually, the Prussian emperor became a mythical figure in Touba's mind as well. Rain would come to Iran with Kaiser Wilhelm, prices would fall, Almas Khatoun's madness would subside, and welfare and plentitude would return to every home. After a while, Prince Feraydun recovered. He began to appear in public and even sent a representative to the shah requesting a pardon. By and by he was permitted to participate quietly in the royal court's activities.

The life of the household improved slightly. But the prince was expected to send expensive gifts to the court, which he was unable to afford, and it was difficult to find an appropriate job. He was finally offered a governing position in a backward area in the province of Azerbaijan. The advantage to this appointment was that the state was in proximity to the prince's own property and thus he could, with Mirza Abuzar's assistance, manage his own estate. It was during this time that Aqdas Ol-Moluk was born and Moones O-Doleh was planted in her mother's womb.

These days Touba would once in a while be invited to parties at court. The new shah was still a child, so the remaining wives of the previous shahs, Mozafar O-Din Shah and Mohammad Ali Shah, managed the harem. Touba had just given birth to her fourth child. She was usually invited to the court parties, but the events exhausted her. She had no attendants or servants to help her with the children. She would end up going to the parties alone, or she would take the children and be burdened with their care. She did not dare to turn down the invitations. She feared that it would affect the status of her husband, who had finally secured himself a job after all the years of idleness and desertion. The remaining queens of the preceding kings had each established a small court of their own. They had little wealth to spare, but they could not bear to let a party go by. Dead egos permeated the atmosphere. Newcomers had to be cautious upon arrival at these courts to praise every one of these ladies and visit each quarter equally in order to not offend anyone or arouse vindictiveness. Touba did not feel up to it. She preferred to return to her weaving in order to secure her children's future welfare. She had once played the tar at one of the court parties and had sung the poetry of Rumi to the rhythmic music. The memory remained fresh with the ladies, and they repeatedly requested her to play and sing again. She would occasionally indulge them, and in her mind ruminate once again on her past dream of going out to search for God.

The last time she had gone to a court party they had again asked her to play. But she was not in the mood. She asked to be excused, and instead the ladies asked one of the women to dance. The woman wanted to but she kept procrastinating and coquetting, when perhaps the one hundred and seventh queen declared, "I order you to dance." This sentence created an upheaval in Touba. She took advantage of the crowded party and snuck out, never to return again. On her way home she promised herself that someday she would sit by the side of the road, like wandering musicians do, and play for people, just as a form of self-punishment. Thus, her visits to the royal court ended.

Mirza Kazem mentioned that Mr. Khiabani's fame and influence had spread in Azerbaijan, and the shah no longer held to his crown. However, Touba and Mirza Kazem had both had lost their excessive attraction for Mr. Khiabani. Mirza Kazem's mind was working well these days. He knew that being a follower of a hot-blooded person would lead only to quagmires and complications. He did like to impress his cousin with grandiose talk, but he would not take liberties. But Touba had other reasons for her change in beliefs. She was immersed up to her neck in life's problems and could not afford the luxury of returning to her old fancies. She had created a huge bundle of dreams during the four years of inactivity sitting in the corner of Haji Mahmud's house. Now, the very bundles created in her imagination were the source of her handicrafts and her earnings. Whenever she got tired and her children gave her a rough time, or when her aunt stretched her patience to the limit, or when not a drop of rain fell and water became scarce, she thought that someday, after the children were established in life, she still would go in search of God. Meanwhile she must continue to weave, cook, and sweep. She must whirl in this eternal circle and return to the starting place. She had never learned to enjoy repetition. Consequently, she never wove the same patterned carpet twice; it bored her. If it was necessary to weave a pair, she would let others do the job and she herself would start a new one. But it was not always possible to get away with that trick. Repetition was an eternal law in her life. It was the law in everyone's life. Touba did not know why she was so serious with other women. She laughed very little and was impatient with women's silliness. A few times, on rare occasions, she organized plays and birthday celebrations. The first time she did it with grace and patience and some formality, but after a while she only did it because she was asked to. She saw herself on a road that did not move forward but turned in place. It would have pleased her if she could have continued to move forward; it did not matter where she was going, as long as she was moving on. But it became more and more difficult each day. These days, when people talked about Mr. Khiabani she no longer had the image of him as pure light. But she believed that Mr. Khiabani's presence brought a change in the monotony of life. She did not know how, but the thought of him still excited her. Mirza Kazem had told her that Mr. Khiabani was now in Azerbaijan, a king who needs no crown. Indeed, what if Mr. Khiabani became a king? The rumor was that the shah was powerless. He was unable to manage the country. What was wrong with the idea of Mr. Khiabani becoming the shah?

After her husband escaped the wrath of the followers of Mr. Khiabani and returned to Tehran, he explained to his stupid wife that if Mr. Khiabani were to become shah, the whole Qajar dynasty, and, of course the prince and his descendants, would lose their lucky star and become paupers by the roadside. The prince had grown impatient with all women's stupidity. His renewed poverty and the loss of the mediocre job he had procured caused havoc with his nerves. Every day he would spend an hour cursing Mr. Khiabani and his predecessors. He now believed that Mr. Khiabani was a paid Russian agent. When Touba reminded him that a few years ago he had accused the man of being a British agent, the prince merely shrugged and said, "A servant is always a servant, and could serve two masters." The prince pointed to Mirza Abuzar as an example. He had doglike devotion to the prince, yet he was crazy with love for Mr. Khiabani. The prince had left Mirza Abuzar behind in Azerbaijan, so that with the love that he carried for Mr. Khiabani he might be able to save some of the prince's estate from being confiscated by peasants. And indeed the pestering peasants had gone wild. During one of their uprisings, in an attack on the mansion of one of the prince's half-sisters, a peasant had dared to demand, in Turkish, that he wanted the princess as his share of the spoils. "These were all caused by that bastard, that nasty and damned Mr. Khiabani the spy."

Conflicting stories came out of Russia. A flood of Russians was escaping over the border to Iran. Mr. Biyuck's family appeared in Touba's household. They had heard from a distant relative of Touba's that there was an empty room in her house. Touba agreed to rent the two rooms, which had been occupied by Haji Mostafa in the old days, and the prince was not happy about it. He had never lived with neighbors in the same house. The idea of having tenants truly embarrassed him. But, he had no money to give to his wife, so he had to keep quiet.

The prince had recently developed the habit of cursing some new creatures named Bolsheviks. After the second prayer, in the position of prostration, he usually discussed his affairs with God. He talked with God as though he was speaking with a close friend who had not been paying enough attention. He would say, "Dear God, I know that I am your special servant. I know that you love me. I know that your grace has always been directed at me, and that you have been so kind to me that if I live a million years I will not be able to repay you. Oh great God, you know yourself that you must save people from the Bolshevik devils. You know, don't you?" He would continue, "God, please send us your messenger Wilhelm, for we are losing patience." Sometimes, when Touba was in the room and he wished her to hear certain things, he would say, "God, please return Mr. Biyuck and his family to Baku. Let our home become ours again. Bring some reason into the minds of these old-fashioned veil-wearing women, and send me a huge sum of money so that the veil-wearing women will start respecting their men again." Touba would smile, repressing her anger. She liked the manner in which the prince did his prayers. She often tried to be in the room at these times in order to listen to the man's heart-to-heart conversations with God. Then a three-way conversation would ensue between God, Touba, and the prince. Touba would say, "Oh great master, explain to this prince that I can't feed the children with empty promises. With the rent from Mr. Biyuck I can buy a morsel of bread and meat to fill their insatiable stomachs." And then the prince would respond, "Oh God who holds the fate of beggars and kings, explain to these old-fashioned, veil-wearing, unwise women, who become more and more stupid as they get older, that they should not annoy their husbands. Make them understand that when Wilhelm, your own emissary, arrives, everything shall change. Explain to them that the atheist Bolsheviks who have dried up the Russian people's income have also frozen her husband's income." The woman would retort, "God, explain to this fun-loving prince that if a man wished to be the breadwinner of the family he would make flour out of stone, turn the stone flour into bread, and thus save his wife and children's reputation in public."

The prince would then dress up, put his hat on, and head for Turan O-Saltaneh's home to squeeze some money out of his sister, pinch a couple of servants here and there, and go even further if one gave him the okay. Of course, he never gave any of this money to his wife. In his mind he was getting even with her for her narrow-mindedness.

Then came Monsieur Boghosian, an Armenian emigrant who could hardly speak any Persian. He had heard that Touba had an upstairs room for rent. He explained in his broken Persian that the Bolsheviks break women up and divide them among themselves. Touba understood that they break women up from the middle. But of course, she could not understand the purpose of such an act. She had asked for an explanation from Monsieur Boghosian. He said, "They share everything, so everyone gets something," and added, "Shame on them."

Fear of the Bolsheviks filled Touba, which for the prince was a great advantage. He developed a friendship with the Armenian man. They became drinking partners and discussed the Bolsheviks in the Turkish language. Gradually the Bolshevik fever spread to Touba and the rest of the family. The prince spread the word that Mr. Khiabani was the absolute servant of the Bolsheviks and that he had been trained by them in Caucasia to come here and divide up the women. The prince was well aware of Touba's misconception about this, and used it to his benefit.

The other character in the prince's dervishes' triangle was Dervish Hasan. He was a ragged man who spoke wisely, and the prince thought of him as the Shams Tabrizi of the era, the natural heir of the famous Sufi master and an inspiring friend to Rumi. Upon entering the house, Dervish Hasan always cried out, "Oh, Creator!" His voice was loud and clear enough to freeze everyone at attention. Before entering, he usually lingered in the outer entrance hall, leaning against the wall as he sang, with a pleasant voice, a litany for the Lord: "His Excellency of Justice, the God whose glory shines from here to the Pleiades, destroyer of tyrants, embracer of orphans, healer of broken hearts, your worshipping servant asks permission to enter." The prince would bow to the dervish, and the dervish in turn would respectfully bow to young and old. He would then take off his cotton shoes by the entrance to the room and sink into his place by the door. If Monsieur Boghosian came in, they would continue their discussion in Turkish.

Dervish Hasan saw a different meaning hidden in Bolshevism. "This curtain has many layers," he would say. Bolshevism was the whip of God and a part of the wheel of the universe. Whenever the wheel did not turn appropriately, someone like the Bolsheviks would appear and reorganize everything—perhaps aggressively and brutally, but decisively! The prince listened very patiently to Dervish Hasan's words. He saw hidden secrets in them. He knew that the dervish could not speak plainly, without philosophizing. He had to speak in such complexity that no one, at times not even he himself, could understand it. Listening to these talks was a necessity for the prince, since he was incapable of thinking in this manner. It was essential that someone else should enter the mess of words and come out at the other end with some nugget of truth. He felt that here was a trusting and virtuous person who understood the truth and in time would inform him. For this reason, he sought out Dervish Hasan's opinions. But whenever Touba entered the room, or her shadow appeared behind the curtain, the prince felt anxious. He would signal Dervish Hasan to cut it short. Dervish Hasan, who was a mystic in character and was aware of the affinity of the lady of the house to himself, would cut his talk short, but in a way that allowed Touba to hear a few of the words and sentences of the dying discussion.

Touba seemed disturbed these days. In the past, since the incident at the cemetery, whenever she felt the need she had sought refuge in her thoughts to Mr. Khiabani, who appeared in the form of rays of light. Although she was shocked and momentarily disconcerted by her husband's negative depiction of Mr. Khiabani, she was still capable of clearly separating Mr. Khiabani's position from that of the other creatures in her life. But the appearance of poverty, which increased daily with the Bolsheviks' rise to power; the desperate refugees escaping Russia, including the ones who now found their safety in her house, and the association of Bolshevism with the name of the man who stood for her as light—this created enormous confusion in her.

Mr. Biyuck's wife told horrifying stories about the Bolsheviks. All of her family's belongings had been plundered. The woman had only managed to hide a diamond under her tongue, the rest had all been taken. The story grew more dramatic each time she told it: now, their house had possessed seven doors; in a few months' time it would have seven gates. Their lives had been so terribly devastated that they now had to live in only two rented rooms. Even if she was exaggerating, what about Monsieur Boghosian's reports? Didn't he say that they divided women? She had by now come to understand the meaning of *divide*. Nevertheless, the dramatic shock of the image she had pictured the first time she heard this term remained with her.

Dervish Hasan tackled these anxieties. He had an inverse form of logic. He searched in his mind to confront the meaning of Bolshevism in an appropriate manner: first to give an account of it, then peel away the meaning, and finally bare its truths. Yet he didn't feel that he was able to reveal all of the meanings. His audiences were inconsistent, and they often were content with superficial, quick conclusions. He explained, "Bolshevism is the whip of God." Once when Touba was in the room she asked, " If Bolshevism is the whip of God, then why do they not believe in God?" Dervish Hasan suddenly spread his eyes wide open and stated that this was another one of the ways that God manifests his glory. "Truth reveals itself inversely in this world. His glory has willed to destroy His own self, and replace himself with his own glory." And Touba's head spun in confusion. Dervish Hasan smiled kindly, and suggested that if the woman would have the honor to meet His Holiness Geda Alishah, the Sufi master, her problems would be solved.

Prince Feraydun was not happy with these discussions. On the one hand, he wished to be involved in Sufi poetry, song, and dance; on the other hand, he did not feel comfortable about a woman learning the secrets of "The Truth." A woman had her own specific duties. If she were to overlook or not fulfill her duties, the world would be utter chaos.

Dervish Hasan understood things differently. He believed that members of this world were responsible for specific duties, but among them there was a group, whether man or woman, who lived under constant trial and tribulation and were wanderers. If this group did not have any means of expression, it would fall to denigration and meanness, or to madness and debility. Such disturbed ones needed to be protected as if under an umbrella, and people would also be glad to be free of them. In Dervish Hasan's opinion, Touba's personality fitted this group. Her scatteredness; her excessive tendency toward manual work; her playing of the tar, carpet-weaving, and recently, reciting poetry in secret; and her mad devotion to and belief in Mr. Khiabani (a problem that once in a while the prince referred to by satirizing her)—all led Dervish Hasan to the enclosed circle of the woman's soul. From Dervish Hasan's point of view, the incident at the cemetery and the woman's dangerous persistence in her hunger strike to the point of suicide were all signs of her abnormality. These also indicated that she must be of the particular group who have no choice but to follow the path of Sufi tradition, for in no other way could they find happiness.

The desire to visit Master Geda Alishah burned in Touba. She talked of him at every turn, causing Prince Feraydun to lose his patience. He had received orders to return quickly to his official duties in his assigned region. He was told to try to make peace with the peasants, and considering his calm personality, he would probably succeed. He was advised to speak badly of the government and the shah if necessary. He was to get along with the peasants until they slowly came around and gave in to the system. He was also

charged to watch very carefully for the Russian's and for Mr. Khiabani's agents, because the situation there was far too risky. The
prince had no interest in risky or dangerous missions. He had once
been involved in a dangerous mission, and spent years abroad, and
his family had been devastated. But he had to get away from the
poverty at home, Almas Khatoun's tasteless food, Touba's continuous rug-weaving, the noise and raucousness of Mr. Biyuck's children
and his wife's fetishism of rinsing and purification. He had to leave
behind Auntie's crazy behavior and Yaghut's forever stupefied face.
He had to survive, somehow, the loss of his servant Mostafa, who
had quit serving him and taken an office job in a ministry; the loss
of Morteza, who had followed suit and now hardly ever touched the
tar; Mansur Mirza's unwashed eyes and his constant disgusting love
affairs and bragging to cover up his impotency; Turan O-Saltaneh's
upturned nose and pseudo-court cronies. And last but not least, he
had to run from a wife who, if she ever stopped working at the loom,
was completely immersed in dreams about Master Geda Alishah. All
these were the signs that he must go.

Touba was adamant about going to the western province of Kermanshah to visit Geda Alishah, who according to Dervish Hasan's
report intended to live in the southeastern city of Kerman for the
next three years. She had never in her life gone any further than the
nearby cities of Qom and Ray, and the desire for pilgrimages to
Mashad, Karbala, and Mecca burned in her now more than ever
before. Dervish Hasan regularly added fuel to the fire of her desire.

Touba had gone behind the curtain while working on a piece of
embroidery. She listened to the discussion between Prince Feraydun
and Dervish Hasan. The prince's mood was worse than ever. Nowadays he felt there was no air left to breathe. There was no money to
organize parties in the tradition of the dervish circles of men, and
most of his friends were no longer in the city anyway. To him, the
woman's shadow behind the curtain seemed like an impenetrable
castle, which now felt like prison walls. Touba was so good when she
was young and he was wealthy. When she was young she was the
song of birds; whether she talked about Rumi or about pots and
pans, she was sweet. Nowadays, whatever she said was like a knife in

Prince Feraydun's heart. Suddenly he said, "Dervish Hasan, women are indeed shit." Dervish Hasan's response was brutal, considering the woman's heavy presence behind curtain. He said: "From this very place of shit we are thrown, head on, into this world of sinners." Touba's hand holding the embroidery needle stopped in midair. She pressed her lips together in anger, and felt her spirit doubling over in her body. She could not believe that the prince had spent all these years thinking of her as shit. The prince retorted, "Whether she has soiled us or not, she is nothing but shit, besides, this is all bullshit, the sperm comes from the man, the woman is the filth in which the sperm falls, and it is only because of the light of man's sperm that this shit house becomes capable of reproducing." Dervish Hasan disagreed. He explained, "Women and children are innocent by nature, eternally innocent. It is men who foul their innocent beings. Initially the woman is born holy. She is a mirror reflecting the depths. If there was foulness in man, woman would reflect it, and if he were spun of light, she would reflect light."

The prince quickly brought the discussion to an end and instantly decided to return to his government position and never again sit with the dervish. Dervish Hasan noticed the coldness in the prince and got up to take his leave. The prince was alarmed by Dervish Hasan's quick response; it was unexpected. And it was at that instant that Touba decided to go to Kermanshah. She resolved to take her aunt and the children as well. She hoped perhaps the master's holiness could cure the poor aunt. Yaghut could come along as the male chaperone needed on the trip. She had a little savings that could cover the cost.

Dervish Hasan left with the habitual salutations of "Truth, Truth." Touba entered the room and announced that she was going to Kermanshah on a pilgrimage to Master Geda Alishah. The prince sniggered, "The master does not receive everybody." He had been trying for ten years to achieve permission to be received, but with no success. But Touba was firmly set in her decision. At that moment, a messenger arrived to invite the prince and his wife to Prince Gil's home. The couple's mood changed; smiles on their faces revealed their hope, desire, and happiness.

Years had passed since their last visit. Touba thought how strange Prince Gil was, and his wife even more so. Where had they been all these years? Many times she had thought of inviting them back. But her husband discouraged her. Prince Gil never went to a feast, and if he wished to see anyone, he either invited them to his own home or visited them unannounced. Feraydun Mirza knew Prince Gil's habits well.

No longer in possession of a carriage, or the little carriage shed at Madam Pump's house, or horses, the couple started walking in the long afternoon. The husband suggested that they make their way slowly to Lalehzar Street and enjoy it. The city was engulfed in famine again. People queued up in long lines by the bakeries. Touba remembered fifteen years ago, the little boy by the bazaar corner begging for bread. She now wore a short veil and did not have to view the world through the dark face cover of those days. The city had also changed. A few cars moved through the streets. There were posts along the side of the streets, holding up electrical wire and some other wires as well; the prince explained that these were for a kind of telegraph that went to houses.

By sunset they had reached Lalehzar Street. On the first street corner a large crowd had amassed around a liver kebab stand. The hungry eyes of the people inspired a deep sadness. Touba thanked God for the roof over her head and some income from the shops that fed her children. She prayed and blessed the deceased Haji Mahmud for his thoughtfulness in salvaging her paternal inheritance for her.

They arrived once again at the large, green, engraved gate. The prince pulled the rope and the bell rang. The atmosphere changed completely when the servant opened the gate and they entered the green hallway. It was as though the house was in another city and another world. Music could be heard from the main building. It was not the sound of a tar or tambourine; it was a sound that Touba had never heard before. And the music was of a different kind. The building was illuminated. Touba thought her eyes were misleading her. Women, "half-naked," in Western-style dresses, which Touba had seen in Madam Orus's fashion magazine, swayed in different directions. Men wore Western clothing, and their suit tails were split open like swallow tails. Their white shirts were pulled up to their necks and white bow-ties were stuck in the middle. They looked like swallows or black crows with white chests. Some others had rounded tails and were flat-chested, white as a drum. Some wore Russian military uniforms. Prince Feraydun Mirza in his old-fashioned military jacket and Touba in her black chador were as oddly out of place as two ducklings among a school of swallows and hoopoes.

The newcomers walked forward together hesitantly. The prince whispered that perhaps Prince Gil had invited them by mistake for the wrong night. However, Prince Gil's appearance on the terrace put an end to their thoughts. He was also dressed in the old-fashioned military jacket. His wife, Layla, had on the same old blue silk dress, and to be more distinctive she had wrapped a half tiara of paisley-shaped diamonds on her forehead, the grips hooked and tied to a black velvet band under her wild loose hair. Prince Gil and his wife welcomed Feraydun Mirza and Touba joyfully. Once again the black servant woman exchanged Touba's black chador for one of blue silk chiffon. Guests paid very little attention to the newcomers.

The decor had changed in the guest salon. There was no sign of the large cushions, and Western furniture occupied the various corners. There was no furniture in the center of the salon. Instead, men and women squeezed and swayed around one another, with shoes on. Touba was unsure whether or not she should take off her shoes. Layla, without being asked, explained, "Do as you wish, with or without shoes." Touba thought that if she took her shoes off, she would be stepping on the carpet that had been polluted by the guests' shoes. She decided to keep her shoes on and stepped on the carpet, fully conscious of what pain had gone into weaving it, how many backs had been bent and how many eyes had lost sight. The carpet was silk, and Touba knew the effort was tenfold more than for a woolen one. She had been working on a couple of silken rugs for Manzar O-Saltaneh's trousseau; she was not yet even halfway finished.

Touba stood clumsily in the middle of the crowd for a long time, until finally she found an empty easy chair in a corner and sat in it awkwardly. She was not used to furniture and felt stiff. A respectable-looking man carrying a tray of full glasses bent down in front of her. The only difference between him and the other men was his black bow tie. Touba respectfully stood up for him and greeted him. The man stood in surprise, apologized for disturbing her, and held the tray covered with glasses full of different colored liquids out to her again. Touba picked a yellow-colored one automatically, to get rid of the man. It was orange juice. A group of men gathered around some objects that she soon discovered were musical instruments. The men made sounds out of the instruments, which were entirely strange to Touba. They finally fell in tune, nodded to one another, and then one of the men with a stick in hand stood in front of them. With the tip of his stick he tapped a wooden board that stood on a long post, and soon a delightful music filled the hall. Men bowed in front of women, which absolutely amazed Touba, then they joined hands and began to dance. Touba felt anxious and depressed at the same time. It seemed to her that she was participating in a genie's wedding in a bathhouse. The party, though very glamorous, yet aroused in her a strange sensation. Prince Gil's wife was now dancing with a stranger, and the prince himself was busy dancing with some other woman. Feraydun Mirza approached his wife, like a savior. He bent down and whispered in her ears that this party was a Western kind. The prince had seen a few such parties in Russia. He seemed very happy, and parted from his wife quickly. In his heart, he was scolding Prince Gil for inviting his clumsy wife to such a party.

The men and women danced together through a few songs. The party had picked up and the sound of laughter could be heard from different corners. The crowd was drinking a lot of wine, and Touba, sitting on the easy chair observing the crowd's behavior, was beginning to lighten up. She was slowly beginning to consider herself as one of them. Some people spoke with her briefly, in a kind and friendly manner. She knew none of them. A few men invited her to dance. She got rid of them clumsily. But all these events helped her to gradually join in the spirit of the party. The moon rose slowly. She remembered that the last party at Prince Gil's was also on a night of the full moon.

The orchestra finished playing and the waiters went around

inviting the guests to the dinner tables. Touba noticed tables surrounded by six or eight chairs. Crystal vases filled with flowers decorated the center of the tables but she did not know some of the flowers' names. The man who had offered drinks to her politely led her to one of the tables. Other guests moved around the tables in search of their seats. The servant stopped by one of the tables, pulled out a chair, and gestured to her that she could sit if she wished. Touba sat, and before she was completely seated, the man carefully pushed her chair slightly forward and so that Touba was at the appropriate proximity to the table. In front of her, on the table, stood different sized plates sequenced from large to small. On each side of the plates were placed various sizes of forks, and at the upper part of the plates a few narrow and wide knives. On top plate stood a skillfully gathered napkin, which appeared like a white flower, and in the middle of it, was a folded card. A calligrapher had beautifully inscribed *Touba*, and slightly below it, in larger script, *Shams Ol-Moluk*, her other name. There was no food on the table. Touba looked around herself; on either side of her sat a man. Through the centerpiece flowers she could see Prince Gil sitting across from her, talking with a woman next to him. The woman was a foreigner, with blond hair and blue eyes, and a bundle of fake pansies decorating the side of her head. The woman kept moving her hand wildly, telling the prince a story with great excitement. A fan moved up and down with her hand movements, and once in a while she spread it and fanned herself. A white-gloved man poured white wine for the ladies from a bottle that had a white cloth wrapped around its neck, and a few steps behind him another servant filled the glasses for men in a similar fashion. When they had finished their work, they stepped back. Prince Gil stood up and there was silence everywhere. The prince smiled and began, "Ladies and gentlemen, the life for this kind of party has ended in Russia. In honor of my Russian friends, some present tonight, I have invited you all here to spend time together. I believe the life that yields such parties is coming to an end most everywhere in the world, therefore I hope you all have a memorable evening." Touba was thinking, But such parties had never existed in Iran, when the prince continued: "Of course, this is a sample of the kind of party that should become a trend in Iran. Since we are behind, we will have to quickly adjust and copy manners of others. Therefore, even if the parties are ending in Russia, I see no problem in starting them up here. Have a pleasant time." The prince then began to speak in a foreign language. The Russian guests laughed heartily at times. It was clear that the Prince Gil was giving a different speech for them. In the end, the prince lifted his glass and everyone joined him by raising theirs. Men were standing. Touba also lifted her glass automatically and brought it to her lips.

Conversation continued immediately after the men sat down. Almost everyone spoke with those who sat beside them. Touba noticed the servants walking around the tables with platters of food in gloved hands. The man sitting next to her picked his white napkin up and spread it on his lap. Touba copied him. In her heart, she felt thankful to him. From then on she watched the man and did everything exactly as he did. Her anxiety subsided. The servant politely picked up her plate and held it aside, while another servant arranged some pieces of fish and vegetables on it. The first servant picked up all other plates in front of Touba and placed them above the knives, then arranged the one with the fish in front of her. The man sitting next to her asked the prince if he knew anything about the Bolsheviks. The prince acknowledged by nodding, and smiled at Touba. He said he knew, and once more looked in Touba's eyes. He said that years before he had befriended a staunch Bolshevik warrior. The guests around the prince were keen to hear his tale. The prince began to speak.

"I was returning from Berlin to Tehran, via Moscow. I had a bad cold, and kept sneezing. Many tiresome days of traveling were ahead, from Berlin to Moscow and from Moscow to Baku. The illness had depressed me. Across from me in the train car sat a young man, about twenty-seven or twenty-eight and very polite. The man introduced himself to me after he noticed my constant sneezing. I do not remember his last name, but his first name was Ivan. He told me that he had just finished medical school in Paris and was on his way back to Russia. This was the year 1904. Ivan gave me some tablets and some syrup from his bag, which miraculously ended my sneezing and cleared my nasal passages. You can imagine what a relief this was. There was a snowstorm going on outside. The train had to make frequent stops so that the men could clear the rails. A few times even the passengers got out to help them. Imagine the circumstances, and having a cold as well. Well, Ivan's convenient presence saved me from the miserable cold, and we began to talk.

"Ivan told me that he was a Social Democrat. In those days, all Communists, even Bolsheviks, were called Social Democrats. After he told me what he was, he asked after my affiliation. I felt like laughing, as he continued looking at me kindly. He seemed very naïve to me, though he exuded seriousness while he talked, and the strength of his belief was clear. I told him that I was an Iranian prince. Ivan raised his eyebrows in surprise. He was surprised that I spoke French so well. I told him that I spoke French and German just as well as Persian, Turkish, and Arabic, and many other languages. Ivan seemed slightly bewildered. But I sensed a slight disdain toward me in his eyes. He did not approve of my royal affiliation. I told him it was not my fault for being a prince. I was born a prince, it was not a political view I had chosen, and if necessary I could be a good Social Democrat, if only he would guide me. Ivan thought for a while. Obviously, he was considering whether or not it was correct to give guidance to a prince. Then he decided to enlighten me, perhaps because he concluded that while I was a prince, I also came from a backward country, so perhaps his ideology would interest to me.

"He explained to me very sincerely that Social Democrats believed in the equality of all mankind and in protecting and defending the rights of workers and laborers who had been oppressed for centuries. Also peasants and women—in short, they protected all deprived groups, classes, and genders, as part of the struggle for equality. I listened to him calmly, and it occurred to me that I had seen him somewhere before. His face looked very familiar.

"When he finished talking, I told him that I did not agree with him and did not believe in equality. I explained that according to a very complex law, people were born unequal, including men and women, who were quite different from each other, and in fact this very difference was the element that allowed the growth and perpetuation of mankind. But the issue did not stop just with men and women. There was inequality in everything, and at first sight that was not a negative thing since it was very useful to society and to nature. Ivan listened carefully, and I could see hatred slowly emerging in his eyes. I said if Ivan wished to, he could see this law in the jungle. The young man ground his teeth and asked if I was a defender of the law of the jungle: that the strong tear the weak, that might is right. I simply told him yes, I was a defender of the law of the jungle, but what I had in mind was the law of nature. Had he ever seen how the young seedlings by the large trees struggle to reach light? They compete with one another to grew, don't they? Their growth is only possible if, among the many trees competing for light, some succeed and some die. There are two possibilities, either the seedling is lost and destroyed, or it ascends and reaches grandeur. Ivan continued listening, but was resolute in his disagreement. He said that this law did not apply to human society. From his point of view, humans could not be compared with trees. I told him that I believed everything had room for comparison. I said that the grandeur of the snow was in its fall. It was no use for the wind to feel sorry for the falling snow and drive it upward, for then it would be a storm, just as it was at that moment outside the windows of the train as we stood immobile.

"Ivan looked outside. I had noticed that despite his determined appearance, my words were taking effect. Ivan belonged to that group of people who have to be busy with something to feel alive, and thus hang on to their dogmatic beliefs fanatically and defend them with their lives. This fanaticism is for them a nest in which they can first hatch and then protect their young, into the next generation and on into perpetuity. There was nothing wrong with such an approach, but I doubt that he could, with that lifestyle and belief, live with me in the same shack. And the reason I doubt it is that I personally do not fit into any specific category of belief. I have never had a garden in which to plant my seedlings. Indeed, I have largely been destructive of other people's nests or gardens. In fact, I continue to destroy them because I hate the confining boundaries of nests.

"Ivan looked at the storm outside for a long time. The horrendous cold cut through to our bones, despite our fur coats. After a while, he turned to me and said, 'Just as the storm follows the law of storms, humans must obey human law. Often social laws contradict human law. Social laws are created by ruling classes in order to enslave humans. Humans are duty-bound to fight for their lost freedom and against all forms of slavery. They therefore must rebel against the ruling classes.' He said that in the course of history, millions like him had turned the wheels of society so a small number of selfish and bigoted people like me would have pampered and comfortable lives. I told him that was exactly the point: A person such as I, a naturally born prince, had no need to partake in turning the wheels of society, because he knew the wheels turned, whether he participated in it or not. But someone like him was always worried about it and therefore forced himself to work like a donkey to power the mill. His life consisted of a donkey's life, turning the wheel with a lowered head, on occasion looking for food. It was natural that someone like me would come along and harness him. And obviously, here, I laughed at him. 'I would not even have to do very much to put a harness on your neck. Someone like you builds your own saddle, and another one like you weaves the bridle, and then I get to ride on you.'

"Ivan's color reddened; he stood up, took me by the collar and lifted me from my seat. I did not resist his actions. He slowly began to realize that I was physically stronger than he was, and that I showed no resistance not out of weakness, but for other reasons. He let go of my collar and hit me with his iron fist, smashing me into my seat. I smiled at him, feeling no anger toward him, and told him, 'Even if you kill me, I still exist. You have killed God to free yourself of me, but what you have not understood is that the same material that you trust and believe in has created me as I am. Why don't you respect this order of things?' The young man took a deep breath. His nostrils were swollen with anger. He said, 'Perhaps you are right, and here sits a donkey turning the mill. But the donkey has learned from the porcupine to cover his body with poisoned needles; and while busily working and turning the wheel, with head down, to keep throwing needles at people like you.' He said that Social Democracy was indeed the poisoned needles with which he took aim at me. I prayed sincerely for his success. And I told him that I too was sick and tired of the way I was, but for some mysterious reason, I and my type continuously discovered the secret of riding men like him. It was not my doing that I recognized the order.

"Ivan pretended that he had fallen asleep. In fact, the young man was by now convinced that he should not take me seriously. After all, he was a Russian, a neighbor to Europe; overall, he was a European, a Master of the World. And who was I? A prince in a backward country who spoke nonsense. Even if my ideas were correct, it mattered little to him. I was a weakling in this competition. But gentlemen, I had spoken of a general order. A matter that I thought he, in his innocence, had not paid enough attention to. It was not our personal opinions and relationship under discussion in that Russian train. Rather, I had tried to explain to him a universal process. Anyhow, he slept, and I spent a long time watching his calm demeanor and with every passing moment I felt I had seen him before. The next morning we did not pick up on our previous discussion. And you may not believe it, but for the rest of the trip to Moscow we traveled as two very close friends and had no difficulty." The prince drank some wine and took a deep breath, and said, "I think this Ivan, considering his personality, joined the Bolsheviks later on."

Layla's soft but continuous laughter could be heard from a distance. Dinner had come to an end and from a corner of the garden came the sound of Persian tambour and tar music. A woman was singing a light popular song and the party was becoming more informal. Some headed for the garden and some relaxed in the armchairs. Touba went to the window and sat in an armchair. The electric lamps were turned off, and instead candles burned here and there. Candles also floated on the pool, creating a romantic reflection on the water. Touba felt the moonlight piercing needlelike through her body, as she did at every full moon. She also felt the heavy sensation of a watchful eye upon her. She looked involuntarily to her right. Prince Gil was leaning in the dark corner by the window, staring at her. Touba rose to show her respect, but the Prince waved his hand, motioning to her to relax. He came and sat by her on the window ledge.

Touba saw Layla dancing toward them with a drummer behind her, playing. She saw her husband following Layla, along with some other men, and competing with them to be closest to her. Layla glided forward, her hair, arms, and legs all flowing. She had her castanets on her fingers again, and with every move she made sounds with them. A herd of men followed her, wildly and crazily. Layla made a full circle around the oval pool and the herd followed her all the way. Touba was not the jealous type—and even if she had been, she would have felt no jealousy toward Layla. The woman did not seem human. None of her behavior was like that of any other women. But Touba did not like to see her husband in this state.

She puckered her lips tightly and turned her eyes to the prince, who had been looking at her, and at his own wife intermittently. In order to increase her resistance to the prince's piercing stare, Touba asked the prince if he had really seen the Russian man before the train ride. The prince nodded his head affirmatively. He had seen him, he said, "Seven hundred years ago in the deserts of Turkistan." Touba continued to listen to the prince, falling into her usual habit of believing men. If the prince had said he had seen the man, and that it was seven hundred years ago, perhaps then it was true. She asked how he had seen him. The prince responded that it was a long story, and asked if Touba was prepared to hear a lengthy and tiresome tale.

In the cellar, Feraydun Mirza was down on all fours, giving a ride to Layla. She had promised to let him kiss the tip of her hair if he gave her a ride, and he had accepted.

Prince Gil told Touba: "I have to begin from the point at which my spiritual Sufi master went mad somewhere in the Roman Empire. As soon as we heard the news, we headed out bareheaded and barefooted to help him. In reality, I don't to this day know if we were running to save him or fleeing from the Mongols. I was an ironsmith in a small town in the province of Khorasan when from one direction came the news of the Mongol's attack, and from another, the news of our Master's madness and lovesickness. We left our clan and families and headed for Rome on foot. Every stop along the way, we warned of the Mongol's advances, of their burning and looting. We hoped that people would try to take some measures toward securing their own safety. What an empty thought! They usually listened to us with pallid faces, and then returned to their work. People of peasant stock are born to be enslaved. I know that most of them were massacred by the Mongols, whereas they could have escaped. I now think that in fact we had used the Master as an excuse to escape, but since our excuse was the Master, he was thus also our destination.

"We found him in the outskirts of one of the cities in the eastern part of the Roman Empire. He was raising pigs. He had fallen in love with a Christian girl who had brought the pig farm as her dowry. The Master attended the pigs while the girl lived in the city. We watched him in amazement and wondered at the wisdom that might be hidden in his action. He worked in silence, and we reproached and rebuked him day and night, or at times counseled him, hoping that he would stop behaving in what seemed to us an inappropriate manner for a dervish. We were told that he had burned his dervish robe, drank wine, and wore a Christian girdle. Can you imagine how we felt? I told you I did not know if I was escaping the Mongols, or if I was in need of the Master's consolation. But either way, our destination was the Master, and that destination had become a lost and empty shell.

"I made up my mind to kill the girl. I had to show the Master that a vessel containing blood and flesh could not have so much value. One night, I left the pig farm and headed for the city. I knew the lady's address. I pursued her for six or seven days until I found her. She danced in a tavern. She was cruelly beautiful. Yet I knew I could kill her. Perhaps it was because I knew she could not be mine. She belonged to the Master anyway; even if I took her body, her spirit belonged to the Master. During the days that I lay in ambush for her, I spent some time thinking of the Master's condition. He was a worldly Master, so how could he be so simple and so completely undone by her? Or perhaps it was the girl who was wasting away for him? Nevertheless, none of my thoughts could divert me from my decision.

"I had chosen a particular night to murder the girl. I was lurking in the bend of the alley, so that when she came out of the dance hall, covered in her veil, I could stab her in the heart with a dagger and escape. This woman was not worthy of being murdered in public. She was to die in a manner that would imply her powerlessness. This, I hoped, might win back our Master.

"I was standing in a darkened doorway when the girl turned down the alley and came toward me. I assure you, I was in a calm state. I did not feel the feelings of a murderer, nor did my heart palpitate. I simply believed that I must press the dagger into her heart. You know, it was a cold, frozen sense of conviction, like a ritual that I was due to perform. But precisely when the girl drew close enough, and I had lifted the dagger to plunge it into her heart, the Master's voice froze me in place, 'What are you doing, you son of Adam?' My hand hung in midair and the girl stood still, head lowered, as though she was expecting an inevitable end. The Master asked who had motivated me to act this way. I had no answer. I brought the dagger down and stood in indecision, wavering between the woman and the Master's voice. The girl raised her face cover and looked at me carefully. In the moonlight, the black of her eyes shone. She had a look of regret and pity in her eyes. I could not bear this. I was angry this time when I raised the dagger. The girl remained silent, awaiting her destiny. The Master harped at me once again, 'What are you doing, you ghoul?' And then, in a voice filled with anger, he ordered the woman to go. Calmly, without hurrying, the girl brought her face cover down and departed in silence. The Master told me that there were issues that I was not capable of understanding, things that perhaps I would never understand. He ordered me to leave that city for good, so that he would never set eyes on me again. I had consequently lost the chance of becoming a follower. At that moment I was not aware what this would mean in the long run.

"My companions and I joined a gypsy tribe and headed for Turkistan via the Slavic plains. I wished to go to the end of the earth, to leave the Mongols behind. With the gypsies, I traveled through China and reached the fabulous Caucasus Mountains. As I traveled, I built metal instruments for people. The peasants were afraid of us.

"We generally set up camp outside small villages. I tell you that if on occasion I found peasant girls by the spring, I mixed with them, and after satisfying myself I would discard them like refuse. I killed them. If their destiny was to be murdered by the Mongols, then better to be rid of their lives by me. Many of them willingly lay on the ground so I could grip their throats with my fingers. I was death itself."

Touba felt a cold wave go up her spine. She was freezing. Layla had come up from the cellar. She was dancing a gypsy-style dance. A man from the Western musical group played the violin for her. The woman twisted and turned like a snake, moving forward. By now, her sheeplike followers had doubled in number. Prince Gil was looking in her direction; he had stopped talking in order to watch his wife's dance. The woman circled the oblong water fountain and disappeared among the trees. The prince said, "The Mongols always arrived either before or after us. Everyone was filled with disrespect, dishonor, fear, and madness following from fear, which is even worse. Many of the girls by the spring willingly submitted to intercourse, as though life had come to an end and they wished to have the last taste.

"We reached Khorasan, and my persistence in searching for my relatives proved hopeless; I could not even find my place in the city. I separated from the others and headed toward Turkistan on foot. I felt more secure that way. My attraction to women had subsided, and anyway there was no woman left who could provoke my desire. Perhaps it was in Turkistan, or in northern Khorasan—I do not remember clearly where it was—that I saw them: A man and a woman, in fact a boy of eighteen or nineteen and a girl no more than fourteen or fifteen, who had escaped death at the hands of the Mongols on their wedding night. The young lad's father, a miller, had led them to the sheep manger by the mountainside. He had given them a week to spend as husband and wife and told them to savor this one week, for the pain and misery of life would begin after that. The young couple returned to their village after a week of lovemaking and were welcomed by the putrid stink of death. Not a live woman or man, not a dog or cat could be seen. They found the putrid, inflated carcasses of the village people, the burglarized and burned-down homes, the annihilated sheep and the scorched earth. The dumbfounded couple packed up their things and began vagabonding in the wilderness, hoping to find an inhabited hamlet. Their hope was to reach Bukhara. They had seen no one on the roads to ask the way. Many times they had to hide in wells and ditches to avoid Mongols who were riding by. They sought a human being to stand next to and relieve their loneliness, and they found me. Like two lambs, they took refuge with me, as though I stood for their father and mother and their clan, all at once.

"To tell the truth, I did briefly imagine that I had a tribe of my own. If I had found a few sheep and goats, our group would have been complete. But we traveled at night and hid in ditches and crevices during the day. The closer we came to Bukhara, the slower we advanced. Mongols' activity in the area was widespread. The woman became a hindrance. She was fat and incompetent. She had no sense of initiative. Either I had to guide her or her husband, who was as shy and coy as she, had to do the job. I had in mind to organize a small group of strong warriors to attack the Mongols. But the woman was always the embodiment of burdensomeness. Sometimes I though that perhaps her lack of mobility and inefficiency was caused by pregnancy. Perhaps she was pregnant. In any case, advancing rapidly toward the city was not possible, and it was in Bukhara that I could search for fresh warriors to implement my plan: I began to think of woman-killing once more, and this time it was not to save the Master so much as to save myself and the girl's husband, for if one worked on him he could perhaps become a warrior, and if he did not become a warrior, he could at least attend to menial jobs.

"After days of slow travel and hiding in ditches and pits, I finally decided to kill the girl. At dawn, when it was still dark, I sent her husband to gather wood and sticks to prepare breakfast. The young man was afraid of the Mongols and did not want to be too far from us, yet my order could not be disobeyed. The girl undid the flour sack that she had been carrying on her back to start making dough. I called her to me. She came like a lamb. She was disgustingly submissive. Without ceremony, I inserted the dagger deep into her heart. I believe she was dead at the first instant, though her eyes

remained open, with the same amazed expression they had held at
the last moment, when she had looked at the dagger and me. I flung
her body into an irrigation ditch nearby and sat down to wait for her
husband. He was rapidly approaching from a distance with a bundle
of twigs and wood on his back. He reached me sooner that I expected and looked around quizzically. At first I told him that the Mongols had taken his wife. His face went white and he began stuttering.
I told him that we must revenge her blood. I skipped breakfast in
order to get away quickly from that dangerous place. He followed
me, confused and disturbed. After three or four days and nights of
walking, I told him the truth.

"Wouldn't you know it, Touba, at first he did not believe me? He
understood my logic. But each time after my long speech he would
repeat, 'But she is my wife.' He always spoke of her in the present
tense, as though she were still alive. From his confused and deranged
words, I finally concluded that he wanted to say that no matter how
many Mongols existed in this world or how many calamities might
befall them, this girl remained his wife. She had to bring his children
into this world so that the wheels of fortune would turn. It wasn't
clear where this young lad, whose mustache hadn't even yet appeared,
had heard that he must take responsibility for turning the wheels of
the world, or partake in their turning. I sometimes think that this category of people often compare themselves to God, the Turner of the
Wheel. Apparently, the discoverer of the Turner of the Wheel was the
old spinner who planted this idea in her children, grandchildren, and
their descendants. Amin, this trusting peon shepherd, believed the
logic that the girl was his wife and he her keeper, and that he was
responsible for her. As though such a thing as Mongols did not exist
and his homeland and his village had not been turned to dust and all
its people not killed; as though the only things that existed were he
and his wife and the wheel to be turned. Now, with the woman gone,
the wheel had stopped turning and his mind had come to a stop. A
vicious circle. He had to be a man with a woman; they had to beget
children, plow the earth, and herd the sheep. Their children had to
follow the same pattern so the turning of the wheel would not stop,
and every so often a Mongol would come and massacre them. I want-

ed to make a warrior out of the boy, but in the end, I left a madman behind. Each day, as we drew closer the city, the lad came some steps closer to mental breakdown. As though his circle of connection to the world was this miserable seven-penny-worth girl. Each day he would decide to return the distance we had covered and search for the wells where he thought he might find her. Many nights he would suddenly get lost in the dark and I would have to go searching for him. After the murder of the girl, I had become truly attached to this boy. I felt as if he were my private property and I suffered deeply because I could not save him from himself.

"By the time we reached Bukhara, the boy had gone totally mad. Bukhara was our destination, for there I intended to visit the Grand Master. I wanted to consult with him about the warrior group I planned to organize. I dragged the crazy youth after me in the devastated and desolate city, where the public spaces were filled with fear. The Mongols were leaving to search for loot in China. They passed by the city in groups, and as they moved further away, more numbers of natives appeared from behind hills and from ditches. Finding the Master's home was easy. He was the only important individual who had survived without hiding. The people gathered around him the way sunflowers turn toward the sun.

"The Master hosted a reception for the sake of a young man in love, as absurd as it was to love in Mongol times. A crowd had gathered at the Sufi center. Perhaps all the living people of Bukhara were there. We arrived exactly at the time when they had seated the young lover in the middle. We mingled in with the crowd and, like the others, silently observed. The Master signaled with his hand and they brought out a servant girl. She was very beautiful. She moved softly. They seated her next to the Master. He took the girl's hand in his own and with a small dagger cut into her wrist. The girl sighed and her blood burst out. I noticed the young man trembling. The crowd was murmuring and then everyone fell silent. The girl was slowly turning yellow. Fear of dying had changed her appearance. She now seemed ugly. At the appropriate moment, the Master circled his fingers around the girl's wound. Someone brought a cloth and bandaged her. The girl fainted. In a powerful voice, the Master told the young man that this ugly demon was the same angel to whom he had lost his heart.

"I was watching Amin, the shepherd boy, from the corner of my eye. He was carefully watching the scene. It seemed as though his madness had subsided. The Master was advising the young lover. I don't know what was going through that youth's mind, but he was listening to the Master in absolute silence with his head bent down. The Master was saying that one should sacrifice false love for genuine love, and the people of the world uselessly attached themselves to falsehoods. These were bad, bad times, and whoever drowned himself in falsehoods was wandering from the path. 'You must focus the eyes of the heart onto the eternal truth and not pay any attention to the joys and sorrows of this false world.' The Master's warm and penetrating voice, like a high-flying eagle, held the crowd's attention. My traveling companion had his whole heart and mind tuned to this voice and once in a while he shook his head submissively.

"The young lover was taken away and the crowd dispersed. I requested an audience. The Master received me immediately, and I paid my respects. I had left Amin behind, for I planned to ask for advice from the Master regarding his condition. At first, I recounted the Roman experience. He listened to me in deep silence. When I finished speaking, he said that he understood my action. I was amazed. He had nearly killed a girl in order to destroy a youth's love for her, whereas he accepted my crazy love for my Master without argument. He understood why I had tried to kill the girl to free my Master from his false love. He explained that similar circumstances could require different actions. Every event occurs in its place and demands its own particular response. I knew the old man was right. He then looked into me with his penetrating eyes. He said there was no time for love in Bukhara, but in Rome there was much room for loving. Here, the Master had only nearly killed the girl, but she was kept alive. In a few days, the girl would recuperate—that is, if meanwhile the Mongols did not come and cut her up with their swords.

"Then I told him of the rest of the trip and of my intention to train warriors and fight the Mongols. The Master spent a long time in silence and then said, 'One who does not know love cannot fight.'

For war you needed a sense of hate, and you could only own hate if you owned love. He said even if I did succeed in organizing a group of warriors, which he did not think I could, there would always be a wide gap between my men and me. I asked him if a man like Genghis, such a bloodthirsty and war-hungry man, knew anything about love. The Master looked at me with penetrating eyes and said, 'Genghis's whole presence is filled with love, only it is a sickly love that arises from barren lands, and therefore his hatred is ferocious and bloody.'

"I no longer dared to recount Amin's tale. I could no longer support the principles on which I had killed the girl, even though the Master had committed more or less the same act in my own presence. In his opinion, I could not organize warrior groups, and if he did not approve of the act, then it was impossible to achieve it in Bukhara. Therefore, Amin would remain a constant burden in my life. Eventually, I found the courage and recounted the youth's tale. The Master listened with his head in his hands. When I finished, he asked how I could expect to organize warriors when I could not lead a fourteen-year-old bride from the wilderness to town. I reminded him that I had earlier observed his bleeding ceremony with the young girl. He said that once again, I was not perceiving the differences between similar events. The young bride was Amin's wife and would have borne children for him, whereas this servant girl whom he had bled was loved by two men to the point of madness. Such a silly infatuation might have its place in a time of peace, but in this day and age—the Master slapped his hand on a short stool in front of him—and here, in Bukhara! It was useless, and damaging to this world and the next. For the first time he looked at me. I could see that a valley separated us. He ordered me to leave Bukhara, and never to return as long as I was such a stubborn individualist. In a city so afflicted, he said, the presence of men like me would only cause more evil and misfortune. This city was in need of men filled with love who were willing to give their lives. He told me to leave Amin with him and depart the city. He said all of that believing that the spirit of the wilderness had driven me to madness. And he truly believed that the wilderness, the desert, the prairie, and everything had souls.

"Looking back and examining my life, I understood that I did not hate women because they dispossess men of their warrior power, but because they are one of the major causes of men's entering into war. Barren deserts and poverty also play a role in my hatred. I saw myself as an avenger against women in the name of the barren earth. I do hate birth, but I am also afraid of death, therefore I cannot conceive of unity in reproducing, and I also do not grasp the value of wilderness.

"I watched his eyes. The Master was part Turk and he looked slightly like the Mongols. I was wondering how, with his wilderness qualities, he saw me as a desert. He read my mind. He said that he was of the desert, but in his spirit he had always hidden in a green grass meadow. Was it not for the protection of my freedom, he asked, that I had killed the woman? Was it not because, contrary to the shepherd Amin, I did not wish to take on the responsibility of herding the flock? And I did not wish to lose sleep, like the farmer who spends the night attending the wheat? Didn't I do it to remain free? Didn't I believe that if I was to exist at all, I had to be the man in charge? Didn't I consider the woman an invisible chain on my ankle?

"'Go to India!' the Master declared. He did not look at me any longer. With a lowered head, I took my leave of him. Before leaving the Sufi center, I looked for Amin. He was sitting under a tree. His eyes were on me as I approached. We looked at one another for a good while, and then I headed for the Chinese border beginning my journey toward India.

"You see, Touba? When I was leaving Ivan, at a depot in a village near Moscow, the young man stepped off the train, and arranged his luggage on the platform, and the train whistled to depart into the far below zero freezing cold and driving snow. At the last moment, Ivan looked at me, and this time I saw Amin in his eyes. I am certain that he also recognized me. But it was too late. Perhaps if the recognition had come earlier, he would have relieved me of myself. But it came too late. We looked at each other for a long time, while the snow fell and the wheels of the train accelerated and the distance grew between us."

Layla approached the prince and threw her arm over his shoulder. She was sweaty and her hair was disheveled. The paisley crown on her forehead was drooping slightly. She murmured that he needed to throw Touba's husband out of the house for she, Layla, did not feel like seeing him anymore. The prince merely shrugged his shoulder. Touba's body was cold, yet she felt as though she had a fever. From where he was standing by the window, the prince ordered one of the servants to prepare a carriage for Feraydun Mirza and his wife. Layla had left them once more, but they could hear her laughter. The servants were carrying the drunken Feraydun Mirza toward a carriage. Touba stood up and prepared to leave. The prince followed her to the veranda in silence. He stood there as Touba descended the stairs. Before departing through the green passageway, she looked at him once more, and just as he had when she first saw him, he seemed like a lion in the depths of a dark forest. She wondered whether or not she had met the prince prior to these times. The prince's face seemed attached to some ancient memory, but she could not focus well enough to recall it. She climbed into the carriage and sat next to her drunk and sleeping husband. Before the carriage began to move, he was snoring.

Touba had definitely made up her mind to visit His Holiness Geda Alishah in the city of Kermanshah, where he intended to sojourn for the next three years. Prince Feraydun, short-tempered and impatient, was packing for his return to Azerbaijan, and had no time or energy to deal with his wife's emotional upheavals. He did not understand that the woman had lost her spiritual strength. The allegation that Mr. Khiabani was a Bolshevik, of the same Bolsheviks that divided women, the fearful stories of Mr. Biyuck's family and Monsieur Boghosian, Prince Gil's stories and his strange feasts—all these combined, and most of all their poverty, were driving her to the edge.

Touba did not have enough money for the trip. But she was thinking that if she practiced frugality, a quality inherent in her, she could still make the journey. If she were to wait until the children grew up, and for her aunt to either get well or die, it might be twenty years before she could visit Geda Alishah. And if she could not pay him a visit, then she had no will to weave rugs or cook food, and attending to the chores of the day was beyond her power. She imagined a major change looming, something like a Mongolian attack, something that would deeply impact her life. She wanted to know what was going to happen before it did, and for that she needed to see someone who knew more than she did and would not lie to her. Obviously, her husband was not that person. As their circumstances grew worse, the possibility of depending on him only decreased. It seemed that the prince was only dependable when good fortune was on his side. This was the man who on the nuptial night had thrown Touba's veil over his hat, to show that the owner of the veil was ruler of the heart belonging to the owner of the hat, and if anyone were to be disrespectful to this woman, he would be chopped to pieces. This same man now disregarded the frequent visits Touba made to the outside world for shopping purposes. He did not pay any money for household expenses, and even at times borrowed money from her. His excuse was that as a member of the royal court, he needed to be dressed appropriately in order to find a respectable job. He felt embarrassed to go to the stores, for he was a prince, and royalty must send their servants to do the shopping. He also sent Yaghut on so many errands to different cities that the man was never there, and when he was home, he was cursing his dark fate. Almas Khatoun was not capable of shopping; she was the bird in the kitchen, where she felt at home. Auntie had gone mad, and the children were too small. Touba had to go to the shops, and negotiate and deal with the tenants of the stores and with Monsieur Boghosian upstairs. Touba collected the rent from him and from Mr. Biyuck, and each time she would turn into a bad-tempered, manlike woman—a woman who she sometimes could not bear herself. Touba, in these times, was in need of support. Mr. Khiabani was more or less a lost cause. But Touba leaned on Dervish Hasan's talk, hanging tight to the dream of Master Geda Alishah. He was a star shining in the sky of Kermanshah. Just as once upon a time all roads led to Rome, now for Touba they all led to Kermanshah.

In midsummer, Touba took a carpet from the loom and sold it to

Mr. Biyuck. She collected the rent for the rooms and the shops, put the money all in a sack, asked the way to the bus station, and reserved bus seats for herself, the children, Auntie, and Yaghut for a departure time a few days hence. Almas was to stay home to tend to matters there and could eat at Mr. Biyuck's table. That night there was a terrible fight between Touba and the prince. He was leaving for Azerbaijan in a few days, and he had planned to take Yaghut in order to look respectable, arriving there with an attendant. The battle ended in Touba's favor. She was to send Yaghut to him in a month's time. The prince accepted but unconsciously held a grudge against her. The following days were filled with packing the travel necessities for everyone. She had to do everything herself. She wrapped her own, Auntie's, and the children's clothes all in a large cloth; it looked like a mountain. She placed blankets, mattresses, and other bedding in a wrapping and Yaghut tied it all up. Then it was time to organize pots and pans for cooking, and basins and pitchers to wash their bodies and their clothes. Various piles of household goods collected on the veranda, requiring three porters to carry them to the bus station. Yaghut hired some porters from the street, and after ceremonial prayers and passing under the Qur'an held by Mr. Biyuck's wife, the pilgrims left for their trip. Even though she had not slept all night and was exhausted from organizing and preparing for the trip, Touba had suddenly acquired unusual power, and her heart palpitated at the thought of important events ahead. They stopped three times on the way to the bus station. Once for Habibolah to pee in the gutter, once for Aqdas Ol-Moluk to recover from her falling down and crying hard, and once to exchange greetings with Madam Amineh, Touba's father's cousin. On this occasion they lingered longer. Madam Amineh had set out at sunrise to the vicinity of the shrine of Shah Abdolazim to purchase plaster, load it on donkeys, and bring it to renovate her house. Her life was similar to Touba's and out of either obligation or personal desire she had taken on the man's duties in her home, to make up for the shortcomings of her opium-addicted husband. She was not too dissatisfied with her lot since she was not the housewife type and was actually made for more important tasks. But such opportunities did not exist for women, so she compensated by attending to the construction of her house, to gardening, and to the management of their small estate in Ray City. In Madam Amineh's opinion, it was absolute foolishness on the part of her cousin Touba to travel to Kermanshah to visit Master Geda Alishah. She thought Touba could wait three years until the Master came to Tehran. Touba explained that she could not wait that long, for she needed him now. Madam Amineh shrugged her shoulders. She knew she had to wrap up their conversation so that her cousin could get to the station. She wished them a good trip, they said their farewells and then Touba and her little caravan proceeded.

The bus station was a jumbled mass of people, yelling and climbing over one another. The assistant driver organized and secured Touba's and her family's bundles, then permitted the family to sit on the loads next to one another. Then he organized the packages of another family beside theirs. Gradually, about twenty-five or more people were packed in, sitting on the floor in the covered section of the bus. It was clear that it was going to be an uncomfortable ride at least until the city of Hamedan, where they would pass the night. As more people came, the assistant driver seated some on the flat bed of the back of the bus, securing them in place with ropes. In this way, the bus held fifty passengers. This was the arrangement only until the city of Qazvin. Yaghut spent the trip to Qazvin bouncing up and down on a metal bench, cursing his black life and everyone around him in his black language. A prayer was said aloud when the driver sat in his seat. People prayed in a unified voice, then began repeating the protection prayer to themselves, and repeated God's name while the bus took off on the dusty road filled with bumps and potholes. Before the bus left the city, people said many more prayers, and Touba told the woman next to her that she was going on a pilgrimage to kiss the feet of Master Geda Alishah. The woman responded that after the Prophet and his family there was no other holiness in this world, and that Touba was going on the wrong path and soon would have to pay for her sin. Touba cringed at the thought that she was going to have to spend the next two days with this humorless companion, who probably intended to preach to her.

The bus sped down the road at forty kilometers an hour, stirring up clouds of dust, and the woman beside Touba continuously spoke of the holy saints of Islam. Touba also heard Yaghut's curses and the retorts of those around him, who were fed up with his constant complaints. Touba kept explaining to the woman that she had never in her life strayed from devotion to God. She explained that only God could heal her pains and solve her difficulties. At times the two women entered into arguments, and the other passengers—who were not interested in these disagreements, considering their own pain from the long and bumpy bus ride—would put an end to the arguments with a loud prayer. They stopped for lunch at a coffee-house near Qazvin, and the crowd left the bus with great difficulty, dragging their sleepy feet and tired bodies. Aqdas Ol-Moluk and Moones O-Doleh were crying. Auntie had for the present forgotten the idea of climbing the rope of light, and seemed miraculously sane. She walked the children around the bus to get their legs moving, and kept slapping her own legs under her chador to awaken circulation. Among the packed loads of paraphernalia, Touba found the pot of meatballs that Almas Khatoun had cooked the previous night. When she lifted the pot lid, the stale smell of unaired food reached her nostrils, and she left the lid open for a good while to air the food. Yaghut spread a rug under a tree and, happy to be comfortable at last, cheerfully helped to organize the dishes and food for lunch. Even though everyone was tired, the joy of traveling had settled onto one and all. They ate half the meatballs with pickles and kept the other half for dinner. The driver, who had gone into the coffeehouse to smoke opium, stretched out by the fire and had no desire to drive anymore. Some of the passengers who were in a rush kept sending messengers to him requesting that he resume his driving, but the messengers failed to rouse him. By four in the afternoon, the driver finally stretched and got up. The assistant had loaded everyone back onto the bus an hour before. When the driver, the light of their sun, finally appeared through the coffeehouse door, the passengers offered up a few more prayers. Languidly, he placed himself in his seat. The assistant driver cranked the engine, and when the bus lurched into motion, he had to run after it and jump onto the foot board. Yaghut immediately resumed his complaints about all the bumps and potholes.

In Qazvin, it was discovered that the bus needed repair. The bus was guided to a traveler's inn, and there, while the assistant driver arranged the tools for the repair, the driver went to the inn's coffee-house to smoke opium again.

Touba emptied the remainder of the meatballs into a bowl and washed the pot. She instructed Yaghut to go shopping in order to have bread and cheese and sesame paste for the rest of the trip to Kerman-shah. Touba was completely exhausted, yet she had to wash the children's clothes. The children were also tired, and kept fidgeting and grumbling. She gave them some nuts to keep them happy. Gradually their energy returned, and they joined the other children in rabble-rousing, claiming the inn's courtyard as their domain. At this point the assistant driver explained that they had to spend the night in Qazvin while they waited for the bus to be fixed. The passengers accepted this without complaint. They did not wish to spend any more time sitting on their bundles cross-legged, begging to reach Hamedan. Soon most of them fell asleep, except for some of the women, who were busy washing their children's clothes or cooking food.

In this way, the exhausting two-day trip took four days. The children felt nauseous and Habibolah had a fever. Yaghut cursed the world. But Auntie was the amazing one. She kept getting more and more sane, and Touba considered this as one of the miracles inher-ent in approaching the circle of light of Geda Alishah. The ill-tempered woman sitting next to Touba persisted with her arguments, and one of the men among the rope passengers, upon finding out that Touba's husband was a prince, expressed his desire to marry Manzar O-Saltaneh. He owned some shops in Kermanshah, he had a house full of carpets, and the food in his house was cooked with the best of Kermanshah's lard. Manzar O-Saltaneh, who was no more than nine or ten years old, held tightly on to her veil for the thought of being married to the man turned her stomach. Habibo-lah was often listless, asleep in his mother's aching arms, and Aqdas Ol-Moluk had to be audience to Yaghut's complaints. But Moones O-Doleh, only four years old, was quiet. She often smiled and was happy to be traveling with her mother. Touba thought to herself that the girl had inherited her mother's personality, and was not concerned with the material comforts of life.

Upon their arrival in Kermanshah, after they managed to get away from Manzar O-Saltaneh's would-be suitor, ask forgiveness from the ill-tempered woman, pay the customary tips to the assistant driver who had lowered their baggage, and say farewell to the driver who was about to start another opium session in the coffeehouse of the bus station, they suddenly realized they were completely alone and had nowhere to go. However, they slowly overcame their fear. Asking around, they found the address of a dilapidated roadside inn. They took a room, which was next to the bathrooms, where the stink and flies drove everyone crazy. The next day they asked around and gained Master Geda Alishah's address. They were told that he was residing in the village of Bisotoun. They all felt awful, for now they had to retrace their tracks. They found some donkeys and loaded the luggage and the children and Auntie on the animals. Touba and Yaghut followed them on foot. The return trip to Bisotoun took three more days. Touba felt deeply regretful at times. She had not thought that visiting Master Geda Alishah would involve so much pain. In her heart she agreed with Madam Amineh, who had tried so hard to prevent their setting out on the trip. She had told them: "It is not good. A veiled woman cannot go on a trip. There will be one thousand and one problems. Thieves might ambush you at night. You might run into ruthless people." Touba had relied on the bus. In comparison to donkeys, horses, and camels, a bus looked like a miracle, and every time she had seen a vehicle of the kind, she had saluted God's grandeur. Now, however, having tasted the bitter reality of a tiring bus ride, the driver's disdainful attitude, the bus breaking down every step of the way, Touba experienced the desolation of a veiled woman. All of her hope had come to rest on Yaghut, whom she had not previously valued.

They reached Bisotoun with great difficulty. They asked the way, and arrived at the Sufi center of the Master Geda Alishah totally exhausted. The custodian felt sorry for this large and distressed family, and permitted them to stay in one of the pilgrim rooms. Habibolah, who had fainted on Yaghut's shoulder, was laid down in bed. The custodian brought the child a steaming hot liquid. Touba herself also fell into the bed that Auntie had arranged for her, where she slept for twenty-four hours straight beside her sick son.

Upon waking the next day, the son and the mother seemed much better. Touba was in close proximity to her beloved Master, and if only she willed, she could see him. For the first time in her life, she could do what she wished, but the knowledge of access to her own will frightened her. She now felt no desire to visit the Master. She was afraid of the unknown. She was not sure what would happen. Some of the stories she had read in Rumi's books came to mind. What if the master would not believe in her and her sincerity? What if he required of her to sacrifice her four children for his sake? Did she, Touba, have the right to leave her family's faith in his hands?

After she had given the children breakfast, and dressed them to go and play with other children in the yard, and left Habibolah to Auntie's care, and sent Yaghut out shopping, and placed the veil on her head to go and see the Master, she realized that she was scared to death. With shaky knees and with the custodian's guidance, she headed for the center's main building. A large crowd of men and women had gathered there. The custodian guided Touba to the women's waiting room. She sat there for an hour, trying to overcome her anxiety, but she was not very successful. By noon, a woman came and told her that she could recite her noon prayers in the room with the pool. Touba quickly stood and headed for the room. She assumed that now all the other women would follow her to perform their prayers. But no one accompanied her. The woman guided Touba to the pool room and closed the door behind her. Touba stood in the middle of the room and didn't know what to do. She finally began praying as she had been instructed. She took her chador and socks off and went toward the pool for ablution. She had just washed her face when she heard the footsteps of a man on the stairway. She stopped her ablution prayer and said aloud, "There is a woman here," so that the owner of the footsteps would be aware he was entering a room with an unveiled woman in it. But the footsteps continued, as if he was hard of hearing. She left the ablution half-finished, ran to her chador and pulled it on inside out, also put her socks on, and headed for the stairway. There she saw a man whom she quickly concluded must be Master Geda Alishah. The middle-aged man was standing on one step, but was stamping his feet in place to create the impression of walking. Touba said a greeting and stood a few steps from him with a shaking heart. The man stopped stamping his feet. There was silence as he looked at Touba with his deep penetrating eyes. Touba looked down. As the silence continued, her anxiety deepened. Then she lifted her eyes, for she thought that the master wished her to look up. The man continued staring at her, then asked, "Is it not amazing that one at prayer would be afraid of footsteps?" Touba answered that the footsteps of a man caused her fear. But the man said, "In prayer, if one is seeking to be received by God, who is of course present every second, when performing the ablution for prayer one must be so deeply immersed in the act that no action or no noise should disturb one."

Touba felt ashamed, and wished she could sink deep into the ground. The Master said, "You are yet young. You have not been relieved of youth's anxiety and expectancy. Let us say that this path is yet too soon for you, although I heard you had a very difficult trip." The woman nodded her head in acknowledgment. The Master continued, "Well, well, it was not fair to cause so much pain for the little ones in order to see me."

Touba lowered her head. The Master came one step down and Touba's heart gave out. He said, "We have women visitors, but not of your kind. They are women whose husbands are dead, women without support, or women who have lost everything. Therefore, their difficult journey does not frighten them. But you are committed to your children and husband, is that not so?" Touba lowered her head again. The Master said, "Return now, and come back in ten years. You shall find your own path."

As he prepared to leave, he told her that he had arranged for one of his relatives to take them back to Tehran, after the child regained his health. For the next few days, she and her family were to be the guests of the Sufi center. Touba told him about Auntie's condition and also inquired about Mr. Khiabani. Regarding the former, he

133

said, "The old woman is lost in herself; sorrow is causing her to dete-
riorate. Give her something to occupy herself with. She needs to
work constantly to come out of herself." He said he would pray for
her, and would also give her some blessed sugar candy. He would see
Auntie in the afternoon and pray for her and bless the candy in her
presence to make it more effective. Concerning the latter, Mr. Khiabani, the Master said, "He is lost in others and has forgotten himself.
He should attend to himself a little more. But alas . . ." He said
nothing more, and the word "alas" tolled like a bell in Touba's mind,
years later, when she heard of Mr. Khiabani's death. The master
probably already knew of his death. As he reached the door, the master turned and looked at Touba. He looked at her kindly and without reproach. He once more repeated that Touba should return to
him in ten years.

The return trip was easy. It was as though they had endured such a
long and rough road on the way there in order to return on a short
and smooth one. Touba was, after all of this, even more bitter. She
didn't wish to talk to anyone about her conversation with the Master. After she sent Yaghut to Azerbaijan, she busied herself and Auntie with rug-weaving. She had registered Habibolah and Aqdas Ol-
Moluk's names in school and the children, accompanied by Manzar,
headed out every morning. Moones was the little one left at home
playing around the women, and she sometimes joined them in
weaving and work as much as she could.

The women kept weaving continuously. It was in the formation
of the patterns of the rugs that Touba could organize her thoughts.
She thought about Auntie, confused and stranded in her own world,
just like a piece of the pattern on a carpet that was not yet completed. Mr. Khiabani, on the other hand, was deeply connected to others, like the background of the carpet, which contained the pattern
and complex design; he did not exist except as a whole, and therefore he was magnificent and yet humble.

But where was Touba? She could not find herself in any pattern
of the carpet. She thought, "I am a weaver." She was implementing

a design, but which design? The ones that the expert designer had put on the paper—but again, where had the designer gotten the pattern? Indeed, where did he get his ideas? Of course this one was a pomegranate flower, this one an Arabesque, and the other a pine tree. But the pomegranate flower did not look like a pomegranate—it did and it didn't. The master carpet designer had gotten it from somewhere else. His hand knew the design before he was born, before having seen the pomegranate flower. She thought of taking painting classes and making her own carpet designs. She felt a need to design with her hands what her mind saw. But when Auntie mumbled her gibberish, Touba's mind became distracted. She would get up to water the garden, to check the kitchen, wash some clothes, and free her mind from the carpet design.

After a couple of months, the prince sent some rice and lard and wheat for the house, delivered by Yaghut. The man had hardly unloaded his wares before, failing to greet anyone, he ran to his wife in the kitchen to tell her that the prince had married a fourteen-year-old peasant girl. But he had made so many strange faces that Touba had followed him and hidden herself behind the door, where she heard Yaghut's loud voice reveal his master's secrets, though the master had specifically forbidden him to tell anyone. The prince had married the daughter of the headman of one of the villages in his regional authority. The girl was merely fourteen, fair-skinned with rosy cheeks, and had been promised to her second cousin when the prince had shown his kind interest and taken her as his wife.

Listening to Yaghut, Touba aged twenty years in just those few minutes. The prince did bother her at times. His lack of attention to the affairs of the house and money would make Touba angry. But she had never thought of the possibility of his taking a second wife. The man was about sixty-one years old. At the time of his marriage to Touba, many of the relatives had commented on the extreme age discrepancy. Yet she had decided to follow her destiny and get married. She could not believe that he would go and get married again, and to a fourteen-year-old girl for that matter. She headed to the stairs, confused and dizzy. She wanted to hide in the corner of her room, but she felt nauseated. She ran toward the bathroom, but had only made it down the stairs before throwing up. She grabbed at her stomach; it went up and down, as if clothes were being washed in her stomach. She threw up once more, and then left the bathroom consumed with anger. She went up to her room and fell to her knees. She still felt sick to her stomach. She had to do something. She walked back and forth in the room for a long time. The children were in school and Moones was busy playing with her cotton doll quietly in a corner. Once in a while she looked at her mother, who wore a frowning, angry faced as she walked up and down the room.

Touba suddenly decided to go visit Madam Amineh. The woman was the wisest person Touba knew. Talking with her mother was no use. She would probably listen in silence and then say that a woman must put up with her destiny, and if one's tapestry of fate is woven of black, then it is black, and a woman who has already had two lives should not push her luck. But Madam Amineh always had a bundle of clever ideas and original words. Touba put on her chador and was halfway down the stairs when she changed her mind. What could the woman tell her? The problem was not yet clear in her own mind. She returned to her room, folded her chador and put it back in the chest. Confused and stunned, she was about to sit down when she heard the voice of Mr. Biyuck's wife.

The Turkish-speaking woman, who still could hardly speak Persian, entered with a face covered in a bright smile. The woman said hello, and Touba, still in her stupefied state, directed her to the back of the room to sit and lean on a large cushion. Touba poured a cup of tea from the samovar and apologized for not having any fruit or sweets to offer, and yet she was all the time dumbfounded and about to begin mourning. Mr. Biyuck's wife, who was unfamiliar with Tehrani manners, did not notice her landlady's obvious distress, and so cleared her throat and said that she was actually paying this visit to the prince's wife for a very well-meaning reason. It took about an hour for Touba to figure out that, in her broken Persian, the woman was asking for Manzar O-Saltaneh's hand as a fiancée for her fourteen-year-old son. The woman liked the girl because she had fair skin and golden hair and looked like the women of Azerbaijan. And if Touba would agree, they could exchange vows now, and would wait until the girl reached thirteen before they had the reception ceremony. Touba, deep in her own thoughts, responded that in her opinion this was a fortunate match, but she could not decide alone—but at the same moment she was thinking how wonderful it would be if each of her girls was married right now. She could then head to the wilderness after Mr. Khiabani or follow Master Geda Alishah, and free herself from all of life's predicaments. She explained that the girl had a father and it was Prince Feraydun Mirza who would need to decide on this matter. Deep in her heart, she was certain the prince would not agree to it. Mr. Biyuck's wife left the room slightly hopeful, partly doubtful and anxious.

Once she was alone, Touba's mind again flooded with disturbing thoughts. Desire for vengeance burned in her. She wished to do something against the prince that they would write about in history books. Anger was building up in her every minute, and the sense of suddenly aging was killing her. The sudden appearance of a suitor for Manzar O-Saltaneh was something that was not unusual for her beautiful daughter, but it always made her feel older. She herself was hardly more than thirty. Of course, once a woman reached twenty, most assumed that the good part of her life was over. But she was still full of warmth and energy. Her femininity bloomed around the prince, but not always to its full potential. The prince was often absent. He had spent a few years in Russia, and other long periods in the provinces. Nevertheless, when he was there, Touba was content. Once in a while she heard rumors about his playing around with other women. The details of the nuptial night, when the prince had slept with the black servant of Madam Saltanat, the famous woman of Tehran, had finally reached Touba's ears. But the prince could always find a philosophical explanation for all these events, and therefore Touba had never been hurt. Of course, she would not let herself be upset by such things. She was so confused and preoccupied with her own personal thoughts that she had not much time or patience to attend to his affairs. For a long time, when the prince lived with hopes and dreams of Kaiser Wilhelm, Touba had also occupied her dreams with Wilhelm. She was constantly worried for Wilhelm and his conquests. She believed the more she thought of

Kaiser Wilhelm, the more chance there would be that the savior would come and deliver Iran from its enemies. When she discovered that Russia and England were Wilhelm's enemies, and that Mr. Khiabani was against Wilhelm, her castle of dreams was toppled over. She didn't know why she thought about these matters. She never discussed her thoughts with other women, and never had a chance to talk with men. It was all inside her own mind. Her mind participated in world affairs and questioned the ins and outs of all problems, but rarely were her thoughts verbalized. And if ever she did have to talk, then she began to stutter to the point that the men felt the same sympathy and concern for her as an elder feels for children. She therefore preferred to keep silent.

But now all these thoughts were nothing but smoke. Suddenly the reality of a fourteen-year-old second wife swept away all other thoughts. She wondered what others would say.

In the afternoon her brother-in-law, Prince Manouchehr Mirza, came to visit her. He had heard that Feraydun Mirza had taken another wife and was designated by close relatives to see how his sister-in-law was dealing with this matter. Prince Manouchehr Mirza was arrogant, haughty, and proud. He always dressed in his military uniform and carried his saber. Walking around with the saber gave him great pleasure. Touba heard his loud greetings from the door. He frowned when he saw some of Mr. Biyuck's relatives. He hated his brother for having tenants, and hated them as well. Having tenants was not appropriate to the status of his family, but he also had no solution for it. He sat down on the chair near the table. Touba went to pour tea and he extended some attention to Habibolah Mirza. The boy asked if his uncle saw the men who were in the curtain, and he pointed toward the curtain that covered the storage area in the room. The curtain had the picture of Majnoun sitting among the animals on it. The prince looked at the curtain suspiciously. Now that his brother had married again, it was not impossible that some men would be hiding behind the curtain. The prince stood up with his hand on his saber and approached the curtain. Touba, who had frowned since the arrival of the brother-in-law and was looking for the opportunity to pour her rebukes of her husband onto his brother, suddenly felt anxious. She knew very well that there were no men behind the curtain, but she could not bear this much suspicion from her brother-in-law. It is possible that a man as arrogant as the prince, though he might not find men behind the curtain, might search into Touba's mind and come across Mr. Khiabani and Master Geda Alishah. In absolute amazement, she realized that she owed part of her everyday life to these two men of her imagination. When the prince was done inspecting behind the curtain, Touba asked Habibolah Mirza which men he had in mind and the boy pointed at the curtain again. The prince paused, still suspicious. Touba encouraged her son to go to the curtain and show them the man or men. The boy ran to the curtain and pointed out Majnoun, and also an Arab man who was lost among the palm trees, sitting on a camel looking at Majnoun in wonder.

The prince calmed down, and Touba did not press the matter any further. Then the boy made another announcement; he asked if his uncle knew that Manzar O-Saltaneh was to become a bride. The prince looked at Touba in surprise and asked, "Whom is the girl supposed to marry?" Habibolah Mirza quickly replied that his sister had been asked for by Mr. Biyuck's son, and said how nice this boy was. He always gave Habibolah sweets. The prince put his hand on his saber again and confronted his sister-in-law, asking, "Is this true?" Touba said yes, it was true. They had asked for her daughter's hand, but she had not yet answered. The prince, whose face was inflamed with anger, asked what the boy's name was. "It is Mohsen," she replied. He then pulled the saber from its sheath, opened the door, and headed down the stairs. Filled with fear, Touba ran to the terrace. For a few seconds she had forgotten the existence of the second wife. The prince reached the windows on the tenant's side of the house, and with the tip of his saber banged on the window. The glass cracked and immediately Mr. Biyuck's wife's face appeared. The prince, in a thunderous voice, demanded to see Mohsen. He shouted that if he is a man, he should come out to the court and show himself. All Mr. Biyuck's wife could manage was to send her son from the back door to his father's shop and tell him to keep out of sight for a few days. The other members of Mr. Biyuck's family hid in the back room. The woman, with what little courage she yet had left in her, came to the window and in Turkish kept begging the prince to overcome his anger. Prince Manouchehr Mirza, who became redder each second, told the woman, in Turkish, that by tomorrow morning she had better get her things out of the house and move the hell out of there. He twisted his saber a few times around his head and instilled fear in everyone. He then returned to the room. In all his excitement on the way back, he tipped a bowl of pomegranate seeds prepared for the celebration of the winter solstice all over the carpet. Saber in hand, he sat down on the chair and let out a deep sigh. Madam Shams Ol-Moluk as he usually addressed his sister-in-law, stood in front of him, and stared at him in rage. What did the prince want, anyway, she screamed. First he went searching for men behind the curtains, as though he had not yet come to know his sister-in-law's personality. Then he went out there and drew his sword on innocent people. Why should people, and why should Touba, the daughter of Adib, who was in pursuit of God and had dedicated her life to the Supreme One, suffer so much? Now, if Mr. Biyuck were to leave, where was she going to get the money to feed her children? Why did Prince Feraydun, who takes a fourteen-year-old girl for a wife, not think about providing for his children? Was Touba a slave, to continuously sit at the carpet-weaving loom and give her life for a prince who was a womanizer, or played politics and took refuge behind the czar of Russia? Or for a prince who, as soon as his life took a turn, in his old age took a fourteen-year-old wife? Besides, what wrong could one find in Mr. Biyuck and his wife? These were hardworking, honest, respectable people. Had they committed a crime or taken the belongings of an orphan that they should be so unjustly attacked?

Touba kept shouting and picked up the pomegranate seeds, and Prince Manouchehr Mirza did not stay to hear the rest of her words. When he descended the stairs, by the fountain, he looked at Mr. Biyuck's window. He saw the whole family gathered there again, listening to Touba's screams and rants, though they pulled back as soon as they saw him approaching. The prince had enough time to pull his saber halfway from the sheath as a rude signal to the woman.

By the time the sad Prince Manouchehr Mirza arrived at the Armenian cafe on Baharestan Square and had the cafe owner serve him some wine, poured out of a teapot into a cup, Mr. Biyuck had told his wife and children to get their things together so they could leave that damned house. Then he returned to the bazaar so that, with the help of acquaintances, he could find a new house and put an end to the matter by the next day, and thereby save his son's life. Prince Manouchehr Mirza gradually calmed down and stopped pulling his hair. The prince had discovered kernels of truth in Touba's words. He had come to realize that the Qajar dynasty's government was declining, after ruling Iran for all of the nineteenth century. The previous year's coup d'etat had popularized the name of a strong army commander, while the young Qajar shah who clung to power had become sick and even obsessive, and therefore did not issue any significant royal commands. He had just come from Europe and he wished to return there again. The shah did not care much for the rivalries going on among the princes and Manouchehr Mirza was certain that if the shah were to hear about his sword escapade involving Mr. Biyuck's family, he would be unhappy.

Prince Manouchehr Mirza thought to himself that he had to find appropriate husbands for his brother's daughters before it was too late. Prince Hesam O-Din Mirza, who had just returned from England, was a good choice as husband to the jovial and beautiful Manzar O-Saltaneh. The young prince was no longer able to speak Persian very well but he had attained a respectable rank in the military. He was simple, kind, and the appropriate age of eighteen. If they waited a couple of years, Manzar O-Saltaneh would turn thirteen, and then the marriage ceremony could take place. For Aqdas Ol-Moluk he was considering Turan O-Saltaneh's son. The boy was about fourteen or fifteen and could easily wait a few years until Aqdas Ol-Moluk reached marrying age. But it was necessary that the naming party be organized so that not every scoundrel would have the audacity to come asking for the hands of these princely children. This left Moones, who was only four years old, and in time a good husband would also be appropriated for her. With these thoughts in mind, the prince headed for Turan O-Saltaneh's home.

The next day, when Mr. Biyuck's family was moving out, Turan O-Saltaneh came to visit Touba. She said that now Shams Ol-Moluk must surely understand her hopeless life. Now she could understand how much agony Turan O-Saltaneh had had to endure from her husband's behavior—her lecherous husband had played around with women and upset her so much that she could hardly sleep or eat. Touba glanced at the princess's chubby body. It did not seem as if any loss of weight had occurred. The princess said that on her way there she had gone to Arfah O-Doleh's house to discuss the wedding of Manzar O-Saltaneh and Hesam O-Din. The family welcomed this marriage; the only condition was that they were to see the future bride in the bathhouse, and Turan O-Saltaneh had invited everyone for Friday to her private bathhouse to show the twelve-year-old Manzar O-Saltaneh to the groom's family. She spoke a while about the merits of Hesam O-Din Mirza, and then asked for Aqdas Ol-Moluk's hand for her own son, Abol Hasan Mirza. Suddenly Touba's daughters, who until then had been playing with dolls and running after one another, had found husbands. Touba, however, did not wish to give her daughters as wives to the princes. She well understood that the Qajar dynasty was declining, and deep in her heart she was weary of the licentiousness of the princes. Nevertheless, she was powerless to stop the course of events.

By two in the afternoon, she had said farewell to Mr. Biyuck's family and asked their forgiveness. She then, according to Turan O-Saltaneh's orders, put on her crêpe de chine dress and prettiest chador and let Turan O-Saltaneh arrange her hair as she pleased while she listened to the princess lecture to her about how a woman must be coquettish and charming. She said that although Touba was beautiful, she was not paying enough attention to her beauty and charm. The two women entered Turan O-Saltaneh's carriage to go to Madam Lazarian, the photographer, to take pictures. Madam Lazarian undid the front of Touba's dress a bit and pulled the fabric down to bare her shoulders. She pushed and pulled Touba's head left and right, ordered her to smile, then told her not to smile, and then she took photographs in two poses, of her standing and sitting, with flowers and without. Turan O-Saltaneh was photographed also. Afterward they rode around Lalehzar Avenue, and Turan O-Saltaneh suggested that they bring their feet a little forward to show their legs. Some men tipped their hats to the women, to which they responded by turning their heads away haughtily. A dignitary on horseback rode beside their carriage for a long while and watched them amorously from the corner of his eye. Turan O-Saltaneh said that now Shams Ol-Moluk could see her own worth, and that if she wished she could make servants of a herd of men. She should not be sorrowful over her husband's new marriage, since all men were the same. Later in the afternoon she dropped Touba off with the promise that the next day she would return and take her to Lalehzar Avenue again.

In a state of trance, Touba said goodbye and returned to the house, and for the first time it dawned on her what had happened to her. When Manzar O-Saltaneh, who was anxious about her marriage, asked a question, Touba scolded her and punished all the children. Anger tormented her like a tempestuous sea boiling in her stomach, and she hated everyone. The children ran from her like chickens attacked by a fox, for Touba struck out at them mercilessly. She kept pushing Almas Khatoun to the side. Unable to free herself from the anger boiling within her, she began tearing her crêpe de chine veil while it was still on her head. Then, feeling hollow and hopeless, she put her head in her hands and began sobbing violently. The children then gathered around her and joined in crying.

Touba imagined that everyone was speaking about her—and indeed, everyone was doing so. She had become an interesting subject of gossip among the women whose husbands were not princes. She tried to feign tranquility and indifference whenever relatives and friends were around. But it didn't work. They often looked at her kindly and smiled; then they sighed and talked about fate and cruel fortunes. They continued in this manner until she was forced to speak about her life. She had to speak about her husband's new wife, a woman she had never met. She did not believe that a fourteen-year-old girl could be malicious, yet what had happened was making her hate all young people. She felt as though they were taking her place. She looked at herself in the mirror and had to accept that she was growing old. She became rather obsessed with examining herself, and this would lead her to ask, "What have I done to deserve this? Have I not put up with poverty?" Madam Amineh said, "My dear, this is the camel that sleeps at every woman's door." In response, Touba asked why it had not slept in front of Madam Amineh's house. Shrugging her shoulders, Madam Amineh replied that her husband needed a bomb just to move him from the bed to do his opium smoking. It was obvious that the camel would not sleep at her door. Everyone has her own misery, she said. It was in this phenomenon that everyone was equal. Did Touba know anyone who was fortunate? We all have our complaints. Madam Amineh would prefer that her husband take a second wife, if he would only stop smoking opium. On the other hand, Touba would prefer that her husband become an opium addict rather than a womanizer.

Not many months had passed since the departure of Mr. Biyuck and his family when Mirza Abuzar, the overseer of the prince's estates, came with his family from Azerbaijan. Mirza Abuzar stood in the courtyard looking sorrowful. His sister, Madam Alavieh and her fourteen-year-old daughter, Setareh, and eight-year-old son, Ismael, gathered around him like helpless chicks seeking protection. Mirza Abuzar explained that they had had to escape Azerbaijan because of an uprising. He said that Mr. Khiabani had been murdered, and the killer was the scientist. No one could believe it. Mirza Abuzar sat by the poolside and began crying uncontrollably. Madam Alavieh and Setareh also joined in crying, and Ismael stood under the pine tree in silence with a frown on his face.

Touba crouched by Mirza Abuzar's feet and listened to him sadly. Mirza Abuzar had been serving the prince when he heard about the attack of the government forces in Tabriz. The concern for his sister and her children and, deep down, his worries for Mr. Khiabani led him to the city. He arrived there after the uprising was over and the city was being occupied by the government forces. Mirza Abuzar had only had enough time to get his family out and bring them to Tehran. Their house had been completely sacked. Mirza Abuzar would be grateful to the prince's lady if she would take these orphans under her wing. His formal manner of talking did not match his mournful demeanor. Touba, who was looking for sorrow, took the death of Mr. Khiabani to heart and became deeply depressed. Now she hated not only her husband; the feeling spread to encompass all aristocracy. She asked why Mirza Abuzar's house had been plundered. Mirza Abuzar explained that the children had been standing by the front door watching the marching soldiers when Setareh laughed at a soldier who had slipped and fallen. Suddenly, the soldier attacked the house. This all happened just before the death of Mr. Khiabani. Ismael had escaped from the roof and hidden, but Setareh and Madam Alavieh received beatings. Touba looked at Madam Alavieh. The woman smiled and began speaking in a strange language. Mirza Abuzar pointed to his head and shook it regretfully. He whispered that the woman was not mentally sound, and therefore Mirza Abuzar had brought them to Tehran so the orphans, whose uncle was always traveling, could live under the prince's lady's kindness. Touba looked at Setareh, who reminded her of the meaning of her name, star. The girl looked about fourteen or fifteen, just like her husband's new wife. She frowned unconsciously. The young girl fearfully hid behind her mother. Mirza Abuzar said that with the lady's permission, he would stay for a couple of months to arrange the affairs of his sister's family. Touba was thinking about how she had carried the burden of her crazy aunt for all those years, and now she had to deal with another one. She thought of naming the second one the Turkish Aunt, then she could call her own the Persian Aunt. She imagined the two crazy aunts each filling the sides of a scale while she stood up at the center to keep them balanced. She didn't know if she should laugh or cry. She told Mirza Abuzar that they could settle in Mr. Biyuck's rooms.

The phrase "crazy aunts" quickly spread through the house, as though these Persian and Turkish crazy aunts had lived next to one another for thousands of years. Ismael was enrolled in a school. The boy who hardly spoke now had to study and converse in Persian, but he showed remarkable potential. From the very first days he impressed his teachers. Gradually, it became clear that Habibolah couldn't stand Ismael. In the past, Habibolah had been the only male child, loved and respected by the family, but now he had competition. The new boy was respected for being calm and quiet and for his intellectual achievements. Ismael soon showed that though he was small, he was capable of acting like a grown man. He would line up the children and lead them to school in the mornings and bring them home in the afternoon. He took care of minor shopping for Touba, and therefore relieved her of a major burden. Habibolah Mirza could not bear all of this. He wished to treat the boy as a servant, but the boy, though small, had penetrating eyes and naturally gained the respect of others. The girls simply developed the habit of abiding by his wishes as to what games to play, where to go and not to go. Though the two boys never fought, they maintained a very cold relationship. They obviously could not tolerate one another. Yet it was only Habibolah who showed his feelings openly.

Touba became depressed. She could not weave rugs. Her heart was not in it. She equated herself with a crumbling castle. She suddenly felt estranged from everyone. Slowly, she came to the conclusion that she must get a divorce from her husband. As long as she did not have a divorce, she could not attend to her daily responsibilities. Her outings with Turan O-Saltaneh soon came to an end. Touba did not have a coquettish personality. It seemed a worthless act to sit in the carriage next to the princess and ride up and down Lalehzar Avenue, looking at men who were not supposed to be a part of her life. After a few of these outings, she excused herself for reasons of work and other duties and gradually rid herself of her angry and vengeful feelings toward the princess.

Although Touba could not fill her husband's absence with any other man, she felt good seeing Mirza Kazem express his care for her in his eyes. On occasion Mirza Kazem came to deliver wool or attend to the accounts and sales of the carpets. He knew that Prince Feraydun Mirza had taken a second wife and through his facial expressions he made Touba understand that he sympathized. Touba sometimes unconsciously looked kindly at Mirza Kazem, and felt that in some small way she was getting back at her husband. Even though her husband had taken a fourteen-year-old wife and his own daughters were going to be brides, she enjoyed knowing that she could still look young and interest other men.

One day she made up her mind, to go over to Madam Amineh to consult with her, and ended up smoking a cigarette with her. Madam Amineh sat in front of her listening carefully to Touba's woes. A small tray filled with cigarette holders, tobacco, and rolling papers was in front of her, and every so often she would roll a cigarette and smoke. When Touba finished her woeful story, Amineh stood up and went toward the window, opened it, looked up at the sky and cried out, "O God, in the name of this day, take revenge for all those oppressed by the oppressors, and O God, put an end to all stupid men." She wanted to say "put to death," but changed her mind. Prince Feraydun Mirza was the father of Touba's children, after all, and therefore she did not feel right in cursing him. She finally organized her sentence as follows: "God, do something so that when men come to be men they also gain some brains." Touba could not help but laugh. Madam Amineh returned to her place after her communion with God, and while she shook her head regretfully, she rolled two cigarettes, pressed them into the cigarette holders and offered one to Touba. For the first time in her life, Touba was smoking, and soon she was also coughing. But she liked the dizzy feeling it gave her. Touba became a smoker from that moment on, and she also decided to get her divorce from the prince. Madam Amineh's advice to stay with him did not have any affect on her. Touba had made up her mind long before, but now it was clear what she needed to do. She decided to discuss the matter with Prince Feraydun Mirza himself, since he was soon coming to Tehran. Mirza Abuzar had heard that the prince was quietly looking for a house in which to place his new wife. The prince rather simplistically believed that his wife had no knowledge of the second marriage, and thought that even if she were to find out, surely he would be able to bring her to her senses with the use of his manly power and some concerted effort.

Prince Feraydun Mirza appeared about ten days after Touba became a smoker. Mirza Abuzar met his master at the edge of the city and the prince left his new wife and child in Mirza Abuzar's care, instructing him to take them to Turan O-Saltaneh. The prince himself headed straight for the bathhouse. He changed his clothes, and with a perfumed body came to Touba's home in order to begin the painstaking process of reconciliation.

Touba's heart stopped when he knocked at the door. She knew his manner of knocking. Instead of opening the door, she got up from the loom and ran to her room. She organized her face and hair, put on her black chadoi, and sat by the wall, holding her veil tight around her face. She heard Almas Khatoun open the door for the prince, and in her usual stuttering manner, give serious response to his jokes while the prince laughed aloud. She heard Moones shouting, "Daddy, Daddy," and the Turkish Aunt speaking Turkish, and the Persian Aunt answering the prince's questions about whether or not she had yet climbed the rope of light. Almas Khatoun informed the prince that the other children were in school. He was happy to hear that Mr. Biyuck's family had moved out. He said that he had heard of that development from his brother. Then he asked for Lady Shams Ol-Moluk. Touba noticed that everyone became quiet. She could tell they were whispering in the courtyard. Then she heard the prince's light footsteps, which contrary to his age, sounded just as youthful as ever. He knocked at her door, and without waiting for permission, he entered. Touba thought, I will soon teach him not to again enter a room of a women who is not *mahram*. The prince looked around eagerly. Touba was leaning against the wall near the door, and could not be easily seen. She had calculated all of this to keep the prince in his place. As soon as he saw Touba, the man let out an exagerrated cry of happiness. He said, "What joy, my own wife? How good to see one's own wife again." But it was obvious that he did not dare come too close. In order to gather courage he walked around the room. Everything in the room was the same except for a new rug, which they had just taken off the loom. The prince spent fifteen minutes speaking in admiration of the rug. He spoke so much of its beauty that Touba almost forgot why she was sitting so tense and silent in the corner. With great difficulty, she restrained herself from speaking with him. Finally, he turned to Touba. He glued his sweet honey eyes on her and said, "What a dam! What a Wall of China! My wife has placed herself inside a castle. Now, with what shall I pull her out of there, or how can I crush the wall and take her?" As he spoke, he approached her, coming within two steps of her. He went down on his knees and spoke very politely. The prince had decided to use a strategy of attrition, and try slowly to penetrate the walls she had erected between them, even though he sensed that they were indeed quite solid and perhaps impassable.

Prince Feraydun Mirza took out a very beautiful velveteen box and placed it on the carpet in front of her. He said, "I told a jeweler I have a wife who is pure gold. Her hair is braided gold, her skin genuine marble, her eyes black onyx. She is a precious gift, a rare treasure. Her tears are pearls, gems, and diamonds, her smile is a bouquet of flowers. Now what shall I buy her?" The jeweler said, "I have strung her very tears together."

Feraydun Mirza opened the velveteen box. A three-tiered pearl necklace lay glowing in the middle of the box. Touba was immediately spellbound by the necklace. The prince was pleased with her response and inched one step closer. Touba who had read his mind, took her eyes off the pearls and pulled the veil even tighter around her face. The prince pushed the box closer to her with the tip of his finger. He said that this present was unworthy of his heart, Lady Shams Ol-Moluk, but it was the gesture that counts and he could not offer more than this, though all the world's jewels would not be enough for her because she herself was the greatest gem on the entire earth. Touba frowned. She said there was no need for jewelry and she could manage without it. Prince Feraydun Mirza said she could sell the necklace if she wished, and with the money purchase two houses and not deal with tenants any longer. Touba said she preferred to live off of her own labor, and the prince smiled in surprise. He said that he believed her problems were all related to monetary matters, and if these issues were to be resolved she would have no worries. Touba replied that she did worry about money, but that she would not tolerate a second wife.

At this, Prince Feraydun Mirza raised his eyebrows and said, "What second wife?" They argued for half an hour about the existence of another wife. The prince denied it. "Shams Ol-Moluk should know that men have their flirtations," he said, "but in the end they return home." He did not know, or could not tell Touba,

SHAHRNUSH PARSIPUR

that taking a second wife for him was more of a spiritual or political move than a reflection of physical desires. He had to prove his princely power to the peasants, and it was part of his position as a prince that he extend a protective umbrella over his subjects. Princes took peasant wives in order to feel connected to the peasants, and the peasants' interests were secured through their representatives who served the princes. In general, then, the princes should be kind to the people. Prince Feraydun Mirza did not know how to put all this in words. He felt these things instinctively, and could not explain them to Touba. And even if he had known how to explain them, he would not have told her.

But Touba also knew her own territory, her home. And in one home, two wives were a crowd. She would not be able to share her husband with anyone. Her psyche would get all mixed up. She felt embarrassed around everyone—and why not? She was being over-looked and she was jealous. The thought of the prince having inter-course with another woman made her physically ill. She regularly dreamt of murdering the prince for his liaisons. She experienced the dreams many times, but would not admit that she enjoyed them. At times she wished intensely to cut him to pieces and send each por-tion to a different city to hang by the city gates and herald to the world that this was the reward for a man who takes a second wife. She told no one that in her mind she had stabbed him with a knife, a sword, and a cleaver, and that she had pummeled him with a ham-mer and her fists.

Prince Feraydun Mirza finally acknowledged that he had taken a second wife, but immediately stated that what was important was that she was not important at all. She was not equal to Shams Ol-Moluk's little finger. He asked Shams Ol-Moluk if she would agree to accept the woman as a servant. What would be wrong with that? She would just hang around. The prince did not tell her that he thought his new wife was more beautiful than Shams Ol-Moluk. Touba answered that she had no need for a servant and that she knew best how to manage her own life.

The prince grew impatient. Touba shut the lid on the velveteen box and returned it to him. She said that if the prince would send her divorce documents by courier when they had been completed, she would be grateful. The prince was tired. He had never in his life learned to compromise. There were many women willing to do anything for him, and all his life he was used to having others try to ingratiate themselves to him. He put the box in his pocket and got up. As he turned to go, he said that one of these days, when she stopped being angry, he would come back. He walked out of the room and Touba heard the front door slam. She then burst out in sobs. Even though she had kicked the man out and asked for a divorce, she had hoped he would get on his knees and beg her for forgiveness. It was possible that she would have forgiven him, of course. But no, it was not possible. She would never have forgiven him. She now cried madly. She kept pushing away Almas Khatoun and the Turkish and Persian aunts' attempts to console her. Setareh was standing behind the door, and looked in innocently. Seeing the young girl caused her anger to rise again, and the girl, even in her childish world, could feel the woman's hatred toward her. She pulled back innocently. She imagined reasons why Touba was angry with her, but Touba only hated her youth and childishness.

Touba felt paralyzed for the rest of the day. After a long cry in the afternoon, she stared at a point in the growing darkness. The children lurked around her like birds that have lost their nest. They were afraid to come too close to her. Finally, she decided to fast for the coming month. She got up and looked at everyone with a frown. The house was buried in silence. Even the Persian Aunt kept calm and knew not to complain.

In the first two days after the prince's visit, nothing happened. Touba fasted each day and the house was buried in a gray fog of sorrow. When she got up at sunrise for prayer she ate one small meal that carried her through to sunset. Unconsciously, she was seeking the peace and quiet of that early hour. She desperately needed to have some time to herself to think, and there never was any time for that during the day.

On the third day she rose early, before sunrise, and made her way to the cellar, where a dim light shining under the door surprised her. It was unusual for anyone to go to the washbasin in the cellar that early. She stood still in silence for a long time and looked at the light. Gradually, fear overcame her. She thought of screaming, then changed her mind and carefully approached the cellar. She saw the figure of a man sitting at the steps of the washbasin with his head in his hands. Light shone on his face. Touba looked for a while. She could slowly tell that it was Mirza Abuzar, who was sitting motionless and silent on the steps, holding his head. Touba rearranged her chador, sat by the stairs, and called Mirza Abuzar. The man did not answer her. Touba noticed that his shoulders trembled and he was crying bitterly in silence. She got up and went down the stairs toward him. A lantern burned by his side, and Touba noticed a dark pile on the floor near the washbasin. She went down and stepped into the basin. Her foot touched a soft object. She stepped back and could vaguely distinguish a hand at the bottom. She could hardly breathe. She picked up the lantern and looked more carefully. Setareh was lying at the bottom of the basin, her veil pulled aside. One of her braids lay on her neck, down over her girlish flowery dress. Lower down, the girl's stomach was torn open; blood was still spilling out.

Touba's heart sank. She almost fell down, and she wanted to hit herself on the head. The lantern shook uncontrollably in her hand. The smell of blood filled her nostrils. Engulfed in fear, she turned and looked at Mirza Abuzar. The man lifted his head, his face covered in tears. Choked by his tears, he said, "She was pregnant, Madam." Touba sank down beside the corpse. Mirza Abuzar asked, "What could I have done? What could I have done with her and what could I have told people?" Touba was trembling. She put the lantern down. She locked her arms around her feet. She was shaking all over and approaching serious spasms. Mirza Abuzar was choked with grief. He said again, "What could I have done with her?" Touba took a deep breath. Unconsciously she leaned against the wall behind her. She heard Mirza Abuzar's whispering voice telling her about the girl. After the attack on his sister's home in Tabriz, Mirza Abuzar had noticed that Setareh had become nervous and clumsy. He had asked his sister about the girl, but she did not have a good memory; she always lived in the present, and never remembered anything. Mirza Abuzar had not pursued the matter any further. He had thought that once they reached Tehran, the shock of the attack would diminish. In Tehran, however, the girl remained tense and reclusive. He noticed that she cried at night, and gradually, after a couple of months of doubt, he realized what had happened. Once he had seen the girl throwing up by the basin. That night, after dinner, he had ordered the girl to stand in front of him. He told her to take off her chador. This had failed to prove anything to him, but what he had asked was enough to make the girl burst out in tears. The child had wrapped her arms around her belly and run to hide in the back pantry. Mirza Abuzar had sent Ismael on some errand and, after slapping the girl a few times, he had demanded the truth. Choking on her tears, the girl had told him that on the day of the attack, she had been raped by some of the soldiers. Mirza Abuzar had hit his own head and had sat like a statue of anger, thinking about his misfortune. What was to become of Setareh? Initially, he had thought of taking her to one of the provinces to just let her loose. But what would become of her? With a bastard child in her, what fate awaited her? Could she get a husband? What man would be willing to raise another's bastard child, especially one from so many fathers? Bastard after bastard. In the middle of the night Mirza Abuzar had made his decision and told Setareh to get up. The girl got up silently and obediently. Mirza Abuzar picked up the lantern and left the room ahead of the girl. He was holding the knife that he had taken from the kitchen. In the dark by the stairs he waited a long time for the girl, who could not find her shoes. Finally he held up the lantern and the child found her shoes and headed down the stairs. Mirza Abuzar went toward the cellar, entered it, and placed the lantern on the side step of the basin, and the girl followed him and stopped in the basin. When her uncle told her to lie down there, she had complied. Mirza Abuzar had thought for a long time, should he slit her throat or stab her in the heart? He could not bear the kicking and struggle that might go with cutting her throat, and had thought, "I will finish her faster if I stab her in the heart." So he drove the knife into her heart at one go. He said she had died immediately. She had not suffered very much. With another stab he cut up her stomach, with the idea of making sure that the child would not suffer much either. He said, "Madam, the baby was innocent. Those bastards who commit such dishonorable acts don't think of this part of it, a miserable child."

Touba laid her head on her arm and rocked back and forth. What should she do? She had never paid much attention to Setareh because the girl reminded her of the other wife. Now she was spread here on the floor, young and innocent. Her beautiful face seemed to be asleep. She almost had a smile on her face. Touba whispered, "God forgive me, forgive me." Then she almost screamed, "Forgive me!" She was filled with the sense of guilt. She wanted to ask Mirza Abuzar why he had not discussed the matter with her. Then she thought, if he had mentioned it, would she have done anything? A living girl who has a bastard child in her is hateful and defiled. The same girl, however, if she is killed like this, will be chosen to be among the Pure Ones. She was realizing that she probably would have done nothing for the girl, or could have done nothing. She tried to put herself in Mirza Abuzar's place. She truly felt sorry for him.

Suddenly she realized that dawn had broken. Now the house would wake up. She had to do something. She had to do something for Mirza Abuzar and the girl. If news of this spread through town or if the children were to see this precious corpse, what would happen? She got up. Her brain was automatically engaged. She had to stop the children from approaching the washbasin area. She took off her chador and covered the corpse. She told Mirza Abuzar to sit there and not to move. She went to her room and pulled another chador over her head. She must get the children off to school. She rushed to the kitchen in a great hurry, before Almas Khatoun was awake, and she got the samovar ready and fixed the tea. She got the children's breakfast spread out in the room, woke them up, and got them to wash their faces by the little pool in the yard. She stopped Ismael from his usual habit of going to the washbasin. Because Ismael did not want to encounter Habibolah Mirza, it was his routine to wash at the basin, but Touba was in the yard, guarding it from everyone. The children did not suspect anything. Then she quickly got Almas Khatoun ready, and saw her and the Turkish Aunt off to Shahabdol Azim Bazaar to buy some cloth for Ismael and visit the shrine. This left the Persian Aunt. Almas Khatoun would not let the crazy aunt come along with them. She was afraid of her crazy behavior in the streets. The Turkish Aunt did not behave strangely; she just didn't remember anything.

After Touba got rid of everyone but the Persian Aunt, she focused once again on the main problem. She decided to bury the girl under the pomegranate tree. The body could not leave the house. If it did, everyone in the city would know what happened. The innocent girl's reputation would be ruined, and Mirza Abuzar would be put under lock and key. It would be a pity for such a thing to happen to an innocent and honest man.

She went to the cellar, brought out a shovel and pick, and asked Mirza Abuzar to help her dig a grave. Auntie was sitting on the steps clapping, her hair spread across her shoulders. It was all right for Auntie to be seen unveiled by everyone. They spent an hour digging a deep grave. Now they had to bring the body. Mirza Abuzar said, "She should be properly washed" and his tears flooded his face again. Touba said, "The girl doesn't need purification. She was martyred, and the bloody dress of the martyr is her coffin." They went to the washbasin. Touba wrapped her chador more tightly around the girl, and Mirza held her in his arms. She was light and pure. He climbed up the stairs. On the last step he bent his head to pass through the low door frame. Mirza Abuzar put the body beside the grave before he went down into the hole. Auntie had stopped clapping and watched them attentively. Touba said, "Dear Auntie, be careful not to say a word or I will cut off your rope." Auntie said she would not say a word and kept repeating in a low voice: "Poor girl, poor girl." Mirza Abuzar lifted the body in his arms and brought her into the grave. At first the girl's head disappeared, then her torso, and finally her feet. The corpse lay in the grave; only a portion of the chador was still outside it. Touba slid the chador into the grave. She instructed Mirza Abuzar to reveal her face and lay her on her right side so that the girl's work would be easier in the other world. Mirza Abuzar did these things accordingly. Then they covered the corpse with earth until the grave filled up. They smoothed the surface of the earth. Touba brought two pots filled with poinsettias and they planted the flowers on the grave. She swept the yard and Mirza Abuzar went to wash the basin.

Touba kept thinking of one thing: the need to wash herself. She wished to go and wash herself like she had never washed before. The lower part of her dress was bloody. She went to her room, took off her clothes, and put on another set. She quickly prepared her own and Auntie's bath bundles and came down the stairs. Mirza Abuzar asked humbly if he could perform the ablution on himself at the washbasin. She nodded her head in agreement, then said that he must leave the house and never return again. The man agreed with his head bent down. He said this very day he would go to the prince and hand over to him all books and papers regarding the estate. Then he said, "Madam!" Touba turned to him, and he knelt down by her feet, held the bottom of her chador and kissed it, and cried incessantly, his body convulsing in pain. Touba let him cry until he was calm, then she pulled the corner of her chador out of his hand and headed for the bathhouse with the Persian Aunt.

By nighttime, a messenger came to the house with the news that that morning the lady, the prince's wife, had come to the bathhouse and sat in silence by the hot water pool all day, where she neither washed herself nor let anyone else wash her. Meanwhile, her—god forbid—crazy aunt either kept clapping or sat crying next to her. Almas Khatoun left the Turkish Aunt in charge of the children. She sent Yaghut after Prince Feraydun Mirza and went herself into the bathhouse. She begged long enough to succeed in rinsing the two women and then positioned the crazy and half-crazy women on either side of herself and dragged them home. The bathhouse attendant put the two women's bath bundles on his head and followed Almas Khatoun. The rumor quickly spread in the bathhouse that the prince's wife had gone mad since her husband had taken a second wife.

They put Touba to bed with a very high fever. Prince Feraydun Mirza had already arrived and anxiously sent Yaghut after a European doctor. Touba could not answer the doctor's questions. Her teeth chattered unceasingly. The prince was confused. That very afternoon he had lost his Mirza Abuzar for good, and now his wife looked as though she was at the end of her life. Everything seemed so very strange. The doctor prescribed some medication and waited until Touba stopped trembling and fell into a disturbed sleep. The Doctor told the prince that it was all due to nervous stress. At midnight the prince slid into her bed in order to cure his wife with the best medicine he knew of.

In the morning, when Touba woke, she noticed that her head was on the prince's arm. She could hear the prince breathing heavily, and the shadow of the pomegranate branches trembled on the sunlit wall. Touba felt transported ten years into the past. As in the habit of those days, she locked her legs about the prince's body and slid her head between his body and arm. Then she saw Setareh in her mind's eye, and jumped like a person electrified. She looked at the prince, who now appeared a stranger to her. It happened suddenly. She got dressed with amazing speed; she slipped and tripped a few times, thus transferring her anxiety to the man, who had also awakened. He remained in bed trying to maintain a smile. But the woman no longer felt feverish, and she remembered nothing about the previous night. She had her chador over her head and stumbled, out of the room to sit in her usual place along the wall near the door. She heard noises from the prince's direction and felt as if there was a whole sea between her and that room. She even wondered if she would ever be able to return to her own room if the prince were to remain there. The prince came out looking fresh and joyful. He felt successful. He was not normally much of a thinker anyway, and to him it seemed that all was taken care of. He smiled at Touba, went toward the window and said, "Spring is coming. One of these days I will send someone to turn the earth over in the garden." In her mind, Touba screamed "Gardener!" and jumped up. If a gardener were to come, he would discover the body. Touba was certain that a gardener, a builder, an irrigation worker, or anyone who knew the hidden corners of the house would sense the existence of the corpse. The house could not hide its secrets from these people. It would reveal the truth, and the girl's reputation would be ruined. She said, "No!"

The prince turned around to look at her. Touba responded cold-ly and seriously. "No one will step into this house. Not a gardener, nor a builder, nor an irrigation worker! I will take care of everything myself!" "But I am the man of this house" said the prince. "No you are not," she replied. And for the first time, anger clouded the prince's face, and he turned red. He shouted that Touba was too proud of her knickknacks, and had ruined his nerves. He said that if he, the prince, wished to, he could take all this away from her and tear it apart. He had not done so because of his noble heart. His aristocratic upbringing did not permit him to trouble a veiled woman. But Touba felt that if she were to drive the prince crazy, then he might lose control and do something to her that they would write about in history books. Touba jumped up, brought her hand out of her chador, and screamed, "Of course you are a prince of the Qajar dynasty. You seem to have a tail and hoofs. But as you can see, this house does not have the crystal chandeliers of Turan O-Saltaneh's home, nor does it have a guest garden and private residences. Nevertheless, it is my house; I have to raise my children here, and I can take care of it. Never mind helping us; we don't have our hopes set on you. Just don't cause us problems." The prince shouted that he would burn a hole in her heart by taking the children. This was the last time that she would see them. Her hair would become as white as her teeth, and her eyes could burn a hole through the door waiting for them to return, but she would never see the children again. In the midst of his ferocious anger he shouted at Almas Khatoun to put down whatever she had in her hands and get the children ready to get out of this sorrow-ridden disgrace of a place. The panic-stricken woman quickly obeyed his orders, and Touba's spirit lifted with joy. If the children were to leave, even if only for one day, she could have some quiet time. Then she could definitely connect to the spirit of the girl under the pomegranate tree.

The girl's spirit had been looming around the house ever since it had left her body yesterday by the washbasin. Touba knew that from now on she would have a guardian angel. She believed that the girl's virginal innocence was the sacrificial offering that would protect the house. Hadn't Mirza Abuzar killed her so a bastard seed would not germinate? Now the girl and the unborn fetus were the guardians of the house, like the young boy who had interceded with God for rain at the time of the famine. He had pleaded at God's court, shouting, "Lord, Lord, look at me. See how tattered and hungry I am. Thirst is killing me. Send some rain." Touba knew this secret. Touba knew that the girl was at God's court crying. She was shouting, "But for what sin?" This way, God's loving umbrella would protect them. The house under the rays of God was filled with light. From now on, there would never come another drought, and no one would kill anyone in this house. Once the girl looked at a murderer, the knife would drop. The house was the proof of God's truth. If a gardener were to come here and through his professional instincts find the corpse under the earth, he would go to Davoud Khan's tea house on the street corner, sit there, and reveal that there was a corpse in the garden. They would come and pull the body from the earth, out of the roots of the pomegranate tree, and then all of the strange eyes would see her. No, no, that could not be.

Almas Khatoun took Moones's hand to leave for Turan O-Saltaneh's home. In accordance with the prince's orders, at noontime she was also to pick up the children from school and take them there. As Almas Khatoun closed the door behind her, Touba was thinking of Mr. Khiabani. Her whole being desired to see Mr. Khiabani back from death, to tell him her secrets. She didn't feel as close to Master Geda Alishah, but perhaps it was possible to tell him, too.

A shy voice called her from behind the door. For a second, she thought that Setareh had returned. Her heart stopped. But it was the Turkish Aunt. She was asking in Turkish if the lady, the prince's wife, had seen Setareh. Touba could only make out a few of her words. The Turkish Aunt came into the room. Touba said that Setareh had gone to Tabriz with her uncle. The woman had understood the words "Setareh," "uncle," and "Tabriz." She scratched her head and lifted her eyebrows. She decided to wait until the afternoon, when Ismael would come from school and act as her translator.

That night, Ismael answered the door. The house was quiet. The Persian Aunt had hidden herself in the cellar. Touba had told Ismael that his uncle and Setareh had suddenly been called to Tabriz because there was a husband-to-be who was very anxious for

Setareh. The boy had neither believed nor disbelieved. The adults had said something and he listened. In a strange home, you didn't ask too many questions.

Now, Prince Gil and his wife, Layla, were at the door. Ismael looked toward Touba, who was sitting on the steps staring at the pomegranate tree. Prince Gil and his wife entered without asking anything of the boy. Layla shouted from the yard, "Greetings, Touba! How are you dealing with loneliness?" The woman came out of her glazed stare slowly and noticed the prince at the bottom of the stairs looking at her. For the first time she was in a position to look at the prince from above. It seemed to her that the prince was slightly nervous and uncertain. Prince Gil said, "I have to talk with you, Shams Ol-Moluk." When Touba pulled the chador over her face, he said, "No, I did not come to coax you into a reconciliation. I have no patience for this type of thing." Prince Gil ascended the stairs. Touba stood up, and moved over to let the prince into the room. Touba saw Layla go to the pomegranate tree and put her hand on its textured, narrow stem. She thought to herself, "She knows, she definitely knows." Touba did not invite Layla into the room. She was free and wild. She always went wherever she wanted and would come in when she wished. Now she was walking around the yard, letting the boy, Ismael, take a good long look at her. She knew the boy had never in his life seen as beautiful a woman as she.

Without ceremony, Prince Gil sat down in a corner. It had been years since they had seen each other, but the prince had not changed. He stretched his feet and looked through the open door. It was the beginning of spring and the air was filled with the faint fragrance of flowers mixed with the smell of wet mud. The sorrow that was visible on his face did not coincide with his calm appearance. Touba was seated in front of Prince Gil. Often, even though she resisted, her mind wandered. Confused images merged in her mind: of Setareh's body, the prince, and a bright and clear image of a boy who had once died for lack of a piece of bread. Touba felt she had betrayed herself. She felt ashamed. When she was younger, she had wished to pursue worshipping God, but had never done so. She had wished to go on a walking pilgrimage, but had never done that either. Now the one thought dominating her mind was the problem of a second wife and marriage. Touba was sick of herself. This thought overpowered even the thought of Setareh's corpse. She thought of how small and pitiful she was. She tried to close her eyes and imagine herself growing larger, big enough to be able to see Prince Feraydun and his second wife as small as flies. She knew this was the only way for her overcome her vengeful feelings. Otherwise, she might end up inserting needles into the children's brains, like the half-witted women of the Qajar court. She would talk behind people's backs, suck on sweets, color her hair with henna and her eyes with kohl, cover herself with rose flower essence, fix herself up in elaborate dresses, and go from one house to another, talking nonsense. Then the thought of the girl with the torn stomach in the washbasin occupied her mind. Touba was bending down to look, and she could see the boy's eyes staring at his hands with his head resting on his chest. Then Mr. Khiabani's image would appear, standing in the rain, leaning on his hand by the wall, gazing straight ahead, not seeing her. The man was now rotting under the earth. His image was grand and eminent in every mind, in Touba's mind and perhaps in the thoughts of Mirza Abuzar.

Touba moaned. Prince Gil said, "Shams Ol-Moluk, I need your advice about Layla. I don't know what to do with her." The woman shook her head impatiently. She was so immersed in her own problems that she had no room for those of others. The prince said, "I know you have no patience for me, but my problem is similar to your own. There is something on your mind, isn't that so? You just don't know what to do, how to solve the problems; you don't know what is right and what is wrong. You wish you could lose yourself, isn't that so?"

Touba hid her face in her veil, involuntarily putting her head on her knees. She said that something like a piece of china had broken into a thousand pieces in her heart, and she couldn't put the pieces back together again. Prince Gil nodded in understanding. He said, "It is like a clear mirror that is then covered with dirt, vomit, blood and mud. It is unclear, and it will not ever again reflect images." Touba said that in addition, the mirror was all charred, so that no one could now prove that it once was a mirror at all. It was a shell.

Prince Gil said, "One feels sorry for the loss of childish innocence. You can't prove that you were innocent once." Touba told the prince that she was afraid, that she couldn't free herself from intensely troubling thoughts. She had an urge to kill, to destroy something, someone, or even many people. She said that her boundaries had been invaded, and she wished to defend them—but she didn't know if she had the right to do that or not.

Prince Gil said, "It is bad to kill, for when you do so, the corpse lives on in your mind, continuing its life. Its thoughts, history, tribe, and clan are transferred to you. If you have killed in a ritualistic ceremony, if you are trapped in a tradition that has approved of such murder, then you can no longer sit and enjoy the smell of grass that permeates the air. You have to rely on your white hair, carry a walking stick, and attempt to maintain a calm demeanor. When people see you, they have to say, look at what a respectable man he is, he has defended his honor. The respectable man has of course lost his chance to live freely. There are always eyes filled with sympathy, respect, and fear watching him. However, if a group participates in a killing, whether one or many, in this case the sin is lighter. You sit in ceremony joined by others. You grow your beard long or cut it short. You let your hair hang loose or shave your head, and along with the rest of the group, your eyes go ice cold. The significance of the murder is reduced. In the group, they will often all laugh at the murdered one, but then in private cry inwardly, and drink in secret behind walls. Sleep brings nightmares, and each day you are drawn deeper into your group in order to share the sense of guilt. Now you all sit together to agree on certain concepts and defend certain principles. You all insist on those principles emphatically. And again, you return home to drink in private."

Touba had lifted her head, listening carefully to Prince Gil. Her dark eyes were glued to the prince's eyes. The man was very strong, but he seemed to endure the woman's stare with difficulty. Prince Gil said, "It is worse when you act on your own. You get involved in a matter that is not really your business, and though an inner feeling tells you that you have this right, you see something in the essence of your being or in your nature that tells you it is not appropriate to get involved. You aim to correct it and take the first step, second step, and suddenly you fall over into the void, as though your feet had been swept from under you." Touba's eyes were fixed unquestioningly on the prince. He said "I know you are very busy, and I won't keep you long. There is something I have to tell you. Then I will leave. Do you remember I once told you a story? It was the story of a Master in Bukhara. But I did not finish the story. Since that day, my heart has been restless, needing to tell you the end of the story. I have to tell someone so I can solve the problem. Surely you must feel the same way. Sometimes, you must wish to speak with someone. I am the same as you. Unfortunately, I can't speak with just anyone, for you know they will not understand me. Often in the middle of my talk they get distracted. Once in a while they get stuck on a detail and the rest of the discussion goes nowhere."

Touba shook her head, confused. Prince Gil could feel her confusion. He smiled; they had connected with one another. He said, "You know, when I left Bukhara, I went to China. Mongols were at the height of their bloody campaign. Shams Ol-Moluk, would you believe it, in one city six thousand Chinese virgins threw themselves down from the city tower in order not to get caught by the Mongols? Because of this, I was carrying the corpse of a newly wedded bride on my shoulders. In those days people killed without reason, as though blood had become a perfume and everyone needed to smell that fragrance. But pay attention, for they were killing in accordance with their traditions. Some man named Genghis Khan had taken upon himself the blame for the killings. If there was to be a punishment or a judgment, all the others would be exempt. Only one person was to stand to answer for the crimes. And in fact, I thought at times that if I were one of Genghis's men, I would also kill. Why? I saw that they lived in the wilderness, dry and infertile, and were constantly struggling against hunger. The people who had captured better lands would not share. They went hungry generation after generation. The Chinese had built a wall against them, and on this side of the wall great dams of human beings were building up. There, in Mongolia, each man who died would leave his wives, daughters, and women servants to the Khan. Gradually, the

Khan was endowed with a harem filled with hungry women he did not need and could not feed. There was no land for these useless beings to till and thus no food to eat. When death came to the Khan, all these women would be slaughtered on his grave as a sacrifice, and hundreds of hungry stomachs would join the Khan to go to the sky with him. Mongols had therefore become savages. One day these unsheathed swords, which had cut their own women and children down, turned to the neighboring tribes and built piles of human corpses. They came, pillaged, and burned. The world became one huge pasture from which to fill their stomachs.

"The Chinese wisely called Genghis the Son of the Sky. They gave him the same title as their emperors. And here in Khorasan he was called the Whip of God. You see, if I were a Mongol, I would also enjoy these titles. Some of their benefits would rub off on me, and their glory would entitle me to drink not behind doors, but in public. If I had a title like that in my group, I would have to live up to that name for two hundred years. I would have to be scary, be the thief of women and beautiful boys, be an enemy of wheat, and continuously impose suffering on the children of Cain for the murder of my great grand ancestor Abel.

"But I was not a Mongolian. My ancestors had broken their backs in the wheat fields. We had jointly pushed forward and achieved a small and fragile existence. Our wives bore children and handled herds of servants. These servants sweated under the sun and we gazed at the ironstone for thousands of years wondering what to do with it. We kneaded earth into water, broke our fingernails, built fragile sickles from argillite and fired them in kilns to attack the wheat. We were the keepers of the secret of wheat, and our wives breastfed our children and we watered our wheat by rain water or irrigation. Then we began separating the iron from the ironstone in order to build the sickles.

"Then the Mongol came to take our women. Pay attention, Touba. At this time, I killed the shepherd Amin's wife in order to become a Mongol. The smell of milk from women's breasts sickened me, their protruding bellies seemed ugly to me. Their slowness drove me crazy. I felt enslaved, I saw the Mongol riding on horseback, and hated myself for taking refuge in caves and holes. I hated myself for bending my back hiding whenever I saw one of them. My stomach turned as I saw men and women of the villages crying and lamenting upon the approach of the Mongols. I wished to choke these helpless sheep. I wished to become a wolf. I wished they would become wolves. The secret of wheat would recede in my memory. I hated wheat, I preferred to steal it from people rather than waste away while growing it. Fertile women and fertile land mixed in my mind.

"But Touba, I could not influence the descendants of Cain. In search of meaning I had killed Amin's wife and that half-crazy Master of Bukhara had driven me away from the dervishes. The mystics held the secret of wheat, and they had torn their heart with daggers to keep the secret deep in the niches of their hearts. They now walked around with open hearts. Because a light emanated from their hearts, people became their followers. They were often the very first ones who initiated lamentations and threw dust on their heads. Those present obeyed them. They then would gather in the depths of cellars and reveal the secret of wheat. They dressed the secret with symbolic words. The newcomer would become stupefied by the symbolic word. Years would pass while a person slowly focused on it. By the time his hair turned white, he could comprehend something. I agree it was hard work. But the attraction of becoming a Mongol was driving me crazy. I had killed the woman, and amidst the bloodshed, among bodies that spread across the earth, I trudged forward, and her corpse became heavier every minute. The master had rejected me; I moved alone. You see, I had committed the murder alone. This had nothing to do with the rituals of collective murder. I had to carry the burden alone, and it weighed as heavy as the world. Think of a half-living person carrying a half-dead one. The master had only made her half dead. I had killed her. He had committed a public act, therefore a public ritual had emerged. She was ugly, she was in unison with the devil, and she was foolish and mindless. They had to belittle her, make her crawl and assume the life of a vegetable, aimlessly; become colorless like the tree sap and, like the roots of a tree, crawl under the earth. They had to make her sit at the bottom of a well, keep her in the depth of the sea, put her in the bottle; she was half-dead, but not dead. But I had killed her, and she became heavier each second. My back was bending, and yet I continued.

"I looked about and traveled on until I reached the freezing peaks of the Himalayas. The woman by now seemed like a huge giant supported by a minuscule man—me. Her feminine nature lacked any sense of progression, it was static. She procreated in inertia. But because I had killed her, instead of numerical increase she was increasing in size, every second becoming heavier. She was a heavy mass that had no intention to cooperate, and it eventually seemed as though she had been on my back since birth and was growing there. I no longer had the desire to become a Mongol. I was not Mongol, and I was not to become one. I had been born in the land of wheat, but without knowing her, I had killed her, as if this had to happen so that she could grow huge and take the whole world under her reign. I don't know how long it took to reach the meadows of the wheat land. I circled India and saw no Mongol. The lushness of nature, naked and bold in continuous growth, gave me a different outlook. I had fallen in love with India and passed through its forests. Gradually I was getting lost in this eternal greenery.

"The dead woman suddenly let go of me. Just as she had once been heavy and burdensome, she escaped me easily and quietly. She left so suddenly, it was as if she had never been, and since my mind had grown very tired, I forgot her disappearance, as one sleeps after a hard work day and does not remember one's dreams. But now another misery occurred: lightness. I had no weight; I was taken off the ground and robed in a vacuum. My body parts were pulling apart and I suffered great pain. As I traveled through the forests, mosquitoes bit me, and I had to break through branches. I was in agony. Then suddenly, in the midst of the greenery, the whiteness of a flower amazed me. I moved on, through the swamps, and suddenly a huge mass of flowers would appear in front of me. I would sit by the swamp and follow the roots in the depths of clear waters as they reached down into the eternal depths.

"I would go to temples also. You, too, would like to go to temples. You are in love with God, in the way you seek his manifestation. I know that you find him in the buzzing sound of the wings of a bee. I have seen people who after periods of sorrow and bloodshed stand by a sunflower and are awed and filled with joy. The flower emanates a very mild perfume that only the very sensitive nose can smell. The gold and black sunlike face of the flower invites the bees to itself. It has spent all its moments thinking of the sunshine. You recover the reflected light in its petals as temples recover countless moments spent by the sunflower. Temples are the same as the sunflower.

"There at a temple, women were preparing to dance at a feast. I saw a woman very much like our Layla. I felt I knew her. The memory lived somewhere in the distance of my mind. The woman danced, and in the waves of her dance, she carried me to the past, to a long-ago past. Somewhere in this past, I had lost someone like her. The thought of why I had lost her disturbed me. I spent many days searching for this woman of the past. The temple woman was unattainable, much like the forest filled with mosquitoes and the white swamp flowers that had deep roots in unknown waters. She was like a green ghost that appears in the flight of the bird above the forest. Then you saw here and there, on her body, flowers—spots of red, orange, and white. She looked like the image of a mythological figure composed of many animals and flowers, and projecting almost all of their fragrances. But she also was like our Layla—perhaps she was her sister, or of her clan. They shared the same blood, but I knew it was not she. That woman of the past was pulling me out of the forest. I knew that I had to leave the enchanted green fields behind. I knew that the woman was in the desert. A vague memory told me I had lost her in the desert.

"I traveled slowly until I reached the deserts of Baluchistan. This woman always appears to the one who has experienced both the forest and the desert. She is the double being of nearness and distance. I was one of the thousands having this experience. As I left the barren desert for the caravans, a kind of sickness came over me, the sickness of that woman, and I knew I must come to this side of the country to find her.

"I stopped in Ray City. The woman was there, in Ray, somewhere. I settled into a hut in the outskirts of the city. Soon some men came to visit me. They were homeless wanderers. A common secret pulled them to me. I tried to draw a picture of the woman for them. The inspiration of a potter kept coming to my mind. The woman lived in the particles of red earth, she seemed like a glazed color, her spirit was in a stream because it could not exist in a vast sea or a large river. The stream brought her spirit from the peak of the mountain, and poured it on the thirsty, dry, and feverish fields. The spirit of the woman turned to steam under the rootless rays of the sun. People dug deep tunnels under the earth to hide the steaming spirit in the earth's depths. There it slowly hummed and flowed. Wherever it surfaced, it mixed with the blue sky, became blue. With light it became dark blue and grew to become black. Black would take over; yet in this semi-desert the sun was the absolute ruler. Nevertheless, I knew that even if the woman was unattainable, she at least must be painted. She could not remain hidden forever. Whenever she was not there something was missing. I felt like crawling to a shady corner in sorrow to think about her. The way she looked dead, she drove me to opium addiction.

"It happened one night that someone, a distant relative, perhaps a forgotten uncle, gave me a vase. The design on the vase drove me crazy. It was the same woman! She was standing by a stream offering a flower to an old man. It was the very same lost woman. After nights and days of searching, I found that same stream and dug the ground next to it and found a suitcase. I took the case to my hut. The cut-up body of the woman was in it. I put the parts together. I went to wash my hands, and when I returned, the woman was sitting behind the door. It was my very Layla.

"As soon as I saw her, I knew my misfortune had begun with my birth. She was not static, she was dynamic and moving. This being had its own will. It had left its corpse so quickly behind that I understood the meaning of physics at first sight. Her desert spirit was wild. It enjoyed harming others. One glimpse of her was enough to make me kill her again. But the woman had rotted under the earth for thousands of years. She had the experience of thousands of years of rotting and becoming earth. I had to look at her for a long time. I had to touch her."

Layla had turned around in the yard. The pomegranate tree depressed her. She had moved toward Ismael, who was standing quietly and calmly by the washbasin looking shyly at the woman. She was kneeling in front of the boy, holding his hand. She asked him, "I am beautiful, aren't I?" The child bashfully agreed by lowering his head. The woman sang a song in Turkish and in sorrow she had said, "Son of man, love me so I can drown myself in your sorrow." Every word of the poem had dropped into Ismael's blood. The child felt like crying. The house was swallowing him up. The sudden disappearance of Setareh and his uncle and the other children was driving him mad. He felt sorry for his mother. And now the beautiful woman had called on him to love her so she could drown in his misery. He shyly allowed the woman to hold his hands. The woman's hand was slippery and soft as effluent water. The child imagined rain. It seemed to him the sky shook from the thunder of black clouds. Raindrops fell on his face. He was trembling. The rain came in a rush, and a lightning bolt hit in the middle of the yard. Then light flooded the entire space. The boy saw that the woman was as beautiful as the jasmine flower that blooms in the dawn's dew. It went dark again, and the woman was still holding his hands. The boy wished to be sleeping in his bed, to close his eyes and to imprison the glowing image in them. The woman whispered to him to go to bed. The child went upstairs sleepily, slipped into the bed next to his mother, and listened to the sound of rain.

Touba swallowed the lump in her throat. The sound of thunder filled the room; the spring showers let loose without warning. Prince Gil smiled bitterly and said, "You know, Shams Ol-Moluk, bringing to life a dead corpse is a doomed act. Death should be left to itself. Death occurs at the moment of death. Sometimes it is necessary, sometimes cruel. But bringing dead corpses back to life is a terrible evil."

Prince Gil had turned and was looking at his wandering wife in the yard. He said, "Often I think of killing her. In fact, I am stuck in that moment when she was first sitting by the hut, once again alive. The person or persons who had killed her had probably done so necessarily, but in reality the question is: Why did she continue living in my mind even after death? Why did I go to India? Why was this dancer so much like her? There are questions for which I have the answers, but every time I wish to express them, I stutter."

Touba heard Prince Gil's words though she was deep in her own thoughts. She felt her head filling with corpses, it was as though her mind was becoming a graveyard of corpses. She wished to tell the prince to leave. Prince Gil always scared her.

Prince Gil said, "Your husband appointed me to ask you to please come to your senses. It appears I am his last hope. Now I tell you, if you feel you must live with him, go ahead and do it; if not, then leave him. But know that bitter events will follow from that decision. You know you are a woman. The order of things is such that you will be left alone from here on, and this is obligatory. This society cannot tolerate a single woman in search of love; if you wish to do this, they will drag your name through the mud. You will become the infamous one, your children will turn their backs on you, your relatives will pull away from you. You see, it is a life of loneliness, but once and for all it should be you who says no. I also once said no, and a part of me died, but now it is your turn. So know that saying no means hardship and bitterness. But Touba, do not ever bring a corpse back to life, and do not ever try to live with a corpse. If you want my advice, let the living procreate. They create according to the spirit of the time. But a corpse always lives in the past. A corpse is a reminder of a series of savored memories. These memories will always hang on your neck like a ghost made of lead."

Along with the lightning and thunder outside, Touba felt a flash in her mind; what was in the dark came to light. "When you procreate, there is freshness in being, but the main part of this being consists of repetitions. And in this circle of repetitions, we seek help from the dead. Prince Gil, the presence of your wife is dear, she brings with her a soft breeze and joy. Of course, she can steal a man away from someone like me. Perhaps she can steal many. But for how long? Someday she will be enlightened and then become ordinary, and will not steal anymore. But her presence will give off joy into the world, for she is like flowing water. She moves forth, purifies the air, gives life to earth. One must be patient."

3

Madam Amineh sat on the edge of the pool and opened her veil. Touba had just stopped washing clothes, and had gone inside to fetch some mint ice drinks. Madam Amineh had arrived to tell them to stop whatever they were doing and come with her to Amirieh Street to see something extraordinary. The late spring heat felt stifling, and she drank a full bowl of the mint ice Touba brought. The clothes were sitting half-washed in the basin, but Touba dried her hands and went upstairs, and dressed and veiled herself. Madam Amineh had encouraged Moones to come along as well, so the three of them set off for Amirieh Street, arriving there at four o'clock. Madam Amineh said, "Look!" Workers from the south, still in their traditional Bakhtiari dress, were paving the road. Part of the road was already covered by asphalt. The rest was tarred and heavy steamrollers were smoothing over the rough spots. Madam Amineh called Touba over to her. She moved to the roadside stream, took some water in her palm, and poured it over the asphalt. It neither made mud nor raised any dust. The three looked at the new road with amazement and approval.

They decided to have some ice cream at a shop that just opened on Amirieh Street. It had pink painted walls, and the upstairs was arranged for women and family. When the women went up and sat by the window, watching the pavers work. Madam Amineh said that when she could manage to build on her land, she planned to have an asphalt roof put on her house. That way, it would never leak and they could do away with the adobe covering. Touba thought that asphalt must be too heavy for the roof. Perhaps the wooden beams would not hold such weight, and it would collapse. Madam Amineh smiled; Touba was out of touch. "Nowadays," she said, "steel bars are used in construction, so roofs do not collapse."

The women returned by six that afternoon. Moones ran down to the cellar to check on the Turkish Aunt, and Touba went back to washing clothes. Ismael had come back from high school and was doing his homework by lamplight; it grew dark very quickly in the cellar. Moones did not usually bother to veil her face from Ismael. She asked how Auntie was doing. The old woman was lying in her bed and breathing heavily. Her lungs were damaged, and she breathed with difficulty. Ismael said she had shown no sign of improvement, and Moones went to the kitchen to bring her some vegetable soup. Touba had finished the clothes and was hanging them on the line. Moones was carrying a bowl of soup to the cellar when her brother, Habibolah Mirza, entered the house. He frowned when he saw her and murmured to his mother that the presence of a sixteen-year-old girl with a young man in the cellar was bound not to have good results. Touba explained that the girl was attending to the Turkish Aunt, who was on her deathbed.

Habibolah said that his sister Manzar O-Saltaneh had told him that her mother and Moones must go to her house. Prince Feraydun Mirza was going to be there, and Touba should be careful not to do anything that would upset him. The prince had come to discuss an important matter. It concerned Moones. Touba listened attentively to what her son said. She had already heard the news that the prince was looking around for a husband for Moones. It was understood that there would be much gossip if the girl reached twenty years of age without a husband. Moones, who also understood this, came into the room to put on her best dress, but her heart was sinking. She knew they were going to marry her off and she could do nothing about it. For a while she walked around in dazed confusion, before silently settling into a corner.

The arrival of Madam Amineh, and then Habibolah, had ruined

Touba's plans. She had been planning to go visit Master Geda Alishah. For several years now, she had been a follower of the Master's and repeated the mantra he had given her. When Touba had seen the Master again in Tehran, some time after her pilgrimage to Kermanshah, she was already familiar with the Master's way of thinking. The Master had told her, "Now is the time. It is time to be initiated." And so Touba had gone through the initiation. She knew dervishes repeat mantras. This was essential. The Master had given her the mantra "Truth, Truth, God, Truth," and Touba repeated her mantra with great devotion. She believed that if she observed all elements of piety, then all secrets would be revealed to her. This thought caused her to tremble. Nevertheless, she felt ready to sit in the circle of those who possessed the secret.

During the critical period that followed her divorce and the murder of Setareh, Touba had often daydreamed that she saw the girl walking in the yard. In these daydreams, as the months passed, Setareh's belly grew larger. When the girl's pregnancy reached its ninth month, Touba developed a fever; the idea that Setareh would give birth to a child caused a rash on her body. She had no image of the child. But the girl's pregnancy seemed like her own. The far distant dream of her girlhood, when she had waited for the Holy Ghost to breathe into her and hoped she would give birth to a Messiah, now seemed actualized in the maternity of the dead girl. But the ninth month came and went, many months and years passed, and still Setareh did not deliver, though her belly still grew larger and larger.

In those days, they said that Shams Ol-Moluk had gone mad because she kept tying petitionary notes onto the pomegranate tree as if by some miracle it would fulfill her wishes. She had received a letter from Mirza Abuzar. He had written:

To the Grande Dame, respectful leader, Mistress Shams Ol-Moluk, the precious wife of His Excellency, the Prince on high, Feraydun Mirza Kamal O-Doleh of great ascendancy.

If you ask the condition of this poor, totally guilty soul, completely immersed in sin, God willing I am not too bad, although the sorrow of days and hardship of times has bent my back. I spend my days under the beneficence and shadow of the trees at the mausoleum of the generous Grand Master, whom you well know and there is no need to name him. The Grand Lady should know that every night I stare at the stars and shed tears. I wish that the Lord would grant you health, and trusting the truth that is God, I hope my unbalanced, crazed sister spends her life in comfort and peace under your presence, for you, dear Lady, well know that the poor woman has endured much pain and sorrow. My dear Lady, I leave the unfortunate orphan Ismael to your kind benevolence and, God willing, I hope your loving kindness will spread on him like an umbrella of protection and he will be able to return all your kindness with due respect and obedience in the future. I send my greetings to the respectful young lady Manzar O-Saltaneh, respectful young lady Aqdas Ol-Moluk, young lady Moones O-Doleh, and the young prince, the carrier of the sword of time, Prince Habibolah Mirza Khan, the leader. Dear Lady, I humbly request your kind deliverance of my greetings to Almas Khatoun and Yaghut. I hope under the benevolence of high truth, that the world and life will always be sweet. Even heaven could not bear the burden given to my name by fate. Dear respectful Lady, my heart bleeds. Day and night I cry tears of blood. I have come by the Master's mausoleum for devotion and I hope my life's rope will be cut soon. If suicide were appropriate in Islam, I would kill myself and free myself of this painful life. I send my greetings to Lady Madam Amineh and my greetings to his royal Prince when you see him.

> With my prayers and your servant,
> Mirza Abuzar Tabrizi,
> Monday the fourth

Touba buried the letter in Setareh's grave so that she could read it and it would serve as a verification of the uncle's innocence in God's court. But Touba would never be able to tell whether or not Setareh had read the letter. She did not talk even in Touba's daydreams. In

Shams Ol-Moluk's mental wanderings, Setareh walked with great difficulty. After a few years, she did not walk at all. She sat under the tree, her huge stomach covering half the yard. Touba tried to avoid bumping into the girl's stomach. Part of the yard, she believed, now belonged to Setareh, and her walks through the yard soon developed their own particular pattern. The only person who followed the same route as Touba was the Persian Aunt. The old woman did not know what was on that side of the yard—or if she knew, she never acknowledged it. But she imitated what her niece did, and refrained from passing through the same part of the yard. The children, however, did not follow the rules of the yard, and they were often punished for it. Touba knew that the children were unaware of Setareh's presence, but she wanted to force them to respect the girl's boundaries. Any time Ismael went near that corner of the yard, an enormous anger would come over Touba. She expected the boy to know where his sister was, and it upset her that he did not know. The boy got more and more used to behaving as the lady of the house wished, in order to prevent being chastised. Eventually, he learned not to go to that side of the yard at all.

When the last heir to the Qajar dynasty, Ahmad Shah, went to Europe, and the military leader Reza Khan became shah in 1925, Prince Feraydun lost his small principality in Azerbaijan. He had already lost his pride. He kept the children for one year just to make Touba miserable; then the children began returning home.

One year had been time enough for Ismael to learn how to act as mediator among the three crazy, imbalanced women with whom he lived. The boy followed all three women's orders. He attended to the needs of his mother, his abundance of common sense making up for what she lacked. He was always patient with his mother, and he placed himself between her and anyone who tried to bother her. Once one of the local shopkeepers tied a water pitcher to his mother's chador. The pitcher dragged behind her noisily as she walked. She wondered why people looked at her so strangely on the way home. Ismael undid the knot, and from then on did not let her go shopping. When he returned from school, he would quickly attend to his chores. He would sweep the yard for Touba or his mother and sometimes sit next to Touba to weave on the loom. Touba soon began to realize that her housework would not get done if Ismael were not around.

When the children returned home, Almas Khatoun decided to stay at Prince Feraydun's home. Touba was left to care for the house and the children single-handedly and Ismael began to play an even more important role. He took the children to school in the morning and brought them back in the afternoon. Moones accepted this new situation comfortably, but Habibolah was not happy about it. On the one hand, as the son of a Prince Feraydun, he liked to have a servant accompanying him to school. On the other hand, it was obvious that Ismael's manners were not servile; although he was very young, he was in charge. Habibolah complained and finally demanded to go to school alone. He felt humiliated taking his sisters to school, but also could not bear the idea that Ismael would do it. He dreamed of Yaghut or Almas Khatoun, who had truly behaved as loyal servants. When he remembered the day that his father, the prince, was fired from his government position and his mother quickly changed the children's last name to her own in order to prevent any harassment from the new regime, Habibolah felt deep shame. He craved to have a horse and to ride like a prince. His sister Manzar O-Saltaneh was lucky that she had married in the last year of the Qajar dynasty. The bridegroom was the young Prince Hesam O-Din Mirza, who was British-educated. During those critical years of regime change, before his marriage, Prince Hesam O-Din Mirza had came to visit his little golden-haired wife-to-be every two weeks. He wore a military uniform and spoke Persian with a British accent. He would hand his horse's reins to his attendant at the entry hall and then head for the guestroom. Five minutes later, his fiancée would join him, dressed in flowery, full pantaloons and a white silk chador. She would sit in front of him for half an hour, during which they might exchange a few words once in a while. The marriage took place about six months before the downfall of Ahmad Shah, so the bride rode in the queen's carriage to her future life. The street was decorated with lights and all the merchants burned wild roses for their scent and for good luck. Everyone felt that Manzar O-Saltaneh's marriage was fortuitous.

Soon after Aqdas Ol-Moluk was married, Reza Shah seized power from the Qajars and established a new dynasty. Turan O-Saltaneh decided to immigrate to Paris to join Ahmad Shah in exile, taking her son and her new daughter-in-law with her. It was now eight years since Shams Ol-Moluk had last seen her daughter.

During his free time, Habibolah would lie in his room and dream covetously of the glorious days of his family's past. Who could believe the day would come when his father, Prince Feraydun, would not be respectfully greeted by shopkeepers? Who would have thought that a peon nothing boy from Azerbaijan, who just a few years ago could hardly speak any Persian, would come along and become his mother's intimate companion? "Ismael, come here, go there, my boy. Ismael, dear, do this job, and don't do that"—as though Ismael was his mother's own son, and he was the son of a second wife.

Touba saw Setareh in Ismael. She felt the boy was *mahram* to her. She often confided in him, talking about the ways and beliefs of dervishes. She impatiently waited for the day when Ismael would reach maturity so that she could reveal to him her secret about Setareh. But the boy was dreaming about Moones, the only girl child who was yet at home. The dream had first entered his mind the day the Persian Aunt's body was discovered. Auntie had been missing for two days and they had searched everywhere. Suddenly, then Moones had cried out, and everyone had run to the water reservoir. A corner of Auntie's colorful dress was floating on top of the water. Crying, Moones put her head on Ismael's chest, and the boy softly patted her head to calm her. He had fallen in love with her then—a connection that was never to be undone. They never spoke of it to each other. It was a silent understanding.

Habibolah Mirza came to fetch Touba and Moones; Manzar O-Saltaneh had invited them all to her home for a party. In the street, they called for a carriage. Habibolah helped his mother and sister in and then sat across from them. Moones was dressed up and had on a crêpe de chine chador. She was looking at the shops, the street, the teahouse man sweeping and hosing down the area in the front of his shop. A faint cloud of dust rose. Someday, when the asphalt covered their street, there would be no more dust. In Amirieh Street, they rode over newly laid asphalt, and Touba leaned over to get a better look. It was indeed amazing; there was not one particle of dust anywhere. Moones thought the horses would probably slip on it, and in fact they did slip every once in a while. Touba commented that Reza Shah Pahlavi was truly a great man. In the past year, when she had gone on a pilgrimage to Mashed to the tomb of Imam Reza, she had noticed how safe the roads were, the sense of security the travelers felt; everyone talked about it all the way there. In earlier days, you would be stopped some eight times by highway thieves along the way. Nowadays, the bus with its wooden chairs seemed like a palace compared to the old lorries. Even covered with dust, the pilgrims had been joyful and content to send their prayers. Now Touba believed that Reza Shah was responsible for the asphalt, just as he was behind the road's safety and security. This shah was working out quite well. People said he was an executioner, but Touba thought he was doing a fine job. A woman could stay out late and feel safe; this, in and of itself, was a great thing. Touba leaned back in her seat in the carriage, feeling content. They had passed the asphalted road and were now going through a bumpy new road that was named Shah Avenue. They were going toward Manzar O-Saltaneh's home, which was situated on Sezavar Street, near where workers were building a university.

Princess Manzar waved at her mother and sister from behind the window where she was standing with her hair uncovered. She even appeared without a veil by the door when the attendant opened it. She pulled her sister quickly to the side to tell her that Mr. Khansari did not approve of veiling, but rather supported the policy of unveiling. In the bedroom, she took off Moone's chador, and arranged her hair, placing two golden pins on the side. The girl looked like a princess from a Qajar drawing. In the mirror she saw Manzar with her golden hair, looking like a European woman. Meanwhile, Touba talked with her son-in-law. Hesam O-Din Mirza had grown a mustache, thin and long, as was the current fashion in Europe. Dressed in a military uniform, he looked splendid. He was a good son-in-law.

When they had all sat down together, Manzar O-Saltaneh showed them the photographs that Aqdas Ol-Moluk had sent from Paris. They were all standing by the Eiffel Tower: Turan O-Saltaneh, her older daughter, her younger son, and her husband Abol Hasan Mirza. Next to them stood a European lady that Manzar O-Saltaneh said was Aqdas Ol-Moluk. She hardly looked like the Aqdas Ol-Moluk of eight years ago. The young prince, Touba's grandson, stood in front of his father, Abol Hasan Mirza. Mansour Mirza was not in the picture; it was he who had taken the photograph. There were many different shots to look at, and seeing the photographs caused great excitement. The secret dream of journeying to Paris was triggered in every mind. Touba took one of the photographs to frame and hang above her mantelpiece.

There was a knock at the door. Mr. Khansari and Prince Feraydun had arrived. Moones heard the knock and the servant's footsteps going to open the door. She heard her father's voice and a strange man's voice exchanging greetings with Prince Hesam O-Din Mirza and Manzar O-Saltaneh. She saw Habibolah go joyfully toward the hall to greet the newcomers. She grasped the arm of her chair tensely and stared at a point on the carpet. Then she heard everyone coming noisily into the guest salon.

Mr. Khansari entered the room after Prince Hesam O-Din Mirza and Manzar O-Saltaneh, and greeted Moones and Touba, who had already stood up. He was more than fifty years old. He was thin and tall and his narrow lips were pressed together, a trace of a faint smile visible. He was wearing European clothes and a tie. He looked odd standing next to Prince Hesam O-Din Mirza, in his old-fashioned Iranian *sardari* dress. Manzar O-Saltaneh whispered in Moones's ear that the gentleman was an important member of the Ministry of Foreign Affairs in the present government. Mr. Khansari shook hands with everyone, including Moones. Upon seeing her, he frowned, wondering what he was to do with such a young bride. He had never married because in his youth he had heard that marriage reduces one's longevity. Now he had accepted the idea because Prince Feraydun had pressured him and also because he wished to have children.

Moones had frozen. She had expected anything but this. For a moment she thought of sneaking out of the room while everyone was busy talking and fleeing back home. It was a useless thought. She read in the man's face that if she were to do this, he would not come after her. He didn't seem like the type of man who would imprison little girls in his house or go from one woman's arms to another like her father did. He was very serious, and this quality frightened her. Dinner was soon served, in the European fashion, sitting around a table. Manzar O-Saltaneh took the soup tureen from the attendant and placed it in front of Hesam O-Din Mirza. The young military man stood up and spooned soup into each soup bowl as he had learned in England. They were not wealthy enough to have servants wearing white gloves. The young prince had decided that he would do things just as his school's headmaster had done at his own family dinner.

Prince Hesam O-Din Mirza started the conversation with talk of the current government initiative to do away with the veil. He wondered if it was really true or if it was merely a street-corner rumor. Habibolah Mirza said that everyone was speaking about that very subject. He wondered if anyone had heard Aref's new poem about the topic? Manzar O-Saltaneh said she had just bought the record, and got up to place it on the gramophone. Prince Hesam O-Din Mirza was looking at Mr. Khansari questioningly. Mr. Khansari said that he had heard the rumor also but thought it might be more than a rumor. The prince asked, "How do they plan to do such a thing? Is such an act possible in a country like Iran?" Mr. Khansari said that anything His Majesty Reza Shah desired to do was possible. He was an iron-willed man and supervised everything closely. Besides, Iran must follow in the footsteps of the more powerful countries of the world, and part of their accruing power came from the equality between males and females. Iranians were descended from the accomplished and erudite Aryan race, who had arrived in Iran from the north and the east, and sought to emulate people of their own kind. Prince Hesam O-Din Mirza's eyes were glued on Mr. Khansari and shone with admiration. His eyes were a beautiful hazel and a trace of his Mongol ancestors could be seen in the shape of his eyes and cheek. Prince Hesam

O-Din Mirza, feeling joyful about his special, exclusive race, agreed wholeheartedly with Mr. Khansari.

The soup was soon finished. Moones wanted to have more, but was afraid of disrupting the progress of her sister's dinner. The attendant collected the dishes. He was not doing his job well, and it annoyed Manzar O-Saltaneh. Platters full of cutlets and chicken with walnut sauce were set on the table. Prince Hesam O-Din Mirza had given up serving the food but everyone else waited for Shams Ol-Moluk to serve herself, except Prince Feraydun, who filled his plate, not paying attention to his ex-wife or others. Hesam O-Din Mirza and Manzar O-Saltaneh looked at one another. Hesam O-Din Mirza smiled patiently and Manzar O-Saltaneh asked her mother to begin helping herself. She also invited Mr. Khansari, but the man delayed, politely letting the women go first. As they began to eat, Prince Hesam O-Din Mirza asked Mr. Khansari if, since he worked at the Ministry of Foreign Affairs, it was possible that he might go on an official trip. Mr. Khansari said that he intended to transfer to the Ministry of Interior. He hoped to get an assignment in Isfahan to get away from the capital city. He said he liked the weather in Isfahan, and had spent some time there in his youth. He glanced in Moones's direction when he said this. The girl, lost in her own confused thoughts, showed no reaction. Mr. Khansari was beginning to change his mind about the marriage. The girl was very young, and he was impatient with youth. Yet he felt if he did not fulfill the obligation, Prince Feraydun would be very disappointed. When he had earlier commented on the girl's youth to the prince, the prince had responded that the woman's youthful breath would make the old man young again. So Mr. Khansari kept silent.

After dinner, they returned to the guest salon where ice cream was served. Manzar O-Saltaneh was sitting in an easy chair, her legs together. She held the crystal ice cream bowl in her left hand. In all her movements there was an elegance and touch of aristocracy. Her husband was sitting on the arm of her easy chair, his legs crossed, busy talking with Mr. Khansari. Moones, holding her ice cream bowl, went toward the aquarium, where two fish swirled around each other with a graceful dignity. The girl noticed that Mr.

Khansari looked like the fish. Now she saw herself as a fish, but didn't know which water she was supposed to swim in. Feeling melancholy, she returned to an easy chair and sank deeply into it.

The conversation had turned to Hitler, who was gaining more power and fame every day. Hesam O-Din Mirza's mustache was a copy of Hitler's. Mr. Khansari didn't have a mustache and he was pressing his narrow fishy lips together. He remained carefully silent while Prince Feraydun Mirza heatedly defended Hitler. Diplomatic life had taught Mr. Khansari to evaluate world affairs before falling in love with political leaders. From his vantage point, he could observe that although the powers of Russia—or now, the Soviet Union—had recently dwindled in Iran, certain people were still eagerly looking in that direction. He was also well informed about British influence. Deep down he also had a lot of respect for Hitler, but preferred to keep his feelings to himself and not reveal them to anyone. Nevertheless, a faint smile of satisfaction could be traced on his lips. Prince Feraydun Mirza was certain his son-in-law was in agreement with him. He continued defending Hitler joyfully. He believed that Hitler was the rightful successor to Kaiser Wilhelm. Basically, Germans were a great race. They had been successful in rebuilding after the near-total destruction of World War I. Who would have believed that in such a short time they could overcome all of that destruction and be able to reassert themselves again so boldly on the world political scene? If they could accomplish such a huge task, what else lay in store?

The men began comparing Hitler and Mussolini. According to Mr. Khansari, the natures of these two men and their followers were similar. Prince Feraydun Mirza, in expressing his heartfelt support for Hitler, also pointed to British power. He considered the British conspiracy responsible for the fall of his family. All his life he had felt the presence of this powerful foreign government. He deeply believed that every minor political incident in Iran and in the world at large had been somehow cooked up by the British. This made him love Hitler even more. If this man grew stronger and Iran sided with him, then the British presence in Iran would come to an end. Enjoying the thought of that, Prince Feraydun resettled himself in his seat to make himself more comfortable.

Manzar O-Saltaneh had taken her sister to her bedroom again to offer her two bottles of fingernail polish from her vanity table. This way, her hands would stand out more. She showed off her own polished fingernails to Moones, and Moones admired them. Moones put the two bottles into her small velvet purse, which her mother had made for her. Together they returned to the guest salon.

Touba sat quietly, wrapped in her chador, resting in an easy chair. She was listening to the men talk. She also felt that she was beginning to like Hitler, because she thought he could give the Bolsheviks a truly rough time. He would also make it difficult for the English. Iran then would regain the power of its old kingdom. She had hung a large calendar on the wall of her room displaying kings of the ancient dynasties, from Kayoumars to the present Reza Shah Pahlavi, in oval shaped frames. Reza Shah filled the oval in the middle and the other shahs surrounded him like little stars around the sun. Touba also liked Reza Shah. She, like everyone else, was afraid of him, and yet deep down liked him. Since his ascension, she had been able to make two trips to Mashad and Shiraz, accompanied only by one of her daughters, without fear of thieves. Reza Shah had not even harmed her children, who were Qajar descendants. It was unusual that a monarch in power would not harm, destroy, blind, or cripple the members of the previous dynasty. She had changed the children's last name as a precaution, but no one had troubled them. Even Prince Feraydun carried on with his life without fear of imprisonment. Of course, people were filled with fear. They talked of Sergeant Mokhtari and the secret police, of the air injections, and strange deaths that had occurred. But what did it matter? The ones who died were important individuals. The shah left ordinary people alone. Touba talked with Ismael about these matters. The young man did not like Reza Shah, and spoke with words bigger than his mouth. Touba thought it seemed strange that he did not appreciate his great leader.

The party seemed flat, although Manzar O-Saltaneh tried her best to enliven the conversation, and Prince Hesam O-Din Mirza and Habibolah Mirza told some jokes. But on the important matter at hand, everyone agreed. It was obvious that Mr. Khansari would accept any demand, and that Prince Feraydun would not burden him with too many expectations. Prince Feraydun would be satisfied as long as his daughter was placed in a respectable marriage, as long as Shams Ol-Moluk's last daughter was settled. Then, he thought, he could breathe a sigh of relief. He had been afraid that his children would not all be settled before his death. He now had four more children from his new wife, but they were all still young. When he thought of them, every now and then, he just shrugged his shoulders. He could not fight fate. Children were meant to be born, even in times of financial stress. He wanted to believe that things would somehow work out for the best.

Later in the evening, after all had said their farewells, Mr. Khansari took Touba, Habibolah, Mirza, and Moones home in a carriage. He did not have a private carriage because he planned to buy a car, but he had rented a carriage for that evening. He invited the ladies and Habibolah to the cinema on the following evening. He was to pick them up at five.

Moones was disturbed that evening and could not sleep. Marriage seemed to her like a giant. She neither liked nor was afraid of Mr. Khansari, but she felt that she did not wish to be his wife. Yet, she was ready at five o'clock, along with her mother and Habibolah. Mr. Khansari exchanged greetings with them at the door, and refused their invitation to enter the house. The women fixed their face covers. Habibolah wore a bowtie and a Pahlavi hat, just as Mr. Khansari did. Mr. Khansari had again rented a carriage. They went to the movies and Mr. Khansari bought the tickets. Upon entering the cinema, Touba wondered if she should take off her shoes, but it appeared that everyone had left their shoes on. Men sat on the right side of the room and women on the left. The electric lights turned off and a lion on the wall made the motions of a roar without any noise. Touba stared in amazement. Some writing appeared and disappeared. A little man wearing an odd hat and shoes and carrying a stick walked on the wall. He jumped up and down and did strange things. He was very comical, but Touba did not laugh. She was deep in God's grandeur. How could it be that an image walked on the white screen? The previous night Habibolah had spent a long time explaining the meaning of the images for her. But the secret and symbols she saw continued to amaze her. Following her first experience with asphalt, this was another significant moment of her life. A long shapeless object came toward her from the wall. She thought of getting up and running away. Moones said it was a locomotive. The black moving object passed them and nothing happened, no one was crushed. Cinema, Touba thought, was a strange thing.

After the movie, Mr. Khansari walked them home. At the door he shook Habibolah's hand politely and they separated. The agreement had been made. Now all that remained was for Mr. Khansari and Prince Feraydun to make arrangements for the wedding.

The next day, Prince Feraydun visited their home. Touba put her chador on to receive him. She wondered how she had once been *mahram* with him, this man who was now so strange to her. She watched him through her chador, which was pulled tightly around her face, without letting the prince see that she was looking at him. Although the man was old, he was still handsome. For a second, she thought how nice it could have been if they had grown old together. She then drove the thought out of her mind. Prince Feraydun could still anger her. Every time she though of his second marriage, she felt enraged. She had also seen the prince's new children. They were beautiful—almost as beautiful as her own. The first time she had seen them, she had thought, These brothers and sisters will support one another in the future and become strong, like a tribe. But would that really be the case? The older children of the prince, from his previous marriages, played no part in the lives of Touba and her children. They all had gone their own way. She believed that children belonged to their mothers; her own children revolved around her. Throughout history, many princelings had been harmed or hindered because they had different mothers. Fortunately, in her world, the struggle for power had very little significance. Her children were removed from the politics of the day, and life moved on calmly.

Prince Feraydun seated Touba and Moones in front of him and began to speak of Mr. Khansari's good soul and distinguished family. He wanted to know the girl's opinion. Moones asked for one week to think about it, but the prince thought a week was too long.

One night and day were enough time for her to make up her mind. The problem was easily solved: either she was to marry him or refuse. He spoke as if there was no obligation, but Moones knew that she would have to become his wife.

After Prince Feraydun left, the girl headed to the cellar to visit the Turkish Aunt. Ismael was sitting behind a small table on the floor studying by lamp light. Moones extended her hand from beneath her chador to show the boy her polished fingernails. Ismael did not like the polished fingernails, so he lowered his head. Moones told him that she had a night and a day to respond to Mr. Khansari's marriage invitation. Ismael looked at her. The girl said she would say no if he wanted her to do so. She said she would commit suicide by taking opium rather than submit to the marriage. It was the first time she had expressed her desire for him. They had never talked of their love for each other. Love had nested in the corner of their hearts, like an illusion. They both knew it was impossible for them to be together.

The young man leaned on the wall behind him. The dampness from the wall bothered his back. If the girl were to say no to the marriage, everyone would want to know why she had refused, and in the end they would figure out that it was because of Ismael. He imagined Prince Feraydun or Habibolah Mirza or Hesam O-Din Mirza strangling him while screaming in Persian or Turkish, "You bastard! Is this how you show gratitude to your benefactors?" He pictured himself sitting in police headquarters with a bloodied head and face, the chief of police repeatedly slapping him, and demanding of him what he had done to the girl. No, this was not possible. They wouldn't even let it get to that point. They would have other ways of dealing with him. They would one day beat him in the street until he vomited blood. Or they would denigrate him privately: perhaps all the close relatives would gather in the courtyard and shove him back and forth, saying "Look at him, look at this bastard. How dare he!" He remembered the story of Mr. Biyuck's son. For a quarter of an hour he had been staring into space, and he was startled when Habibolah knocked at the door. He knew that Habibolah Mirza was not pleased with Moones spending time with him in the cellar. He said, "Go get married. Go. It is absolutely impossible."

Moones was not concerned about the differences in their backgrounds. She had never believed this was important. She had still been a child when the dynasties changed, so she had no memories of the court parties. She had learned in school that the Qajars were decadent; deep down, she even felt embarrassed by her heritage. Now she thought that Ismael simply did not want her. She felt rejected. She sent word through her brother that she would consent to the marriage.

The wedding party was held in Touba's home. A tent was spread over the courtyard and many rows of chairs arranged. The living room was decorated for the wedding ceremony. Ismael attended to the guests, but his head was always lowered. He did not like to look at Mr. Khansari. The party was not joyful. The age of the groom and his friends spread a cold feeling into everyone's hearts and Mr. Khansari's serious look and unsmiling countenance silenced even those women who usually liked to ululate at such occasions.

When most of the guests had left, the more intimate friends and family members began to prepare to accompany the bride to the groom's house. Dinner was served at his house, and Touba was to spend the night there as well. She had consulted with her Master regarding Moones's marriage. The Master had sent the comment that every marriage is of good omen, but that the groom's age was too advanced. The Master kept his thoughts to himself in order not to disrupt the wedding, but his frowning face spoke of his lack of belief in the future of this marriage. Touba chose to take the Master's silence as a sign that he consented.

Touba had long been overwhelmed with a desire to tell the Master the story of Setareh. She felt she should not be obliged to carry this secret alone forever, and wished desperately to share it with someone. The Master, whose breath matched the cosmos, could undoubtedly carry Setareh's secret in the depth of his heart. But then what would become of the girl's sanctity? Touba had resisted the desire to tell him. The first person who should know this secret was Ismael, but clearly the time was not yet right. Touba wondered if Setareh would give her a sign when it was time to tell the secret. Perhaps the sign would come on Moones's wedding night. Setareh sat there all night under the tree with her pregnant belly, her territory transgressed by the comings and goings of guests. That same night, Touba heard Habibolah Mirza refer to the tree jokingly as the holy pomegranate. As long as Habibolah was there, Touba could not tell the secret to Ismael. There could be no strangers in the house when the story was revealed.

After the bride and guests departed, Ismael and his sick mother were left alone at home. Two servants stayed to help him gather up the tables and chairs. He now felt his spirit constricted in his body. He believed that he had an invisible hump on his back, and the harder he tried to get rid of it, the more rooted it became. He felt no anger, but was enslaved by sorrow. The house was eating him up, and for the first time he thought about his uncle and Setareh. How alone he felt in this world. If this stupid mother were to die, then no one except Prince Feraydun's family could vouch for his existence in the universe. As he organized everything quickly and methodically, he thought, "Who am I?"

After finishing everything and returning to the cellar, he decided to follow the advice of his friends. The group of them had been gathering to read newspapers and books and to study French and German. When he was involved in these gatherings, he felt he was somebody in the world. Instead of relatives, he had friends who considered him their equal. A few teachers were also in the group. Ismael decided that he would enter the university. He wanted to know everything. But he knew that he must definitely do something about his invisible hump. He was afraid he would bend under the weight of it. It was clear that he could not always walk around with this hump on his back. He was also certain that as long as his mother was alive the hump would not go away. He did not hate her—he loved her, and indeed felt sympathy for her in his heart—but what had the woman given him but loneliness? What had she offered that he could believe in? Her prayers? When he would ask her the meaning of the words, she gazed blankly and shrugged her shoulders. She bent up and down in prayer according to habit, speaking words without any idea of their meaning. What could he make of her obliviousness? A woman who did not realize that there was a water pitcher tied to her chador, or a hat on top of it—or who put the hookah cap on backward and wondered why the water wouldn't bubble. Now his mother was snoring in bed. Tomorrow, because Touba would not be home, he would have to miss school to take care of her, and it was final exams time. Without Moones, the empty house was getting to him, as if the walls were closing in to choke him. He wished he could escape. He thought how good it would be if he could go to the wilderness and scream. In order to keep himself from screaming, Ismael pulled his knees closer into his chest. His muscles were tense from the pressure he was exerting on his body. He calmed himself with the thought that the day after tomorrow he would join his friends. They knew what was good and what was bad.

Who would have believed that healthy Prince Feraydun and the sick Turkish Aunt would die on the same day? Three months after Moones's wedding, Prince Feraydun had a heart attack on the way to Mashhad, in the city of Neishahpour. On that same day, in the first month of fall, the Turkish Aunt also took her last breath. Touba was there at her side, she saw steam coming out of her mouth. Fearful, she had raised her head to ask someone for help. The aunt's nose sharpened and her breathing turned to snoring. Habibolah Mirza and Ismael were both at the university. This was their first month as university students, and Touba felt very proud—but she also felt terribly alone. Touba poured the holy water that she had prepared the night before into the aunt's throat. She then began reciting the Qur'an and sobbing. In her mind, she saw Setareh sitting under the tree smiling at her mother's death. She thought, "The dead one accepts the other's death joyfully." This aunt was dying a saint's death. It was impossible to think she had ever committed a sin.

At noon, when the boys returned home, the body lay eastward toward Mecca. The boys became anxious because they both had to go back to the university. Habibolah returned, but Ismael remained to help with the arrangements for his mother's burial. When the undertakers were carrying the woman's coffin out of the cellar, repeating short prayers together, Ismael began to cry. A chapter of his life was ending. Only he and Touba were accompanying the body. They went to the cemetery, placed her in a grave, and performed the appropriate prayers. Ismael only pretended to say the prayers. Since rejoining his group of friends after Moones's wedding, he had gradually distanced himself from religion, but did not want to tell this to Touba for fear that she would be horrified.

The old aunt was buried with little ceremony. As they poured the last bit of earth on her, Ismael felt free of half of his invisible hump. Now, he thought, after finishing the university, he could go to Germany to complete his education. On the way home from the cemetery, he helped Touba jump over a little stream. Unconsciously, he knew that this woman, an extension of his own mother's presence, would not permit him to go his own way. An old connection still kept him tied to this family.

They were walking under the autumn sun. Touba was speaking of the aunt's kindness and generosity when, in a moment of silence, Ismael asked if Touba had any news of his uncle and Setareh. The woman's body suddenly tensed up. She turned around and looked at the boy's completely innocent face. She wondered how it was possible for the boy not to sense Setareh's presence in the house. She was about to begin telling the truth when she remembered that he had just started at the university. If she only waited a little longer, until he finished, it would be better. If she told him now, it could cause a shock that would affect his studies. She remained silent, and after a moment she repeated the same story of Setareh's marriage and travel to Azerbaijan. This time Ismael did not believe the story, but he too remained silent, not knowing why.

Ismael sensed that his mind was separating from his mother. The farther he went from the cemetery, the more distant he felt from the old woman now under the earth. Instead, his friends' happy gatherings, their talk of everyone and everything, became more prominent in his mind. He wondered if Touba knew that there existed men in this world who wanted to change the order of things—to remove the existing idea of the cosmos and replace it with another one. If this old woman knew this, he thought, she would have a heart attack. How could he tell her of these truths when she constantly talked about the love of God? He had learned that Touba was on the path toward uniting with God. But what kind of union was this? Words that had so much meaning for him as a child were losing their meaning now. A few times, it had occurred to him to tell her that God did not exist, but each time he had closed his mouth quickly.

Touba began to speak instead. She was saying that Ismael could now live in one of the two rooms that Mr. Biyuck's family had once rented, and that Ismael and Setareh and their mother and uncle had spent some time in. It was not right for him to sleep in the cellar where his mother had died. The young man sighed with relief. The atmosphere in the cellar was damp and oppressive and made him tired, and he could never invite his friends there. The move would bring him one step closer to independence. Still, he vaguely knew that he would never leave that house even if every part of him demanded it. There he belonged to Moones, even if she herself was living elsewhere. It was his mother's home, and it was here that her life had ended. And finally, it was Touba's home, where in his child-hood, she with her charcoal eyes and fair hair, which was now white, had so many times told the story of uniting with God. Ismael could not leave that house; therefore, it was better to live in a more appropriate room. He accepted Touba's suggestion, and the reflection of happiness in his face made her feel happy also.

A few days later, when news of Prince Feraydun's death reached Tehran, only Habibolah could go to bury his father. The prince's new children were too young; Moones was in Isfahan, and Manzar O-Saltaneh was pregnant. Habibolah was crushed by the death of his father. He felt that the last memory of the family's grandeur was buried with the prince. He was deep in sorrow, and all through his trip on the bus he thought about how unfairly life had treated him.

When the family had tried to bury the Turkish Aunt next to the Persian Aunt beside a popular shrine, they discovered that the ceme-tery and the shrine had been demolished to make homes. Now his father was to be buried in Neishahpour. Habibolah felt this was a sign of the entire society falling apart. A whole tradition was being destroyed, and now people like himself had to struggle a lot more for recognition and identity. Habibolah knew that he must marry. He had set his mind on marrying a relative to prevent the further disin-tegration of his family's stature. He felt obliged to defend himself and his family against the forces of change that sought to uproot everything. A frown had appeared on his face. He made a pact with himself to stand firm and resist the corrosion of traditions.

Two months later, when all the rumors about the removal of the veil were turning out to be true—and just two days before the law went into effect—Madam Amineh came to visit Touba. They sat together and talked, placed cigarettes in wooden cigarette holders and smoked. What should they wear? Madam Amineh knew she must buy a hat. Manzar O-Saltaneh came to their rescue, taking them to Lalehzar Street to purchased hats. They also bought felt cloth, and sewed overdresses that fell to their ankles. A week passed, and Touba did not leave the house. From here and there news came to her that the city was changing. Finally, Madam Amineh came to her rescue again. She came wearing her long overdress and hat, looking very strange. She dressed Touba just as she herself was dressed and the two women stepped out of the house. Madam Amineh was self-possessed, but Touba's heart beat fast. They had intended to go shopping on Amirieh Street, but later changed their minds and went on foot to Manzar O-Saltaneh's home. The women everywhere were dressed oddly. Often they wore their husband's hat over their scarf-covered heads. Many wore men's overcoats, and people stole glances at one another on the sly. The streets were full of police, and they pursued women who still wore the chador or persisted in keeping on their headscarves. Madam Amineh commented that Reza Shah was a very strange man: whatever he desired, he did. It made no difference to Madam Amineh whether she was veiled or unveiled. She was so deeply involved in work that she could head out of the house in any shape or manner.

Touba was as indifferent to this issue as she was to any kind of problem. By the time she returned home that same day, it felt as if she had lived all her life without the veil. In the past, she had seen women at parties without veils. Her mind had always remained focused on the issue of drawing close to God, and this focus kept her from dwelling on such earthly concerns. So the unveiling was a simple event, one that happened very quickly; and just like that, the old manner of dress no longer concerned her.

During his first year at the university, Habibolah Mirza married Tabandeh, the daughter of a relative on his father's side. He bought a house near the university so he would be close to work and his classes. In his former home there remained only Touba, Ismael, and the house itself, which for the first time became entirely Setareh's domain. During her long, lonely hours, Touba realized that Setareh did indeed speak. The girl often expressed angst. She did not know when her child would be born and Touba consoled her. It was of course unusual that a human being carry a child for more than nine months. But could the dead do it? In Setareh's case, the pregnancy had lasted for years and years. Was it really possible? The girl's pregnancy occupied a major part of the Touba's mind. She didn't want to do anything but sit and think about the secret of the girl's pregnancy. What was to become of this child?

Perhaps when the child came, it would take revenge on all of the Cossack soldiers. The child might hang the father upside down and cut up his body piece by piece. But there were no more Cossack soldiers. Setareh had become pregnant during the Qajar dynasty, Touba thought. The Qajar's henchmen, the Cossacks, had been the cause of Setareh's death. But now that there remained no Cossack and no Qajar, Touba wondered if she would give birth at all. Perhaps the child wouldn't be born because it had no cause to take up.

In this way, along with Setareh, Touba remained in the house for two years. Gradually, she even ceased going to visit her Sufi master. She also spoke very little with Ismael. The house became Setareh's abode, and Touba was just the keeper of it. When Ismael came home, he would go straight to his room. Touba knew when he was home only by seeing the light on in his room. They got used to eating alone and to seeing each other rarely. Touba noticed that Ismael sometimes brought his friends to the house. She could see their heads through the window and hear their music. She knew that Ismael had purchased a gramophone. It was just like the record player at Manzar O-Saltaneh's home. On its big horn there was the image of a dog looking into a big horn, and again on that horn was a dog looking into a big horn. Touba could not see any more layers of images, but she knew they were there and she thought about the inner landscapes of truth. It was just as dervishes believed and as her master, Dervish Hasan, had told her. There were many layers inside truth and, like curtains, they would be lifted one by one.

How much could a human know? This woman, Touba, who could even see the dead—how much could she know? For example, of the dead Setareh and the living Setareh, how much did she really know? The Setareh who lived had kept that life hidden from Touba. The dead Setareh was totally concealed, yet her belly grew larger; it was about to cover the whole courtyard. In one of Ismael's magazines, Touba had read that a woman had recently been discovered in Europe who could stop people in their tracks just by the glow of her eyes. No one had the courage to look into her spellbinding eyes, and the woman had to wear dark glasses so that they would not disturb people. Later, in some place called the circus, she trained lions and tigers. She would enter the cage, and take her glasses off, and the animals would freeze in their places. The woman was found dead one day in her room. The doctors said that the magnetic energy in her grew to the point that her small body could not resist it, and thus she died at a very early age. Touba felt mesmerized by this story. For many hours she sat by the mirror and stared into her eyes to see whether they emanated magnetic waves. Unfortunately, she was totally devoid of this energy. Of course, she did speak with the dead. Often she was tempted to go and visit the Master. But she felt if she were to return she would have to reveal Setareh's secret. She couldn't be in the Master's presence and not be truthful.

She sat at the loom again, to weave a new rug. It was for Ismael, to be presented to him at his wedding. Touba intended to tell him of Setareh's secret at the same time. This thought was her only deliverance. When she sat at the loom in the cellar, Setareh would appear and sit by the wood-latticed window. This Setareh was not pregnant; she was the fourteen-year-old Setareh. The pregnant Setareh was always under the tree.

Touba asked Setareh if Manzar O-Saltaneh would bear a boy or a girl. Setareh responded that she would search in the uterus. Shortly afterward she returned and said the baby was a girl. Touba told Manzar O-Saltaneh that she would have a baby girl, and when she did bear a girl, all the family and friends were amazed. Touba predicted that Tabandeh, on the other hand would bear a boy and, indeed, she did. Touba also predicted that in the affairs of the world there would be bad news, that there would be war. And soon people were talking about the Spanish Civil War. Little by little, Touba began to be treated with respect as a seer and a dervish—a gifted mystic.

At times Touba would ask the fourteen-year-old girl by the window why her child was never born. The girl would shamefully shrug her shoulders and say that she was not pregnant. Touba would think, The other, the other, the Setareh under the tree. And the image of Setareh sitting under the tree would slowly disappear. Touba would think, Then the child will not be born? and the thought gave her a calm satisfaction. The fourteen-year-old Setareh walked up and down in the yard, went to the cellar washbasin to look at the shadow of her own body, then sat on the steps in sorrow. Whenever Touba asked her a question, she gave her the answer. In this way, Touba's fame as a mystic was spreading.

Another two years passed, and one day Moones returned. Holding her suitcase, she stood at the door. Touba had never before seen her daughter without her veil outside of the house, and for a moment she did not recognize her. The girl whispered that she could no longer accept the conditions in Mr. Khansari's house. Touba's mind flew to the nuptial morning when Mr. Khansari had departed from the house at six o'clock in order to take his usual morning walk and Touba had gone into the bridal room looking for the famous bloodstained kerchief. Moones had explained that her husband had decided to wait and consummate the marriage in Isfahan because he did not like the commotion and the pressure of expectations made on him. Therefore, she had gone to Isfahan as a virgin, only to return three years later as a half-virgin—with a divorced woman's reputation, but not her experience—holding a suitcase at her mother's door with her head bowed, her nerves ruined.

Touba let Moones in, but she had become an old, bitter woman who did not wish to let anyone into her private sanctuary. She told

Moones that she was now too old and did not have the patience to mother anyone. The girl shook her head, holding back the lump in her throat. She swore that she had no intention of bothering her mother and had already done a lot of thinking. She wanted to live in the cellar where the Turkish Aunt had passed away. She possessed recommendations from Mr. Khansari for a typing class and a bank position. She said she would soon get a job. What frightful audacity, Touba thought, and how dangerous. Her daughter wanted to work, but it was unheard of for a woman to work in an office, next to men. What would people say? They probably would equate the girl with a prostitute. To make matters worse, now that Moones was sitting with her, she could not speak with Setareh, although Setareh was there, calmly sitting on the threshold, just as she used to sit by the cellar window. She was looking at Moones lovingly. Setareh seemed to like Moones. When Touba looked at Setareh quizzically, the young girl said, "What is wrong with having her here?" Touba replied, "Does it really not matter?" Moones instinctively turned around toward the door to see this invisible conversant. There was no one there.

The small lock on the house door made a clicking sound. It was the familiar sound of Ismael returning at noon. He was heading toward his room when Touba called him back. He came toward Touba and his eyes fell on the beautiful woman whose photograph he had seen on the mantelpiece in Touba's room—the photograph of Moones after her unveiling. He greeted her hastily, so distracted that as he entered, he hit his head on the door frame. He held on to the door frame reflexively to let the darkness and sparkling stars before his eyes disappear. Meanwhile Moones had risen to greet him, and they were on the verge of embracing one another passionately. How everything changes. Only three years ago, he hadn't dared to even imagine touching her hand. Now, going to university, going out with friends, going to parties where young men and women regularly danced the tango, and going on mountain-climbing excursions—all had changed something in him. He was no longer inferior, no longer bowed. He didn't even think of such things. He was quite the gentleman in his tailor-made suit, and now he was in a position to look down from above, although he always remained humble. He managed to greet her and to shake hands as was the custom of the day.

Touba told him that Moones had returned to live in the house. She asked that on his way to the university, Ismael go to Manzar O-Saltaneh and inform her. Ismael stood up quickly. He couldn't bear to remain in the room. He wished desperately to be alone. Since it was not possible to embrace the girl, he must take refuge in his private solemnity. He nodded his head to acknowledge Touba's demands and, with a quick farewell, took refuge in his room. He went to the mirror and leaned his face against it, so that the cool glass would calm his feverish body. After he felt better, he looked at himself in the mirror. In the reflection, he could see the courtyard and the entrance to the cellar. Branches from the pomegranate tree covered part of the door. He thought that when Moones began living in the cellar perhaps he could enter the mirror, and through the door there he could reach the girl. He warmed up the leftovers from the previous night's dinner and ate them for lunch, then he ran out of the house to deliver Touba's message to Manzar O-Saltaneh. The house was coming alive again.

In the afternoon when he returned, Moones's sisters and brother with their spouses and children were all there, and the sound of laughter could be heard coming from inside. For an instant, Ismael remembered the bygone years when they had joyfully chased each other around. Manzar O-Saltaneh noticed his arrival and invited him to the room. Ismael approached the entrance to the living room, and greeted her with a smile. Hesam O-Din Mirza, Moones, and Tabandeh stood up to show him their respect. Manzar O-Saltaneh rose halfway, and Habibolah Mirza remembered that he had placed his cigarettes somewhere behind him, and searched about uselessly for the packet. Ismael greeted everyone and joined the crowd. Prior to his arrival, they had been talking about Yaghut's children. What rascals they had turned out to be. Ismael remembered how they used to play the Wolf and the Shepherd. Almas Khatoon had once been the wolf and Ismael the shepherd. The children lined up behind him as the sheep, and excitedly turned this way and that way until Almas Khatoun grabbed one of them—often one of her own children or Moones, who was the youngest. How well Ismael shepherded his herd and how intently he protected the children from Almas Khatoun, who rolled her large eyes to scare the children.

They then spoke of the Persian Aunt, of her unfortunate death and the discovery of her body in the house water reservoir. Manzar O-Saltaneh remembered that three days prior to the Persian Aunt's disappearance, she had kept repeating, "I should go, I should finally climb the rope of light." But Habibolah's opinion was that these words proved nothing. The woman had always wanted to climb the rope of light. She had thought of this in her final days just as she had on all previous days—only instead of ascending, she had descended.

When the conversation turned to Setareh, Touba quickly stood up to leave the room, with the excuse that she needed to water the gardens. Manzar O-Saltaneh asked if Ismael had really had no news of his sister. The young man shrugged his shoulders regretfully. He had theorized that on their way to Azerbaijan his uncle and his sister had been attacked by highwaymen. Habibolah thought this theory was logical, though their bodies should have been discovered. Ismael said that in those chaotic days, if some ignoble individuals had killed them and left their bodies in a ditch, then they might not have been found. Touba returned to the room to ask Ismael to come and help her lift a large water container. The discussion had become confused, anyway. This kind of thing had happened before: It seemed that they were never able to talk about Setareh or Mirza Abuzar, who had disappeared so suddenly. Every time the topic arose, Touba would go into deep silence or find an excuse to leave.

At sunset, all of the visitors left. Steam was rising from the brick tiles in the yard as the muggy heat of the long afternoon subsided and the cool of the evening was approaching. After accompanying the guests to the house door, Touba returned quickly to perform her afternoon and evening prayers and Ismael and Moones found a few moments alone. Strange feelings had come over both of them. Something was about to happen, and no one in the world could stop it. Ismael asked her if she was well. Moones first said that she was well, then said that she was not. She shook her head nervously.

Ismael asked her if he could see her the next day, because he felt that he must see her. Moones nodded her head quickly in agreement. They arranged to meet at ten in the morning, at the corner of Ferdousi and Berlin streets. Moones then returned to her room and began aimlessly moving objects around. She took the dirty dishes to the pool in the yard and washed them. She let Ismael watch her from the window. She went to the kitchen to fix something for dinner, but she didn't know what to make; she had forgotten how things were arranged in the house. She finally just sat on the bottom step of the kitchen and stared at the wall ahead of her.

Moones thought of the future, approaching her, dark and elusive. Unconsciously, she edged toward a future she could not even remotely envision. Since childhood she'd had the feeling that she must go toward Ismael. An attraction drew her to him. She didn't know if this was good or bad. But it was the reason she had left her husband. It was the reason she wanted to work, and had left Isfahan to come to Tehran. For this reason she wished that moment to go to Ismael's room, sit there and listen to him talk, it didn't matter what he said, not at all. Only as long as he talked. She wished to speak there. To say that she felt weak, needed someone to lean on. She felt the ground absent beneath her feet. She thought Ismael was a grand being who could fill all empty spaces in the world.

When her mother descended the stairs, Moones suddenly trembled. She wished to hold her mother's skirt and say, "I don't know what is the matter, but I feel I want to cry." But there was a whole sea of distance between them. They were in two different worlds. Touba asked her if she wanted to finish the leftovers from lunch or would she prefer some fried eggs? Moones said it made no difference what she ate, food did not matter to her. Touba told Moones to return to her room, change her clothes, and get some sleep, because she had not had a chance to rest since the morning. Moones obeyed like a child; she went back to the room, changed her clothes, and sat in a corner hugging her knees.

Both women spent the night in restless slumber, and in the morning each left the house separately. At five minutes to ten, Moones reached the corner of Berlin Street and saw Ismael, looking pale and nervous and busying himself with window-shopping. Without acknowledging one another, they began walking side-by-side. They went through back streets to avoid any encounters with friends or relatives. Ismael asked Moones why she had gotten divorced. Moones explained briefly that Mr. Khansari was a good man and a good friend but could not be a complete husband. Ismael did not inquire any further. They continued walking next to one another; just this was enough for both of them. Moones explained that she wanted to go to typing classes. She wished to begin that very day, and later, by Mr. Khansari's recommendation, she wished to start working in a bank. Ismael could well understand all this. The woman had to have an income. Prince Feraydun Mirza had left nothing for his children. The younger ones lived in hardship, their necessities were provided only with great difficulty. He asked if Moones intended to marry again. She answered that yes, she would, if there would be an interested husband. Ismael asked if he could be that interested husband. Moones told him this could be so, only if no one were to find out. They both knew why. Her family had an ego the size of an elephant's nose. Ismael was the son of the Turkish Aunt. No matter that he was the top student at the university or had lifted himself into a socially high position; he remained the son of the Turkish Aunt. Such things did not matter in the least to Moones, since she had spent her whole childhood dreaming of marrying Ismael. But the others would not understand this, including even Touba, who recently had tried to direct Ismael's attention to the older daughter of Morteza, the old tar player. Morteza was now retired from his administrative job, but he had a comfortable life and his children who were all studious and had good futures ahead of them.

Moones and Ismael decided that Ismael would talk with his friends and try to find a solution. They agreed to meet in the street on certain days. Moones was to wear a hat with a wide brim and a dress that she would never wear at family gatherings. Neither one was willing to bow to the difficulties that their relationship created; having once lost one another, they did not want to ever again experience the bitterness of being apart.

They parted in front of the typing school and Moones went up the stairs. She presented her introductory letters to the director of the school, and a quarter of an hour later she was sitting in front of the black machine full of buttons, practicing the first lesson. The machine amazed her. She pressed buttons and words appeared on the drum in front of her. The machine's secret was simple, yet it created a sense of power in her. The day before, her sister Manzar O-Saltaneh had warned her many times that it was shameful for any woman to work in an office, let alone the daughter of Prince Feraydun Mirza of the royal family. There were only a very few women working in the offices and they were often from Christian families. Even the Jews would not let their daughters work in public places. Moones had ignored all of Manzar O-Saltaneh's objections. She absolutely wanted to work and absolutely wanted to become Ismael's wife. She absolutely wanted to bear Ismael's children, and did all of this toward that end. Now that she sat by the black machine and created words, just as she had wanted to, the unexpected sense of power grew in her. The hurdles she might have to overcome were unimportant. If necessary, she could even move mountains. At the end of the session, when she got up from her seat, she held her head up high. Manzar O-Saltaneh did not understand the value of being independent and self-sufficient. The night before, Moones had been anxious about seeing Ismael and attending the class. Thinking of going to the typing class scared her so much that in some moments she thought of giving up on the whole idea. Her mind had also been distracted by thoughts of the meeting with Ismael and the idea of marriage. However, half an hour into the class she had command of the buttons, and with it moved toward command of her whole being. As she progressed in typing day-by-day, her love for Ismael grew.

Moones had settled into the cellar. She had placed a wooden bed on one side to protect herself from the dampness. A rug was spread on the floor and a small mirror hung on the wall, her clothes were stacked on a large antique chair, and the rest of her belongings were kept in bundles and a suitcase. Each morning she woke with the hope of seeing Ismael's face, and he often appeared by her window for the same reason. When she waved to him, her heart filled with joy. Ismael didn't respond because his room was just across from Touba's. Moones washed, dressed, and went to her mother's room for breakfast. Preparation of breakfast was up to Touba and clearing up afterward was Moones's responsibility. Then she would run to get to her new job at the bank on time. And at lunchtime she headed to the back streets to meet with Ismael. Ismael prepared lunches with the small income he earned from teaching. He would make them little sandwiches. Or sometimes they went to Khachik Café on Lalehzar Street. The happy Armenian proprietor would smile at them kindly. He would seat them in the back of the restaurant so they could hold hands, trembling.

Ismael had talked with his friends and they had made the arrangements. They had found a cleric in Ray City who could perform their marriage. They planned to officially register their marriage and take all of the usual steps of a wedding, only they would not announce it publicly. Time would take care of the rest.

Abdullah and Taymour, close friends of Ismael, were to be in charge of initial preparations. The three studied French and German together, though they were in disagreement about the necessity of studying English. They read books together. They had reviewed history and philosophy. They were dependable men. It was agreed that Moones would ask for two days' leave from her office. The first day they would go to the cleric and then have lunch at a French restaurant. The second day was to be the conjugal day for the couple, in Taymour's room. Abdullah lived with his parents, but Taymour lived alone. He had already mentioned to the landlord that a husband and wife who were friends of his would be coming from Shiraz and because he was busy at the university, he would not be able to receive them. The landlord was to give the keys to the couple so they could rest in his room until Taymour arrived.

Setareh did not talk with Touba anymore. The girl had become secretive and introverted. She wore a sweet smile, but every time Touba asked her a question she would quickly repeat, "Later, later I will tell you." Touba was gradually losing her ability to foretell the future. She knew the loss of this ability had to do with Moones's return. At first she resented it, but over time she learned to tolerate her daughter's presence, and even be happy that she was there. Moones was a great help. She personally took care of cleaning and even some of the cooking. When she received her first paycheck, she bought some cloth for her mother. Touba felt very proud of her daughter. She had been repeating her mantra after prayers when Moones handed her the cloth. Touba glanced at the cloth from behind her glasses, then went on with her mantra with renewed concentration. Meanwhile, Moones dreamt of a waterfall in the mountains, a mountain north of Tehran, a cottage in the valley of the mountain, the chimes of the bells on sheep collars, and a shepherd playing the flute while she sat by the window knitting. Once in a while she looked up at the moon in the sky. At times she looked across the house at Ismael sitting behind his desk writing and she would reduce her distance from him with a simple sigh. She would lower her head and kiss the back of his masculine neck, and then a soft breeze blew, the grass trembled in the wind, and the music of the sheep bells faded in the distance.

Now Touba unwrapped the package of cloth and examined it. It was material selected with good taste, enough to make a skirt. Setareh would definitely like it. She was there, sitting by the door frame, looking at the mother and daughter. It was strange how much Setareh liked Moones. Setareh's eyes were often glued to Moones, which upset Touba. Then the door lock clicked and Moones in her mind was already embracing Ismael as she walked downstairs. She imagined that Ismael was crying out inside, "Where is Moones, where is Moones?" In her excitement, Moones shouted out loud, "In you, in you." Touba looked at her in surprise. Moones apologized hastily and ran to the cellar to prepare for her secret wedding the next day.

The wedding ceremony went smoothly. The cleric knew his duties. Abdullah and Taymour acted as witnesses, and the calm appearance of Moones and Ismael gave the cleric confidence. After all, he was doing nothing wrong; he was providing the appropriate legal and ethical conditions for a couple to become intimate. This is how he reassured himself, and he received a large sum of money for performing the wedding. After the wedding, they returned to Tehran. Abdullah had borrowed someone's car for the journey. The car provided a greater sense of security. Ismael thought that if they had lived in the era of the horse and donkey, he could have never married Moones. He would have needed a whole tribe backing him up, with fast horses, and in addition, he would have needed to accept the eternal enmity of Moones's tribe. He thought of the battles and feuds that such marriages entailed. Suddenly he laughed and shared his thoughts with his friends. To pass the time they imagined what it would have been like. The men would have had to wear dark costumes and masks. Moones, with the excuse of bringing water from the well, would leave her home. Of course, if she were—as indeed she was—the daughter of a prince, she would have had to weave a rope from her hair or from her father's cummerbund or something else, and hang it from the castle's window. She would need to involve her nurse in this escape. They would have had to pay off some of the guards. After passing all these obstacles, the family feuds would begin.

They laughed a lot and spent a happy lunchtime at the French restaurant. They all felt confident, filled with the warmth and joy of an unusual act. They had arranged their schedule so that they arrived back at the end of Moones's working day, and she could return home as usual. If Touba happened not to be home, Moones could visit Ismael in his room, or the other way around. But this was not possible on their wedding day. The old woman spent her nights praying until dawn. She would go to bed after the morning prayers, then wake up again later in the morning. All her activity took place during the night, as though she was guarding the night and the sanctuary it offered. Moones lay in her bed and stared at Ismael's room. He paced in the dark. Tomorrow they were to go to Taymour's house. Ismael was to take a suitcase along in order to make it look as if they were returning from a journey, and they would have all day until the afternoon to be alone together. Neither one knew that this would be their first and last private time together.

In the morning, Moones told her mother that after work she would go to the home of one of her office friends and spend the afternoon there. She dressed as usual and left the house, paying no special attention to Ismael. She took a carriage to Amirieh Street to wait for Ismael. He soon arrived and together they headed to Taymour's house, which was nearby. The landlord's wife felt suspicious about them. Nevertheless, she gave them the key, and the nervous couple entered the room and locked the door—only to open it again and again in the first hour for the inquisitive woman, who kept invading their privacy with various excuses: Would they like some tea? Why had they come to Tehran? What relationship did they have with Taymour? How are things in Shiraz? And would they be kind enough to have lunch at her house? Finally, Ismael took courage and told her that they were very tired and in need of rest, and would like to sleep the whole day in order to get some things done when Taymour came, since this was their reason for coming from Shiraz. The woman looked at them suspiciously, but agreed to leave them alone to sleep. They opened Taymour's bedding and lay down together. They were fulfilling a fifteen-year need, and their bodies fit well together. Then Moones had cried, and Ismael had joined her. These tears were to be their eternal bond.

They talked about ways that they could be together. Ismael said he wished to get his doctorate in philosophy and he wanted to do it in France or Germany. They could travel abroad, and live together without worrying about the criticism of friends and relatives. "But with what money?" asked Moones. "We can save some," Ismael assured her. He was currently studying, though he had missed some classes. He said he would find a way at night to get to the cellar, behind the old woman's back. Thus they must always speak quietly in order to prevent Touba from finding out their secret. They wished they knew how to place the woman under a spell or hypnotize her so they could have free time together. Perhaps it was best to let her know about everything, because otherwise how would they ever find a way in which to be alone? Moones said, "If we were to someday get a house, it would have to be in Shemiran, where there are small alleys, where I can live in a cottage and hear the sound of sheep bells." Ismael, on the other hand, wanted to live around the university, since he was certain that someday he would teach there.

The secret love blossomed, though their nights were full of anxiety. Exhaustion slowly overtook the young couple. They stayed awake, watching for the moments when Touba might sleep. Sometimes Moones would go to Ismael's room, and at times Ismael went to her. They could not arrange mutual activities very easily at all. They had to go to see a movie separately and then talk of it together at night. Moones was in love with Greta Garbo—what lovely characters she played! Ismael retold the story of *Les Miserables* for Moones, and also gave her the book as a gift. In his opinion, Harry Bauer was the best actor who had ever lived. Happiness crawled over Moones's skin like small ants and gave her strange sensations. In the mornings at breakfast, she wanted to shout and run to her husband's room. She wanted to wash her husband's clothes, and fix his breakfast and make lunch for him. She needed Ismael to compliment her cooking, and at night she yearned to sit by her husband and do her sewing or knitting. None of this was possible. Rebellion welled up in her. She was forced to endure long hours of family gatherings where her sister and brother often offered to look for a new husband for her. They were embarrassed that she worked in a bank and apologetically explained to interested suitors that their sister, of course, had broken many traditions. But Moones politely refused the gentlemen callers. With difficulty, she resisted marrying Tabandeh's brother. She regularly saved half her salary in a small metallic box into which Ismael also deposited money. They still did not know if they would live in Iran or go abroad. Many times they had thought of announcing their marriage, but something always frightened them.

On the the twentieth of March 1939 Ismael did not come home. The next day would be New Year's Day, the first day of spring, and Moones had decorated a small traditional *Now Ruz* table with items that started with the letter S. Touba didn't care for such secular holidays, but Moones thought this was a good opportunity to bring the old woman and Ismael together. She was tempted to use the happy occasion to tell Touba their secret. She encouraged Ismael to be ready to put up with the woman's anger and scolding until she gradually came around and accepted the situation. If they could solve the problems inside the house, then the problems from outside would no longer be important, and Manzar O-Saltaneh and Habibolah Mirza would also gradually come to accept their love. It was possible that they would not talk with them for a while, or turn red with shame and talk behind their backs; but in the end, they would have to accept it.

When Ismael failed to come home, Moones lay awake all night. Anxiety was eating her up. At dawn, she caught her mother by surprise while she was doing her ablution before prayers. "What has happened to Ismael?" she demanded to know. Touba said that prior to Moones's arrival Ismael would often not come home for days at a time, so she was not concerned. She looked at the girl suspiciously. Then she turned around to look for Setareh, but Setareh was not in her usual place. Touba's concern grew despite her efforts to rationalize Ismael's absence, so a short while later, when there was knocking at the door, the mother and daughter both ran to open it. Two uniformed policemen and one in plainclothes stood at the door. They asked if it was true that Ismael Kazemi lived in this house. The women acknowledged this, and the men explained they had orders to search his house. They entered without invitation, breaking the lock on the door in the process, and in one hour had turned his room upside down. They had collected almost all his books together to take them with them. The women stood nervously in the yard. The men sealed the door, and said no one was permitted to enter "this infidel's room." This was how their new year began.

At ten in the morning, Moones ran to Abdullah's house to inquire about the whereabouts of one friend from the other. About ten steps before reaching his house, she stopped in her tracks. The policemen were also there. She returned home very upset and headed straight to the washbasin to throw up. Some instinct told her she was nurturing Ismael's child.

Touba had started praying to ask God's help for Ismael. By concentrating on her prayers she hoped to get Setareh to reappear. Certainly something terrible had happened; something so significant she could not yet grasp the depths of its effect. Why had they arrested Ismael? Had he stolen something? He didn't seem like that kind of person. In all the years that he had grown up in this house, he had never stolen anything. She told Moones that she planned to go to the police station and tell them that Ismael was not a thief and had never been one. Moones replied that this was not the issue. In her opinion, it was political. She knew of her husband's meetings. Hearing of them only now, Touba was shaken. Ismael and politics? Was he a shah or a cabinet minister to want to get mixed up in politics? Ismael was only a university student, and there was nothing wrong with that. Her own son was a university student and no one ever came to arrest him. Moones said that they probably thought he was a Bolshevik. She explained that Ismael was not a Bolshevik, but he did read their books. Touba was so shocked that she felt dizzy. Since the day of Mirza Kazem's visits and after her divorce from Prince Feraydun, she had not heard much about the Bolsheviks. Madam Amineh believed that the Bolsheviks intended to take over the world. She had heard from her husband that this was a fear expressed in world political circles. It was certain that the Bolsheviks had this in mind—but what was a Bolshevik? Touba regretted that she had never tried to understand their philosophy. After the issue of dividing women, she had avoided such matters. She had shown some curiosity because of Mr. Khiabani, but nothing concerning Mr. Khiabani was clear. Some said he worked for the British, and others thought he served the Russians, and some believed he was a Bolshevik. Touba knew that Mr. Khiabani was just himself and nothing else, and based on this belief, she had not concerned herself with anything further. In the years after her divorce, she had been busy raising the children and living with the unfolding secret of Setareh, and had never spent time thinking of these matters. She had heard Ismael mention that Reza Shah was a brutal dictator, but many had said this. The few times that she saw Prince Feraydun prior to his death, he had said the same thing. Even Hesam O-Din Mirza believed that Reza Shah took things too far and was too stubborn. They said that he had taken all of the land of the state of Mazandaran for himself. It was not only Ismael who complained. But Bolshevism was something else. She had to do research. She asked Moones what Bolshevism meant. Moones explained that it stood for the equality of all human beings. She didn't know much more and had only learned that much from Ismael. The girl was so agitated and disturbed that she could not speak about anything, especially the subject of Bolsheviks, but Touba was suddenly obsessed with Bolshevism. She had to discover the secret of its meaning.

Besides, she had to deal with Ismael's situation. But how, and by what means? Touba knew nothing, and Moones could not even reveal that at least one other friend of his had also been arrested.

In the afternoon, Habibolah arrived carrying a special edition newspaper. It reported that a Communist cell intent upon over-throwing the royal crown had been discovered and squashed. Moones held the paper in her trembling hands and read it. She read Ismael's name over and over, about a hundred times. to make certain that it was truly him. And indeed, three more familiar names fol-lowed his. She began shaking, sat in the corner of the room to pre-vent fainting, and noticed that Habibolah looked at her with suspi-cious eyes and a grimace on his face. She wanted to shout, "But I am pregnant." But, of course, she could never do that. What a tragedy! Now what was she to do?

Through the five days of the new year holiday, Moones paced back and forth in her cellar room. She had to attend all of the cus-tomary *Now Ruz* celebration visits and hear how harshly everyone spoke of Ismael's behavior. Many of her relatives had grown angry at this bold and godless man. What a snake they had nurtured. They remarked that it seemed true that a wolf's child will always be a wolf, even if raised by humans. Such an ungrateful son could only have come from a mother as stupid as his. Touba sat silently, her lips pressed together. She was not interested in these witch-hunting con-versations and her source of support in such matters, Setareh, had suddenly disappeared. Ismael was not a wolf. This was the boy who had eaten at her table, who had read to her from Attar's books on the *Lives of the Sufi Saints* and Rumi's poetry, who had told her of the life and struggles of the martyr Halaj, and had aroused her sympathy to the point of tears.

None of her children could understand her mystical experiences. She had not seen Habibolah pay any attention to her mystic inter-ests; neither had Manzar O-Saltaneh or Aqdas Ol-Moluk, who was farther away. Moones had some affinity, a perception particular to herself that might be mystical. But Ismael was the only one who paid attention to her. She even told him of her spiritual journeys. To him alone had she revealed what happened the day that she was in the presence of Master Geda Alishah. Pretending to be angry, the Master had shouted "Madam Touba!" The woman had lifted her head and seen that the Master was levitating, floating at a level as high as the ceiling. To whom else could she have told this? She had not even told Madam Amineh, who was a willing listener. But she had told Ismael. And what about the experience of one night waking up and seeing that the Master was sitting next to her bed. He stated that it was two in the morning and asked her to remember him. The next day the Master had asked her, "By the way, how were you feeling last night at two o'clock?" She burned now thinking of it. To whom else but Ismael could she reveal that she had such visions, and receive a reassuring nod and a smile, and sense a willingness in her listener to believe everything? This boy who was so studious and intelligent still had a weakness that overpowered all his positive qualities: He was simple. Simple in accepting, he accepted everything. As if he had come to this world to accept.

After being brutally beaten, Ismael sat across from his inquisitor, trying to answer his questions. Where did he first meet his friends? What were they doing together? What did they read? With whom were they in contact? From the inquisitor's questions, Ismael perceived that he already had a lot of knowledge. Ismael, anyway, had nothing to hide. He never considered himself as being engaged in political activity. He saw himself simply as a student of such things, an explorer. The dream of becoming a university professor had whetted his appetite for knowledge and, not being fed enough from standard sources such as school, he had turned to other outlets, including private gatherings. His thoughts about Moones were driving him crazy. Could he tell the inquisitor that since he married Moones he had been attending the gatherings much less frequently? Could he tell them that the woman was each moment filling the vacuum in his life and they had plans to go live quietly in a cottage in the mountains? In other words, he had thought only of acting on and fulfilling her dreams. There was nothing wrong with her fantasy; they could go there and start a small life for themselves. Concern over how much Moones must be missing him filled his mind. His whole being desired to fly to her. He hoped that all this would end quickly, like a nightmare, and he would be able to return to the house that, although filled with problems, was light and beautiful in comparison with life in prison. He already missed the old house in which he had grown up. He missed Touba. He even missed the penetrating looks she had cast from behind her glasses, which had bothered him so much lately. During his childhood, those eyes had somehow suspended themselves in the atmosphere and followed him everywhere. They were the eyes of his conscience. Now he understood that they had come to be an integral part of his being.

Ismael was instructed by the inquisitor to write up his confession and state that he had met most of his friends in high school and at the university. He wrote that he read books because he wished to continue his education in hopes of later teaching in the same university. He wrote that he had no family, which he felt had immediately ruined his chances at a good life. In reality, he had lost any respect he may have had in his family; yet even if they tore him limb from limb, he refused to drag that family into this and get Moones in trouble. He therefore wrote that he had turned into a ruthless being, who had no shame and wanted to destroy the country. All he had wanted was progress and an improved life for himself and for everyone else. What bothered him was backwardness, decadent traditions, and matters of that kind.

Late at night, when Ismael was finally dragged to his dirty, dark, solitary prison cell and dropped exhausted onto the oily, flea-ridden mattress, he began to cry uncontrollably. He was glad that he was alone and no one could see him. He could not stop his tears. He felt ashamed and demeaned. He had no parents. He could not remember his father, or his mother—that simple, backward woman who had no memory. She didn't even remember her own daughter who had disappeared. Suddenly he jumped up. He had a sister. What if his sister would appear out of nowhere and come to visit him? He was certain that if he could see Setareh, he could send messages to Moones through her. And what about his uncle? He was not the kind of man to leave him alone in this world. What had become of them? His mind began to focus on the disappearance of his uncle and Setareh. They, along with Moones, were his only emotional connections. How could he find them? Could Moones find out where he was? Would she come after him? Did she have the courage to find him? Could she shout that Ismael was her husband, and try to free him? These useless thoughts filled his mind over the next few months, and as time passed with no contact with his few remaining loved ones, he felt more and more alone.

Moones pined for Ismael, but she got into the habit of hiding her feelings behind a mask that she put on when she rose each morning. The source of her worst mental torture was the child calmly growing inside of her. Habibolah had discovered where the prisoners were kept. At first they were inside the Palace of Justice Prison; then they were transferred to the Qasr Prison. Moones had a few times taken a carriage and passed by the prison. She had even spoken with the prisoners' families who gathered there, but she did not dare to go any further and visit her husband. The news would spread in no time that she had visited a convict. She might even lose her job at the bank. But worst of all, she didn't know what to do about her baby.

Day by day, Moones became thinner and weaker. Touba suggested that they go to visit Master Geda Alishah together. She herself had recently reduced the frequency of her visits to the Master. In the many years that she had attended the gatherings and been in the presence of the Master, she had often experienced visions and arrived at mystical states of being. But because she always had to sit with the ladies and join in their prattle, the visits tired her. She wished to find a personal means of discovering the mystic world, but no alternative path was ever revealed to her. It was said that if one does not reach the absolute state of purity and ascent, secrets might nevertheless reveal themselves, but for Touba nothing revealed itself. Touba continued to come and go in sorrow because she remained unenlightened. Finally, one day in private with the Master, she asked why the secrets were not being revealed to her. The Master, smiling, had responded that he was not God and was not able to reveal any secrets to anyone. Those who were worthy would at the appropriate moment comprehend the stages toward enlightenment and be content with their rewards. There is a hierarchy in everything, and this was also true in mysticism. It was not possible to complete the stages out of order, nor was it possible for everyone to reach the highest levels of communion with God. But Touba had seen men who attended the meetings and rapidly ascended to enlightenment. However, they only attained this level of success in private with the Master. She had slowly come to believe that the Master kept the truths hidden from women, particularly from her. Her natural wariness toward men, which had increased since her experience with Prince Feraydun, hightened her suspicions. Eventually she felt it was best not to go as often to see the Master. She had decided to be content with reading books and to live in her own individual dreams.

Setareh had grown larger in those days. Touba experienced this and other kinds of visions. There was a secret in the world to which only she and one absent man, who might be dead or alive had access. A pregnant girl was under the earth in her very own courtyard. It was possible that one day she would bud along with the grass and grow again. This girl had the house under her dominion. For Touba, the house could not exist without the presence of Setareh's wandering spirit. The Master had once inquired, through one of his students, as to why Touba's visits had become scarce, and Touba had then gone to visit. The Master had received her in private, had smiled kindly, and had told her in a suggestive manner that God had left the weight of the world on the shoulders of the son of Adam, and the son of Adam was nurtured and grew in the arms of a woman; consequently the main burdens in life were on women. But if women wished to know more, they of course could. The only problem was that from then on they would become wanderers, and their lack of physical strength made this kind of nomadic life difficult for them. Mental disturbance, he warned, could result. But there were women who could succeed in knowing. They had to be brave, have patience, bear difficulties, and do as they were told. It was just before this meeting of reconciliation that the Master had appeared in Touba's imagination at 2 a.m. to let her know that she was on his mind. And it was at the meeting that the Master levitated up into the air, and his hand rose up and touched the ceiling. But even before this, even without going to meetings regularly, she had discovered the appearance of a small true light as proof of God's presence.

As Moones melted away with worry, Touba gradually began to believe that her daughter was in love with Ismael. Without mentioning his name, Touba suggested that she and Moones go to visit Master Geda Alishah together. Moones rejected the idea. She was preoccupied with an idea that was slowly filling her mind: the need to free herself of the child. The child that she loved so much and had so many dreams for was now an ogre, a giant, a specter that with its appearance would turn her entire world into smoke. She had heard here and there how to get rid of an unwanted child. Once she had soaked a kilo of wild barberries in water and eaten it all in one sitting, but to no avail. She was constantly tempted to use a sharp instrument on herself. She planned to do it on a Thursday night. She thought, naively, that she would then have Friday to rest before work again on Saturday.

Setareh had, by then, returned to Touba after so many months away. Touba was at her prayer mat and had just prostrated herself saying her last prayer, when the girl murmured to her, "Touba, Touba, the baby will no longer be born." Touba's heart sank. Setareh had returned to the house only to put an end to her dream. It was through Setareh that God had bestowed grace upon her. This girl and her constant presence in the courtyard had enriched so much of her life. In the past few months, Setareh had not revealed secrets and Touba's ability at fortune-telling had left her, so, the woman's heart had filled with joy at the girl's return. But the news she brought was unwelcome; the child would never be born. Setareh looked with concern at the cellar door. Touba stood, undid her chador, and headed to the cellar. She placed the night lamp by the door and entered. The cellar was dark. She heard Moones moaning and crying. She brought the lamp forward. The girl was rolling in blood and moaning in pain. Touba struck herself in the head. The memory of Setareh's killing by the washbasin came to her. She said, "Get up! Get up!" With difficulty she wrapped the girl in a chador. They quickly left the house and passed through the neighborhood, trying not to attract attention. Touba hired a carriage to go to the American hospital. She knew the more foreign the hospital was, the better. She had to cover up this problem or suffer from public dishonor.

The Armenian doctor was alarmed when he saw Moones. The young woman was as white as a corpse from the graveyard. She was all blue around the eyes, and even though she had wrapped many pieces of cloth around herself, she was still covered in blood. The doctor said, "Surgery!" and they took Moones directly to an operating room.

Touba sat next to the waiting room window, looking into the dark night. This turn of events hit her like an earthquake. She knew from the beginning that the girl's return to the house was not a good omen. Moones had married and should have accepted her fate. Touba had forgotten that in order to separate from Haji Mahmud, she herself had gone on a hunger strike. She no longer believed that humans could fight and hang on to any branch in hopes of saving themselves from destruction. She had so little interest in Moones's return that when the girl chose to live in the cellar, away from her mother, Touba had agreed. Touba had even thought her daughter's bank position somewhat useful. The girl paid her own expenses. It was the first time in family history that a woman had earned her own income outside the home in a manner that did not include rug weaving. Touba had accepted it all, and had kept silent in spite of people's belittling talk. But she could neither accept Ismael's situation nor endure this much disrepute. In the carriage, Moones had told her that she was Ismael's legal wife, but even that was not enough to calm Touba. She kept asking herself, Why did Setareh die? Why had Touba helped Mirza Abuzar bury the girl's body under the pomegranate tree? All in order to prevent public dishonor. In all these years, she had never thought that Setareh could have had her child and gone on living. It was a social law that ill-spent sperm must be extinguished at its very root. The girl had been an innocent fourteen-year-old, but that did not change anything. The uncle was obliged to kill her. What could one do with an illegitimate child? And now Touba was being repaid for all her hard work. The damned Ismael, whom she had raised with her own hands—this was how he showed his gratitude. Perhaps people were right. This boy was not trustworthy. He was the child of a wolf. He had done the same to Moones as had been done to his sister. Of course, one could not call this a rape. Moones had received the man willingly. But what difference did it make? Did Ismael, even if Moones wished it, have the right to act in such a way? She had raised him badly. She had thought of him too highly and told him too many of her secrets. This was the person to whom she had chosen to reveal them—to this boy who was suspected of being a Bolshevik. How stupid she had been. Though he smiled in her presence when she told him of her visions and spiritual journeys, he had probably gone on to laugh behind her back. When he and his godless friends got together, they must have found it hilarious. The woman was filled with anger. What a snake she had nurtured! As if it was not enough for her to carry the burden of his family secrets for a lifetime, now he had dishonored her own daughter.

The girl was not a girl, but a monster. She had negated everything. How horrible; this was how one behaved when there was no more faith. Every act became permissible. People acted like animals in a jungle. No order, no calm remained. It was the fault of the Europeans. They had come and brought movies. Some people had radios and listened to European stations. Women had become so impudent that some did not even wear hats anymore. Their hair was out in the open for all to see. Their clothes became shorter every day, revealing their legs to everyone, familiar or strange. They went to offices, acted like men. And every day, they grew more disrespectful than the day before. Now, what was Touba to do? How could she lift her head among friends and family? Moones had married. Her child was legally pure. But what difference did all that make? What kind of marriage could this be, if concluded in secret and continued in hiding? Moones was now paying for her insolence, and she deserved it.

By dawn, Moones had been transferred to a regular room. She seemed colorless, bloodless. She was still unconscious, yet even in that state teardrops rolled from the corners of her eyes. The English nurse said something in a foreign language. Then the doctor came into the room. He said that Moones would never be able to have children. In order to save her life, they had been forced to perform a hysterectomy. This news made Touba happy. A nervous smile danced upon her face. Moones, then, was genuinely paying for her filthy lifestyle, and she could no longer cause public shame. She was now sterile. A woman without a husband was better off this way. Touba could not accept that Ismael was Moones's husband. She did not see anything wrong in him, and deep down in her heart she even had a strong affection for him, but she could not think of him as her son-in-law. Now, at least, even if the man remained her daughter's husband, he could not produce any progeny to add to the family. He had taken a bigger bite than he could swallow, and now it was stuck there in his throat.

On Saturday morning, Touba had to go to the bank and explain that her daughter was sick. The girl had to stay in the hospital for at least a week. Touba told Habibolah that Moones had gone for a week to the mausoleum of Shahabdol Azim to give alms, but this only increased the man's suspicions about his sister. Touba grew more hateful of Ismael and the Bolsheviks. She now truly believed they were the number-one enemy of herself and the family. She wished she could speak with Hesam O-Din and Habibolah, but she was afraid. She was afraid their male pride would move them to drastic action and matters would be made worse. But she had to talk with someone about this terrible turn of events. Of course, Ismael was paying for his sins. He was caught in prison like a filthy mouse in a trap. He probably would be beaten so terribly that he would tuck in his tail and run. But no, he mustn't run away. He must stay and bear Touba's scolding. Now Touba could find the courage to tell him that his sister was buried under piles of earth, that they had done to his sister what he had done to her daughter.

Three days later, when she brought Moones home, scolding and belittling her daughter became Touba's pastime. She had to take care of a woman who had ruined the family's reputation. What a curse and an indignity! Moones sank deeper into herself with every passing minute. She had learned that she would never be able to bear a child. She now thought of herself as a major sinner who had earned the most terrible kind of damnation. Gradually, fear replaced her love for Ismael, because of the way people talked about the Bolsheviks. Ismael of course had never told her that he was a Bolshevik, but his way of talking was definitely different from others'. He had even expressed doubt in the existence of God. The girl wondered if Ismael had been honest with her. How much did she really know about him? Had she become a servant to her imagination? Had she not destroyed her own life and the possibility of motherhood forever because of these illusions she held about him? What was the fault of the child who had begun to grow in her uterus that it had deserved to die? Wouldn't only a professional murderer kill her own child? A murderer. A sick person. A crazy person. A psychopath, a stupid person, a useless, perverse, heartless person? She felt she was a lump of filth that had no power to resist an impermissible love. What was sex after all? Was it not but the filthy outcome of lust? How could she have ever thought she had the right to go live in the mountains? Had it not always been said that sex was a sin? Had not Adam and Eve been thrown out of paradise because of it? Had not God explained to his beings that they were not to gravitate toward such unsanctioned acts? How simple it was. She had contemplated for years what it would be like to be with Ismael. Three years she had brooded at Mr. Khansari's home and thought only about Ismael—and all for what? All for the sake of coming to Tehran and ruining her life.

Moones returned to work at the bank with a lowered head. Smiles no longer graced her lips. The energy and joy that she had previously felt at work were now replaced with sadness and self-contempt. She no longer thought about seeing Ismael, and night and day she struggled with a vision she had experienced one week after her abortion. Before going to sleep she had first seen the shadow of a large being standing at the door to the cellar. The shadow gradually took on color and a clearer form and Moones saw what she later only referred to as the Angel of God. The Angel of God held something in its left hand that dripped blood. Moones's heart sank. This specter became more solid on successive nights. Slowly, the object in the angel's left hand developed into the shape of a bloodied child and words came to Moones's ears like the toll of bells: "What have you done with God's charge?" The young woman had to get up. There was no sleeping with this thing in her room. In order to escape the specter, she stood to do night prayers, and each night her prayers became longer. During her prayers, the angel would not appear, but if she said no prayers, then it would say, "This is your load of sin in my left hand." What scared Moones more than anything was the process of the image taking shape. It had not appeared in full form in the beginning. At first, it was only a shadow; then it became an angel; then the blood dripped from its left hand until the child's body took shape; then it spoke the words. Moones prayed and prayed to the point of fainting at her prayer mat. In the morning, she awoke disoriented and afraid. She bore the scolds and frowning looks of Touba, set off for the bank like a robot, pressed on the buttons of the typewriter with only a hazy comprehension of what she was doing, and returned home to put up with the psychological torture of the angel in the heart of the night. She desperately wished to sleep in Touba's bedroom. But the frowning old woman had built a wall between herself and her daughter. Soon Moones's clothes hung on her; she looked like a wooden stick with arms and legs. She had gotten used to standing for her prayers; this way, the angel would stay away until she fainted at the mat. Touba noticed that the girl prayed ceaselessly, bowing down and sitting up over and over again. She could hear her prayers full of pleas. She felt sorry for her but did not think it right to express affection. She thought this way the girl would better purify herself of her sins.

One night the angel appeared in the middle of Moones's prayers. She did not expect this, and she screamed like a mad animal. Under no circumstances could she accept the angel's presence. Her screams were howls from somewhere deep inside, and even she herself wondered where the sound was coming from. It was as though every cell in her body took up the cry. As Touba ran toward the cellar, she saw that Setareh was crying. Through her tears, the girl repeated, "You are bad, Touba, very bad." Touba was shocked. She had always thought of herself as good. Her actions had always been met with approval. She had received much respect—in her youth because of wisdom, beauty, and knowledge, and later for showing so much character in the separation from her husband and for being a dependable old woman. She was also respected for her ablility to predict the future and receive pure visions. She had always been good. Now the girl who represented Touba's inner being had accused her of being bad.

She came to the cellar and embraced her screaming, fear-ridden daughter. Touba held Moones close for the first time in many years. She spoke kind words, and the girl, burning with fever and seemingly on her deathbed, began slowly to come to life due to the presence of her mother. They cried together for a while. The girl said that the Angel of God had been assigned to torture her. She had been enduring terrible suffering and then more suffering for the sake of her forbidden love.

Touba's voice, like the sound of a moving stream, covered the girl's body and rolled over her. Her words rose like warm water rising from the depths of unknown gold mines within a woman who had never experienced true love except in her imagination. Touba was saying that humans were driven out of paradise for this very reason. Love burned like a flame. Moones burned because she was in love. Now she had to direct her love toward the supreme creator in order to be able to bear the weight of her past. In Touba's opinion, what had appeared to Moones was not the Angel of God but a representative of Satan, as witnessed by the fact that he had not been able to pursue the girl while she was occupied with her prayers. She said that most probably Moones had not focused properly in the last prayer, and while she was distracted from her prayers, Satan had appeared to her. Moones remembered that in the last prayer, without intending it, her thoughts had been flying toward Ismael. She did not admit this to her mother. She still could not confess her love in Touba's presence. If she did so, the love would be defiled. This was something between her and Ismael; no other being could know anything about it. Even now, gray layers of ice had covered it.

Touba and Moones agreed that they would go to visit Master Geda Alishah together. They arranged to go the very next day, after Moones finished her work. They hoped that the Master could help Moones. The assembly around the Master was always filled with women burning in the fire of love.

Moones slept not only in her mother's room, but in her bed as well. The Angel of God could not enter that side of the house. It was the first night in a long time that Moones slept peacefully. The next day she worked calmly, and in the afternoon she had the energy to visit the Master. Moones and Touba found that the Master's room was full of people. Men and women were seated everywhere. Some women had their headscarves on, contrary to the orders of the government regarding unveiling. Moones and Touba kept their hats on and took their seats quietly. Touba had asked for permission to be received in private and she was soon sent to see the Master. In her absence, a man sitting next to Moones began speaking with her. He said that he saw the pain of love in the young woman's face. He believed that love had brought her to the Master's presence. Listening to him, Moones had difficulty holding back her tears. The man said that he himself was a moth burned by the flames of love. He no longer had wings or feathers left and had become the shadow of the meaning of Truth. Suddenly, without embarrassment or inhibition, the man began to tell Moones his life story.

He was a minor cleric. His life had begun in a village around the city of Hamedan. In his youth he held classes and taught lessons to the children, until the Westerners came. Stopping outside the village, they set up their tents and used the measuring equipment they had with them. Apparently, they intended to excavate the hill nearby. They said it contained ancient remains. In a very short time, the young cleric had gone crazy for a woman who was a member of the excavating group. During the day, she rode on horseback through the fields and let her golden hair blow with the wind. Sometimes she would ride through the village and amaze all the men and women. The cleric spent hours on the roof of his house watching the woman. He realized that when he sat this way watching her, the people could see what he was doing and know that he had fallen for this foreign woman. So he dug a hole in the wall where he could watch for the woman. From the hole he had a view of part of the wall of the house across the way and all of the field beyond it. The woman often did her riding in this field. Sometimes he spent a whole day lying in wait for the woman to pass in front of his eyes for just one minute, far away and unapproachable. He had never dared to go near her, and his status as a teacher would not permit him to join the crowd of curious observers, though he always wished he could. The woman had gradually become the muse of every man in the village. And then one day she left just as abruptly as she had arrived. Since then the cleric's life had been chaos. He had turned to wine, and became the disgrace of the village. One day he thought it best to pack up and leave for Tehran, with the hope deep in his heart that he might be able to find the woman there. He had been in Tehran for some time before he finally happened upon the Master.

Moones asked if the man had looked for the woman. Did he search for her? The man shrugged his shoulders. Where could he look for her? Could he search the whole of England? And what would the English tell him? Would they not laugh at him? Moones thought of herself and of how she had considered using her time to search for Ismael. How insanely she had given in to everything in order to have him. She thought if she had been born a man, she would never step outside the realm of love. She would endure it no matter how miserable it became. If she were a man, she could stand at the crossroads in the bazaar and engage in competition with all the other macho men who claimed to be protecting people and won them over. She could convince everyone to accept her love.

But she was a woman. Her world was limited, restricted. She had never thought that as soon as she was barren, all her power would be lost. Now she could become two, three, a thousand people. It was never necessary to give in to her romantic dreams. She would have to live in a crowd and coordinate her steps with those of the crowd. If the crowd went to the left, she would have to go to the left. She would have to keep her breasts full of milk for the children to drink. If necessary, she would have to take stale bread out of garbage and eat it to keep her breasts full of milk, because the children wanted milk from her. She felt proud of her humility, and proud of her body's eternal drought. What she had now was honesty. She had generously and sincerely offered that honesty for the bastards at the bazaar corner. Now she was infertile. She was like a dry desert. She was afraid. Her mind attempted to rebuild itself, to come out of misery, but it seemed impossible. Alone, with lowered head and hunched back, she had been able to make her mother a friend again. Her female fate was to bend, to become small, to fold; thus people would leave her alone and let her share herself in other ways. Love for her had to be of another kind. This love was a stranger to night-time restlessness. It had no knowledge of trembling bodies and palpitating hearts. It was directed at reaching out rather than union. It worked according to a strategy that was opposite to that of the human male. It was not expected to arrive at union through love. On the contrary, it had to multiply itself, creating parts that spread all over; then they would be sewn together by some method to prevent their falling apart and causing chaos. Therefore, she could not laugh when she wished. She could not eat when she wished. She needed to draw a circle and put her genie—the evil and fire of her worldly desires—firmly under her control.

Touba went in to the Master, and like a dam released, told the whole story to him. The Master understood well what she was saying. As he listened, he shook his head with sorrow. He called Moones in. He said that in his opinion, Moones should hold on to her man. He said she must not leave her man alone in the midst of loneliness and imprisonment. It was not necessary to announce her marriage, but she could behave in such a manner that gradually people would accept the situation. Touba and her family had to accept that nothing impure or illegal had happened. The Master listened sadly to the part about the baby. He said that Moones had done wrong to break from the family circle that fate had built. The Master believed that human beings are obliged to accept their personal limits.

It was like being born a hunchback, or being short or tall. Each of these conditions places a fate before a human being. If one sensed the power, one could try to break free of destiny. But this required education and knowledge, which only some people possessed. It was as though the world was filled with a series of nets that had an infinite number of holes and little bells hung from every hole. Every being was fated to move in a specific direction. If an individual decided to pass through any other hole but that which fate had provided him, the little bells would begin to chime. One or two bells did not matter. But if a human being continued to be autonomous and left the crowd, many bells would begin to chime, to the point where their strange noise would disturb the entire society. Then people would leave their work to come and find out who had caused the disturbance. Moones's husband was this kind of person, fighting his fate. But the Master had, from the content of Moones and Touba's talk, come to understand that Ismael was not a bad man. The Master said, "The world is changing. When something new arrives, people think that now all is changed and everything is permissible, not realizing that if somehow things have developed as they have, it was meant to be so. One goes through great trouble to create a new design. Beyond the gate of being, the bones of thousands on the path burn and dry up in the cruel rays of the sun. A thousand heroes with seven arms may use their armor to open a road to a little village. What they often do not notice is that true survival is accomplished through patience and tolerance. It is easy to upturn all foundations, but if one day out of that chaos you try to construct a new world and a new fate, suddenly those invisible nets, covered by the little bells, reappear again. Everything will find its own natural way, and the rebel will be left behind, sorrowful and regretful, even though he might be able to calm the pain of his regret by hanging on to new nets."

From the Master's point of view, Ismael was not very much at fault. In the confusion of life, Ismael had simply gone in the wrong direction. He had cut with tradition to do something unusual, and of course there was the matter of love. The Master was willing to allow room for love when it came to youth. It was tolerable to him. But Moones had become the servant of fear and had ruined her future. In the Master's opinion, however, there was a solution for this, too. To make up for things, she could embrace other children. The Master became excited at this point. He said that woman's nature is the same as the earth, awaiting seeds and fertilization. If the land is infertile, it becomes a wasteland. Slowly it becomes parched and salty, and any seed that lands on it dies. But Moones had the possibility of replacing her physical infertility with spiritual fertility. She now must sow the seeds of kindness and love. She could grow

large and embrace all of nature in her loving arms. The Master
ordered her to go visit her husband. He told her to repeat a specific
prayer to negate the being that seemed to her to be the Angel of
God, because the Master also believed that God's angels would not
bother a woman who was desperate and desolate. Logically, the
angels of God were not hurtful. The Master became devoted to
the idea of Moones following a mystic path. He was convinced that
the young woman could reach a high level of devotion and become
a true follower.

Moones felt completely calm when she left the Master. The gathering had affected her profoundly, and she now knew what she must
do. She already knew that Tuesday was the visiting day at the prison.
Moones asked for a day off from work and early in the morning she
set off to visit Ismael. In her hand she grasped her birth certificate,
on which her marriage was registered, as proof of her right to see
her husband. She tried to calm herself by placing this hand on her
heart.

When Ismael was called for a visitation, he froze in his place.
Nearly a year had gone by, and he had come to consider himself lost
to the world. He was even a burden to the other prisoners. They
took care of his costs because he had no family coming forward to
pay for him. He was bothered by this fact, and he had limited his
needs to the point that he was often hungry. He could not eat the
prison food. He was used to cleanliness. He followed almost fetishis-
tically the sanitary and health directions he had studied in school.
What they gave him as food turned his stomach. Every time he
found a hair, a pebble, or charcoal in his food, he would lose his
appetite for several days. Often he would limit himself to eating only
the bread, and so he was loosing weight. This was all obvious to the
others, and it bothered Ismael that everyone knew of his shortcomings. He was placed among the poorest prisoners. The bitterness of
the experience had made him more bitter. He felt so lacking in support that at times he wished to lean on a hay straw or a branch of
weeping willow, as either would be more than he had.

He didn't know who his visitor could be. According to the order
of law he was now a Bolshevik. He had been separated from one

group only to be forced into another, though he was truly not a member of either. He didn't know what to do with his recollections of Touba's spiritual journeys and visions. These filled his childhood memories. At the same time, he had been arguing with his friends about philosophy and politics. They had taught him what they could. Their learning had excited him; there seemed to be nothing wrong in what he heard. It seemed like a smooth road that would lead humanity to its final, better destination. Now at night, as he lay alone in his bed, Moones would come to him, a woman who did not fit any worldly category. For her sake, he had gone against all rules and had allowed himself to desire to be with her. And a little further away stood Touba, the rock that he had leaned on through all of his childhood. In those childhood days, how badly he had wanted to be hugged by her and caressed by her motherly touch. Lack of love had driven him crazy. He had slowly learned from his friends how to pull a veil of coldness and indifference over this sensation. In the midst of all these ruminations, once in a while, came the image of a woman who looked ethereal—a woman he had seen as a child, in full moonlight. This was Layla, whose presence shimmered in the moonlight that shone on the old courtyard. This was the one who had, after Setareh's departure, come to sing him a song.

Ismael had learned to respect women. All his life consisted of women. All his life he had taken care of a retarded mother and, often with great longing, had held on to of the memory of a sister who had one day disappeared as though the wind had carried her away. He often thought that he would grow just large enough to become an umbrella protecting them from the sun. He now felt guilty. He had ruined the lives of at least two of these women. He had felt so important and powerful next to Moones. If he could buy her a present, he felt proud. He had often pictured himself in a home with Moones and their children. He had many times pictured Touba looking at him proudly and showing off her son-in-law, a university professor. And he had believed that with effort, lots of hard work, and brain power, he would create a good life for himself and his family.

His friends had said that everything must change from the ground up, and he had accepted their views. He had thought of carrying his own small part in life on his back, and dreamt of changing the foundations of everything in the manner of a great man. In his dreams, he kept people in the palm of his hand to protect them while he renovated their individual homes. He also built bathhouses for people, schools, and provided them with factories and guilds. He fought for their rights and meanwhile raised his own children.

These dreams were all crushed when one day one of the uneducated guards had spat on him. In fact, every aspect of prison was teaching him that people are not small beings that he could, like a giant, lift into his palm and transform through education. Whatever and whoever people might be, if they felt that their peace of mind was in danger, they would scream and resist. People's bodies were also about the same size as his, and some even slightly larger. People could spit at him and refuse his well-intentioned plans for them. People shared a common instinct that was based on protecting their own rights. It was not so simple to just accept a great, kind giant happily. In fact, the giant would have to prove his greatness at the start. But was he really a giant? Ismael understood that he knew only a very small part of the truth, and even what truth he had was suspect, perhaps false. His oversized mental image of himself was slowly breaking down, diminishing. In the past, he had never had to prove himself. When he told Touba fabulous things—for instance— such as that there are many small living beings in the water that are carriers of various diseases— the woman would raise her eyebrows and fall into thought. Ismael felt smart and thought it was appropriate to think as he did. It seemed to him that whatever he told anyone, it would be accepted because he believed in it and in his own goodwill. Now he had been forced to prove himself at every turn. Every sentence, every idea was discussed, often for hours, and he realized that he was not being listened to as closely as in the past. In prison Ismael had come face-to-face with poverty, orphans, and humility. When they called him for visitation, he struggled between two worlds.

He passed the prison courtyard proudly, noticing that his friends were looking at him in surprise. No one expected that he would have a visitor. When he entered the hallway he rushed forward, at times ahead of the warden, to reach the door. He stood in the doorway and noticed Moones sitting demurely on the bench, wrapped in a gray coat and matching hat. For a moment, they looked at each other in amazement. It felt embarrassing and shameful, but the warden would not leave until he had satisfied his curiosity about this long-in-coming first visit. He stood between the two of them, watching them greedily, wearing a contemptuous smile. Who was this visitor? A lady from high society, surely. Now he could tell this to everyone—and indeed, this visit fueled a week of gossip for the warden.

The man and woman felt his presence between them. They greeted one another calmly. Ismael inquired after everyone's health. Moones answered, then told him that she had brought him pastries, fruit, clothes, and money, and mentioned the amount. Ismael shook his head and said he did not want to cause her any trouble. Moones replied that it was no trouble and she felt happy to bring him some presents. She asked if she could come to visit him on Fridays. Both looked at the warden questioningly. The warden mumbled that it might be possible; perhaps it could be arranged. That had to be decided in the higher offices of the prison. Moones stated self-assuredly that she would take care of it. Sunlight was shining brightly on the little muddy pool visible through the window. Ismael absorbed the reflection of the light through every pore of his body. The warmth of love crawled under his skin and when he looked at Moones again, he transferred the heat to her. A morning sunbeam struck Moones's body like a caress. It was clear they still loved one another. Nothing could ruin this love. They filled their meeting with small talk. Moones had purposefully neglected to mention the child. She had no intention of ever mentioning it.

Ismael walked back to the ward as if in a dream. One year of separation from the mute outside world was ending. Ismael did have someone to think about him, someone more important than the rest of the world. He must keep her. Ismael's fingers were unconsciously gathered into fists. Even if they cut him up he must keep her. This only connection with the living world could replace all of the characters that lived in his mind.

Moones went straight from the prison to see Mr. Khansari. This man was the wisest being she knew, and they had been friends enough that he would understand her problem, this troubling love. Mr. Khansari was not a jealous man, but rather very realistic. He knew from the beginning that he had engaged in an improper marriage. He always believed that he had ruined a young girl's life and felt quite regretful. He welcomed her kindly and said he would help if he could. He listened intently as she rapidly recounted the story of the marriage and described Ismael's current situation. She skipped over the pregnancy and abortion because there was nothing to do about that now. Mr. Khansari explained to Moones that the people like her husband were very dangerous from the government's viewpoint. Nevertheless, perhaps some arrangements could be made to provide the prisoner with better conditions. He promised to do something on behalf of Moones's desire to visit Ismael on Fridays.

Ismael's transfer to a better ward changed the warden's treatment of him. The orphaned prisoner now had an owner, and therefore was less of a victim to the whims of the herds. Prior to Moones's first visit, Ismael had been a suspicious revolutionary prisoner who exchanged books secretly. If he ever got ahold of pen and paper, he took notes and would teach and study among the other prisoners. He continued to do this, but now his whole being craved to be outside the prison. The desire to hold his wife in his arms consumed him. He had someone to think about him. His eyes shone, as if he had a constant fever. On Fridays, as soon as the visits ended, he began counting the minutes until the next visit. He could now offer sweets, pastries, and fruit to his friends. He could buy better food with the money he now had. He also smoked. Ismael spent two and a half years buoyed by the woman's visits, and became more and more a servant to his love for Moones.

Moones's life circled around home, office, prison, and the Sufi center. She commuted almost solely between these four places. When her brothers and sisters saw her, they would lower their voices. Now everyone knew she was Ismael's wife, but no one mentioned this fact to anyone else. From the very beginning, she got everyone used to the reality through her actions, rather than by talking about it at length. For a long time they were all confused. Many times

Habibolah Mirza intended to slap his sister in the face, but he couldn't. Each time he positioned himself to act, she moved. Habibolah's imaginary hand would fly through the air. Gradually, the brother's anger subsided. In fact, the woman had not committed such a great sin. She had of course married someone he had always hated, but whether he liked it or not Ismael had become a part of the family. From the first day of Ismael's arrival to the house, these truths should have been considered, but they weren't. With regret, Habibolah noticed that questionable creatures like Ismael were climbing the ladder of success. These people perhaps could not even name their grandfather, for either they did not know him or, if they did, he was not worth mentioning. But they climbed the ladder of success all the same. Their clothes were in order, they spoke in an educated manner, and often they were better educated than he was. The young man sadly resigned himself to these things. The world's order was messed up and vagabonds were infiltrating from every direction. Habibolah shrugged his shoulders in private at this state of affairs. Slowly he learned not to think of them, and eventually he began to limit his interaction with other family members.

Gradually, people began to stress the positive qualities in Ismael. He was certainly a good-looking man, and certainly he had a good education and superb knowledge. They also knew that he was not really so fatherless or motherless, after all. His father had been an important merchant who went bankrupt because of the Bolshevik revolution. Due to the shock of this experience, his mother had lost her memory toward the end of her life. His sister, supposedly, was now the wife of an important landowner in Azerbaijan and held high status in her own area. All of the positive rumors, spread by Manzar O-Saltaneh and Habibolah, reverberated and were eventually taken for truth. In order to make the man acceptable to the family they had to build him up.

Before Ismael left the prison he had been turned into an important person, just shy of a hero, that no one needed to fear. They did not use the term *Bolshevik* in association with him anymore. They said he was a progressive thinker and like all such people, he was dissatisfied with most systems. Had it not always been this way?

Humans who know too much suffer. Ismael suffered from the stupidity of others who could not accept proven truths. Madam Amineh shook her head patiently, sighed, and said that wise people always suffered and had troubles.

The family was gradually immersed in the aura of Ismael's knowledge, yet every member remained somewhat cautious. They had to accept this man of wisdom because he was the husband of a family member, but they felt they also needed to distance themselves from him because there were certain things they did not know. They suspected, for instance, that he might be close to some foreigners. It was always this way: some citizens helped to ruin their country by giving their power to this or that government. Would Ismael do such a thing, even though his father had suffered badly from the Bolsheviks and his mother had consequently lost her mental balance? Everyone knew very well that such a thing would likely never happen, yet there remained a very small chance that it would. One could dangle a sense of caution between the gates of truth and lies. They asked of themselves: Why had he gone to prison? And they answered themselves: He was a book reader and intellectual, therefore he became the target of the government's suspicion. All that talk about Bolshevism was hearsay. What did Bolshevik mean anyway? Even in Russia, this word was meaningless. Ismael was not a Bolshevik. Ismael was an intelligent person who disliked groundless theories and nonsensical talk about God and religion. Although Madam Amineh did not reach agreement with anyone, she had committed herself to mention these matters wherever she could, so that the whole situation could be placed in the past. And why had Moones and Ismael married on the sly? Well, the reason was clear: Moones had just gotten divorced from her husband, and it was not right for the woman to marry immediately after separation—but they lived in the same house and this was not appropriate either. They thought it best to go through the legal part of the marriage before they got their own home, to which they would have invited everybody.

Back in the prison, Ismael did not know he had become favored again in the family. He was merely anxious to reconstruct the bridges between himself and Moones and his friends. These were friends who had been tortured and each day became firmer in their beliefs and tried to take Ismael along with them. Moones, by her continuous rotation between house, office, prison, and the Sufi center was immersed deeper in mystical prayers. The woman could now love Ismael through her mystical thoughts. She did not know that her relatives were talking about her marriage. She was not aware of anything. She had her own mental world alongside her mother's mental world. She believed that her marriage with Ismael had occurred eons ago. Eternal fate had led Ismael to her home. This fate had taken all of his family from him so he could spread his umbrella over Moones. They had grown up together. The same eternal faith had wanted Moones to lose her fertility; most probably she was meant to accomplish something more important. An unknown and unrecognizable power had wanted her not to bear children. This power wanted her all to itself. Holy Mary, the Virgin Mother, had lost her ability to speak directly with God after giving birth to Christ. Similarly, all-powerful fate had wished Moones to be completely devoted to it. It had made Ismael an intermediary. The man was a bridge that directed her to the higher love. As for Ismael as a husband—well, she had to test her ability to live a life of abstinence. She had been weak once, and had been punished for it. Moones felt that fate wished her to be close to material love, but keep all of her attention focused on eternal love. It was in this area that the young woman had to pass the test of fortitude.

Touba busied herself with Setareh and sometimes envied the mystical progress of her daughter, who now wrote poetry and had premonitions of things that would happen in the future. Touba wondered if her daughter had been able to dig a passageway to Setareh's presence. Jealously, she wished to hide Setareh from anyone else's view. In all these years, she had never permitted a mason or gardener to enter the house. She still believed that these kinds of people would be able to sense the spirit of the house that if they came to the house, they would somehow discover the girl's body. The girl brought sanctity to the house. If they were to discover her, the house would collapse. Touba had come to believe that during the transfer from the Qajar dynasty to the Pahlavi regime, the girl's honor had protected her house and her children. She could not tell her children not to leave the house, but she knew that she herself must not leave, and that she must not ever tell the girl's secret to anyone. She believed Setareh was the reason why she failed to benefit from Master Geda Alishah's presence. It was Setareh herself who wanted to be Touba's protector, here in this world and in the next. It was Setareh who would tell her the future, and it was she who lived in the most hidden recess of her conscience. But was Moones in contact with Setareh? Many times Touba had tried to find out. She would ask Moones how she achieved her visions of future events. Moones would say that a voice simply whispered in her ear. Undoubtedly, it had to be Setareh. Touba believed that Moones knew about the secret of Setareh.

Meanwhile, as a smoke screen, the relatives had composed a complex story of Ismael and Moones's marriage. It was similar to the star-crossed romance story of *Layli and Majnoun*, and Madam Amineh, the narrator of the story, without discussing matters with her second cousin, had tried to save the family's reputation and each day the story acquired further embellishment.

In this atmosphere, just a few days after Reza Shah Pahlavi was to leave the country, forced out by the Allied forces as war raged around the world, Moones woke up one morning and said, "Ismael will be freed today." She did not bother to go to her office, but instead took a carriage directly to the prison. On the way she constantly repeated the prayer invoking God's presence, "Oh God, the intercessor, the bestower . . ." She was correct. She had not been there more than an hour when Ismael stepped out of the prison gate. He held a suitcase in his hand and looked around, confused, until he saw Moones coming toward him. He was flushed, and he stammered when he spoke. For several years now, he had seen her only in the presence of a third party. Now that they were alone and nothing divided them, he did not know what to do or say. He stood as quiet as a bashful child and didn't know what to do with his hands. He was afraid to hold her hand and have strangers see him. A vague image of returning to the prison came into his mind. Unsure of what to do, he let Moones handle everything as she thought appropriate.

Moones had not sent the carriage off, fully trusting that he would come out. They now sat in the carriage and looked out at British, American, and Russian soldiers. In one week, the city's appearance had become European. Moones asked Ismael if he had ever seen so many foreigners. He looked around and said he now was looking at them. The foreigners were much lighter in complexion than they were. Moones confessed that she had felt anxious since the foreigners arrived. She said that people had expected the city to be bombed, and now they were wondering what was going to happen.

Hesam O-Din Mirza had gone personally to remove all of Hitler's photographs from the walls of his sister's room and destroy them. The girl believed in Hitler, and whatever money she received she spent buying Hitler's pictures. Indeed, almost everyone had a picture of Hitler. Ismael smiled bitterly, for he had never felt attracted to Hitler and now, in the street, he saw Hesam O-Din Mirza passing and noticed that he had changed out of his military uniform. Indeed, the whole army was hiding itself. The shah, who had built such close ties with Germany and its dictator, had now departed, so there was no need to resist the Allied forces that were entering the country. Moones said that Mr. Khansari had taken leave from his office until it all calmed down. Ismael said that Mr. Khansari had provided his bail, and he blushed again. He didn't feel he could tell his wife how much it bothered him that she had asked for her ex-husband's assistance. Without desiring it, he had become Mr. Khansari's favored friend, and he didn't know what to do about it in the future. Moones thought she really should go right away and express her deep gratitude to Mr. Khansari. Ismael wanted to go to a cafe so they could be alone for a while before going home. They went to Naderi Avenue to drink some tea in a cafe there.

The cafe was full of Americans. Ismael and Moones felt like strangers—strangers to each other and to the people surrounding them. They sat across from one another and looked at white cups filled with tea. Slices of lemon floated on the tea and lumps of sugar stood on the table in clean containers. Most of the Americans wore military uniforms. Some were reading the paper. A few American women and a couple of Iranian women, heavily made up, sat at other tables. Habibolah Mirza had told her that at night there was live music in this restaurant, and everyone danced right there in public. Moones commented on how tall the Americans were, much taller than the Russians or the British. Ismael agreed. Moones said without any introduction, "I had a child." The man's heart stopped beating. He asked, "Where is the child?" The young woman laughed bitterly. Trying not to look at Ismael's eyes, she kept her eyes on other tables. She saw an American officer lift his cup, but before he drank from it, his hand froze. Some news in the foreign-language paper had caught his attention. He kept on reading while holding the cup in midair. Moones focused her eyes on their own tea. It was getting cold. She told the story in very few words, she did not wish to emphasize it too much. If she emphasized it, then the circle she had built for herself would fall apart and she would be back at the beginning. When she said that she could never have any children, tears filled her eyes, but she fought them back. One night, one of these future nights, she would cry in Ismael's arms. The man quickly said that children did not matter to him at all. Moones was the most important being in his life. He was telling the truth and a lie at the same time, for he had many times pictured himself as a father.

As a giant, Ismael had imagined having his wife and children on his back and the people in the palm of his hand as he calmly worked to change everything from the foundation up. When the guard had spit on him, he had slowly lowered his hand to the ground to let the people go, and to let himself do some more thinking. But he had still imagined his family on his back. Now the children were sliding down and dissolving in midair like soap bubbles. Ismael, who was no longer a giant, sat straighter in his seat. He felt lighter—a very painful lightness. The atmosphere was no longer strangling him, instead, he felt afraid of floating up from the ground, dangling in midair. Moones whispered that if Ismael would like to, he could marry another woman in order to have children with her. Ismael tried to smile. He needed to say something to calm the fragile, shaking woman, to reassure her. But he could not smile. His lips trembled a few times, and finally a faint smile began to appear on his lips. Music was playing on the gramophone, a kind of music that he later on learned was Latin American. He said that although he had great respect for Moones and loved her, if she were to continue to talk like this, he would loose his patience. He said he would love a different single strand of Moones's hair every day and when they reached a hundred and twenty years of age, he still would have worshipped only half of her hair, thus, the love they shared would keep him well-occupied. Moones did not believe him, but she was beginning to come around. She had shared her most awful secret and he had not left her. She said that Ismael must come to attend Master Geda Alishah's meetings. She said that the Master had helped her a great deal.

A woman in a chador was standing behind the glass window of the cafe looking at them. She seemed to be a beggar. Ismael was amazed at her clothing. Moones explained that since Reza Shah's departure, many women had returned to the chador. Madam Amineh was wearing it again; her own mother, as well. But being unveiled had also established itself as a custom. Almost all young women and some older ones remained unveiled.

It came time to return home. Ismael picked up his suitcase, and they left the cafe. They took a carriage again, passing through waves of soldiers from every nation, women with and without veils, and a mass of beggars. It passed through Ismael's mind that his second reunion of the day, the one yet to take place with Touba, was going to be very difficult. The closer they came to the house, the more nervous he felt. He understood that Moones's family now knew the story of their marriage, but the initial confrontation was still going to be hard.

They walked the length of the alley in silence. Shopkeepers who saw him became excited and exchanged greetings. They were brief, since they noticed that the couple was anxious to get home. Moones knocked at the door. A few minutes passed in silence and anxiety. Then they heard the door latch turning and saw Touba's face appear from behind the door. The glare on her glasses hid her eyes, but something danced upon her lips that was not clearly either a smile or a frown. Ismael bent down and kissed her hand. Touba wanted to pull her hand away, but the man did not let it go. The first obstacle had been surmounted. Touba turned back into the house, letting

Ismael and Moones follow her. Ismael was happy that they had gone to a cafe before coming home. The manner in which Touba welcomed them might have ruined everything between him and Moones. He left his suitcase by the door of his room and accompanied Moones as she moved toward the old woman's room. By the door, Touba told Moones to stay outside because there was something important she needed to tell Ismael. The man followed her into the room and reclined on a cushion, under her critical eyes.

Touba sat on the other side of the room. They spent a few minutes in silence. Then the old woman asked if she had ever, in all these years, done anything that would give him the impression that he was an orphan or poor. The man could not at that moment think clearly enough to search his memories, but doubtless he had spent his childhood as a servant. He said no. She asked if it was fair that he should mislead her daughter and create such public dishonor. His throat went dry. He wanted to answer, but the woman went ahead and asked if was it right that he take advantage of a young woman who was alone and divorced from an older man. Ismael flushed all over, and with a voice tinged with anger he responded that he had never taken advantage of anyone. He and Moones had jointly agreed to marry and this was an eternal union. He said that they had felt this affinity for one another since childhood, though they had never talked about it or asked for advice. Touba asked if it was right that a man accused of being a Bolshevik, an enemy of the people, be her son-in-law. Ismael shook his head impatiently. He said that these were incorrect accusations. He asked what Touba really knew about Bolsheviks. The woman changed the subject, and angrily asked if he had ever thought about where his sister Setareh was? Ismael, losing his patience, began to rise but, before he could leave the old woman, pointing at the tree in the garden, shouted, "There! Under the earth of the pomegranate tree."

Moones was nervously walking around the courtyard. She wanted to unlock Ismael's room so that they could clean it together. During Ismael's imprisonment, no one had never entered that room. In her and Touba's opinion, there were secrets in the room that should be revealed only in Ismael's presence. She was shocked to hear her mother's sudden shouts. But she did not understand the entire sentence. Moones stopped where she was and waited to see if the conflict would go far enough that she needed to interfere. Ismael, at first, did not understand anything. Following the woman's aged finger, he looked in the direction of the pomegranate tree. Touba poured out the twenty-year-old secret feverishly, barely controlling her anger. She told him the story of that early morning when she found the girl at the washbasin, killed by her uncle.

Ismael rapidly descended through the well of time to his childhood, to that strange day, when he was seven or eight years old, when he had been forbidden to do absolutions at the washbasin. He remembered the day very well. He remembered that his uncle's back was to him, and that Touba's hand had pressed hard on the back of his own neck while she repeated, "Go to the pool! To the pool!" She had pushed away him toward the pool. In those days he did not yet speak Persian very well, so things eluded him. Now, gradually, it fully dawned on him that his sister was buried deep under the pomegranate tree, sleeping among its roots. He had heard rumors that the girl had become pregnant by Cossacks, or a Cossack. He had heard it said that he, Ismael, had done to Touba's family what the Cossacks had done to his sister. Ismael knew that Moones would never be able to have children. Was he supposed to believe that if he had killed the girl it would have been better than causing her such a tragedy?

The pressure in Ismael's chest grew stronger every second. Touba was taking her revenge for everything. She had now shared her secret with the person who, more than anyone else, should know it. She felt her back straightening. It seemed to her that she was no longer an accomplice in Setareh's murder. Simultaneously, she knew that Setareh had left the house forever, and this realization brought her great sorrow. Now Setareh was merely a body under tons of earth, and Ismael had become the owner of a dead sister, burdened with the memories of her tragic death. The weight of the presence of the dead, instead of making Ismael feel heavy, made him feel still lighter. Now he was not only dangling in midair but also twirling around himself. He heard sounds in his mind, as though bubbles were bursting in there. If there was any secret, it now belonged to him.

With the discovery that she had lost Setareh, Touba suddenly fell silent. She saw Ismael, who was crushed under the burden of her talk. She did not know exactly what she had done to the man. Instinctively, she reached for her chador, pulled it over her head, and headed out of the house. She needed to go for a walk.

Moones came into the room and asked Ismael what Touba had said to him. She saw that Ismael was upset and told him that he should not bother himself too much about anything Touba said. The woman was old, tired, and traditional, and thus unable to understand their love. The young man, sitting hunched over, seemed to have suddenly aged ten years. His mind was filled with memories of a pomegranate tree, and a forgotten face was also beginning to take form in his mind. Setareh had begun to appear to him, and he knew that he should not reveal the secret to Moones. This was his and Touba's secret to share. He now knew that he would have to live in this morbid old house forever. He now understood why the old woman would not allow a builder or gardener into her house. This was why she took care of all the repairs herself.

Gone was his dream of going to Germany to study philosophy, the dream of a newly built house for himself and Moones, the dream of happy, mischievous children. Gone too was the hope of his sister ever reappearing, along with the dream of changing the very basis of his life, the dream of breaking the mysterious code of the sphere. Gradually, he put aside all thoughts of a new world order or even of a new personal one, a life where people would gather for friendly intellectual discussions.

The windows were kept open in the summer. Through them, one could see rectangular flower beds, the octagonal blue cement pool, the not-very-professionally plastered, carved columns of the terrace, the door, and the green windows of the rooms on the south side of the house. A piece of sky was reflected in the pool, where mosquitoes laid their eggs, the algae twisted around itself, and occasionally some red-and-black fish surfaced to make bubbles in the water. Persian music could be heard floating over the wall from the neighbor's house, where a woman was also singing. On Ismael's gramophone, a recording of Beethoven's Ninth Symphony was playing. Ismael sat on an easy chair looking at the cracked, half-full pool, a tray of yogurt, fresh herbs, cheese, and vodka before him. Holding his glass, he scrutinized the dilapidated house. Not far from him sat Moones, doing her mending at a sewing machine. Touba was walking through the garden spreading fertilizer on the grass, the flower beds, and the flower pots by the pool. The fertilizer came from one of the sewage wells that she had emptied into one of the cellars twenty-five years ago to let it air out. Every time Ismael passed this cellar, he turned his head away in disgust. One could still see in the fertilizer, the shells of sunflower and melon seeds. He wondered at the amount of seeds consumed by humans in the old days. It seemed as though the fate of the people in this society had been tied to seeds since the beginning of time. He thought it must have been due to malnutrition; that they had tried to compensate for their nutritional deficits by consuming the seeds of watermelon, pumpkin and Persian melon. Hence the waste, which the old woman used as fertilizer, was filled with seed shells. After Touba had finished spreading fertilizer on the plants, she began to water them. Ismael thought, "Now the fertilizer will seep into the pool, and then they will wash the plates, pots and pans in this same pool, whose water is filled with algae, slime, and human waste."

He took the record off the gramophone, and Beethoven was silenced. He thought he should not listen to Beethoven when the water was extremely dirty and human waste was pouring into the pool. He felt it would be disrespectful to Beethoven, although he put up with the sound of the sewing machine. He knew that his wife was tuned into her own thoughts, turning over in her mind many things, such as problems at the office. In his opinion, these were matters not foreign to Beethoven's music and could all be melded together. For some reason, however, the fertilizer full of seed shells in the pool disturbed his serenity.

The more Ismael tried, the less successful he was in changing the old woman's ways. He had wanted to build a washbasin next to the pool, but she had resisted. Touba wanted to continue to use the hand pumping system, even though it froze in the winter. She insisted that they all wash their hands and faces in the washbasin in the downstairs apartment. He had tried to tile the washbasin and stucco the walls and ceiling to make it easier to clean, but she had resisted. She argued that if the well's connection to the wash area ever became clogged, then they would have to break through the tiles, and that would be costly.

He had wanted to cobblestone the alley leading to the house to avoid the ankle-deep mud that built up in the winter. She had resisted because the water canal might also get blocked, and breaking through the cobblestones to fix it would again be costly. He had suggested that they at least cover the alley with bricks, so that if the water canal blocked, then only a few bricks would need to be removed to gain access to the water's passageway. Again she had disagreed.

Although Ismael had long ago lowered his giant-sized hand to let people follow their own way in life, once in a while, no matter how much he had been reduced in stature, he wished he could lift his small-sized hand to bring it down on some people's heads. He thought he needed to take Touba by her shoulders, back her against a wall and tell her "Lady, sometimes it is necessary to mend, to build, to change, to renovate." Then maybe he could get it into her head. But she was adamantly against any "fixing," so they did not have this discussion often.

They kept Setareh's secret between them, and the old woman had by force convinced him that no mason should come to her house. She said a mason gives life to a house, which would otherwise be nothing but a barren shell. The mason sets a foundation and constructs a building brick-by-brick, and soon something resembling a house is made. Such a person would undoubtedly sense the heart of a house. Hadn't Ismael paid attention to the fact that the girl's spirit wandered through the house? Obviously not. The old woman reproached him for losing touch with the spiritual world. It was as a consequence of this, she said, that the material world had torn him apart.

Ismael looked at the sagging walls, thinking that this year's rain and snow, or perhaps next year's, would finally topple everything. He knew that he could never leave the house; his sister had tied him to it, and then, of course, there was Moones. He could have taken Moones and left, since she did not mind the idea of moving to their own house. Both of them were fed up with the old woman's habits and "proprieties." But then there was Setareh.

Ismael placed the vodka glass on the tray and stood up. He had decided to attack the old woman from another angle. He went to the tall open window and said to Moones in a loud voice that he thought this was the year that the walls would crumble. Moones asked, "Why do you think that?" And Ismael, as if Touba did not exist in the world, said, "From a physical point of view the curvature in the wall has reached a point where it will buckle at any moment." He deliberately used technical words to scare Touba. He said, "If not this year, the wall will fall under the weight of next year's rain and snow. Perhaps we could live with a fallen wall, but then the neighbors will be able to see inside the house. They will stare with coveting eyes at our courtyard and garden." As Touba irrigated the garden she listened closely to Ismael. He turned around and swallowed the last of his vodka. He felt bored. The summer afternoon was eating him and he could not even listen to Beethoven anymore. He now had only the dirty water of the pool. He needed to get out to breathe fresh air. Perhaps he would come across a few friends with whom to chat. They liked to call up past memories and analyze current events. Their discussions moved from politics to literature and literature to philosophy. They would provide some mental food to overcome the monotony of life.

For a while, Ismael had associated with the pro-Soviet Tudeh Party and its Communist aims. Some of his friends had joined the party and he was tempted to do the same. But there were things holding him back; he could not tolerate the ambitions of the party officials; or their dependence upon foreigners. Many nights he walked along and thought about these things, when the party, inevitably, was torn by internal divisions, he decided to stay away. Moones did not like the Tudeh Party. She could not tolerate it. She was crazy for Prime Minister Mosaddeq, who had taken power—and the nation's oil—away from the shah and his foreign allies, the British and the Americans. She spoke of him everywhere she went, and she had bought many of his government's bonds. She had tried several times to go and see him. Ismael did not have great faith in Mosaddeq. He believed that the prime minister had made mistakes. But Moones continued to believe that the old politician would prevail. Ismael and Moones disagreed on these issues. In this time of exciting chaos, Ismael left his wife to think and do as she wished.

With his friends, however, he was trying to find the right way forward for his country. But before they could succeed, Mosaddeq's government fell, victim to a coup engineered by the foreign powers he had challenged. Ismael felt deeply depressed. He thought they could have helped the prime minister. He was consumed with the events of the entire decade leading up to Mosaddeq's rise and fall. For a while he tried in vain to find the solution to all of the problems that burdened his mind. He had barely survived the separation from his wife and the sadness of the death of his sister. He had moved from one group to another, from one party to another, only to come back home and sit in his usual chair and resign himself to the fact that there was nothing he could do. He had become like an office employee. He told his wife he was going out to see his friends. He told her not to wait up for him or delay dinner. His destination was the usual place, Monsieur Ardavaz's bar, where he would drink vodka and eat ham sandwiches while discussing current events. He would not return until around nine or ten at night.

The fateful 1940s had passed and the 1950s were already half over. Now men gathered at bars and whispered to one another. Some of Ismael's friends had given up on the discussions and their dreams of activism. Ismael remained baffled. He did not know what to do. His friends were aware that he was responsible for many women at home. Besides, had not his comrades made mistakes in the past? Had they not missed golden opportunities? Nevertheless, he felt he still needed their friendship. When the disappointment of the 1953 coup shocked them to the bone, they all crowded into the bars to drown their sorrows. Alcohol became a daily indulgence behind which they could hide. In order to avoid Geda Alishah, he went to the bars more often. He did not blame Moones for her fondness for the Master; he simply could not accompany her. He was not concerned with the next world. He was more worried about the unsanitary water in the pool and the kinds of microbes that could and probably did thrive there.

Ismael also listened to Moones talking about her supernatural experiments. She could foretell events and amazingly, her predictions often came true, just as his mother-in-law's did. Ismael grew curious about the source of this desire that women seemed to have to predict the future. Women were frightened about their current situations. Thus they were weak, and needed to be surrounded by other weak people. That is why they wanted an enclosed space with their provisions safe inside it, where no one and no war could penetrate. Ismael had no doubt that it was a woman who invented the concepts of storing food, weaving carpets, and knitting clothes. He

was certain that carpet patterns were born out of women's philosophical and mystical deliberations. For thousands of years for example,
the Zoroastrians had used the aigrette design as their sacred cedar;
now it appeared in carpet designs, with many variations, such as the
mother and child design in which the main pattern embraces the
smaller ones. But Ismael could not distinguish these sacred patterns
from regular ones. Women worry about the future of their children,
Ismael thought. And they know that in a time of bloodshed their safe
space will be invaded. In such a mode of thinking, women try to sur-
pass men, to make predictions, to foresee the result of any disaster
ahead of time. Because they are worried about storing food and keeping their homes and children safe, they are only concerned with pre-
dicting the bad things. They know that every event in history has
caused their swollen stomachs to swell with starvation, so they try to
prevent the next event. This would sometimes prove beneficial;
women did sometimes avert disaster. The continuation of that separated branch in the carpet pattern perhaps represented this sort of forward thinking—that which attempted to keep things together and
rule them all in silence and secret. Because women are physically weak,
lacking an iron fist, they know they can accomplish more with their
thinking. They weave a net so invisible that it can trap anything, and
they do it calmly and peacefully, the way one walks on a sophisticated
pattern on a carpet. In this way, women remained the rulers without
even being acknowledged as such. If a man really wanted to make a
change in the world, he had to employ the women's method of looking
forward in time. Ismael imagined himself as a big person, a giant, but
nevertheless a man with womanly sensibilities. He could protect the
patterns of the carpets, the storage of the food. He could let his wife
make predictions.

He was suddenly struck by a second thought. Women made predictions because they were not allowed to have an opinion. He
remembered that in the 1940s, when he was active with political
parties, he could not tolerate women speakers—those women who
stood firm, with open, steady eyes, and talked about minute details
with great care and attention. Now he was enjoying this woman, his
wife, sitting at the sewing machine, spinning its wheel and making

predictions about imminent deaths of family members, droughts, and famine. Throughout history, the female had been prevented from thinking. She was devoid of an individual ego, of an "I." Instead, she was a part of "we," and dissolved into the communal. "We" drew assistance from collective instinct in order to think. Under these conditions, ideas resembled dangling illusions. "We" then appeared in a plethora of sounds, murmuring sounds, that revealed words and somehow inspired the listeners. "I," on the other hand, was concerned with independence but often could not arrive at any solution.

Ismael knew that his wife did not have the courage to think. She had once thought, and had become sterile. Showing independent thinking had turned her into shapeless clay. Now a voice thought for her. A voice told her, "There will be famine." Through the night, the voice would nurture the rationale for the famine in the woman's unconscious. In the morning, without having thought or knowing that she had thought, she would tell to others the voice's revelations. She would not tell everyone. Only those who smiled on her kindly received the word. She was afraid of the rest.

Ismael did not disagree with Moones. She had brought her sterility under control through mysticism. He, too, felt compelled to became gigantic enough to hold all of the children of the world, or to imagine that he had given birth to them. Consequently, he also was in need of Master Geda Alishah. Moones needed to grow larger and larger in her imagination. Yet since such grandeur was not possible for her alone, she had to attach herself to another's greatness.

The problem was that she no longer joyfully met her husband's physical needs. The woman who slept in Ismael's bed at night was of no value as an earthly body. Moones believed more and more, each day, that one must give up the temptations of this world for the sake of the lasting world. She cared nothing for sex. The woman who had expressed such heated passion in the early stages of love was now a mountain of ice who only reluctantly tolerated Ismael's advances.

In the taxi, Ismael closed his eyes for a minute. How terribly he needed to embrace a loving woman. This woman was Moones—but the old Moones. His one and only experience of love was now like a blade of grass suffering through winter in the coldest frozen places of the world. Her numbing coldness was not obvious in the beginning; it had seemed more like embarrassment or shyness. But gradually, it sapped Ismael's energy. It created a sense of paralysis. He wanted to give her a child. If his love could make her uterus fertile, then Moones's ice-cold heart would melt. His mind returned to the first few days after prison when he had been in such turmoil. Touba had ruined it all. By telling him about Setareh, she had rendered him dysfunctional for nearly a month. He had felt ashamed, carrying on his back the sin of his uncle and the unwanted sin of his sister. He had later tried to keep his thoughts of sex distant from himself and his eternal wife. He remembered one night undressing Moones. This was not their custom, but this time, he had kissed his wife all over. He genuinely believed that if he wanted he could impregnate her, but all the time she kept covering her body with her hands and saying that it was a sin. Amidst his passion and desire and the idea that grew in his imagination that he had the power to impregnate her, he had patiently explained to Moones that they were married, and no matter what law she believed in, nothing and no one had the right to interfere in their freedom and privacy. But the woman was afraid of the big eyes of the angel—or the evil spirit—who had ruled her life for so long. Everything had to be done in darkness, all under the cover of the night. Love had no place in daylight. The affair had begun in sin and its fate was to go on in the same way.

Ismael soon learned to distance himself from Moones. It drove him crazy to have his heat frozen by this mountain of ice, so he assigned himself a schedule. He had been accustomed to spending a few hours of his free time around Moones, but now he changed tactics and stayed out late at night to make her worry. When he was next to her, he would steal his mind from her and travel as far away as he possibly could. He had a whole series of colorful imaginary events saved up for these times. He also carefully protected his friendships. He had no desire to lose any of his friends, so every day he was available to them. He did not get the kind of love from them that he missed, but there was at least the possibility of communication. As silent as he was beside Moones, he spoke freely when he was among his friends. They had learned to listen to him. Ismael tried to be the central focus of the group and attempted to unify its uncontrolled elements. He had many times managed to subdue their desire to argue among themselves. He was bothered by their need for conflict and animosity. They had all gotten used to blaming one another for everything that had happened. Ismael tried to acknowledge everyone's point of view. Undoubtedly, there was a middle ground where all could meet, only they did not try because each of them wanted to be in control. Ismael was constantly cooling heated tempers, trying to show them their common ground and bring their discussions back to that terrain. Sometimes he was able to lead them there; but at other times he was not, and the wheels of conflict turned.

After listening to Ismael's warnings about her decaying house, Touba had gone back to her room to worry about the wall. She could not stop thinking about it for even a minute. What would happen if the wall were to topple over? Everyone would be able to look into the yard—the yard that she had been able to guard so jealously through all the years. She had to do something. Whenever she got stuck she would think of Madam Amineh. The woman knew a great deal about the different aspects of building construction. She was now building a three-story house on Reza Shah Avenue. Touba knew that Madam Amineh herself was the overseer at the construction site: Each day, she wrapped her veil around her middle and cooked hearty amounts of potage for the workers to give them the strength to get the job done. Early one morning, Touba pulled her chador over her head and set out for Madam Amineh's building site. The whole way there she was thinking about how was she going to explain to Madam Amineh the need for a trustworthy laborer. She had to say only so much that it would not suggest the secret of the buried corpse, because Madam Amineh had done enough construction and gardening to be able to discover buried people under the earth. But she also had to make the woman understand her need for a very specific type of mason—a person who would keep secrets and talk very little; someone who combined the qualities of Mirza Abuzar, Master Geda Alishah, and Ismael. Of course, Touba might not find a mason who exactly reflected her desire. But perhaps it was possible to find one who was to her liking.

Once at Madam Amineh's home, she was surprised by what she found. The two women sat by the cooking pot and chatted. Madam Amineh complained about her children. They did not help their mother, leaving all the heavy work to her. Madam Amineh complained that God had made things difficult for her by not taking her husband. The man was constantly in bed. He still should have been very active, but the maximum energy he exerted was in going from one side of the room to the other. He now moved directly between the bed and his opium smoking equipment, expecting Madam Amineh to serve the food and drink, clean the place, wash the clothes, and build the new houses. The only thing to be grateful for was that he had retired from his civil service job with respect. Madam Amineh said that all her sisters had lost their husbands just at the right time. But in her case, she was stuck with him because she had such good luck in life. She laughed as she complained. In a contented tone of voice she said that she now believed life was hard, and she was destined to constantly revolve in a vicious circle, repeatedly building, sewing, knitting, cooking, and cursing. She said that in the early stages of her life she had thought that if she were to work very hard for a while, at some point the work would end and she would be able to sit by the window, start the samovar, and drink lots of tea. She would smoke lots of cigarettes and look out at the yard and flowers. She then brought her head close to Touba's ear to tell her that there had been a time when Madam Amineh, this miserable veiled one, had wished to go to Mazandaran and live there. Touba raised her head; she knew nothing about this. Madam Amineh shook her head in confirmation. She had traveled there. She desired to own a simple bungalow and a rice field. She said that at sunset the perfume from the rice fields drove one crazy. One could cook a pot of rice, eat it with dried fish, stretch out one's feet, and spend hours watching the movement of the wind through the rice paddies.

One of the workers came to Madam Amineh to get some money to go buy bread. Then Touba told her that she was worried about the bulging walls. She explained that it was likely they would fall down soon—that if not this year, then perhaps next year. If the walls were to crumble, the house would be lost. Capable and knowledgeable Madam Amineh saw that she had to do something for her ill-housed cousin. She asked if Touba had considered changing houses. After all, she, Moones, and Ismael could move to a new house, a house with a white ceramic washbasin and modern bathroom, in a better area of the city. There she would have better neighbors and none of the problems of the old house. Touba lifted her shoulder and eyebrows. She could not leave her house, she said; she wished to die there. Every event and thought in her life had occurred in that house, and she could not transfer all those good and bad memories anywhere else. She said that when she thought about the house, she remembered its hall full of people who had now died. The dead often surrounded her there, and she liked it. Her mother, for instance, who had died so quietly—perhaps Touba alone remembered to pray for her on Friday nights. If she were to change houses, the dead would loose their place and Touba would lose her memories. Was it possible to live without them?

Madam Amineh had the solution. The work must be taken care of by the efficient hands of Mahmood the mason. This man was hardworking and trustworthy. Better still, he had an important gift, that could no longer be found in anyone those days: He did not know that he was hardworking and trustworthy. He always underestimated his own work. He was a potter who drank from a broken pot. If Touba acted wisely, the work would go smoothly. She could leave everything in Mahmood's hands. But when he said he was done, she should not make it known to him that he had done a good job. If the man knew that his work had pleased her, he would then get excited and drink more. This was his only defect. Cousin Touba must once or twice a day criticize him and place the fear of God in him so that perhaps, she could make the man drink less—or at least, make him feel very guilty when he did drink. This way he would come to work earlier in the mornings and work harder to show that his drinking did not prevent him from working.

Madam Amineh called to Mahmood. He was a man of about forty-seven or forty-eight, yet he seemed older. The man came down from the scaffolding to stand in front of the women. He was holding his hat in his hands and folding it over and over. He was very shy. Madam Amineh said, "Mr. Mahmood, this is Madam Shams Ol-Moluk. She has some building work to be done." Mr. Mahmood, she made clear, must know he was not dealing with just anybody; this was a real lady, a princess, the pride of humanity. If you searched the whole city, you could not find one like her.

If he demonstrated talent and efficiency he would receive just payment, and he would always have some work taking care of at the lady's house in the future. Her house was a very good house because it had a strong foundation, and only needed some cosmetic work to take care of structural deficiencies. This would be a good job for Mr. Mahmood, who was a good man, an honest being—if only he weren't trapped by the poison of drinking. Everyone knew that every Friday he drank to excess. The man blushed red and twisted his hat even more. If only he could get rid of this blemish, then nothing would be wrong with him. Unfortunately, the bastard Satan would take him over and would not let this pure, God-fearing man, who would otherwise live a respectful life of one hundred and twenty years, stay free from drink and thus open the way to heaven for him. Mr. Mahmood smiled faintly, turning his eyes toward the construction site. Touba saw a strong will in the depth of the man's eyes, but on its journey through his bitter life, it had made poor decisions. Madam Amineh asked why Mr. Mahmood drank so much vodka, that evil liquor. "What," she asked, "is in this bitter brew that attracts you so much?" The mason did not wish to answer. He was the type of man who did not like to talk in the company of women. What could he do? He said life made him tired.

It was arranged that the man would come and see Touba's house, and Madam Amineh sent him back to his work. Mahmood, knowing that the women were watching him, walked away nervously. He wished to be away from their penetrating gaze. Touba liked this quality in him. He looked like the type who must definitely be able to keep secrets. Madam Amineh said Mahmood's wife had passed away. She might have had tuberculosis, from how he described the way she coughed and how blood would stain her handkerchief. Two boys and a girl were left behind for Mahmood to raise, and during the day and night they went largely without supervision. Madam Amineh wanted to find him a wife, but he was addicted to that poison. She had heard from the other workers that his drinking did not bother anyone. He did not even go to drink in public places. But he would regularly buy a half-bottle of vodka, take it home and nurse it all night, and then spend all of Friday in bed. This was a significant defect in his character.

Mahmood the mason came to see what needed to be done to Touba's house. Touba was not afraid of him. She could read into the depth of his character and knew that even if he were to discover the girl's body under the tree, he would not reveal it to anyone. He looks like Mirza Abuzar, she thought. If he had been in Mirza Abuzar's place, he would have done the same thing. And afterward he would start drinking. Probably Mirza Abuzar was also drinking every night, in Tabriz or somewhere else, in order to overcome the sorrow of the girl's death.

Mahmood spent a quarter of an hour in each of the cellars. As Touba showed him the decaying parts, he went forward and examined them closely, like a doctor taking the patient's pulse and counting carefully. Perhaps if he had a stethoscope he would place it on the heart of the bricks to understand their pain. They then went to look at the washbasin, and from there to see the three empty water reservoirs in the main courtyard. The reservoirs had stood useless since the city had laid water pipes. Touba suddenly found herself acting in accordance with Ismael's will. She consulted with the mason about the possibility of a Western washbasin being built somewhere in a corner. The mason examined the courtyard and the cellar washbasin carefully. He said yes it could be done. He said if the lady so desired, the cellar washbasin could be turned to a proper bathroom with a sink. Touba said no to the idea of a bathroom. The sink is enough; there was no need for a bathing area. Going to the public bath once a week was sufficient. If Ismael and Moones needed a bathroom, they could take care of it themselves. She would not allow them to build a bathroom in her house, but if they wished, they could borrow a portable bath from the same Westerners whose music they listened to so much, and whose movies they watched so often. They could get the folding kind to keep in the corner of their room, and whenever they wanted it they could open it up to wash themselves. She didn't know where she had picked up the idea of a folding bathroom. Perhaps from a picture she saw in one of Ismael's foreign-language magazines, of a man washing himself in a bath in the middle of the desert. Ismael had explained that there are portable baths that could be placed in houses and even inside cars.

Mahmood the mason inspected the roofs. He told the lady that the adobe on the roofs was in very poor condition. Mahmood believed that the roof over the pantry would fall in this coming winter. The walls were, in his opinion, in even worse condition. A lot of work was needed. Touba asked if Mahmood would take over and organize everything. He agreed to do so. He had two assistants who were very trustworthy. Though their business was concluded, he lingered because he wanted to say something more, and Touba asked him if there was anything else to discuss. He said that his older son went to school every day, but his other two children, Karim who was about three or four, and Maryam, who was about four or five, were without supervision at home. He had come straight from his village to the slum, to live in the home of a relative, and his wife had died there. Now the children ran loose there all day long. He asked if Madam Shams O-Maluk would permit him to bring his children with him so they could play in the yard while he worked. This was a house where he could have his children nearby. Touba agreed to let his children come over while he worked.

In a few days, Mahmood came with his two children. Ismael had not yet gone to work, and Moones was just getting ready to go to the bank. Mahmood's son was quiet and shy, his daughter sickly and thin. She was asleep in her father's arms, her hair all a mess. Ismael and Moones watched them from behind the window. Ismael opened the window to greet Mahmood, and asked about the children. The husband and wife looked at one another. If they had their own children the younger ones would be about the same age. The little girl woke and Moones took her to the room to give her a pastry. While the girl ate, she checked the child's hair carefully. The girl had lice, so

Moones told Mahmood that in the afternoon, when she returned from work, she would take the children to the public bath. Moones asked her mother if she had any mercury in the house. She wanted to kill the lice in the old-fashioned way. In the bank while working, she thought about how the children had no clean clothes to wear after their bath. During her lunch hour, she ran to a nearby store and bought some children's clothes. The children had very suddenly filled her every thought. They had come on their own two feet to open a new room in her life. It was not even necessary to consult with Master Geda Alishah. After she rubbed mercury on the children's heads she took them to the bathhouse and had the washerwomen scrub them thoroughly. The girl quietly tolerated the washing, but the boy cried loudly and incessantly, the soap burning his eyes. He slipped out of the washerwoman's hands and ran to the door, but finally, with great difficulty, both children were bathed.

In the afternoon, the children returned to the house, clean and wearing new clothes. Moones said she would keep the children for the night. Mahmood, embarrassed, explained that there was a third child also. He was older than the others, and quite a rascal. These two were very quiet. Moones told him to bring the third child and let her see him for herself. Mahmood thanked her, but said it was not possible to bring him until Thursday. The two children stayed in Ismael and Moones's room. Before dinner Ismael began reading his paper, at the same time watching the children, who sat silent in the corner of the room. They even kept their breathing low so as not bother Ismael or Moones, and the man's heart trembled for them. He remembered his own childhood: his first year after arriving in Tehran and his many painful experiences. Everything he had encountered here was new and unknown. It was peculiar how he had always been afraid of doing something wrong. "Children, come and look at this picture," he said. A drawing of Donald Duck covered a quarter-page of the newspaper. Ismael told them the duck's name, cut the picture out of the paper, and gave it to them. Moones found a couple of thumbtacks and pinned the picture to the wall. The two little ones stared at it for a long time. Moones gave them chewing gum and noticed that the boy swallowed it after biting on it just a few times. They laughed and slowly they warmed up to one another. At night Moones slept separate from Ismael, and put the children on either side of her. She didn't want them to be scared. If they ended up staying over the long term, she would need to sew them mattresses filled with down.

For the first fifteen days that the mason came and went, the children remained in the house even at night. During the days they hung around with Touba and at night they slept next to Moones. Touba asked them if they knew how to do their prayers. They did not, so she taught them how to pray. Maryam learned quickly, but Karim was still too young to do it properly. She had them stand behind her for prayers. The children followed shyly, and thus obtained their pass to the old woman's heart. The next day Touba went and purchased cloth to make Maryam a prayer chador. The girl loved her chador. Moones taught her to wrap it around her waist and make a long elegant skirt for herself. She also bought a doll for her and a toy car for Karim. The two held on to their toys everywhere they went.

The third child was difficult to handle. Kamal would not go to the bathhouse and would not accept that he had lice. When he was alone with his brother and sister he spat at them and said they were going to become servants of this Ismael and Moones. He tried to pull the toys out of their hands and break them. The children screamed, bringing Touba in. She pulled him off the two smaller children, and he stood in the corner of the yard and bore her scolding. Kamal was just eleven years old, but he had a sister and brother who had died before Maryam and Karim were born. He felt responsible for his younger brother and sister and could not tolerate anyone else taking his place, even though he mistreated them. He couldn't tell Touba this because he did not know the reasons behind his own behavior. He now suffered more than anyone else from his own dirty body and the lice, but because he had stubbornly refused their demands, he painfully put up with his own filth. When summer vacation arrived, his father told him that he must come and live in Touba's house; he could not spend the whole summer alone in the slum. He therefore spent three painful months under the eyes of Touba and the others in the house.

Initially, when they asked his name, he would not tell them. Mahmood had explained that Kamal was stubborn; he studied, but this was the one thing he did without trouble. Otherwise he did not demonstrate any positive qualities. During his time in the house, however, he began changing slowly, maturing unwittingly. He would flip through the pages of Ismael's magazines secretly, and struggle to read them. For the first time in his life he read something besides textbooks. When Ismael noticed Kamal liked reading, he bought the boy some books. Kamal would read the books and return them to Ismael, though most of them were stories and magazines especially for children. Ismael told Kamal that since he had become an honor student in school, his photograph would be published in one of these magazines. He took the boy to the photographer and had his picture taken, and two weeks later it indeed appeared in the magazine. The boy was incredibly moved by this. He spent a long time looking at his own photograph. He could not believe that he had become so famous in the world. A feeling was growing in him; it was love for Ismael. Yet it bothered him that Moones did not pay much attention to him. He spent a long time sitting in one of the cellars thinking. If he were to become an honor student every year, then his photograph would continue to be published in the magazine. He could become famous, but at the same time this Ismael would in a way become his master. Then he would have to do everything the man demanded. Ismael was already telling him not to bother his brother and sister, to go buy something from the store; scolding that if he did not go wash himself at the bathhouse, the lice would suck out all his blood. He finally decided to go and wash himself, but tried not to let them notice. Ismael and Moones pretended that they knew nothing about it, but Touba did not bother with such delicate matters, and after the boy returned from the bathhouse, the old woman had expressed approval. The boy hated Touba, and this only added to his grudge against her.

Although he was not aware of it, Kamal had become the central thought in Ismael's mind. Kamal did not know that Ismael believed the boy was a natural extension of himself. Ismael tried to give him what he himself had never had, but found he could not satisfy the boy. He thought it was because Kamal had never had a retarded mother, and therefore did not feel the burden of life's responsibility. When he noticed that the boy was sulking, he kept some distance. It was best to leave him alone until he came around on his own. Kamal was thus left alone with his thoughts, which were bent on not becoming the servant of this man and woman. His father's constant presence also bothered him enormously. The smile of acquiescence on his father's face was hateful to him. He could not stand it that his father kept saying, "Yes, Sir. Yes, Madam." The man was not a servant. He was working; he knew a trade; he was a mason. He was in fact a great mason, but he was always subordinating himself. Why?

The masonry work was completed at the beginning of autumn. Kamal was to return to school. The mason sadly moved his children back to the slum. It was agreed that he would bring them once a week to visit with the ladies. The house seemed so much more in order now. It had brightened up noticeably when Kamal white-washed the rooms. Ismael's mood had improved with the interior of the house. He could now wash up in the sink, though it had been a year since the city had laid water pipelines. The miserable dirt of the pool did not bother him anymore. The tadpoles could not reproduce as much as they desired. If he continued to work on the old woman, building a modern bathroom would also become possible. He had convinced her to permit electrical wiring in the house last winter. They were relieved of lanterns and kerosene lamps. Actually, Touba had accepted the need for electricity without argument. She was well aware of its importance. She lined up all her lamps in the cellar and covered them with a cloth. But as for the plumbing system, that would mean digging up the alley and the courtyard. This was not agreeable to her. What was wrong with the old-fashioned ways? The water in the house reservoir was perfectly clean. Ismael was talking nonsense, saying it smelled. On this topic she had become an object of ridicule among her daughters, son, and grandchildren, the subject of many family jokes. Not wishing for the jokes to go on, that summer she had finally agreed to upgrade the plumbing system. The water reservoir was now useless, all their water was emptied in order to prevent mold and swamping. Three water reservoirs went to sleep in the depths of the house. The woman felt sad, but she soon got used to piped water. She finally had to accept that the piped water was cleaner than the reservoir water. She was also relieved from buying drinking water everyday. There was no difference any longer between drinking water and water for washing up. The mason had significantly enhanced the house's appearance. A new feeling had blossomed in the house, a new kind of joy had bubbled from its depths. Children's laughter had filled the gray background tones of the house and the light's perfume had emanated from the wall colors. A kind of mental rainbow had covered the house. It was a good summer. At the end of the summer, when the children left the house, Touba was shocked at how much things immediately changed. All the color left the house. Although the children used to make noise in the afternoons and disturbed her afternoon naps, their existence there had kept fear out of the house. The bodies of the past had become distant, and the dead were not constantly around her. Often, without knowing it, she spent a whole week eagerly waiting for Friday, when she would see the children.

The second month of autumn came and went and Mahmood's comings and goings stopped. Moones was worried about the children. She talked to Ismael about her concerns. He, however, was preoccupied with commuting between home, office, and the local bar. He was busy. When the children were there he thought of them, but when they were not there it was as if they had never been. He was coiled deep in his habits to the extent that he could easily forget any new event. He was not as concerned about the children.

By midwinter the mason still had not visited, so one weekend morning the two women put on their chadors and headed for the slum. They took a taxi and got off on a very dusty road. The owner of a small shop directed them to an alley, and from there they stood looking over a open pit with holes dug in its walls. People went in and out of these cavelike places. The women asked around until they reached Mahmood the mason's house. His was not a cave but a mud hut with a window at the bottom of the slum area. Mahmood explained that for three months he had been lying there with his feet swollen. The neighbors provided the children's food but complained about having to do it. Kamal had been taking care of his younger brother and sister as best he could. The women cried for Mahmood, and he cried along with them. Touched by Mahmood's situation, they arranged to transfer the man and the children to their home. The cellar that the Turkish Aunt and then Ismael had lived in was now to become theirs. The more the mason expressed his gratitude, the more Kamal became upset.

When they were settled in the cellar, Kamal told his brother and sister that now this family, their hosts, would go to paradise because they were gracious and God was merciful. But their father, Mahmood, as was the case with their mother, would end up in hell because he had always been poor, and therefore God would not be merciful to him. The children's eyes closed in fear. Maryam's face drained of color. Kamal laughed. Did they really think their mother had gone to hell, or that their father would go as well? Why should they end up in hell? They had done nothing wrong. The more the boy thought about it, the more he could not understand why his family had suffered so much. His reasoning could not rise to this challenging question. When he had seen his photograph printed in the magazine he had thought for a moment that perhaps he was a wealthy boy and was meant to live in a palace, but did not know it. And when he returned to the slum and went back to school, he could no longer be satisfied with that life. Before going to Touba's house, he had known of no other place except the slum. In the only place known to him, he had tried to become greater and larger than anyone else. All the children in school and in the neighborhood followed him. After the miserable summer spent at Touba's home his thoughts changed. Along with his brother and sister, he had accompanied Ismael, Moones, and that old moody woman on visits to different homes. He had seen that children could have a room full of toys, wear patent leather shoes, always have new clothes and change their clothes, if dirty, after playing. After he had returned to the slum, the boy felt suffocated. When his friends fought with one another for one single sweet or a dead mouse, he felt hateful. They did not know better homes. He thought about this issue. He no longer liked to participate in their rough games. On the contrary, he wished to take them by the hand and show them these houses—show them that this was how life was supposed to be. But he did not wish to be like the children who lived in those houses, either. He wanted to grow up in such a manner that the house would itself come and invite him to live in it. He must perform important acts—acts that rendered all houses unimportant in comparison. All the children with their pretty clothes must bow in front of him and say how great he was. The boy was now less stubborn than he had been in the summer. Life was teaching him to take opportunities and use them to his benefit. Now that it was conceivable that he could live in a better place, he needed to do it. He had not asked to live there, but they had brought him. He could grow up as he wished and conquer the world without worrying about his brother and sister.

It was agreed that Maryam should sleep in Moones's room. Touba did not think it was appropriate for a girl to be in the same room with her brothers. Karim was to sleep in Touba's room, since he was little and needed attending to. That left Kamal and Mahmood the mason. No one was willing to take care of the older boy. In the mornings when he woke up, he would take a stale piece of bread and head out of the house. He felt embarrassed to join Touba or Moones and Ismael in their breakfast. On the first few days they invited him to come and eat with them, but he turned down their offers. They later decided to send something—pastry, bread and butter and jam sandwiches, hummus, or meat wrapped in bread—to the cellar as gifts. The child would not eat these things in the house. He did not want anyone to see him eating the presents. Instead, he usually ate them on the way to school.

School was very different in this part of the city. The children here were better groomed and they did not fight over dead mice. Kamal preferred to sit in the back of the class. When his back was to the wall, he felt safe. He did not make friends with anyone. His heart longed for his former friends, especially Ghadir, a boy about his own age who had weak eyes. Kamal often had to help him cross a stream or hop over a rock. The child could see far distances, but could not see near objects. When they were together, Kamal was Ghadir's eyes. Noticing the lady teacher's glasses, the glasses that

Ismael wore to read the newspapers, and the ones Touba always wore, he came to the conclusion that Ghadir needed glasses. He could not stop thinking about his friend's need for glasses. Friday mornings he would get up early to go to the slum to see his friends Ghadir and Akbar. The second one had good eyes and was also strong. He wanted to fight with everyone. He had fought and wrestled with all the kids. He was a natural leader, but Kamal still did all the thinking for the group. He and Akbar took turns being Ghadir's eyes, Kamal on Fridays and Akbar on other days. Now they both were trying to think of a way to get glasses for Ghadir.

One Friday morning, as Kamal was about to leave for the slum, he saw Ismael's glasses on a newspaper lying by the large window. He automatically reached out and picked them up. He didn't know that Touba was watching him from the window across the room. He slipped them into his pocket, and before Touba could open her window and say anything, he had run out of the house. Touba ran to the courtyard. Her movements were now those of an old woman. Her voice had grown thinner as well. She screamed, "Ismael, he took your glasses. I always knew that he was a thief." Ismael had just finished washing up by the sink and was drying himself, a towel around his neck. The old woman quickly reported everything she had seen. Ismael listened calmly. He then told Touba not to say anything about the matter. Most likely there was a reason the boy had taken the glasses. They must wait for him to tell his side of the story. The younger brother and sister heard all of this conversation. Maryam was filled with fear, though little Karim showed no sign that he understood the situation. Not getting any reaction from Ismael, Touba went to the cellar to tell the story to the mason. Mahmood, who had more difficulty walking each day, tried to get up and run after the boy. Touba told him not to bother. The boy would come back and the problem would eventually be cleared up. Ismael pressed his lips together angrily. He told Moones that he was losing his patience. Why wouldn't the old woman let others think for themselves? The glasses belonged to him. It was he who should decide what to do about them. He went to the mason to apologize. He tried to calm the man and asked him not to say anything to the boy. Mahmood began to cry. He insisted that the boy had never been a thief, and Ismael believed that this was true.

Kamal ran all the way to the slum. He found Ghadir sitting on the step by the door of his father's house looking at the wall in front of him. Without a word, he placed the glasses on Ghadir's face. Ghadir was shocked, and his first reaction was to take the glasses off. Kamal said his name and the boy recognized him. The glasses did not help him. He could see no better than before, although he liked the glasses. Kamal said, "They are yours, keep them." But they were too large for the boy's face and he looked like a clown.

Akbar arrived and asked Kamal if he had brought his sparrow. Kamal had trained a sparrow to tell fortunes by picking out of a box slips of paper that had writing on them. He had learned this from a homeless addict with whom he had spent some time working. He broke off small pieces of bread and placed them in the sparrow's cage along with a small bowl of water. In the afternoon, after school, he would take his bird to the street to make some money. It provided him with some pocket money to buy sweets. His friends liked the sparrow. One of their hopes had been to save up the money from the bird show and use it to buy Ghadir's glasses. Akbar said that the lady teacher's glasses were much thicker than these. Ghadir most probably needed thicker glasses. Akbar knew a man selling junk by the railroad yards who also sold some used glasses. They could go there and exchange Ismael's glasses for others that would make Ghadir see better. They started out for the man's junkyard. On the way, Akbar commented that someday he was going to become a great wrestler. Kamal had decided to go to university and learn about everything in the world. Ghadir did not yet know what he wanted; he could not see anything well enough to make a decision about it. He had been in the same class for two years and the teacher still did not understand his sight problem; she just shrugged her shoulders and left him in ignorance.

When they arrived at the junkyard, the old man readily agreed to exchange glasses. It made no difference to him to replace one pair of glasses with another. The kids sat around amid the junk. Akbar, as the leader of the project, placed one pair of glasses after another on Ghadir's face, to see which one would suit him.

After several pairs of glasses had been tried on Ghadir, a miracle occurred. The world suddenly lit up. Ghadir saw his friends' facial details clearly for the first time. He screamed, "I can see, I can see very well!" It was a magnificent moment. The boy had tears of joy in his eyes. Ghadir repeated many times that he could see, not believing at first that it was true. Then the friends began walking back toward home so that he could see everything. At that moment, their eternal bond of friendship was forged. Ghadir said that now he, like Kamal, would go and learn all the knowledge in the world. He wanted to become a maker of glasses or an eye doctor.

In the afternoon Kamal headed toward the house with a hungry stomach. He daydreamed all the way home. He dreamt of one day getting a house and taking Ghadir and Akbar there to live with him. He would also take his brother and sister and father there. They would all become very well-off. Kamal slipped quietly into the house and headed for the cellar to eat the leftovers of his father's lunch and calm his grumbling stomach. When he opened the door to the cellar, a nauseating stench greeted him. Mahmood had not been able to reach the bathroom and had messed himself. He said that if his dear child would help to clean him up before the ladies found out, God would open the seven gates of paradise to him. The child quickly began to help, silently cleaning his father, who was obviously a very, very ill man.

Indeed, Mahmood began to slowly rot away in isolation. The women could no longer take care of him. They had brought the doctor for him a few times, but there was little to be done to reverse Mahmood's decline. Ismael tried to help him on occasion, but the man would not accept it. Sometimes Kamal would clean him, all the time constantly cursing himself and his fate. He was angry with the world and poured it out onto his father. The solution was to eventually admit Mahmood to a hospital. Within just one month, his corpse was handed back to them. Ismael, Moones, and Kamal took the body to the cemetery. Touba stayed behind to take care of the children. As they spread the last shovel of earth over the grave, Mahmood was already becoming a distant memory.

On their way back, Kamal thought he should explain the incident of the glasses to Ismael. His sister had told him that Ismael knew all about the glasses anyway. But he didn't know how to begin. Ismael had never confronted him about it. Kamal had almost begun to talk about it a few times, but something always stopped him, and as they came closer to the house he had less of a desire to tell. He was curious to know how long Ismael would remain silent on the subject. He decided not to say anything until Ismael began the discussion.

From then on, time passed as if a dream. One child had found mother and father; another had a grandmother. The third had no master, but was left alone in an empty cellar with the memories of a father. Touba, Ismael, and Moones would have nothing to do with Kamal. The child had a sharp look in his eyes and he never gave them a straightforward answer. They simply left him alone. He had developed a habit of finding an excuse at mealtimes to visit either Touba's or Moones's kitchen and find himself something to eat. He always ate only so much that they would not complain. They knew this, but pretended not to know. He sometimes did small errands around the house. He would go shopping for Ismael or get a spool of thread for Moones. He would run through many streets to do this, but his help was irregular. On Fridays he would pick up his sparrow and go to the slum. Other days of the week, after school, he was in the local streets with his bird. He considered himself the owner of all of Ismael's old magazines, which accumulated in the corner of his cellar, and he would take a magazine along with him to read as he waited for customers. On Fridays he would give the magazines to Ghadir and Akbar. They would read the magazine and then together they would cut the pictures out of it, divide them between themselves, and use them to cover the walls of their rooms. Their walls were covered with the photographs of the shah and his wife, Lenin, Ava Gardner, Brigit Bardot, a Japanese woman holding her fan, Vajanti Mala, Raj Kapoor, Narges, Jack Palance, Victor Mature, Anthony Quinn and Gina Lollabrigida in the film *The Hunchback of Notre Dame*, and most of all, Fidel Castro. The latter was getting to be very famous. He was a strange man, strong and handsome in a rugged way. Akbar would look at him for long periods of time. He wanted to grow a beard like Fidel's when he was older.

Akbar had found himself a canvas bag, filled it with sand, and hung it on a rope from the ceiling to use as his boxing bag. Kamal wanted to find himself a similar bag. They went to see the junk man again and bought a bag with a hole in it. They patched the hole with some difficulty, then brought the bag to Touba's house. They wanted to fill the sack with sand right there in the cellar to make their job easier. They dug up loose dirt along the cellar wall, careful that the old woman did not see them. They filled the sack and hung it from the ceiling. This activity made them hungry, so Kamal, as usual, sneaked into the kitchen and brought back some bread. Akbar stood by the window looking at the courtyard. This house did not look in any way like the houses in the movies that he, Ghadir, and Kamal went to see in the back street cinemas. Ghadir commented that this was an old house.

Karim had come down the stairs to the pool to do his ablutions before prayer. Turning around, he saw his brother in the cellar. He stood quietly by the window and watched his brother's guests. Akbar asked who the boy was and Kamal said that it was his brother. He was eight years old, and in second grade. Kamal found himself shocked by his own words. The day they came to this house, the boy had been only four. He now went to school and always prayed following the old woman, although prayers were not required for him by their own tradition. He prayed in order to see the shining light of approval in the old woman's eyes. Maryam saw her brother from her godparent's window and curiosity brought her out to the courtyard. She approached the cellar window and shyly watched her older brother and his guests. Kamal said that this was his sister Maryam and Akbar's heart began to beat faster. The nine- or ten-year-old girl with braided hair, wearing clean clothes and a faint smile stood looking at them. Kamal opened the door and told his brother and sister to come in. The children entered shyly. Kamal went to the boxing sack and threw a few punches at it, then told Karim that when he was older he could also come and practice his boxing. Akbar said Maryam could also practice, because these days girls also needed to know how to do it. He had seen a woman boxer in a film and liked the idea. The girl stared at the boxing sack.

Ghadir said again that it was truly an old house. The walls were beginning to bulge again after just four years. Kamal said it was only worth throwing some gasoline on and setting fire to, along with the stuffy, grumbling old woman. Karim's heart stopped at such talk. The old woman was very good. She had always fed him. Why should she be set on fire? Maryam also didn't know why the old woman should be burned. Kamal knew, but would not say any more. Akbar knew also, but he too was silent. Ghadir didn't know much about the old woman. He had spent half his time without eyes and had no relationship with any old women. He shrugged his shoulders indifferently. Kamal suddenly said, "Great, a celebration of burning old women." The two older boys laughed together joyfully, and the other three listened quietly. Then they heard Touba muttering. There was some earth spilled in the yard again. The old woman followed the trail of soil to the cellar. Kamal told Akbar and Ghadir to stand against the cellar wall to hide from her. But since the old woman considered the cellar part of her house, she entered to ask Kamal who had permitted him to spill earth in the yard, and who was supposed to sweep it clean. She saw the two fifteen-year-old boys standing by the wall, and asked who they were. Kamal said they were his friends from school and had come to see his brother and sister. The old woman remarked, "Do they think the house is an inn, where everyone can come and go whenever they feel like it?" She took Karim and Maryam by the hand and left the room, saying, "These friends had better leave right away."

Touba took the two children out to her room and sat them down on the floor. Her eyes were bulging with rage, frightening the children. She told them to watch out and not to spend time with their brother's friends. She didn't trust these boys that he hung around with and wondered where they got their money. She focused her eyes on Maryam. A good girl should know better than to talk with just any boy. If she did, she might fall in a well and never be able to get out. The children must keep their distance from their brother. She said that when God wishes to punish someone, he places a collar on his neck. God allows the disobedient person to dangle in space, doing anything and going anywhere and seeing anyone he wishes. Because, in essence, humans are sinners. The human on whom God has placed the collar will collect nothing but sin, and one day he will have a mountain of sin on his back. He will be crushed by it, become dust under this load, but do you think he can ever free himself from it? No, never. Every cell under the load screams, cries, but regrettably, there is no going back. The person will remain burdened until judgment day, and his cries of regret and pain will continue even after that from the bowels of hell.

Maryam began to cry. She felt sorry for her brother, she didn't know how to save him. That night she cried in Moones's arms. She said her brother's sins would soon add up to a mountain. Moones laughed. She didn't think her mother's words were right. She said God was not so cruel to put a collar on one's neck. Maryam should not worry. There was always a way out, always an angel to save a person. After the girl went to sleep, Moones asked Ismael if anything could be done for Kamal. Ismael said he was not worried about the boy. He said that Kamal seemed to be forming an autonomous life for himself. In his opinion, the boy had an independent personality, which was not necessarily bad. It was just unfortunate that he hid his real personality from the members of the family, and showed only the part that was not pleasant.

Kamal was embarrassed and very angry that the old woman had thrown his friends out. He accompanied Akbar and Ghadir halfway along the road. He swore that someday he would finally kill the woman. The boys told him that it didn't matter; the woman was old, and like all old people, she had become stupid. Ghadir said that his grandfather was constantly grumbling also. Their shack belonged to him, and he always complained that his son and daughter in-law and their children had not gone to find themselves another place to live. Akbar's father was a water bearer in summer and in the winter he sold baked beets. Akbar said that his father was driving him crazy to come and help with the beet-selling in the winters. Kamal said they could all three go get a room together, but first they would need a little money. Kamal explained that he had decided to go find a job in a bicycle shop after school. He could pay for the rent and the other two could get some money together to buy food. They placed their hands on top of one another in the fashion of the soccer teams at school, and made a pledge.

Kamal returned home and, still angry, threw a few punches at the boxing bag. Tonight he would a guest in Moones's kitchen and tomorrow he would go looking for that job. As he turned toward the door, he was surprised to see Ismael there. The man entered the room smiling. He had not seen the cellar in a long time. He asked if Kamal knew that he, Ismael, had spent all of his childhood in this cellar. He automatically went and sat down where he had always sat as a child. He said that his mother was also sick for a long time before her death, just like Kamal's father. He too had been obliged to take care of a parent at a young age. Kamal thought he was lying. He was a respected gentleman; he had a necktie and his shirts were always shining white and his polished shoes never showed a particle of dust. He could not have lived in this cellar. Ismael was saying that perhaps they could do some fun activities together, and have some talks. Ismael thought he had a lot of things to tell Kamal. All his life he had wished to do important things, but the opportunity had never come along. He was not an important or great person, and indeed on the grand scale of things he was very insignificant. But if Kamal would like to have a friend like him, Ismael would be very happy. Kamal kept staring at the wall in front of him.

Ismael opened a magazine he had in his hand and showed Kamal the picture of an old man. He said that today he had remembered something about the old man that might be of interest to Kamal. He said that one day in the year 1919, the conquerors of the First World War had gathered at the Palace of Versailles to divide the world among themselves. This old man, who at the time was a boy of eighteen or nineteen, had gotten on a bicycle and peddled from Paris to Versailles and approached the guards at the palace to request an audience with the head of the conference. The guard tried to explain that such a visit was impossible, but the youth was determined and pressed to see the chief. Finally, someone from the administration staff came to ask what he wanted. The young man introduced himself and said that he was a citizen of Anam and had heard that they were going to divide his country. He therefore had come to warn all the conference participants that they had no right to do such a thing, and that he would not permit it. Probably the administrator had laughed at him. Ismael held the magazine in front of Kamal, poked the photo with his fingertip, and said, "Kamal, this man later on adopted the pseudonym Ho Chi Minh in order to remain unknown and led the Vietnamese Liberation Front against France, driving out his country's colonizers."

Ismael got up, smiling. He said that in the afternoon of the next day they could go to a cafe and talk a little, if Kamal would like that. Kamal said that tomorrow afternoon he needed to work in the bicycle repair shop. Ismael then suggested they go on Friday. Kamal said that on Friday he must see his friends. Ismael asked, "When would be a good time, then?" Without hesitation, Kamal replied, "When this house burns down." Ismael was shocked and asked why the house should catch fire. The boy said, "Because it is very old, it has a stale smell, and it is full of corpses." Ismael sat down where he stood, on one of the steps to the cellar. He didn't wish to sit there; his trousers would get dirty. But he had to sit down. He said, "I can't see how burning down the house would do any good. It of course is not a good house. It is old, but burning it is not an easy job. Besides, what then? The house would just be gone. Do you have a plan to build something in place of the house, Kamal?"

Kamal shrugged his shoulders angrily and said, "That isn't important at all. Something will crop up. After the house has burned and turned to ashes, clean and even land will remain. Then I could think about what should be built in its place." Ismael smiled bitterly. He said, "I don't think that a piece of clean and even land will be left because this earth is full of corpses, and each corpse has enough memory to speak volumes about the world left behind. These memories, good or bad, joined people together. These people had to hide their knowledge of one another deep in their hearts a stranger could come to excavate the earth and stumble upon their secrets . . . their treasures, or something else."

Kamal thought all this was nonsense. The man had become a respected gentleman and he wanted to remain one. He was not free. He was not liberated. He blabbered nonsense. He had a bunch of big-sounding words and sentences, which made sense to him alone. Ismael interrupted his thoughts. He asked if Kamal knew the grumbling old woman had once wanted to seek God. Kamal asked with surprise, "God?" Ismael nodded his head. Kamal asked, "Does God even exist, that she would go after him?" Ismael shrugged his shoulders and said, "She says God exists."

Ismael stood up and left the cellar without another word. He was now aware that for all these years he had been a little bit afraid of Kamal. The boy stored within himself a power like that of a very great waterfall, and it poured forth fearlessly. It was as frightening and noisy as spring thunderstorms. Ismael wondered how he was going to be able to channel the energy of this spring into a dry summer, to calm it. Touba had recently mentioned that it was time to find Kamal a wife. In the old days, the solution for one who was too free-willed was to find him a wife. It was assumed that marriage would calm him down after a while. But where would they find a wife for Kamal? It was not even clear that this was what the boy wanted. He was far too independent. Ismael decided he needed to consult with his friends about Kamal, to find strategies that might help to straighten out this bright but unruly youth.

Kamal went to the bicycle repair shop. He said he would like to work and he was willing to do anything. Fixing a flat tire on a bicycle, the owner looked up at Kamal and told him that the muscle in those arms would have better use in an automobile repair shop. But he agreed to let Kamal start the next day. Kamal left the shop, but before going home, he stopped at the automobile repair shop a hundred yards down the street. He asked if he could be of use in repairing cars. The owner looked at him from behind his glasses. He cleaned his forehead with the back of his oily hands and said, "Yes, you could be, if you have stamina." Kamal said he did. The owner said he could start right away. He had Kamal stand on a large truck tire so that he could free the inner tubes from the ring with a long crowbar. Meanwhile, he asked why Kamal wanted to work. Kamal replied that he needed money to rent a room with his friends. The owner moved the crowbar up and down around the ring. If a small, dark, smoky room in a garage were available, he asked, would Kamal and his friends be able to use it? Kamal's heart beat fast with joy. Of course it would be useful, he said.

At day's end, after giving Kamal twenty tuman as an advance and the promise of a job, the garage owner showed him the room and said he was looking for someone who would live in the room and keep an eye on the garage at night. He felt deep down that Kamal was a hardworking boy, but he expressed concern about his friends. Kamal swore that his friends could also be trusted. The owner said it didn't matter, because if any living thing were to cause him a problem, he was powerful enough to make that thing run for the rest of its life. Then he laughed. He said that when Kamal proved himself to be capable and had been at the job long enough, then he could whitewash or paint the room and fix it up any way he liked. The bathroom was at the other end of the garage, and a little cooking could be done under the stairway that connected the room to the garage. They would just need to buy a small stove and a couple of pots and pans. The owner was very happy that he had happened upon such a helpful and trustworthy fellow. He said that a man must organize his own life slowly, piece by piece. It was not good to expect others to do it for you. He slapped Kamal on his back so hard that electric shocks went through the boy's body. But he didn't feel at all upset. On the contrary, he was coming to like the mechanic very much. The man was what he had needed all his life. This was not the agreeable father who bowed to every insult and only smiled; whose drinking habits were not manly at all, but more like a dog who licked leftovers from the ground; who once in a while cried and forever had a dumbfounded or sad look on his face, which made one think of one's obligations. This man in front of him was a man.

Though he was tired, Kamal went straight to see Akbar and Ghadir. He told them that tomorrow afternoon, if they could, they must come to the garage to let the garage owner have a look at them. Returning home, depending on the twenty tuman, he took a taxi and fell into such a deep sleep that the driver had to poke him several times to wake him.

In the morning, before going to school, he brought his brother and sister to the cellar. He sat them down in the middle of the room and he knelt in front of them. The children looked at him in silence. He said that he must leave, that he had found a job and a room. He revealed that he planned little by little to save for a house, and when he had one, to send for them. The children must know that they did not belong to this house and that Touba was not their master, nor was Ismael or Moones. They had simply had bad luck. They did not have parents and therefore they must live here for now. But they need not worry; as long as Kamal was around, they had nothing to fear. He promised to take them to the movies someday when he was rich, to buy them beautiful clothes and provide them with the most beautiful house. But until then, they must put up with the old woman's complaints and be at Ismael's and Moones's mercy and charity. Maryam commented that they were good people. She said she was certain they loved her. Kamal shook his head vehemently and said that no, they did not love Maryam; they tolerated her because they could not have their own children. They would, he said, kick the children out in a moment if they had children of their own. If they had children, they would never have taken her in to begin with. Now they showed off Maryam in front of people as a way of saying, "See, we also have a child." This was not true love. Did they ever tell people that Maryam's father was a sick alcoholic mason? No, they would never say that. But Maryam must not forget that these were the very people who had killed her father. They could have brought him to a doctor earlier, couldn't they? And why should their mother die of tuberculosis—had a doctor ever examined her? Their father had only been able to carry her on his back to a hospital along with the three children, to keep her there for one week. Kamal said they were young and did not yet understand everything. For example, the doctor had said that their mother's problem originated from poor nutrition. At the time Kamal himself had not known what poor nutrition was. Did the children know now what it meant? The children didn't know. Kamal told them it meant hunger, constant hunger, and he hit the floor with his fist. Karim jumped from his seat. He was afraid of his brother. He didn't like him. He also had memories of the mother Karim was describing. The old woman had always given him food. He did not know the meaning of hunger.

Karim asked, "Why does the old woman keep me if she does not like me?" The old woman didn't need to show him off as her child, he said since she had her own children and grandchildren. Kamal was dumbfounded; he didn't have a ready answer to this. Then, he suddenly remembered the words of his history teacher and retorted, "The old woman is like Hassan Sabbah, who lived in the eleventh century. This Hassan Sabbah asked only to be given a cowhide, and to be allowed to take whatever he could surround with the hide. This wish was granted by his benefactor. But Hassan Sabbah did not place it over anything right away; instead, he pounded the hide to stretch it very thin and then cut the hide to make a long rope. He took the rope and wrapped it around the Alamut Castle." In a similar way, Touba was using her love in a calculating way, to draw a rope around Karim or anyone else she could.

From the yard, Ismael and Moones were calling for the children. It was getting past the time when they needed to leave for school. Kamal quickly told them that he would come in the afternoon to take his personal belongings. He advised them not say anything to the old woman or Ismael or Moones. In the future, when everything was organized, he would return to rescue the children from this sorrowful house. He told them that in his opinion the house was doomed, and that the old witch would someday eat them up.

Karim shrugged his shoulders slowly. He loved the old woman. She fed him, and his pocket was always full of sweet bread. He was even given two rials per day, and if he helped with the construction work, he earned five rials. Touba was forced to do her own masonry since Mahmood's death. She ocassionally patched the roof with adobe or filled the cracks in the pool with cement, and Karim was her assistant. Together they safeguarded the house from collapse. They got along well. The old woman praised Karim in front of anyone who came to her house. She remarked in amazement how interesting it was that all people are born with their innate characteristics. It was not required for a boy to pray until fifteen, but this boy began praying at five years old. This is how God lights up the hearts of his select beings. The boy was filled with joy, and the old woman was truly proud of him. He felt as if he was a gift that God had sent to her. It seemed to Touba that Karim embodied the spirit of the innocent boy who, on that street so long ago, had cried with hunger and

died right there, only to be buried in a seated position. That boy had
now returned to spread justice and equity through the world. When
the old woman looked at him, Karim felt he was big. Although he
was in fact small in stature, she made him feel larger than his years,
and made him believe that he must someday become as large as the
whole world. They often went together to the shrine of Shahabdol
Azim, and Touba had promised that if he became the top student in
his class, next year they would go to Mashad. Perhaps someday
Touba would take him to Master Geda Alishah, and perhaps he
would someday become the greatest orator of the city. She told him
there had once been a great man who had been the greatest orator.
He was Mr. Khiabani. People said incorrect things about him,
spread nonsense that he had been a servant of the British or the Russians, but it was just that people had loose tongues. Karim should
know that all the rumors were false. Mr. Khiabani had been a great
man; he was like light. Karim must become like him—or, if he did
not like it that way, he could become like Master Geda Alishah.

One day she finally took Karim to the Master. Karim saw a very
old man who in his aged state looked like a chicken. Being that it
was the end of autumn, he was sitting beside a heater with a blanket
over his lap. Some of his students were also sitting around the heater
with him, but one side of the heater was left unoccupied so the rest
of the followers sitting by the walls could see him. Women sat on
one side and men on the other. Touba said, "Your Excellency, this is
the boy I mentioned to you." The Master looked at Karim penetrat-
ingly, but with a smile, and Karim dared to lift his head for a
moment and stare into the Master's eyes. Emanating from them was
a strange aura that confused and bothered Karim. Later, much later,
when he had grown up, it seemed to him that the aura had spoken
to him, and it had said, "Of course he is a good boy, but this is not
the one I want."

It was clear even then to the young boy that they had not connected. The Master did not look at Karim, and Karim spent the rest
of the time looking out the window and thinking, Mr. Khiabani
must have been a more important person. This old man seemed to
be hiding something. Kamal sometimes had this same look when he

talked to the two children, as though Kamal was this old man's grandchild.

Karim would still listen politely to the old woman talking about the Master. And he confided in her as well. He told Touba that he did not like Kamal, that Kamal planned to set the house on fire. The woman felt cold sweat break out on her body. When she found out that Kamal was leaving her house for good, she felt relieved. She wanted to change the locks on the door. The boy did not have keys, of course; she had never given him a key. But what if Ismael, out of carelessness, had given him a key at some point during the last few years? She spent a long time explaining the importance of this matter to Ismael, but he did not pay much attention to the old woman's disturbed imagination. Of course he was afraid of Kamal, but not to the extent that he would deem it necessary to change the locks. He had indirectly discovered that Kamal had needed his glasses for a friend. He told the old woman that instead of being afraid of Kamal, she should try to understand him. The boy needed love. He was full of hatred, and they must transform his hatred. The old woman remained afraid.

Maryam continued to live with Moones. She had heard from Moones that Geda Alishah's breath had the power to heal. Every breath that the Master took was synchronized with the breath of the cosmos. If, God forbid, the Master were to die one day, the wheel of the cosmos would stop turning. For this reason, even if he died, his spirit would still inhabit the world. Maryam asked what it meant to have this kind of synchronized breath? Moones explained that the whole world was alive and breathed. As the world breathed, it went through contractions and expansions. A mystic breathed with the world, adapting his breath to the world's breathing; no one could do this perfectly except Master Geda Alishah, who was one with the world. Whether he was a youth or an old man, whether he appeared alive or dead, all was in unison with him. For this reason, the mystic was neither angry nor at peace, neither in love nor in hate. His status was above all these things. He was indifferent toward humanity without being disconnected from it. He let the people's anger, pain, hate, and love collide with the rock of his being. He let everyone pour themselves out like bowls of water into the ocean of his being. He helped people in this manner in order to let them know they were at one with the ocean. Since Maryam was a wise girl, she could work on the path of purity and sincerity, pass through the seven cities of love, and, like the birds in the classic poem "Conference of the Birds" she could reach the peak of Mount Caucasus and from there watch herself in the preexistent mirror. She could come to understand the meaning of unity and synchronize her breathing with the breath of the world, just as the Master had. Maryam could become as great a mystic as Rabieh. She might one day sit with men and with great wise sheiks of mysticism. But if she became attached to appearances, she would be doomed. She would fall into the trembling bowl of material life, and the secrets of this world and the next would remain unknown to her. The young girl did not understand many of Moones's words, but she understood that the woman was opening a doorway to her. She was standing at the threshold and was looking beyond, into a thick fog. She didn't have the courage to cross the threshold, but knew that there was something desirable on the other side.

Ismael was annoyed by these discussions between Moones and Maryam. The mind of a child is a clean slate, impressionable, susceptible to any design. They must go easy on her. There was nothing scary in this world. When Moones was not there, he seated the girl on his lap and they talked together. She was told the story of a little girl named Alice. This Alice once passed through a mirror and on the other side of it she reached a world that did not exist on this earth. The girl listened to him in total amazement. Ismael also explained to her that Alice had strange dreams, like any other child, but life was the very thing that was around them. He told her that a single leaf is as interesting as the wonderful world of Alice on the other side of the mirror. A leaf had such extensive secrets in it that even if Maryam were to spend her whole life studying it, that would still not be enough. Maryam must study, become a doctor or an engineer and cure people's pains or build them houses. She must try to become an inventor and become one of the world's famous scientists. All the miseries of the world were curable by knowledge.

Maryam must not be afraid of knowledge. Even if she were to become a mystic like Geda Alishah, as Moones wished, she must first become educated. Education was a tool that Maryam could use to investigate all the mysteries in the world. Before Maryam tried to synchronize her breathing with the world, she had better look at the leaf of a willow tree, or study the pomegranate tree that every spring blossomed beautifully in their own yard. How many colors could Maryam find in the pomegranate's tree trunk? The girl said she saw brown. He told her that if she looked hard, perhaps she could see the waves of yellow, green, and even other colors, which when they combined formed the brown color of the tree trunk. Maryam could learn all this through education. Knowledge traversed all boundaries. It spread freely in the world and among the people. Human beings leaned on their own kind. One must learn different languages. Every language a person learned brought one closer to truth. Instead of one person, she could become two or three people. She could talk with all the people of the world. Ismael read her books and told her good stories. They also went to the movies, once a week, on the same day that Moones went to see the Master. They saw many movies, such as *The Shepherd Girl, Yasami, Zoro Brothers, Gone With the Wind, The Hunchback of Notre Dame, High Noon,* and *Three Coins in the Fountain.* They usually walked home after the movies, and all along the way Ismael informed her about the directors and producers of the film, or the country where it had been made.

At home, the old woman told Maryam that a good girl always listens to her father and mother. She was now considered Moones's and Ismael's daughter. But her brother Karim was Touba's son, and the other, Kamal, was an orphan. The young girl did not understand these distinctions very clearly. She did notice that Ismael had changed a little. For the girl's sake, he now came home earlier. The child was the image of his lost dreams. Since she was very smart and quick in learning and reciting facts, he felt he could make a scientist out of her, or even a great revolutionary leader. As he shaved, Ismael looked at himself in the mirror. He now had wrinkles around his eyes and bags under them because of his drinking. His hair had thinned out, too. He said to himself, "You look like one of the conservatives."

Touba was in the yard again, spreading fertilizer into the flower pots as stubbornly as before and therefore dirtying the pool water. The house walls were noticeably bulging again. Ismael thought perhaps Kamal was right. Nothing could be done to save the house. It seemed as though it was decaying at its foundations. How could he tell this to the girl? He must tell her, "Maryam, the house is rotten from the foundation up, but it must not be set on fire. It must be rebuilt." But how could they rebuild it? The old woman held the house between her multiple arms like an octopus. And she would not let them leave to build their own house. A brave man would take a pickax to it, but then all his books, his memories of Maryam and Moones's loving care, would get buried under its ruins. Later on, he would have to explain to Maryam that Setareh was asleep under the branches of the pomegranate tree. They would need to have a long talk. But there was no need for such talk now. Whether people knew or did not know, the girl's spirit, and her body under tons of earth, rotated around the sun along with the rest of the planet. This being the case, Ismael realized he had to begin the complex process of fixing the house. The bright young girl, Maryam, transferred her heat and energy to him unconsciously. Together they must draw up a plan. He did not know that Touba was secretly watching him.

For the old woman, the relationship between the girl and her adoptive father was unusual, and not in a positive way. The man could not have a child by his own wife, so he was raising the girl in order to marry her and have a child with her. Poor Moones! Her daughter was servant to Ismael's inner demon. Initially he had caused Moones's sterility, which had led her away from the natural course of life. Now he was getting ready to take a new wife in a few years' time. Moones, Touba thought, was nurturing a snake in her sleeve that would soon be the ruin of her nest. Maryam was not guilty, of course; she had not yet reached the age of understanding. But why did she not understand? In the old days, by the time girls reached nine years old, they knew everything. She was about twelve or thirteen now, so how could she not know? She most certainly had feelings for her adoptive father. He would often take the girl to his own room. Apprehensive about the relationship, Touba tried to create distance between Maryam and Ismael. Ismael could not be permitted to leave her house. The house needed a man. But he must be sure never to overstep his bounds. Touba began telling Maryam to perform her prayers. The girl was uncertain what to do. Moones performed her prayers regularly, but never demanded it of Maryam. Ismael did not pray, and each time the subject came up he said nothing but smiled sarcastically. The old woman said a girl must watch out that God does not put the collar on her neck. She said prayer was a protective shield. When one was inside it, one felt safe, and one became superhuman, beyond the reach of all temptation. Maryam should know that men—all men, without exception—had their eyes set on women and girls. It made no difference to them who the girl or woman was. It was enough for a girl to make a noise in one room for the man in the other room to imagine that the girl had made the noise for him. It was in men's nature to watch women. And it was Touba's duty to look out for Maryam and help her stay away from them. Maryam should know that many girls have caused problems and complicated their lives because of youthful emotions, ignorance, and innocence. All prostitutes had once been innocent girls who unwittingly and unknowingly became servants of their immature emotions. Prayer was like an armor, which would protect one from Satan's temptations. The Prophet had specified that even a brother and sister must not sleep in the same room. Maryam must try not to go to her parents' room too often. She must try never to be alone with her adoptive father. The child blushed with shame. She slowly learned to keep her distance from Ismael, and the old woman joyfully observed this change in her behavior. It would be a good idea if Maryam followed in the footsteps of her younger brother. Karim was superhuman. Praying from the age of five had made a holy being of him. No one was able to cheat him or defeat him because he had faith.

She took the girl to hear religious sermons a few times. Maryam was afraid of the things they said. The world was full of invisible snakes and dragons. Passersby must proceed carefully, to step among the snakes with caution so they would not be bitten. The road of life, she learned, was full of danger and evil. The girl became very scared. She didn't know where to turn for protection. Moones was not preoccupied with such thoughts. She said God makes a super-human of you, and it does not matter how you reach him. One could find God in a church, mosque, synagogue, or temple. These were all manifestations of the same thing. Moones simply urged Maryam to strengthen her faith. Meanwhile Ismael, coaching her on earthly life, urged her to try to stand on her own two feet. It was not the era in which men would come asking for her hand. A woman needed to study and work. If Maryam could become a doctor that would be very good. She could serve humanity, have a good income, and marry an educated man like himself. This would be an ideal life. Moones smiled kindly at Maryam and told her that when she had gone to the slum to visit Maryam's father, she had seen scenes of desperate poverty. Maryam was to be grateful to be free of poverty, but she must do something for the rest who were left behind. She must definitely become a doctor.

Manzar O-Saltaneh was disappointed that the city had grown so large, and people so very busy that they saw each only infrequently. She decided to provide the occasion for them to see one another every so often by hosting large picnic parties. The large family was scattered all over. Once upon a time, everything had been in its place. Everyone knew their limits and no one crossed anyone else's boundary. Now, whenever she went shopping downtown, she could not believe that this was the same city she had grown up in. She could not recognize anyone. It wasn't clear where all these people had come from. Everyone spoke with a different dialect. It was clear that all of Iran was gathered here in Tehran. The country had developed a huge head that was out of proportion with the rest of its body. The head wobbled over the body uncomfortably. Ismael had explained that urbanization was a disease of Third World countries, but since she did not trust Ismael's ideas, she had not given much thought to his words. Still, she truly could not recognize the city.

Fortunately, the telephone connected her to friends and family so that she could inquire after their well-being and exchange news, but she felt she must do something more effective. She had suggested gathering at a hotel once a month. This way, everyone could contribute to the cost of getting together, and no one need bear the burden of providing the space. This proved a difficult plan to implement. The old religious woman did not want to go to a hotel, and the hotel management did not admit women wearing chadors. Without the old woman, you could not claim that all the family and relatives were gathered together. But no one had a large enough house to invite everyone at once. Another solution was a picnic. Each family could bring their own food. Manzar O-Saltaneh paid to rent an entire garden and organized the whole thing. Everyone accepted the invitation, but they could not figure out how to transport themselves there together. The roads going out of town were full of traffic on Fridays. One family member came from the east of the city and another relative from the west, another from the north and the fourth from the south. At last, all the arrangements were made, and everyone was excited about the event.

Ismael, however, had no patience for the picnic. He had never been able to find a way of comfortably mixing with his wife's family. They were always cautious with him. They were polite, but did not consider him one of their own. Their standoffishness only increased after Ismael and Moones adopted the children. The relatives did not consider it respectful to kiss children who were not of their blood. This being the attitude about them, Ismael, Moones, and the children had learned to worry only about their own lives and keep a cold and distanced connection with the rest of the family. In fact, their small family was a misfit everywhere. Ismael knew that if the children were to return to the slum, they would be strangers there. The slum's community did not accept them as their own any longer, either. If he himself returned to Tabriz, he would probably not recognize anything. His fate was decided by the times, and what Ismael most believed in was science and knowledge. From this perspective, he was related to the whole world. Art gave him refuge, as well. He loved the world-renowned Beethoven and consulted with Mozart. His personal friend was Tolstoy, and his other friend translated Hemingway. He listened to Henry Massignon about Halaj, and from Goethe he learned about Hafez. The friendly, worldly family of art always welcomed him. The family of scientists also kept their doors open to him. Ismael shrugged his shoulders in response to his conservative in-laws' cautious manners. He knew that many of the older women among the relatives considered him impure. After he left their homes, they always rinsed the teacups. But he didn't care. These old women were dying out, just as the old woman of their own home was nearing the end of her days.

Ismael remembered his childhood and the amazing enormity of Touba. How they had all respected her and feared her! The old woman was now a wizened being, bent over with a dust bin and little shovel, spreading fertilizer among flower pots. She had swallowed all his youth's energy. But not to fear, he still had enough energy to wait until she died. Besides, he had Maryam. He knew that Touba and Moones, at least, considered him one of themselves. But deep down, and in the end of every calculation, his greatest joy was to count the child as his own. Maryam was the reward for his life.

On the way to the family picnic, the girl sat between Ismael and Moones in the car, with the old woman and Karim in the back. They inched toward the gathering amid a flood of traffic. When they arrived at last, they had to search a long time for a parking place. Two large pans full of food, some blankets, and other materials then needed to be carried to the garden. The hot summer had them sweating. By the time they reached the garden's gate, Ismael said he wanted to take a hike with Maryam, over the mountain that lay before them. He said if they got involved in greetings they would never be able to get away to go on their hike. They could spend a couple of hours hiking, and be back by lunchtime. Moones said she did not mind if the two went off together for a while, but Touba voiced her disapproval. This was a family picnic, and they had come to visit their relatives. They had not come to go mountain climbing. Ismael was always the loner. He pulled away from everyone—and this, of course, caused rumors and discussions. Why could he not try to be like other men? Ismael did not wait to hear any more of the old woman's words. He set off with Maryam at his side. Ismael had forgotten to invite Karim, so the boy walked beside Touba, and was frowning and disappointed. Now that his adoptive father didn't want him, he would stick with the old woman. He knew that she would protect him.

Ismael and Maryam climbed the mountain, with the heat on their heads. Ismael told Maryam that an individual must be as solid as the mountain. One must be a pillar for people to lean on. The mountain was a great teacher. At birth one was at the lowest point. Nature helped one to reach the peak of being. Life was like mountain climbing. Anyone who tired easily would be left behind halfway up. The one who knew the right way to go up the mountain would start off with solid, assured steps, pacing himself and climbing one step at a time until he reached the peak. There were two kinds of mountain climbing, that which occurred in everyday life and that which occurred in the realm of the mind and in the world of science and art. The wise climber integrated the two, and reached unity in the self. Maryam was listening. They had gone high enough that the people below seemed small. The young girl was surprised by the smallness of the people. Ismael explained that because she was small and not yet grown up, everyone seemed big to her. There would come the day that she would see large groups of people as small. The man then climbed a boulder. He stood on top waiting for the girl, but she was stuck halfway up. She felt as though there was no way to go forward or backward. Under her feet was just air, the area around her was full of sharp rocks and scorched by the sun. The dryness of the mountain in the summer frightened her. If she panicked for one second, she could fall. She looked at her father helplessly. Ismael sat down and looked at the girl. He knew the child wanted help. He told her that he could stretch out his arm and pull her out of this purgatory she was stuck in. It was the first time the girl heard the word *purgatory*. But he would not reach out to her, he said. He would let Maryam either fall or save herself, because she would be caught in similar situations many times in life. The child looked under her feet again. She felt dizzy. Ismael said that she had better not look down. Of course, it was empty under her feet, but if she persuaded herself, the emptiness would not frighten her. If Maryam looked carefully, she could quickly figure out where to place her feet.

Maryam looked around her. She could not see any footing. She wanted to cry, but she knew it was useless. Her father had turned cruel and would not help at all. Then she saw a protrusion in the rockface nearby. She held on to the body of the boulder and struggled to balance her foot on this ridge. She took a few small steps, and then her steps came quicker, until she threw herself in Ismael's arms, which were now willing to provide refuge.

There, high upon the mountain, the two of them sat and looked at the beautiful view below. The boulder was no longer scary. Ismael had Maryam's hand in his own, and he told her about the logic of the mountains. The girl felt proud to have overcome the great danger. There was now a stronger bond than ever before between the two of them. Ismael talked softly about Moones and Touba. Moones had suffered much in her life. The girl should understand this. But much of what she said about Master Geda Alishah was not correct. How could it be possible for a human being to perform so many miracles and possess so much grace? Besides, why was there a need for miracles? One had to build one's life with work and effort. Maryam must approach life just as she had today, when she had crossed the boulder. She must study, learn slowly, endure hardship with courage and perserverance. Only in this manner could one become great. And as for Touba, she had become old. She also had once been young, with dreams and hopes. Ismael said that Touba had always wanted to see and touch God. It was ridiculous, because a God that Touba could see and touch, contrary to her own beliefs, would have to have a human shape—a person in the sky, some kind of huge man. He said that this was how women who were searching for something to depend on usually saw things. But Maryam must distance herself from this kind of woman. Either God existed, which meant he was in Maryam just as he was in any rock or boulder, or he did not exist, and then there was no issue. The girl asked if it was possible that God did not exist. Ismael shrugged his shoulders and said he did not know. This was all he could say on the matter. The girl was dumbfounded. It had not once, even for a moment, occurred to her that God might not exist. She had thought a lot about what God looked like. She had sometimes seen him in the

285

shape of a great cloud or, through Touba's influence, as rays of light. But the possibility that he might not exist? Once Touba had told her that in her youth she wanted to become God's wife. This being the case, she had indeed seen God as a huge man. Once Touba had dreamt that the Prophet Mohammad and Imam Ali had filled the sky like stars, and Maryam had pictured God as a great man marked with stars. But that he might not exist? This she had never thought.

The girl returned from the mountain feeling reflective, and troubled. Who was telling the truth? Touba, who was searching for God? Or Moones, who saw Master Geda Alishah as God's image on this earth? Or her father, who said he didn't know anything, and couldn't care less? On the mountain, she had asked if Ismael had ever seen ghosts or angels. Touba had seen some ghosts and heard their voices, too. Ismael laughed. This sort of talk seemed absurd to him. Nevertheless, if one were to build on the imagination, it was possible to see far worse things than ghosts and angels. He had asked, "Maryam, what is so uninteresting about the simple issues of life, that you should throw them aside and pursue a question such as whether ghosts or angels exist?" The child didn't know what to answer. Could she say that she was like a fragile, delicate young branch that must depend on the strong, sturdy body? Would she ever be bold enough to push aside her modesty and say that she wanted to throw herself in his or Moones's arms and hide there? Could she reveal that, when her teeth chattered with fear, the only thought she had was to run and take refuge between the two of them? In fact, when she heard about God from Touba, it comforted her. At nights she talked with God. When she was scared she would say, "O God, who sees me, be with me," and her fear would disappear. She could not tell Ismael any of this. She did not even know what she felt clearly enough to be able to describe it. Descending from the mountain, she thought about Ismael's words: when they were up there, people down below seemed small. If only she could grow as large as the mountain, then everything would be all right. Her body could not grow to that size, but her spirit definitely could. Then no human, no ghost or angel, could ever bother her. Then she could even bring her dead parents back to life—or at least make them rich in the other world, so that they would not suffer sickness. In order to grow as big as the mountain, she decided, she must study as Ismael had said, and learn science.

When the two returned to the park they found the relatives seated around tablecloths that were spread on the ground. There were many cloths spread out around the park, and every family had placed their pots and pans of food on them. The place was abuzz with noise and conversation. As the two passed each group of relatives, they greeted them and asked after their well-being. Habibolah Mirza jovially invited them to sit down with his family. Ismael said he was afraid Moones's feelings would be hurt if they joined Habibolah's family first, before they ate her food. Habibolah's wife was arguing with her children. A little further on, Madam Amineh was telling a story to the women around her. Touba was there among them. The women wore chadors, and one was fanning herself. When the two arrived at her tablecloth, Madam Amineh said, "God bless her, what a girl!" And Maryam laughed. Madam Amineh asked what Maryam was planning to become, and Maryam said she wanted to be a doctor. The women raised their eyebrows in surprise and joy. Manzar O-Saltaneh's daughter was eating lunch with her fiancé nearby in the shade of a tree. Hesam O-Din Mirza was entertaining some of the boys with the story of how his uncle Mohammad Hasan Mirza had transversed a remote swamp. Mohammad Hasan Mirza's own children were all in Europe. Aqdas Ol-Moluk had become a complete Parisian and no longer visited Iran. One of her girls had recently come to Iran to marry her cousin, but she had not come to the picnic. In any case, she had adopted Western ways, and the relatives feared her.

Maryam sat down at her own family's cloth. She was eating and observing the crowd when suddenly she realized that she felt a bit like a stranger toward all of them. As long as she had been a child she did not understand this, but on the mountain, in that lonely moment when it seemed as if she was standing in a vacuum and felt herself in the midst of purgatory, she had suddenly grown up. A hazy image of Kamal, a brother she had not seen for some years, sparked in her memory. She thought that her brother had felt this way, and it was why he had gone away. He also could not mix with this crowd.

Maryam looked at Moones. The woman was smiling, and the girl knew that she was very kind. Moones never desired to hurt anyone, and she was a shy and demure woman. She was always turned into herself, as though she had committed a major sin. Maryam silently vowed that if she someday became a doctor, then she would not let Moones work. She would take care of her and let her stay at home to overcome her exhaustion from the years of hard work. Then Maryam looked past the tree branches and the heads of people moving and talking to where Touba was seated. She thought, Does she love us? The old woman never kissed her or her young brother, but she counseled them as much as she could. She was like the people Maryam saw in the streets. Crossing the street one day she was told by a man, "Dear girl, watch out. You do not want to get run over by cars, use the sidewalk." Touba was like that man. She lived her own life, kept to herself, but sometimes she talked to others. She also scared everyone with her warnings: "Do not run in the yard. Don't eat junk. Nap in the afternoon. Do your prayers. Don't wear short skirts. Don't look at boys and men. Be a good girl and study." Touba was all tongue. She talked without seeing to whom she was speaking.

Maryam looked at Ismael. She was certain the man loved her. But why? Maryam was not his real daughter. Perhaps this love had a motive. She had noticed that what Ismael told her in private was never repeated in the presence of Touba or Moones. He did not even tell Karim these things. She had noticed that Ismael was not much interested in her brother. Even when he was kind to the boy it was for Maryam's sake. So why did he love her? Kamal had said, "This tie-wearing gentleman is full of big words, but his talk is useless." Nevertheless, Maryam decided to become a doctor for the sake of this tie-wearing gentleman.

With each passing minute the girl felt more distanced from the crowd in the garden. She was no longer a part of them; she was looking at them from the margins. She said to herself, I am the daughter of Mahmood the mason. This was the truth. No matter how much she wore pretty clothes or ate good food or studied, she remained the daughter of a mason. She suddenly missed Kamal. Where was her brother? When he had first left the house, he would come to visit them once a week. Many times he had come by their school to greet Karim or Maryam. He always said he had no patience for the people they lived with. Maryam had always wondered what his reason was for keeping himself apart. Later he had disappeared entirely. Now as she distanced herself from the crowd in the garden, she grew closer to that brother's memory and thought she understood his motivation to leave and make his own way in life.

Life changed for Maryam after the hike on the mountain. Once a week she went to the movies with her adoptive father. Moones always said she was busy. She didn't care much for movies, so she stayed home to do her housework. Soon Ismael and Maryam had seen many movies. Karim went with them sometimes, but one day he refused to go. He told his sister he did not wish to go to the inferno after his death. Someone had told him that it was a sin to watch movies and that he should even turn his head the other way when passing by the cinema, for all such sins would be recorded on his chart. Maryam, however, looked forward to the movies. She became familiar with the different movie stars, and they often appeared in her dreams.

In these dreams, Maryam often wore Mexican clothing and waited by their shack for her husband, who was tall and dark with a mustache and a large hat. The man had gone to fight the rebels and was struggling to save their village by the mountainside. People loved him. He was their leader. Sometimes she was a golden-haired lady living in a beautiful mansion somewhere in America. She wore skirts that made a rustling sound and had curls in her hair. She would put on Moones's chador, wrap a string around her middle, and then pull the chador down so it formed a full, gathered long skirt. Dressed in this costume, she imagined herself living the life of a beautiful young American lady. She would let men bow before her and kiss her hand. She then would walk in an imaginary garden, wearing a large hat on the side of her head to prevent the sun from bothering her eyes. She had gone to see *The Cranes Are Flying*. This made her dream of running around imaginary empty streets in Russia with an imaginary fiancé in the morning light. She let the trucks spraying water wet her down. Then a war would start. Hungry and sorrowful, she would go to bomb shelters and drown herself in the memory of her fiancé, who was at the front. At times she wore pants and a gun on her belt, running around the western deserts of America; from under her wide-brimmed hat she would watch the thieves who were planning to rob the bank, then suddenly draw her gun and shoot thirteen of them single-handedly. At the same time, she was the beautiful young woman wearing a long full skirt, carrying her baby, running through the bullets to the safety of a barn. For a whole week she was a woman from India who stood up from the midst of cotton fields, swung her head around, held her fingers to her cheeks and sang, "Na, na, oh," and danced like a wave of water. Her black hair swirled through the air. Suddenly ten or twelve men jumped up from behind the bushes, and while their heads moved delicately on their necks they shouted, "Ya nati, ya nati, oh." She danced across her imaginary fields and the men followed her, dancing as well.

She was a shepherd girl who had been raped by the master's son and now she was homeless in a big city. Whenever she found an empty corner she began to sing. She was a grand hero who could fly by pushing a button on her belt. She was a nun gone to Africa to cure the sick. The Africans were dancing wildly in front of the hospital, and she was watching them from the corner. She loved a young doctor, but because she was a nun, she could not reveal her love. At other times she was a woman partisan in Czechoslovakia. Her golden hair tied on her head, she climbed a mountain route, hiding from the Germans. She carried an important message for the partisans' leader. On the way she was shot, but before she died she was able to relay the message to a shepherd boy, who delivered it to the leader. The young boy left her in the middle of the forest, and Maryam wept for her tragic fate.

All these dreams left Maryam with the sensation that she was definitely meant to do something very important. What that thing would be, she did not know. Running away from thieves or delivering a message or discovering a new world under the sea, flying into the skies or dancing in cotton fields or discovering the north pole—whatever it was, she knew it must be important. In the meantime, she hated everything she saw on her way to school. Why didn't people know something important must be done? They crowded by bakeries for their bread and bought filthy yogurt from dairy stores. They ate poor food but still bore more children. They complained about not having enough money, but they never accepted that they had to change their lives to earn more of it. Maryam was sick of everything.

One day, on the front page of the newspaper, the important task revealed itself to her. Ismael said, "Look what Algeria is doing." Algeria was fighting for its freedom, and the paper spoke of heroic girls who strapped dynamite to their bodies, went among the French, and blew themselves up. Meanwhile, men were arrested and tortured by the dozens by the French occupiers. The picture of Djamila Boupacha, the young woman who stood up to the captors who raped and tortured her in jail, appeared in all the newspapers and magazines. Maryam cut one of them out and stuck it on her wall. She now knew what direction her life would take. Women wearing rustling skirts faded into the background of Maryam's mind. The woman from India spread her hair once more to the wind and slowly disappeared into the cotton field. The gun-toting man from the Wild West took his hat off and faded into Djamila Boupacha's body. She got up and stood staring into Maryam's eyes.

Maryam was fifteen when Kamal returned. He was a full-grown man, polite and dignified. Maryam herself opened the door to him. His laughing eyes revealed his identity. The young girl shouted his name excitedly, "Kamal." He smiled, came in, and kissed his sister. He asked after Karim. The boy was coming down the stairs. He looked at his brother as he would look at a stranger. Kamal asked after their grandmother. Touba was coming out of the bathroom holding a water pot. She had never formed the habit of filling the pot with tap water; she believed the water pot must still be filled at the pool in order to conduct a proper ablution. Touba did not recognize Kamal at first. After she realized who he was, she put the water pot down to sit by the pool's edge and measure up this young well-dressed man who no longer bore any resemblance to the nervous, bad-tempered young boy of the past. When she asked him where he had been all this time, the young man answered that he had been traveling to make a living. Now that he was attending the university, he could no longer travel. Kamal looked around. He asked if Touba didn't think that the house was dilapidated, and inquired whether she planned to do a complete renovation. The old woman shrugged her shoulders and said that she herself was old and when she died her house would likely die with her. For all she cared, they could bury her right here in the middle of the courtyard.

The young man smiled, as if he was probably in agreement with her. He asked if he could live in his old cellar room for a short while until he found himself a place. He said he could pay rent. The old woman told him he could live there under the condition that he not bring anyone to the house. She was too old to be bothered with veiling herself in front of strangers. The young man promised that, with the exception of a couple of his university friends, he would not have guests. Ismael and Moones were pleased to see Kamal—excited, really. They asked about where he had been, what he had done, and why he had not come to visit them. Kamal rattled off some automatic answers. For a while he had rented a room with his friends, then he had gone on some trips. Later he became an assistant to a truck driver and saw many cities. He had traveled in the summers to make money to live on during the school year. Moones was very happy to see that he had succeeded in life. She told Ismael they must take a photograph of him and his brother and sister to have as a keepsake. The young man resisted the idea; he said he did not like pictures. Finally he gave in and offered to bring a camera one day and take a photograph of everyone. Ismael asked about Kamal's course of study, and Kamal said it was mechanical engineering. Ismael announced to him that Maryam planned to become a doctor. Karim desired to become an engineer as well, but he had not yet decided upon a specialty. Kamal seemed truly happy, and the next day he brought his personal belongings. However, he was seen very little around the house and he seemed to have a secretive way about him.

Nevertheless, Kamal found the time to take his brother and sister on occasional outings and talk with them. In his opinion, he told them, the whole city should be set on fire. The city was sick and caused everyone in it to become sick. It had an incurable disease that could only be eradicated by annihilation. In an emotional voice, Kamal told them that if the city were not set on fire soon, he himself would burn. He said it would take a very smart person to fan the flames, to be the one to start the fire. Kamal said they were still young and thus did not understand things.

Maryam did not have a clear image of the city. For her, the city was largely just her house and school and her classmates and a limited number of people who visited, and Moones and Ismael. Yet she had a feeling she understood Kamal's words. Since she had learned about Djamila Boupacha, many things had become clear to her. Karim, still quite young, did not pay attention to these statements. He could not understand why the city should be set on fire. This was the city they lived in. If it caught fire, where would they live? Kamal's attention slowly focused on Maryam. He could see that the young girl was listening to him. She listened to everyone and absorbed all ideas. Kamal called Touba a reactionary, and the girl asked him what a reactionary was. Kamal explained that it meant she was an old-fashioned, self-congratulatory person. He pointed out how the old woman resisted every new thing. "The walls of her own home are rotting and collapsing, the earth in the garden has grown barren and has no strength to feed the plants, and the pool is broken, but she will not allow any improvements. She is afraid of losing her place. Because she is afraid for herself, she makes life miserable for others." This made the old woman a dangerous creature.

Maryam did not sense any thing threatening in Touba. Indeed— and quite amazingly, Touba was coming to like Kamal. The young man did small tasks for her now and then just as Ismael used to do in the old days. The woman was old and tired and needed to lean on someone. The young man was quiet and polite around Touba. He took care of things for her and did her shopping. The old woman was afraid that the taxi drivers might steal her purse, for instance, and the young man would go in the taxi with her to her destination. He would also pick her up and escort her back to the house. But even though he did these things, he spoke badly of her behind her back. He told Maryam that he was like a surgeon who operates on tumors, and in his opinion, Touba was a tumor that must be pulled out of a patient's body. If it had surgery, the house would then be able to breathe. Then the house could be demolished and a new house built—a house without so many cockroaches, ants, and millipedes; a house that wouldn't have so many dilapidated cellars and useless water reservoirs. The house could become a place where humans lived comfortably. Touba was the cause of all the problems in the house. Moones, Kamal said, was also a useless being. She was of course a nice, simple lady, but she had no real purpose. She must be trained and grow out of this aimless dervish state. Kamal was silent on the subject of Ismael. Whenever the topic turned to him, Kamal shrugged his shoulders and did not speak. Maryam pressed him for his views about Ismael, but he would only say that Ismael looked like a conservative. It was not clear what he really thought, and thus he could not be trusted. He talked big but did small things; in this respect, he was a foolish being, a person to be pitied.

The children gradually learned to see many issues from their brother's perspective. Slowly, Maryam and Karim parted from those with whom they had spent their childhood. Before Kamal's return, Maryam had been close to Touba, Ismael, and Moones; she had been one with them. She was now more distant from them. Karim did not show much emotion. He was often silent, and it was not clear what he thought and what he approved of. He was still too young for Kamal to think of him seriously. It was his sister who received most of his attention. The girl was smart and exacting and followed her brother's ideas well. They were not in full agreement on all matters, but they understood one another. Maryam said she didn't want to set the house or the city on fire. She argued that this was not the right way to change the world. Important events were brought about through other means. Maryam suggested that they must find the French and fight them, but there were no French here in Iran. Kamal explained that the Americans were here. Maryam did not understand that there were different conditions in different places. The problems in Iran were different from those in Algeria. Kamal explained that in Cuba people fought against the Americans, and that in Iran people also must fight against them. France and England no longer presented any real danger; they were like Touba and her old house.

When the girl turned seventeen, Kamal's gift to her was a book. It contained most of the ideas he talked about, presented in a more complex and literary way. The girl spent a long time reading the book. She found it boring. It was filled with statistics and numbers and tedious historical facts. It was the history of human society and the proper way of thinking about things. In fact she could not understand the book very well; she wished someone would explain the sentences to her. But she came to trust her brother more after reading it. The things he said had not just been made up by him. They were based on ideas from great people—people who each minute earned more respect in Maryam's mind. The girl now felt as though she lived in-between two different worlds: the physical world, which was always in front of her, and the world of the mind, which was shaped by Kamal's talks and the books he gave her. Kamal had reminded her that their roots were among the poor people.

Did the young girl remember how cruelly her mother had died? The girl had no memory of her mother. How about her father? She did remember him, but just that he had swollen feet. Had she ever understood that if they had had money, neither of their parents would have died? Who was responsible for their death? It was people similar to Touba, Kamal said—people who seemed kind and friendly and even offered shelter to the poor when they were dying, but who really were not kind. The young girl asked how she was to interpret the kindness offered to herself and Karim by Touba, Moones, and Ismael. Kamal only sneered. They were kind in order to get something back. Didn't she and Karim and even Kamal himself work in the house under the command of the old woman?

He asked her whether she knew that their father had killed one of their own brothers. Maryam trembled. Kamal recounted for her a fight that had taken place between his father and mother. Mahmood was unemployed at the time, short-tempered and constantly picking fights with his wife. Maryam was still being breastfed and Kamal was small. They had a two-year-old brother named Karim. Kamal remembered that in a big fight his father had gone toward Maryam saying that he was going to pick her up and throw her. Their mother, horrified, had run and grabbed Maryam and rushed out of the room. Their father, who had obviously gone temporarily insanely, had turned to the two-year-old, picked him up, and thrown him at the wall. After crashing against the wall, the child had fallen down onto his head. Kamal remembered that he had hidden behind a curtain in the room and watched from there. He had wondered when Mahmood would attack him and throw him against the wall. He had seen his mother, holding Maryam, standing at the threshold, mute with shock. She had run toward Karim and tried to embrace the child without putting Maryam down, but she could not hold both of them. So she had hit her own head, again and again, against the wall. At this point, their father apparently came to his senses, picked up Karim, and ran out of the room. Their mother, still holding Maryam, had wandered around the room, continuing to hit herself. They had ended up spending the whole night curled up in the corner of the room, trembling from the cold. Their father had returned in the morning with his dead child, colorless in his arms. He had sat in the corner of the room holding the child, staring in front of himself at a crack in the wall.

The girl hid her head in her hands. Kamal told her that a few years later, when they gave birth to another child, their parents named the newborn Karim as well. It was because of this event—in order to forget it—that the father drank. Kamal said it was all the result of poverty. Poverty brought filth and humiliation, and Satan was born of these things. Kamal said he did not feel like bowing to everyone for the sake of a bite of bread, then going home to bash his wife and children. He wanted to change the world, and he knew that he must first free himself from the current system. Poverty must be burned in its own home in order to be eradicated. The girl finally understood what Kamal had been saying all this time and came to stand on her brother's side.

By the time Maryam was eighteen, she had cut off her relationship with her surrogate family. She lived there without any emotional connections, and did not know why she hid all the changes in herself from Touba and Moones. Ismael, however, understood that she had changed. His sharp eyes could read the girl's every thought. He even talked in ways similar to Kamal. Thus the young girl had reason to accept her brother even more.

It was in her eighteenth year that a serious event took place. She went with Kamal to a newsstand to buy a paper. In it was the list of students who had been accepted to university, and her name was among them. She had passed the entrance exam to the pre-medical college. Kamal said that he had bought a present for this special day. He led her to the upstairs apartment of a small house in the southern part of the city. Kamal told her to keep her head down. A group of men was there, having a discussion, and she must not look at anyone. Maryam stayed in the room alone for a quarter of an hour. Then three men came and told her she could raise her head. All three had masks on. They asked if she would like to do something for herself and for the people. The girl said she would like that very much. They said that her guide within the group would be someone by the name of Abdullah. One of the men took off his mask. Maryam saw a face that was vaguely familiar; she searched deep in her memory and recollected that he had been a childhood friend of her brother. She knew instinctively that she should not let on that she recognized him. She kept the secret to herself. But as time went on, she gradually fell in love with the man. They saw each other once a week and talked. It was Abdullah who revealed certain secrets about the group to her. Each time they met, he gave her small tasks to do. He would also bring her certain books to read, and then they would talk about them. He was certainly the greatest and most important person she had ever met in her life. It was at Abdullah's command that she studied very seriously. She must become a very capable doctor. It was necessary that she increase her knowledge in order to be worthy of undertaking important missions in the future.

Maryam's mind had suddenly flown far beyond the mental boundaries of the house. Moones could not understand these changes in Maryam; she was involved in her own activities. But Touba and Ismael noticed them. They both became conscious that they had lost the girl. Touba was amazed at how drastically the university had changed the girl. Was this serious, frowning bookworm the same happy, shy girl of previous years? Abdullah had warned Maryam about Ismael, saying that in no way could he be trusted. Based on previous experience, people of his age had already gone rotten. They were suspicious and untrustworthy. Maryam created a wall between herself and Ismael. She was no longer kind to her adoptive father, and this pained him greatly. He wondered what had happened.

Kamal decided to leave the house again, this time for good. He told his sister that they would not see one another until the moment with the lit match met the stored dynamite. When the young man was saying farewell to Touba, under the pretense of taking a trip to Bandar Abbas, he mentioned that matches were a good thing. Everything could be set on fire. The woman's melancholic mind heard Kamal's words, not really registering them but feeling unsettled by them all the same.

After Kamal left, Abdullah told Maryam that they must somehow arrange to become husband and wife. Maryam needed to get away from the observing eyes of Touba, and she especially needed to be rid of Ismael. Some important things needed to be done. Abdullah therefore planned to come and ask for Maryam's hand. After that, everything would move forward with minimal formality, and it would have to be done quietly.

One Wednesday Maryam said that a student from the university was coming to ask for her hand in marriage, and she wished to accept. She had become so secretive and unfriendly in the last two years, it left no room for reaction from anyone. Abdullah arrived and everything took place informally. Touba and Moones and Ismael accepted the arrangement. They had to accept. The boy and the girl shut them up every time they opened their mouths. There was no need for a dowry, or even a wedding party. It was to be a civil wedding. This was no era for frivolous spending. What did they have to prove to anyone, anyway? The girl would go to live with her husband. Moones and Ismael asked if they could sometimes visit. No, they could not, the couple replied, because they were going to Tabriz, a long way away.

When Abdullah left, the girl went quickly to her room to study.

She had not read more than a page when there was a knock on the door. She did not know why she was so shaken. She got up and unlocked the door. It was her brother Karim. He was finishing his last year of high school and had a question to ask his sister. He wanted to benefit from her knowledge. He came into the room and sat on her bed. He looked at the photographs on the walls suspiciously. He asked if she was certain she was making the right choice. The girl pretended to be busy in order to avoid answering directly. Karim said he wouldn't allow himself to interfere in her affairs because they had an older brother who could make decisions for his sister, but he felt he needed to tell her that he had reservations about the marriage. Maryam said she had no need to consult anyone else about her decision. Karim suddenly held his sister's hands. He said that he did not trust Kamal and his friends. They were dangerous beyond Maryam's imagination. They were leading her onto a path that Maryam could not at present understand, and it was a fearful path indeed. They were planning to set everything on fire. What was so bad in the world that it must be burned? Of course there was corruption, and it must be fought, but this did not call for such extreme measures. If Maryam turned her back on everyone, she would find herself alone. She would be in a vacuum and she would not be able to save herself. Karim quickly opened his sister's palm and placed a prayer seal in it. The girl tried to pull her hand away, but the boy stubbornly held on to her closed fist. He insisted that the girl must preserve the seal as a memento from her brother. It was Karim's spirit, and it would go with her to the other end of the world and protect her. The girl must hang on to the seal with all her will. She must promise to come visit her brother sometimes. She must not cut off her relationship with Touba, either. The woman had become their grandmother and she was a good woman. Although she was old and grumbled a lot, it was she who had housed them in their childhood and protected them from many dangers. Maryam could always count on Touba, and on her brother Karim.

The girl walked across the room, hiding her emotion. She asked her brother whether someday, if it were necessary, he would go away with her. The boy spent a long time staring in silence at the pattern of flowers on her bedsheet. A fearful struggle raged in his mind, but when he spoke he simply said no. He would not go with her because he did not approve of her ways. Any time Maryam wanted to she could come back to him, and he would welcome her back. But she must not wait too long to return because then it might be too late. Maryam still had the power to stay if she wished. Then he looked into his sister's eyes. He could see that she was absolutely determined to go, and he stood up and left the room in silence. He paced back and forth in the yard for a long time. Was it necessary to inform Ismael, Moones, or Touba of the reality of the situation? He didn't know in fact what was really happening, but he sensed the trouble toward which his sister was headed. As long as Maryam remained in the house, he would have some idea of what was going on, but now he was about to lose his only contact with her. He thought the people of the older generations were right in thinking that a woman's place was in the home. Karim was certain that if the girl left the house, she would descend to the depths of perdition. But he did not have the power to keep his sister at home because the men who now surrounded her were stronger than he was. And it was unlikely that he would even be able to find them. Perhaps it was best to go visit Master Geda Alishah. Someone great must intervene.

By the following week Maryam had left. The old woman sat by the pool at sundown, looking at the empty house. Her daughter was sewing and Karim was studying in the corner of the room. Ismael was out. The old woman felt nostalgic. She could not understand the recent turn of events. When had these children become so independent? In times gone by, no girl would ever have been married off in this manner. Had she done something indecent in agreeing to such a wedding as this? It was done so poorly and unceremoniously. She asked this question of Ismael when he arrived. What had happened to the youth? Ismael sat next to her by the pool. He asked if the old woman ever looked around herself and really truly saw the way things had changed. Did she even see that right here, the house was tumbling down? Who would want to live in a house like this? Was it not time that the old woman called the masons in and rebuilt the house?

The old woman resisted the idea of any renovation. Had Ismael forgotten Setareh's corpse was there, under the earth? Perhaps they could remove the corpse, then call in the builders. The man shook his head impatiently. The woman did not understand that the corpse had decomposed and become part of the earth. Touba became angry. Why didn't Ismael realize that the girl, due to her sacred martyrdom, was the guardian of the house? If she were to be disturbed, then the house would no longer be blessed. People were not stupid to build their houses as they did. They calculated everything. In every village there was a mausoleum. And this house claimed enough respect to be protected by the spirit of a fourteen-year-old child. Ismael became truly impatient. What was the use of all these foul-smelling and rotting water reservoirs? Water now flowed through the pipes. The old woman smiled patiently, as though she were comforting a child. She said there was always a chance that someday water would no longer flow through the pipes. Why did Ismael trust appearances so much? If the water stopped, then the water reservoirs would be appreciated.

Karim had come into the yard and was occupying himself with the flowers in the garden. He listened to what the old woman and Ismael were saying. Ismael felt that it was useless to continue the discussion about the house. Touba asked if Ismael really knew where Maryam had gone. Ismael shrugged his shoulders. He didn't want to talk about it. The woman then asked about Kamal. She said that Kamal had told her, just before leaving, that matches were a good thing because you can set everything on fire with them. Did Ismael understand what he meant? Ismael thought for a moment and then said that, in his opinion, Kamal was a dangerous person. Kamal might be psychologically imbalanced. He suffered from a violent streak. At this point, Karim entered into their conversation. He said that he agreed wholeheartedly with Ismael. He was certain that Kamal had expressed his true feelings for his grandmother, and they were not kind. He also finally told them that his brother had often talked to him and to his sister about setting the house and even the city on fire.

The old woman became very disturbed and approached Karim.

She held Karim's hands in her own trembling ones and asked Karim if he was in agreement with his brother. Karim shook his head vehemently. He felt sorry for the old woman. She was far more helpless than she revealed. For a moment, his heart felt a burning anger. He was now learning how to stand up to his brother. In the past, he had not known what to do. He asked Ismael if it would be advisable for Karim to go find Kamal and have a serious talk with him. Ismael looked at Karim for a long moment in silence. The old woman's spirit was housed in his eyes. The two of them were very much alike. Ismael thought that if the boy were to go and talk to his brother, the house would have a new caretaker and his dream of reconstructing it would vanish forever. But if, just if, the young man could go and bring his brother and sister back to the house, it might be possible for all of them to sit down and talk the old woman into seeing reason. Ismael thought that if only the girl would return to the house once more and bring with her the heat and life of her being, perhaps something could be done to reverse the negative flow of things.

Ismael said he did not know whether what Karim was suggesting was a good idea, because experience had taught him that once people decided upon an act, and once they chose to live in a group and make decisions as a group, it was difficult to influence them as individuals. It was called something like a "mob mentality." But if Karim could manage to influence his brother and sister, it would be a good thing.

Ismael smiled at Karim. He felt that he must treat him politely from now on. This young boy, who until recently had so little significance in the house, had suddenly acquired a new status. Ismael felt a strange fear. He wished that he had included Karim in Maryam's childhood tutelage. The boy did not know many of the things that his brother and sister knew. Instead he had knowledge and experience of matters that the others were complete strangers to that even Ismael himself did not truly understand. He must follow Karim's train of thought for a while, he thought. The old woman had certainly impressed her ways upon the boy. His mind was filled with a confused conglomeration of the innocent Setareh, the hungry boy by the roadside, Mr. Khiabani, and Master Geda Alishah.

Ismael excused himself and went to his room to sit next to his barren wife and read a newspaper in order to hide his anxiety from Karim and the old woman. Contrary to her usual habit, Moones was not sewing, and she was not embroidering either. She was staring at the wall in front of her, thinking. Ismael said that all her talk of Master Geda Alishah had in the end caused Maryam to hate everything. Moones turned to him in anger. She said that she did not see any sign of Geda Alishah being a force in Maryam's life. In fact, it was Ismael's intellectual approach that had turned the girl crazy. Was he not the one who had pushed her into science? Was it not for his sake that the girl had gone into medicine? How could he now hold Moones and Master Geda Alishah responsible? The man buried his nose in the paper to avoid hearing more.

Touba entered Karim's room, very disturbed. Karim was behind his desk studying again. She asked him if he really knew where his brother and sister were. The boy said he did not know, but he thought that they were involved in some dangerous activity. The old woman wondered if she should consult with Master Geda Alishah. Perhaps it would be good to ask him what the young people were up to. The Master could probably provide an explanation.

Over the next few months, Touba paced the yard, confused. She had entered into serious thought about the house. Perhaps Ismael was right: If she repaired the house, the children would not want to leave. At least they would not leave without warning. But how could she renovate it? Where should she begin? What could she do with Setareh's corpse? Only a few things remained that grounded her to life. She felt that if she were to change them, she would forget her soul and her identity. A entire sea of dead people lay behind her. Many of those who could testify that she was Touba, the daughter of Adib, were dead. The few who remained were old and sickly, and most had lost their mental clarity. The only thing she had was the house; this house, in the middle of the city. Although the neighborhood had once been considered high-class, its stature had fallen. Yet the house itself had a solid foundation. It sat soundly in its place. It was her house. Who cared that the teahouse on the corner had been demolished to build a Bank of Saderat, or that Haji Abdol Samad's grocery had become a supermarket? Yagub, the crystal man, no longer came to the alley's corner to spread his old cloth and set out little tea glasses and matching saucers to sell. What happened to him? But, never mind; the house still sat firmly on the ground. Ismael did not understand this; neither did the children. Karim did. Karim understood that he must have something to hold on to. He understood it well, and the old woman was happy. When they talked together, she often criticized Ismael, and he agreed. One needed a place—a solid, dependable place. Long ago people lived in caves. They wished to be surrounded by solidity. You couldn't just live in the street under the sky. Besides, the ceiling's design came from the idea of the sky, only scaled down to protect a small group of people.

One summer night, about a year after Maryam had left the house, Touba sat at the table eating a dinner of eggplant and whey. On the other side of the house, Moones and Ismael's window was open. They were sitting by their little dinner table, eating their food. A star was shining through the leaves of the pomegranate tree and the sky looked velvet black. Suddenly the sound of gunfire came from the street. Touba hearkened to the noise. Karim said offhandedly, "There is that shooting we hear off and on these days." Touba said, "God help us!" They had a few more bites of their dinner, before they heard a knock on the door. Touba saw Ismael get up from the table, pull the curtain aside, and go toward the door. She heard the sound of the door unlocking and then nothing. Touba noticed that Ismael seemed to be having difficulty moving back into his room. Moones stood up at about the same time. Someone wearing a chador was leaning on Ismael. Touba and Karim got up and ran toward Ismael's room. They could see Moones striking her head. They turned at the top of the landing and pulled the curtain open. Ismael had lain the figure wrapped in the chador on the carpet. Touba moved the veil away from the face and saw that it was Maryam. The girl was covered in blood. She was pregnant, but worst of all, she held a gun tightly in her right hand. Ismael brought a pillow and placed it under Maryam's head. The girl breathed heavily. Ismael said he was going to get a doctor. The girl repeated in a frightened voice, "No! No!" Ismael bent to her wishes and knelt beside her. He now opened Maryam's chador. The girl's breasts were covered in blood. The girl said, "My foot, my foot is broken." Ismael said, "Dear Maryam, nothing can be done without a doctor. If you know one of your own, tell me so I can go get him." The girl moved her head from side to side wildly while her body trembled. Ismael tried to pull the gun out of her hand, but he could not pry it loose. She had wrapped her fingers around the weapon so tightly that it was now one with her body. The four of them looked at one another helplessly. The girl wanted to say something. Her mouth moved like a fish in water, but no sound came out. Ismael bent over her, and could barely hear her say, "No one must find out I have come here. It is very dangerous. I got this chador by force from a woman in the street. If somehow you can find her, pay her for it." The sound of police sirens came from the street. Moones asked what they should do. She was rubbing her hands together in severe agitation. The girl then took in one last deep breath and died.

They all spent a long time sitting there looking at her. They could not believe what their eyes saw. Again came the sound of sirens from outside. The sound brought them all to their senses. Then the sound of Karim's teeth chattering made everyone turn toward him. The young man had his arms wrapped tightly around his body, trying to stop his own violent shaking. Moones instinctively went to him and placed her hand on his shoulder. The boy bent over and ran to the door. They saw him vomit in the gutter by the pool. Moones had followed him and was rubbing his shoulders. He said, "I will kill him!" Moones asked, "Who?" He replied, "Kamal, I will kill him!" They had now returned to the room. The young man's tremors had been replaced by numbness. He seemed dumbfounded. Ismael said that Maryam must be buried right there. The old woman asked, "Where?" The man moved his head in the direction of the pomegranate tree. For an instant Touba's eyes and Ismael's met and locked. An old memory awakened. Without a word, each set about their task, Touba brought the shovel and pick, and Ismael dug into the earth beneath the tree as rapidly as he could. He dug exactly where Touba had, with Mirza Abuzar's help, buried

Setareh some forty years ago. Little could be seen in the dark. Sometimes old pieces of cloth came up with the dirt; nothing else seemed to have remained.

Maryam, wrapped in her chador, was brought into the garden. Ismael went down into the grave. The three others placed the corpse in his arms and the man laid her in the bottom of the hole and climbed back out. Then, for some reason they all simultaneously froze in place. Again it was the sound of sirens that brought them back to reality. They filled the grave with earth. They placed some flower pots on top of it. They searched in the dark to make sure everything looked normal. It was only at this point that Moones suddenly lost control. She began trembling like a leaf, and her voice was slowly rising into a scream. Ismael had her in his arms and had to place his hand over her mouth to try to calm her. Her condition was making Karim sick again. The boy ran to the cellar basin and vomited a second time. He then said he must do the ablution of the dead; he must cleanse himself. He went to the kitchen, brought out a bowl, went to the cellar basin, undressed, and poured water over himself. Ismael meanwhile carried Moones to their room and tried to soothe her. After the ablution, Karim went quickly to his room. He had put his clothes on over his wet body. Wet from head to toe, he opened the prayer mat and prayed rapidly. By the time Touba came to the room he had finished a whole set of prayers. In a loud voice, so that the woman could hear, he said, "God, I do not know anything, nothing. I only know that I must kill him. Grant me the power."

The old woman returned to the yard again. She paced back and forth. She could not understand anything. Had the girl lost her chastity? Was her child a bastard? How had she met this fate? Ismael soon joined Touba in the yard. Moones's voice could still be heard, saying that she could not live in this house for one more minute. Touba said to Ismael that what had happened to Maryam must have had something to do with her reputation. The girl must have done something irresponsible, and her husband had killed her. Ismael suddenly turned toward the old woman and grabbed her arms roughly. He screamed into her face, "Ancient woman, you seven-thousand-year-old bitch! Crazy, mad old woman, how can you not understand? How can one become free of you—of the chains you have wrapped around our hands and feet? When will you change? When will you understand the truth?" Brimming with intense hatred, he then pushed the old woman aside. He shouted over his shoulder, "We are going. It is not possible to stay in this house anymore."

Karim's voice could be heard from the terrace. He was saying that he would also go. Ismael returned to his room. He picked up a suitcase and quickly threw his belongings into it. Karim was preparing his own bag in his room. In half an hour they were all ready to go. Touba stood in the middle of the yard, amazed. She didn't know what to do with the house. By the door of the house, Ismael turned to Touba and said that when the old woman decided to demolish the house she should let him know. She asked, "What shall I do with the bodies?" Ismael did not answer. She ran toward Karim and grabbed his arm and asked, "What shall I do all alone?" Karim stopped. He was staring into space, in an unnatural way, as if he had been hypnotized. He said that he must go and find his bastard brother and kill him. He said that if necessary he would go to the end of the world to find him and kill him. He would also seek out Maryam's husband and all the others who used to come to the cellar to visit that bastard. Ismael must help him. If he had really believed in Maryam as his daughter, he must help. Ismael, who was waiting by the door for his wife, said that if he could, he would help Karim. He said he felt that a great catastrophe was at hand. He found himself ready to try to prevent it. The old woman asked, "But what am I supposed to do?" Karim said, "We have to go. We must take care of this. We will come back to the house, one of these days."

Just like that, they were all gone. Touba was left with her pool. All night long, she walked aimlessly around the courtyard. What about this whole matter did she not understand? She had witnessed Ismael whispering often to Maryam, and she had seen the girl talk with her brother. She had always thought that they were speaking of indecent things. She was absolutely certain that Ismael loved the girl. She had always believed that the girl was looking for a mate, and like all of her generation, too many of whom Touba saw in the

street, she was shameless—she had become loose. Then there was
that strange marriage! She ought to have known right then and there
that something was wrong. One thing was clear to her: Everyone
was trying to grab her house. They wanted to disrupt everything.
But they wouldn't dare to because the one who could take her house
from her wasn't yet born. She had been the caretaker of the corpses
in order to keep the house for a lifetime. That was how it should be;
it was for the sake of the house that she tolerated the corpses. She
could kill everybody, participate in any murder, in order to protect
the house. She could turn the house into a cemetery, but it must
remain hers.

At dawn Touba decided to go to Master Geda Alishah's home. She
went to her room, put on a chador, took her purse, and descended
the stairs. She opened the door, and for the sake of caution, she
locked the main lock with a large old key that had not been used in
years. After securing the door with no less than four locks, she headed for the Master's house. Her hands were dirty and covered with
earth. Unlike Karim, she had not thought of cleaning herself after
digging the grave. The rest of her appearance was also quite
disheveled. The city was slowly waking, the buses had begun to roll,
and here and there taxis and private cars sped past. By six in the
morning, she had reached the Master's home. She pressed the door-
bell, and after a long time the Master's wife opened the door. Touba
said that she had come to see the Master on a very important matter.
The wife left and returned after a few minutes to direct her to the
Master's room. Touba entered the room confused, speechless, and
dusty all over. The Master was sitting on a sheepskin rug, leaning
against a large cushion. A book was open in front of him. Touba did
not sit down, preferring to remain standing. The Master focused his
penetrating eyes on her. Touba asked whether the Master knew what
she must do. The woman said she had been caretaker of a house for
about sixty years. In this house, under the earth in the garden, some
corpses had been hidden. Touba was caretaker of these corpses. She
had been caring for the first one for forty years. Since last night she

had become the guardian of another and now she did not know
what to do. The Master asked who the corpses were, the first and the
second. Touba answered that the first one was a fourteen-year-old
girl who had been raped. She had become pregnant as a result, and
her uncle had killed her to wipe away the disgrace this would have
brought onto the family. The second one was a medical student who
had married and left the house entirely by her own volition. She had
returned pregnant, holding a gun, and covered in blood, and had
died without a word. Touba was now afraid of caring for this corpse.
She said she did not have the energy anymore. The house was about
to tumble down and she, Touba, after sixty or seventy years, would
like to finally understand the truth and be at peace. What was the
truth? Why must she care for the house? Why couldn't she follow
her youth's desire to go after truth in the fields and mountains? Why
had she been forced her to stay within a four-walled place, and why
was she now hated for having done this? Why had the Master never
told her the truth? Why had she never been admitted to the circle of
mystery? What did the youth want, and say? Why had they gone
crazy? How could Touba understand the truth? What must she do
for the Master so that he would tell her the truth? She said that she
had always, since childhood, wanted to give birth to a messiah, but
she had taken a husband, again not knowing why, had children
without knowing why, and spent her years of youth raising these
children. Not knowing why all that was required of her. She had
always wished to seek God, always wanted to understand truth, but
no opportunity was afforded her to even learn to understand it
through the books she had inherited from her father. Then these
bodies had been tied onto her back. She had carried the first body all
these years, had cried for her on many occasions in the mosques and
during sermons, and had protected the house's perimeters, not
allowing an unfit eye to view the hidden grave. She had put aside her
dream of searching for God in order to be able to adapt and turn the
wheels of her fortune until the proper time arrived. Now they had
placed a second corpse on her back and left the house. How could
an aged woman carry such a burden?

The Master listened silently. When the woman finished, he

asked her if the girl had really returned carrying a gun, and if Touba knew what the girl had been doing. Touba said the girl had indeed returned holding a gun, and she did not know what the girl had been doing. The Master asked Touba how it could be that she had lived in the same house with the girl all those years but didn't know anything about her. The woman shrugged her shoulders helplessly. She said that the girl had hidden everything from her. The Master said that the truths are these very things—the things right in front of Touba's eyes that she failed to see. He said that every day men and women, old and young, came to him and said that they had buried a corpse under a tree, in a cellar, or in a wasteland. They also did not know why they had to do what they were doing. But they did it and then they became alienated from people. They withdrew from everyone and wished only to immerse themselves in contemplating truth.

Touba looked at the Master in disbelief. She tilted her head upward in defiance, and said that she did not accept the Master's words. The truth was that which, if Touba could only understand it, would free her from the need to question Setareh or follow her. The girl's world would naturally be rendered visible by knowing the truth. The Master smiled patiently. He got up and walked toward Touba, and told her to go and sit in his place. Touba expressed her unwillingness to commit such an act by taking two steps backward. The Master said, "You see, Touba, someone must sit there and understand the truth gradually. Please go sit there. The truth will slowly become clear to you. People come and tell parts of the truth. You are a rug-weaver—why don't you weave them together? You will then grasp what you have been calling the truth." The Master pressed Touba to go sit in his place. But the woman was afraid of the Master's place. She could not bring herself to sit there so she pulled back forcefully. The Master said, "The problem lies in this. You cannot sit there. In particular moments, brief moments, one can bring you to the field, but when the battle is heated there is no room for you. The truth is this: You have to be the caretaker of a house. This is your role. Good or bad, this is how it is."

The Master walked up and down the room, deep in thought.

Touba said that she had never thought she was obliged to do this. For some reason, she had thought that she was doing it of her own free will. The problem now was that she could no longer tolerate these bodies in the house. The house was crumbling. What could she do? The Master said he could not help her with this. He said that he had been aware of Setareh for a while. He, too, knew her, and sometimes he still saw her, with different faces and different shapes, as man or woman. He was also amazed at how she had suddenly come to him, and why she had come to him. The Master said that he had to sit in his place in order for people to come, and tell him what was happening, piece by piece, just as Touba had come. Later on he could tell her what had happened and, as Touba desired, tell her the truth; but at present he could not do anything. He said he had to wait until people came and each one spread some pollen of the memory of Setareh on him. Then he could become pregnant with Setareh, or with the idea of the girl. The old woman stared at her spiritual guide in wonder. The Master smiled, and said it was just as he said—he must become pregnant. He was not afraid of revealing a minor truth for an old student. He wanted her to sit in his place because he thought that for many long years he had acted in her place on the stage of life. Now he was tired. Of course he knew the woman could play her own part, but if she could only find or recognize it, the Master would help her to return to her real place and to sit there. The Master stood in front of her again. He said that if she knew any more about Maryam or her friends she should tell him now. He thought that Touba had sometimes spoken of the girl as having a wild, older brother—was that the case? The woman concurred. The Master wished to see this youth. He remembered that Touba had brought the younger brother to visit him, but he wanted to meet the older one. He had wanted to tell Touba this at the time, but some people suddenly come into the room. The Master had gone to greet them and had then forgotten to inquire about the older boy. The Master now resumed his sad pacing. He said, "It is a shame if I never meet him. But Touba, let me tell you something: I was afraid of him. I thought I couldn't handle him. These kinds of boys, rebellious boys, make me angry—they are too full of themselves. I should have taken him under my wing, but I let him go and he has done himself harm." Touba said that this was right, he was a born thief and murderer. There was fire in his eyes. Then the Master stared into Touba's eyes, and the woman was shocked. His eyes were like Kamal's eyes; they were related somehow, somewhere. And this idea for some reason made her tremble all over.

"It is not as you say it is," the Master said. "You are so afraid and insecure that you cannot be fair toward him. The movement he is involved in frightens you. The truth is that from such movements comes new creation. But—it should be done in an orderly manner. A moving object must follow its own curve. At first you must bow to the crowd, then it must flex. That is how motion and change come to have meaning. The slightest diversion from the goal or aimless action is a waste of time, futile. These feed off themselves, leading to a loss of energy without any replenishment."

The Master said a dust was spreading over the city, as if it was being showered with unknown seeds. Of course, in the logic of the cosmos there was no such thing as unknown, but as each cycle in the world came to an end, unusual events occurred. It was similar to the spring thunder and violent downpours. This was frightening for people. And in fact, they ought to be afraid, because it would be followed by complete change. For a new cycle to begin, one must end. Now a cycle was being completed. Everything was an illusory reflection. In fact, since the beginning, it had been the illusion alone that resembled reality. It was because of this that Touba was so perplexed and felt as though the ground was sinking beneath her feet. For Touba, he said, a new curtain had gone up—a curtain beyond the curtain she was used to. If she still wished to search for God in the fields and deserts or mountains, she must fearlessly approach this new illusion, touch it, and examine it. Roles were changing now: the flute played the shepherd and the grass blew the wind; the sheep ran after the wolf and the fox twirled the lion in its paw. The weak human being was like a soap bubble in the air; it lasted for a moment then burst. The strong human stood firm and observed the illusion.

The Master sat at the side of the room and told Touba to go and sit in his place. The woman stood quietly for a short while, then headed for the door. The sun had risen and the city was crawling with its usual motion and uproar. Touba took off into the streets. The changes were indeed amazing. She no longer recognized the city. There were so many people. All strangers! She recognized no one. She thought she ought to introduce herself to people. She felt a desperate need to tell them who she was, who her father was, what he had done. People must know what a great man he was; they must know that he determined Touba's destiny and the turns of the wheel of her life. What could an old-fashioned woman like Touba do but submit to that destiny? Now everyone would say she was a stupid old woman. Just like in the old days, when she had argued with Ismael about the plumbing. How stupid the people were! She was defending the water reservoirs because these stupid people had forgotten the draught years; they depended on a few drops of water in the pipes. She was afraid that one day they would shut the water off and everything would become a desert, like the area around Karbala, that city where the Shiite imam was martyred. And they thought she was stupid!

She said, "I will show you who is stupid. I will make you fall to your knees and apologize to me." Ismael must understand that she was not responsible. Everything was outside of her control. During all the years that she was protecting the house inside, events were occurring outside. She didn't know anything; she had never had time to know; she was not responsible for knowing. But what about now? Could she still say that she was unaware of the recent events? In truth, even her spiritual Master did not know what was happening. He was waiting for people to come and tell him parts of the story so that he could put it together and retell it. Touba did not dare to sit in his place. She knew she could definitely get crushed under the significance of these matters. Perhaps she could see it in the street now. Perhaps she would understand it now if she had always walked around the streets, if she had stood by the shops and listened to the people, if she had read Ismael's magazines, if she had gone on trips and seen the world. How foolish she had been to hide in the house until events suddenly descended upon her like an avalanche. How she had driven Ismael crazy until he had shouted all those curses at her! How ridiculous that she could only judge everyone for their sexual needs, and yet claim to be searching for God all of the time.

Someone shouted her name. She turned around, and the voice said, "Here!" A man was calling to her from a bench in the median. Someone had finally recognized her. As she moved closer, she recognized Prince Gil. He was sitting on the bench in a park nestled in the middle of several streets branching off in various directions. His face was unshaven, giving a greenish look to his dark complexion. His clothes looked like the outfits of the neighborhood thugs. The heels of his shoes were worn thin and his hat pushed back, as if he had been a gallant rogue all his life and had now decided to become a shopkeeper at the bazaar. Touba, confused, sat next to the prince. She asked if the prince had gone bankrupt, and if that was why he looked the way he did. Prince Gil laughed from deep down; his laughter carried for quite a distance and some pedestrians looked at him in surprise. He said he didn't know what bankruptcy was, but that he was sitting there to watch his harlot wife.

Touba looked around, trying to find Layla. The prince said she would come in a minute. Every day she came in a different car and with a new group of men—a real bitch. The prince said that one of these days he was going to kill her. His eyes looked decisive. Touba was close to vomiting because the smell of Maryam's dead body and blood had returned to her nostrils. The prince said that Touba must be returning from visiting her spiritual Master; she must have gone to ask him about truth. The woman acknowledged that this was what she had done. The prince said that the Master didn't know much, but if the woman would like, he would tell her what went on among the protectors of secrets. Touba bent forward attentively. The prince began to laugh when he noticed the intense look of curiosity in the woman's face. It made him feel like teasing her. He said that in fact her spiritual Master was the follower of others. His custom was to walk always at the end of a line. When the line turned around, as it sometimes does, the Master ended up first in line. This was why he was called Geda Alishah, or Shah Ali the Beggar. He claimed the first person's place, but actually occupied the last place. This was like an imaginary kingship that even the real kings believed in because they always knew him as the last one in line. He was in fact the embodiment of the invisible crowd, a collective state of being contained in the body of a small human. It was a secret kingdom. This crowd was the nucleus of that which was to be born one day, but never would be. If it were born the dimensions would fall apart, convexity would change to concavity. Like a black hole, his gravity would destroy all the parts of reality even as they sought unity. It would turn and twist everything together in order to force unity among all beings. From then on, nothing would be left for him to attempt to unify. After one instant, and only an instant, the turned and twisted particle would explode, scattering everything and everyone once more; the parts would prefer to remain scattered. And at that precise instant, he would be reborn. It was as such that the real kings knew the Master, knew him and knew that he must move to the end of the line.

Touba was so intent upon listening to the prince that her entire body was stretched toward him, leaning to the point of falling off the bench. Prince Gil, who was watching her out of the corner of his eye, said, "This is how they all sit around, and then your Master says, 'Friends, the Prophet Mani borrowed an urn from Noah the Potter, picked up some earth from Babylon, took a seed from Christianity and powder from the Buddhist tradition, mixed them and poured the mixture into the urn. He watered it with the Taoist tradition, and placed this in the semblance of some garden in the land of Ahura Mazda, the wise God. It is in this way that he tries to collect all the scattered grains of the world.' He then says, 'Friends, Mohammad entered the gates of the garden in the tradition of unity, and spread pollen on this collection. One thousand and one flowers grew.' The Master's friends become ecstatic, and he then says, 'Now open the eight windows of eight directions to allow the wind to blow on the branches and get rid of the putrid smell. Let new truth enter the gate. Don't be afraid of it. We shall borrow another urn from Noah the Potter.'"

The woman's heart was beating fast, but she managed to gasp,

"Do they really say this?" The prince shrugged his shoulders. He said he didn't know, but his guess was that they said things similar to this. He then turned to Touba, his eyes shining, and said, "Now your Master is confused. You told him about Maryam and have disturbed him. He will now ask questions to discover Maryam's secret and place it in a corner of the garden of his mind. His concern for unity might blow the girl's body apart on the chance that the secret might be hidden in the corner of her being. Touba, he is actually jealous. He cannot allow his parts, which in his opinion consist of all people and all mountains and all seas and all particles of dust—and indeed everything—to separate from one another. Now a particle of his totality is propelled, his garden is stormy, like the garden of the rebellious Zoroastrian priest Mazdak. I have faith that he will possess the girl again." Touba asked, "And you? Are you concerned for the girl?" The prince looked straight ahead, his forehead wrinkled in thought. Touba said that the girl's death had made her very concerned. She was sure some event was occurring that would shake everything at its foundations, and everything would fall apart.

Prince Gil smiled and a look of patience appeared in his eyes. He said he was not worried at all. His place was clear in the present context, and no one and nothing could take his place. People can be servants or be free, they can use atomic bombs on one another, they can become wild animals like the Mongol invaders, or they can be afraid and follow blindly like sheep. But for him there was no change. He would always be solid, in his place. He looked at Touba and said, "Do to Mongols as Mongols do, and do to a sheep as a wolf does."

The prince then pointed up the street. A green jeep was stopped at the light. Layla was driving it; a man sat next to her and another sat in the back. They had both brought their heads as close as possible to the woman's head. One of them was saying something, and the woman was laughing carelessly. The prince said, "Do you see the bitch? She must die. The bitch must die."

The light turned green and Layla took off quickly, the sound of her engine filling the street. The prince said that they had removed the muffler in order to create more noise. He asked Touba if she didn't think the woman should die. Such an unimportant being, and she had so little shame; she was so wild, such a slut. Touba thought all this was the prince's own fault. Those moonlit nights, those dances, those feasts—all had contributed to this. She shrugged her shoulders. The prince said, "You are mistaken, I had to see her dance again. Sometimes one must refer to one's memories as fuel for thought. Unfortunately, I can't always nurture myself from my own energy. It is like sitting in a closed cellar: slowly the air is used up and you get claustrophobic. At this moment, you need to open a window no matter what, even if there is storm or if it is cold outside. You take in a few breaths of air, and then you have to close the window again. This woman is that cold storm, the tempest, she is . . . everything that is bad." Silence lingered between them. Amidst the noise of the traffic, the heavy silence bore into the two of them like a twisting screw. The prince whispered, "You should know a truth, that you must never have paid much attention to before. I have to dominate. She must obey me. But this slut is extremely independent."

Prince Gil stood up and stretched. He looked just like a vagabond. He said, "I will kill her one of these days." Touba asked, "Why don't you kill yourself?" The prince raised his eyebrows, as if he had not heard clearly. He turned to look at the woman in amazement and asked, "What did you say?" The woman repeated very distinctly, "I said: Why don't you kill yourself?" The prince smiled, trying to appear as if he still had not heard very well, and the smile froze there on his lips as he looked the woman up and down. Suddenly a massive layer of ice covered the prince's eyes. He grinned mercilessly. Touba felt that his teeth were made of iron. He did not look human. He resembled a huge engine that could run over any human being and demolish everything in his path. The man walked off without another word.

Touba was scared, but in her heart she felt satisfied. She had finally said what she had always wanted to say. For a moment, she had become free of Maryam's corpse and the meaning of truth. She got up and headed home. Every step that brought her closer to the house also added to her anxiety and worry. She automatically stopped in front of the Bank of Saderat. She wished that the teahouse was still there so she could ask for help from Davoud Khan, the owner. What an empty thought. Davoud Khan was dead, and the bank employees were working hard, their heads bent low over their desks. The woman dragged herself to the door of her house and pressed the key into the lock. The huge lock turned with a dry sound. She then opened each of the newer locks with smaller key and finally entered.

The half-dilapidated house stood in front of her. Touba put down her purse and sat on the step by the entrance. She recalled the frozen eyes of the prince. She did not know why she, a veiled, old-fashioned woman, could have said what she had said to the prince. She had no right to say it. It was enough that the prince had let her participate in his parties. Touba, the daughter of Adib, must have become very bold and opinionated to suggest to a man like Prince Gil that he should go kill himself instead of killing his wife. Where had this thought originated? Had she never before thought of it? Perhaps she had. She remembered a night when the prince had, for the first time, talked of killing Layla—one night after the death of Setareh. Touba remembered how she loved Layla. Her manner then was like the soft breeze; she was like a twisting vine and as a calm climbing moon. She didn't want the woman to die, and at the time, she was apprehensive of any death. She had told the prince not to kill his wife. Since then they'd had no contact—and now, a day after the second girl's death, he reappeared and revealed his decision to kill his wife. But why should it concern her that the prince might plan to kill his wife? Why did he ask her? Why did the prince tell her these things?

Once again, she remembered the prince's frozen eyes and felt a cold sweat come upon her. What if the prince thought of killing Touba herself? She was probably the only one who knew his secrets. It was therefore probable that he would kill her to keep his wife's murder hidden. Who would even know that Touba had died, at a time when everyone had left her and no one knocked at her door? Perhaps the house would cease to exist—and if it were gone, no one would even notice.

What a vain life. A bitter sensation bore down upon the old

woman. She felt useless. She remembered that in all her life she had
not once looked carefully at a butterfly, never observed the beautiful
wings of a cricket. And worst of all, she had never seen a forest or a
desert, and she did not know the amazing contrast between the two.
She had circled continuously around a house that one day might not
exist. It would be as if it had never been there from the beginning. The
prince, who was not human, had burrowed into her with his staring,
frozen eyes. This prince knew of Maryam's death, knew of the Master.
It was as if he penetrated into human minds and stole their thoughts.
He probably knew Touba's other thoughts, as well. He had probably
guessed that she would like to see Layla once without him around. He
might know now that she had begun to doubt his greatness and
importance. Perhaps she should go and find the prince again. She
could draw on her feminine power and look at the prince admiringly,
just as she had done in the old days when she was in love and over-
flowed with devotion and everything seemed so amazing. However,
one could worship a prince but not a vagabond. He had dragged his
shoes, worn like slippers; his coat collar had been shiny from oil and
dirt; and the ugly noise he had made through his teeth, as though he
was clearing food particles from them, was disgusting. She should fear
this man rather than worship him. He might suddenly pull his knife
out and tear her through her belly. She should hide from him like a
mouse in a hole, rather than respect him. Poor prince, she thought,
how miserable he has become. Nevertheless, perhaps it was not a bad
idea to trick the man—to bow her head, bring her chador over her
face, approach him with her back bent and lowered like a beggar's, and
try to appear as the weaker one. There was no need to communicate
with him ever again. From now on, whenever it was necessary to make
contact, she would turn her head to the side until he passed, and if
they had to talk, she would humbly lower her head and listen.

A dry sound rattled through her throat. She found tears in her
eyes. She disliked herself. All these years the image of a great, important man had absorbed her, until now, in her old age, when she no
longer had any patience, a vagabond came and preached to her. It
must be that she had lost in the gamble of life; otherwise, everything
would be a farce. But what was one to do with a loser?

Sitting on the step by the door, she slowly lost her energy, growing cold. She did not dare to enter any of the rooms. She thought that if Ismael had left with Moones thirty or forty years ago, perhaps she could have freed herself from the deteriorating house. If they had left at that time, she would have cried and screamed for a while. But then one day she would have grown fearful of the enormity of the empty house, and propelled by her own loneliness, she would have left Setareh's corpse and run away. Somehow all would have worked out.

But they had not left, and their love had gradually turned to a swamp. They had, for all those years, hidden their eyes from the old woman so that she would not see the shame in them. And she had enjoyed this aspect of them. How grand and magnanimous she had felt! She was the great one, and the others were small. Now, suddenly, they had abandoned her in the worst state of helplessness. She was in the desert. How could she repair the house? Even Karim had left. She had piled all her hopes on the boy to be her caretaker in her old age. She loved the boy the same way an old farmer would love his plow ox. Now the ox had become rebellious, had gone to kill its brother. Could she not have taken the brother under her wing, so that he would not become a flaming match? What could a veiled old woman do? She started pacing in the courtyard. She thought that she would keep the outside walls at first, and demolish the interior. She would build a many-storied building containing bathrooms with tubs, central heating, and hot and cold water pipes. She would carpet the entire floor. Then, after everything was done, she would destroy the old walls. Ismael had said to contact him whenever she decided to demolish the house. He might return and help her. But perhaps it was better that he did not come back. This was a man who had not been able to honor his trust. Wasn't his sister's corpse rotting under the pomegranate tree? This man was like a traitor. He had never become a father, had spent all his life with a sterile woman; he did not know the meaning of life, did not have a sense of responsibility, knew nothing about mental and physical exhaustion. No, it was not necessary to contact him. It was best if she found Karim. But where could she find him? The boy had two places, home and school. He did not socialize; he was a homebody. He had now chosen to follow Ismael and Moones, to stick with them and perhaps set up a home with them. Karim could not help, either. How about Kamal? Did he know that his sister had died? Could she drag him to the house and tell him that together they ought to become the caretakers of the girl's grave in order to keep her death secret. Where could she find Kamal? As much as Karim was always at home, the other was always away. He could be anywhere. The last time she had seen him, he had said he was going to Bandar Abbas. How could an old veiled woman go to Bandar Abbas, and amidst a sea of people find Kamal? It was not possible. She walked up and down, turning the pages of her life. Slowly, she wore down a path beneath her feet. Then rain came and it turned her path into a deep depression, which turned into a stream, which poured into the garden. Gradually the wall plaster peeled and fell into the yard. Then the hot sun shone on her head and scorched her brain, the water at the bottom of the pool turned into a muddy swamp, and the smell of death filled the house. Still, the woman kept walking.

In her childhood, Touba was important because of her golden hair. People said she resembled the sun engraved on the tile at the entrance to the bathhouse. Her mother inspected her head for lice and combed her hair regularly between baths. Gradually her braids loosened, her hair spread around her shoulders, became tangled, and grew to look like a crown. As children, they would go to the muddy pond to swim. They held the corners of their towels to trap air bubbles in them, then tied the corners to their ankles, and in this way they were bouyed up, somewhere in the middle between the ground and air. They floated loose, twisting and turning in the water, feeling as if they were on an imaginary flight. Her mother would tell her that her father was wise and educated. Her mother had told Prince Feraydun Mirza that Touba's father was an Adib. The prince had inquired, "What does Adib mean?" She had responded, "Well, dear sir, equal to the shah. He wrote poems and was an intellectual."

Touba recalled a time when she had felt embarrassed. As a five-year-old in the arms of her nanny, who lived in a house adjacent to an elephant stable, Touba had seen the movement of the elephant's ears, and felt afraid. She screamed, "Elephant! Elephant!" Now she stood with the sunken ground under her feet, recalling those days when her father taught her the Qur'an and spoke to her about the chapter, "People of the Elephants," and how flying birds with stones had swooped down on the elephants, crushing their heads. It was as though a group of elephants was attacking her from the depths of her childhood. The elephants were crushing the walls of her house, stampeding through the desert where a group of swallows waited to crush their heads. The old woman screamed again, "Elephant!" She wished there was someone there so she could throw herself in his arms and be protected from the elephants.

The prince! Feraydun Mirza arose from the depth of his decayed death and came toward her. His traditional long jacket was mildewed and the emblem of the lion and the sun on his hat was rusty. He opened his arms and his face was filled with a warm smile. The woman asked, "Prince, why did you do this?" Ever since he had married the second wife, she had been bitterly disappointed. Many nights she had remained awake, turning her head from side to side, clenching her teeth and putting her fist on her mouth to stop herself from screaming. She had told no one that she had still felt jealous of the prince long after his death.

The door of the house next to the elephant's stable opened and a Westerner entered. He was there in the room, offering a diamond ring to her father. She recalled the geography lessons, the yellow map of Iran and the globe that was still hidden in her hope chest. She thought again of Haji Mahmud, her husband, and felt her incredible fear of him. She remembered how she had been able to use the sorrow she felt for the dying street boy to free herself of this husband. Why had she not gone in search of God? Was it perhaps because God was everywhere? Was God in her house, also? Or was it fear that had kept her from going in search of God? Why had she never given birth to a messiah? What right did she have to think she could bear a messiah as the holy Mary had? Did Mr. Khiabani have something to do with any of this?

She stopped. She believed that only once she had done the right thing, and that was choosing Mr. Khiabani. She had spent years under the power of a man whom she had seen only twice. She had survived many degradations. She thought of her life with the prince, of living like a princess, giving birth to the royal children, and then becoming poor, becoming a commoner, being forgotten. She knew that in the recent years she had each day sunk deeper into the realm of the forgotten ones. Other people had come and taken over the domain that she had mistakenly thought was hers. A young girl had lived in her mind for forty years. The girl had given meaning to her life and endowed her house with sainthood. She knew that Setareh lived in every warp and weft of the carpets she had woven.

The woman walked back and forth in the yard, and thought how briefly and how humbly she had lived. She had imprisoned others in this spiderlike life of hers. She thought perhaps she was dead and she herself did not know it. She had been walking for months. She had not yet learned the meaning of truth, though she had an image of truth in her mind. Truth was a woven complexity hidden in the corner of a closet. There were important people who knew this, and did not tell her. In the old days the prince, her husband, had such an image of the British. He believed the British knew everything. Later on, when he had come to like Wilhelm, he believed that Wilhelm also knew everything. But he thought Wilhelm would need to have the power over the British in order to tell the truth to everyone, and he had not possessed that power. It was the same during Hitler's time. Her son-in-law, her own son, and many others had waited for Hitler to come and enlighten everyone. He had not arrived.

The woman kept walking back and forth. She had been walking for a couple of years. She looked like a mildewed corpse who would daily go to the local grocer, to buy a cup of yogurt and some syrup and to the baker for half a loaf of bread, eat then, and walk again. Then suddenly, the smiling mouth of a pomegranate stopped her in her tracks.

The pomegranate tree had borne fruit, it was in fact laden with pomegranates. The pomegranates had ripened and cracked open, and their shining red seeds shone in the golden-bright sun. The woman thought that this was the truth, the pomegranate seeds. She had received a vision that truth, the truth which she did not know and yet had spent a lifetime guarding, was born of Saint Pomegranate. She still did not know what truth was, but the tree had given fruit, as it never had before. The tree was completely covered with large pomegranates and was breathing heavily under their weight. The tree was old. It was actually hollow. But for the last time it offered the masterpiece of its existence. The woman thought she should take the truth to the streets so that people could taste the truth. There among the people there were some who knew what truth was. The mystery of her guarding the pomegranate tree was revealing itself to her. There in the street, the people would tell her what truth was.

The woman ran to the cellar, opened the hope chest, searched through it, and pulled out a large sheet. She saw beneath it a tar that she had not touched for some thirty or forty years. Two of the strings had worked loose and spiders had woven their webs around them. She picked up the tar as well, remembering that she had once promised herself to play for people. How late it had all come to her. She placed the tar by the pool and spread the sheet on the ground. She picked the pomegranates and arranged them on the sheet. She could not reach the pomegranates on the highest branches, so she brought a ladder, placed it against the tree, picked the remainder of the fruit, and threw it on the sheet. The pomegranates piled up. She tied the corners of the sheet together and then she tied her chador around her middle. She put her arms through the tied-up sheet, creating a sort of backpack with it, and with difficulty she picked up her tar and went to the door.

Mr. Tahami, the employee of the Bank of Saderat, was astounded when he got off the bus. The night before he had drunk a great deal of vodka in the company of his friends, and as usual, they had wanted to purify the world. They had cried that they must do something about the arts and sciences. The arts had become mediocre; a bunch of cheap singers and composers had dragged music into the mud. On the other hand, scientific work had lost its popularity; everything would end up a copy of the West. They also had to think about literature. Everything was mediocre and people were being fed junk, while those living in their ivory towers created an elusive literature of fear, without knowing what they were doing—and a great deal of favoritism was going on. A genuinely honest person didn't know what he should do. Progress depended on servitude. In short, everything was reaching the point of oppressiveness. A vista had to open, some fresh air needed to be brought in. People ought to talk with one another. This whispering and murmuring instead of open discussion would only serve to eventually blow everything up. Mr. Tahami knew that it was not easy to achieve all that was needed. He had been thinking about getting a second job in the afternoons in order to pay his mortgage, the installments on the freezer, the car, and the washer-and-dryer set. He had nevertheless participated in his friends' discussion and offered some ideas. Returning to the house, he had put up with his wife's complaints and crying. His wife didn't know why she had married only to become a unpaid servant, why she had to wash Mr. Tahami's children's dirty diapers and the dishes and cook food and sweep and was supposed to live in joy just from the idea that she had a husband. When Mr. Tahami lay his body on the bed he thought of taking his wife to the movies the next night to dispel her melancholy mood. In the morning he had gotten up feeling miserable, had damned himself and felt his grumbling wife was justified, but still continued frowning. Now, as he got off the bus near the bank, he saw the ancient woman offering pomegranates to the people.

She had spread her stuff just a few steps from the bus stop and had split the pomegranates with her rough, scabbed fingers and dirty nails, offering pieces to people. Mr. Tahami received a piece also. He noticed that the woman had an old tar beside her. Even though he was late for work, he paused for a while to discern the meaning of this alms-giving. He couldn't figure it out. It was not customary to give pomegranates as alms; he could not remember ever hearing of such a custom. He finally shrugged his shoulders and entered the bank. He was certain that night he would not take his wife to the movies. Not that he wished to drink vodka again, but it would be interesting to talk with his friends about the woman. In the midst of the traffic and noise, it was a subject all to itself.

Meanwhile a group of high school students strolled down the street, kicking a stone along the gutter as they went. The stone rolled to a stop right next to the old woman. They were also given some pomegranate. The woman was undoubtedly mad, but no one laughed. Some people even stood around waiting to see what might happen. The boys heard the high school bell ring and ran off to class. They did not want to leave the scene without seeing what might happen, but there was no time left. Rushing toward their classes at the school, they were able to inform a few of the other boys about the woman. They shared their pomegranate pieces with the others.

A woman carrying bread took a whole pomegranate. She said she wanted to give some to her children. In the mildewed old woman's face she saw a grandeur and magnanimity that she could use. She felt she would definitely have good fortune receiving alms from such a woman. A taxi driver stopped a short distance down the street to check his tires. He also received a piece of pomegranate.

After the last piece of pomegranate was gone, the crowd disappeared just as quickly as it had gathered. It was not possible to hold anyone there. Nothing was left to look at except an old woman and a broken tar. The old woman picked up her tar and boarded a bus. The driver looked at her expectantly. He wanted her bus ticket. The old woman moved toward the back of the bus giving the driver's look no heed, and sat in the only vacant seat. The driver gave up the idea of getting a fee from her.

When the bus began moving a flood of words rushed to the woman's mind. But she could not organize them; she could not form a sentence. She wished for the people to listen. She clapped her hands together a few times and a few turned to look at her. The old woman wanted to speak. Many things fermented in her mind but they did not make sense. She stood up to quiet people's murmuring, and said, "Hum, hum, hum, hay, hop, hay, ho."

Everyone was now looking at her. She said, "I want to tell you that there is something I must say right now." A young woman sitting with her child a few seats further back turned her eyes away. Feeling sorry for the old woman, she looked out the bus window. The old woman said, "That is right, I have to tell. There are bodies in the garden, you know. It has been many years—one only a couple of years, but the other one has been there a long time. I had to take care of them."

The bus driver had to use the brakes, and the old woman was thrown forward. A man held on to her to keep her from falling. The old woman continued, "The prince wants to kill his wife. If he kills her time will stop. Everyone will turn to stone. He might have done it by now."

The man who had prevented her from falling said, "Come, mother. Come, dear." He held on to her hand and carefully helped her get off the bus. He stepped over the gutters and stood by her on the sidewalk and asked, "Where is your house, mother?" The old woman said, "No house, there is no returning now. I must tell the truth." The man asked her to tell him the truth. The old woman suddenly went mute. She looked into the man's eyes. It was not Prince Gil, but his eyes had the look of the prince's eyes. She said, "It is not possible to talk to you anymore. Now we must whisper." A wise look suddenly came upon her; she bowed to the man a few times and stepped slowly backward. She thanked him for helping her, said goodbye, and started walking away.

She held on to her tar, passed a few streets, and turned into a quiet alley. There she sat on the ground and began playing her tar. The cacophony of an out-of-tune tar with two snapped strings filled her ears. She had forgotten the order of the notes. She started singing to encourage herself. Her rough, unharmonious voice mixed with the sound of the tuneless tar. A young boy who was near her spat at her. His spit fell on the hand playing the strings.

It was useless. She leaned the tar against the wall and resumed walking. She had definitely discovered the truth, but could not verbalize it. In order to free herself of the truth, she shook her head a few times. The ambiguity of her thoughts bothered her. A bicyclist coming toward her imagined that she was a common mad dancer; he pushed on her chest in jest. The woman fell flat down in the gutter, and the bicyclist quickly disappeared. The woman was expecting to hear his laughter, but she did not. She lay on her back in the gutter as the polluted muddy water flowed around her. Her body blocked the flow of the water; dammed up, it soon began to run over her face and body. A crumpled, empty pack of Winston cigarettes caught between her eye and her nose. She pressed her arms against the walls of the gutter and struggled to sit up. She sat there until the water rose to the level of her waist. Dripping with water, wet from head to toe, she finally headed toward home.

She shuffled along silently. She had forgotten to shut the door behind her when she went out, and she no longer felt so adamant about shutting it now, either. She went to the pool and sat on the edge, and then she heard the sound of a door shutting. She thought it was Ismael, Moones, or Karim, but it was none of them. It was Layla, hiding under a black chador, but still obviously full of fear. Her dark, frightened eyes shifted from side to side in her painted face. She looked around apprehensively, as though searching for someone hidden there. She tried to overcome her anxiety, approached Touba, and said that she had to hide herself somewhere. Prince Gil was stalking her in order to kill her. The old woman watched in absolute silence while Layla waited desperately for a response. If Touba didn't want to help her, she would leave her house. Touba said that she could stay there, but the prince knew the way to her house and was well aware of everything. Layla laughed. She said that she was not afraid of the prince. Of course the prince was aware of everything—everything except the depth of Layla's being. Touba said that the prince also knew Touba's thoughts, always. He could now search in Touba's thoughts and find Layla here, frightened and anxiety-ridden. Layla smiled and said that it didn't matter what he might know because she could leave immediately. However, Layla said, beginning to pace in the garden, Touba was right: The prince could not find Layla, but he could find Touba and he could locate Layla by reading her thoughts. She said this was why she was afraid of showing herself to anyone, because she might instantly be recognized. Therefore, she had to degrade herself, she had to be a buffoon, lead a dangerous life and pretend to be a prostitute. In this manner she had sometimes preserved her life until the prince became impatient with her excesses. It was possible that Prince Gil would let her be this way to test his own power of endurance, but he would eventually beat her, and he might even kill her.

Layla continued pacing. Her painted makeup was slowly dripping. A simple, clear face appeared beneath the mess. She looked like a virgin who was the image of purity. She said whenever she went back to her real, untouched, pure self, she scared the prince. Her chastity threw the prince off balance; the man rotated constantly around her impenetrable fortress of being in order to find a way in. Often he would begin crying because of his sense of ineptitude. He would think of suffocating her to get rid of the image of her being in his mind, and at times he would feel sickened by her purity. He would then head out into the fields to rebel. He would search after prostitutes and have sex with them by the streams, therefore letting the woman know that this was how he wanted her to be. She thus felt an eternal piety, but the prince felt powerless and crippled, suddenly empty of his manliness. He became attracted to female ways, visited monasteries, engaged in prayers, and drowned himself in amazement and stupefaction. His incapacitation and bewilderment drove him to hatred. At times he came to her, raped her, enslaved her, mocked her in the presence of their many children, told her that she was a weak, crippled, contemptible person. He belittled her to the point that Layla was unable to make ordinary conversation, and her thoughts settled into the deep layers of her being. Over time, she had drawn into herself, turned into a hen dangled by a leg, ready to be attacked by all the cocks in the world.

The woman walked and walked, her face fluctuating between piety and lewdness, like the waves of the sea. Layla said that she had learned not to think of the prince anymore, not to see him. She would sit by the windows and crochet silk, cook and eat for herself, only herself, and only leave the leftovers for the prince and others. She could think but not speak. Others could take advantage of her, but she remained somehow uninvolved. She felt that she loved her cat more than she loved the prince and even appreciated the rug under her feet more than she valued him. She would see the man go to pubs and bars and get drunk. His breath always smelled of pickles, alcohol, or vomit. She then noticed that he was dealing drugs behind the bars. He raised prices on rice and oil and mixed water with milk.

Layla said she would behave like a complete bitch, her lips tight and her nostrils sharp. She would belittle him, walk behind him, and make him feel insecure and disabled. Then the prince would lose his temper. He would scream and holler and badmouth her, or in a moment of anger, pick up a knife and stab at her. She said the prince killed her on a regular basis. The woman would pretend to be dead and let a moment pass, and then the prince would bring her back to life because he could not live a moment without her. She said that the problem was that each time she died she was innocent, but when she came back to life she was not innocent. When she was not there, the sorrow of her absence showered the world with dead ashes and people became ridden with sorrow. They got nowhere, they walked through a vacuum, they wanted her, they cried in her absence—but every time she returned, her light brightened all to the point that they stared, they got anxious, and they reached beyond their means. She said it was not her fault that people acted as they did. She had to move. If she did not, death came to her; if she did not, she felt needles on the soles of her feet. Unwittingly she caused agitation, chaos, even bedlam in others.

She said the problem was that she must always remain the wife of the prince, always love the boy in him, and that the man must always choose her and worship the mother within her. But Layla was now tired. She remembered a day long gone, a distant day when she promenaded in an unknown forest. She had an animal feeling; she was like a fly, or a tiger; she was a leaf of grass, or the trunk of a tree; she was the taste of quinine, the water of a spring; she was the mountain. She loved her man the same way—mountain-like, fly-like—and it was the memory of that eternal love alone that kept her going, kept her alive.

She sat in the corner of the yard, wrapped in her chador, leaning against the wall with her head resting on her knees. She leaned her head back against the wall and stared in sorrow at Touba. Touba asked her how she intended to live in this house, which was toppling over. The news would undoubtedly spread quickly through the city that this house was full of dead bodies. Officials would come and pull the corpses out. It would cause havoc. To prevent chaos, they had to be silent, as they had been before. To prevent chaos they had to keep their secrets in the depths of their being, refrain from speaking aloud, whisper, and never record anything. But all would fall apart if Layla stayed there.

Layla continued looking at Touba sorrowfully. She said she felt the girl's corpse under her feet; it seemed to her that the girl had come close to the memory of her imaginary eternal forest. She had wanted to stand next to the man and then fly with him over mountains or deserts, to fly like eagles, to touch the edge of the rays of the sun and the empty sky—to mold into one. She said it seemed to her that Maryam had been in love. She said the girl's presence was multiplying.

Layla stood up, declaring that she now knew that she must kill herself in order to be born again from the girl's particles. She said that this time she would take the opportunity away from the prince. She would not let him kill her; she would kill herself. She said longingly that if the prince had only heard Touba's message correctly, if he just once killed himself, a new world would emerge.

Layla shook herself violently, and just like that she was cut to pieces. Her blood spread over the walls and her flesh stuck everywhere. Touba was covered in blood, her nostrils filled with the smell of flesh and blood. She covered her eyes from fright. She heard the woman's voice cry her name. Then by some miracle, Layla stood in front of her again. She said, "Only with my death is purity possible. We have to go together to the depths of eternity. Silence is possible only there. He now knows us not."

She pulled the old woman to the depths with her. They traveled down to the roots of the pomegranate tree. Initially Touba could hear the tender sound of a bell, like a pear-shaped drop of water dripping on the surface of a swamp. They spent long moments in absolute silence in order to hear the sound. Touba heard the dripping sound three times. "These are the last moments of Setareh," Layla said. The bell now sounded regularly in the distance. The other body, Maryam, like a tornado announced with thunder, turned into random particles. She was a flood under the dust; she turned and twisted in herself. Layla said, "We are going further down." The lower depths were filled with cries and lamentations. She said, "These souls died mute, and now they are expressing themselves." The torrent of cries and lamentations tore through

Touba. The two sank even deeper into the depths of darkness, into a darkness darker than itself, which was heavy and stagnant and silent. There was in that place a silence to end all silence, a heaviness to end all heaviness. They descended to the depths of metal, to the depths of fire. Particles of Touba's being were turning around themselves, her head and feet were all one. She had become as one singular particle, and she screamed from the pain. She could not bear it. The prince had said that this state would only last a brief moment.

There now appeared a ray of light. Layla said, "It is consciousness." Touba was in a desert and Layla was inside her. Layla said, "Do you remember that we were one? How much we feared our four sons. You enjoyed the dancing wind among the tree leaves, you drank from the springs, somewhat like being in Paradise. Some men came, they embraced you, you slept with them happily, and then the children came, one after another. You cut their umbilical cords with a stone, tied them off, and slowly a tribe formed around you. Your chicks' eyes were glued on you, they clustered around you with open mouths and empty stomachs. You didn't know what to do."

Layla laughed and continued, "Do you remember the time you sat respectfully with the children a few steps from the older son as he was hunting? He ate the meat, sharing it with his friends, and you watched. They threw the bones, and you would collect them and give them to the smaller children. Then you would bury the bones in the ground, hoping that wild goats would grow into a tree that would relieve you and the children of the sorrow of hunger. The second son didn't like eating the leftovers of the older brother's hunt. The boy dreamt of flying like an eagle. He hung bird feathers on himself and danced around the fire. He truly believed that he would be able to fly someday. You and I watched him hopefully, expectantly, as if he could fly, could soar up to the peaks, and could grab the bird's eggs from among the insurmountable boulders, and then hunger would end. We watched him, filled with so much hope that at times it seemed as though he actually had flown.

"Do you remember the third son always hid everything? In the heart of a tree, under a bush—something was hidden in every crevice: a bird's egg, a bone, a piece of meat. Hidden from everyone, he ate alone, sharing with no one. He was a miser. To make matters worse, he also stole from others. You hid everything for fear of him.

"The last son hung on to you, as if you were one spirit in two bodies. He sat next to you politely and watched the hunters eating voraciously. Like you, he would put a handful of bloodied sand into his mouth in order to stop the grumbling in his stomach. Like you, he watched the flying dance of his brother, watched how you dug into the ground and buried the wild goat's bones. From you he learned the secret of planting seeds and fell in love with the earth. Do you remember, from then on, he always accompanied you to the springs? It was with him that you lost love, sacrificed me for food. You gave birth to me, a girl.

"You must have learned from your flying son, because you taught me the dance steps. The hunters would come, and each would give you part of their catch in order to watch my dance. Your older son was among them. I mesmerized them. They would calm down. You had given me all your will to move. You resided on the earth and sent me to the sky. I would close my eyes, call the spirit of the wind, dance among the branches as the wind. Then I tried to pour myself onto earth like raindrops, tried to roll like ocean waves, rise from the horizon like the moon, and disappear beyond the peaks like the sun. They watched in amazement. Each time they came with meat, you and the younger son hid while I slowly worked on the hunters, brought them around to your tribe. You became stronger and became part of the sky.

"But your older son never forgave me when he realized that he had lost his freedom to us. You offered him women and girls, left the best food for him, but he would not forgive you, and he was determined to take his revenge out on me. My eternal husband insulted me. He wanted to pull me down from the sky. Now that he had lost his freedom, he felt power must replace it. He now sent me to the deserts to hunt wild animals. He drew energy from them, until he could command you and all your belongings. We had to do something. We had to kill his wildness. Do you remember that we killed him, the pure, simple one who lived like an animal, the very one who watched the dance? If he hurt anyone it was not intentional.

There was so much love in his eyes that I swooned unconsciously. He clung to me like a lamb, but we killed him.

"Do you remember your older son, how at night he languished in sorrow for his lost half? He wept violently. He had just acquired our disease—the disease of splitting ourselves in half in order to manage the matters of the world. He suffered from the fear of death. He walked around the village at night calling for his wild half. Sometimes he would become crazy, head for the forests, get lost for months and years, and return again. He would hold me in his arms, I who was the murderer of half of his being. When he did this, he frightened me. Out of fear I would begin to dance, and he would calm down and cry. He was caught between the desert and the village.

"One day, the flying boy went to the mountains to become an eagle. He did not return. You and the younger son sat staring at the mountain peaks, and you taught everyone else to look up at the peak. If he were to come one day, the great wild eagle would tear apart all sinners. I danced, and you planted the sense of guilt, created traditions. You gave birth to a girl for the younger son, and she was an obedient and calm girl. The two of them sat on either side of you and stared at the peaks, and I would bring to you the spirits of wild men as offerings. After nights of drunkenness, they headed to your village to watch for an instant how the people stared at the mountain peaks. Your older son was also watching the mountain peaks. He was also seeking the secrets surrounding his lost brother. He gradually came to believe in the great eagle spirit and relied on your magic. There was someone greater than all, there above—more silent, more present, more absent than anyone else." Layla placed her hands on her face. She said, "I saw that brother in the mountains once, frozen in ice while battling a tiger. This was the reason he no longer lived. I told no one that secret, until this moment when I now tell you."

Layla continued, "The desert was buried in a fearful silence, when the older brother believed in the spirit above the peaks, and he became its shadow on this earth. He wondered about the rules of the flying dance, and he made me dance to those steps of his. His watching my dance gave him power to conquer the world. Thus, he needed to steal me from you. The path was doubled in this way: Yours that covered the ground and ours that made its way through the skies."

Layla laughed again and said, "Do you remember how the third boy sold us to the hunters? He wrapped me in a skin and took me as a gift to the older brother, to get some meat in return, and I received meat again in order to reveal the secret of the flying brother for them. But the hunters did nothing against your wishes. You had given birth to me to free yourself of movement; you were now an owner of wheat fields. But they took everything, killed you, divided your spirit in half—just what you, Touba, had asked for. Henceforth you had no life, but your stomach was full. They had me, the living half, to dance for them. They came in herds from the desert to watch me and to grab your younger son's lands. Once in a while I made them war against one another to give you breathing space. For a while this trick worked, until they grew angry at me. Then they brought me down from the sky to prostitute me. Poor woman, they polluted your living half and you grew further away from me. Whenever they came, you gathered your children about you, spread earth on your head, cried out loud for the spirit of your eagle son to witness, and you lamented together.

"Then, in the midst of the night, you hid from the third boy, who stole from you to hand the booty over to the hunters in return for a reward. He also stole from them to receive rewards from you. You would all go to the silo to count the remaining grains of wheat. And I danced continuously, hoping to calm the men from the wilderness. I would grow dizzy, and yet there was no end to them. They mated in the wilderness and poured down on your village. They prostituted me in order to dominate you, and you slapped the faces of your other daughters to warn them of their fearful fates and of the danger of becoming like me. Touba, I took your hatred to my heart. I no longer danced as the waves of the sea, nor as the wind in the branches, nor even like the law of union between the earth and the sky. I only moved enough to keep them calm. I now danced in cities; I hated men and hated you. I had been separated from my pure roots and defiled.

"On the day that the third brother had sold me into slavery and

I was dancing in a brothel, I looked at the men of the wilderness around me. They were all headless, but had complete sexual organs. My will to dance left me. I felt disgusted. However, the habit of moving, which had been negated in you, would not let me be. I turned completely to prayer. The hunters did not believe me. They mocked me. I had your chador on my head and traveled alone through the wilderness. They pursued me to force me to dance. I spread the chador into the air, prayed between the earth and sky. I bewildered them. I crawled on the ground most of the way in order to get to the house of God. I bewildered them, and they wondered what to do. I then took my revenge. I gave birth to you.

"My man hung around me to observe my metamorphosis. The possibility of seeing the old dance drove him mad. But we had left the old purity so that you and your younger son could remain complete, to sow the land, and to stare at the mountain peaks. I no longer danced for him, so he went mad. The semi-dead wildness was burning from within. This half-dead man was in love with the dance of nature. Instead, I gave birth to you. From the very first day of your birth, I belittled you. I avenged on you the aimless dances I had done for the wild ones. You were lowered to nothingness. There was no need to chain your feet; you were already chained to the earth beyond reprieve by the oppression you endured.

"You, poor one, then gave birth to me, a prostitute. One who moved her lower limbs to amaze the wilderness people, in hopes that they would give you part of their loot or meat from the hunt. As such we rolled together to the lowest abyss.

"My eternal husband abandoned me. He wandered around the world, but his life was doomed. The Mongols had come to steal the last of your strength and belongings. I had information about the man who was killing the women by the water springs. He was in the right. He had to kill in order to prevent getting caught by them. But regrettably, he had killed you once, you who had been born of me, who had been so oppressed, belittled, quiet, and helpless. I had created you in this manner in hopes that you would be strong in times of cruelty. I had thought that your weakness would save you. Poor me! For seven thousand years you remained silent. You became as silent as a stone."

Touba was now someone else. She no longer had the need to search for truth. In the wilderness, between those two women, sat a third one who held a weapon in one hand and in the other a fistful of damp earth, a souvenir from someone, something, or someplace. She had a frown as large as an ocean on her face. Touba said, "So is this the one?" She indicated the girl with her head. Layla said, "Yes and no. She was born once, once became pregnant in perfect love, once she gave birth to everyone. But our era comes to an end. After seven thousand years of struggle, something else must now begin. I once killed myself, but now what about you? Are you ready to die?"

Touba lowered her head to acknowledge that she was. Layla said, "You are your own veil. Hafez, oh poet, be gone from our midst!" She heard the sound of an explosion. Touba shot to the surface and noticed that she was spread all over the earth. She was now a thousand earth particles, and she could see through every particle. She saw herself in a wilderness, and the prince had killed a deer. The blood and milk of the doe mixed in waves and covered Touba's being. The woman saw through a thousand eyes, and her look silenced nature. Prince Gil watched over the doe's corpse. Touba had the thought that it would have been a good thing if she had been a hunter. A hunter must kill, even though a mother deer was not to be killed. But this man was not a hunter, and it was not the era of hunting. No one was hungry for venison, so it was wrong to kill.

She heard a sound. At a place a little distance away, some men were being murdered. The men bent over the earth, their blood dampening the soil. Touba cried. The men's blood mixed with the woman's tears and penetrated deep into the earth. It penetrated to the depths of the thundering hurricane. A star sparked; the earth became pregnant. The earth was continuously pregnant. Always in the season of birth, it bore someone from every cell in its body—woman, man, old, young, short, tall.

Layla had returned. She was now fully dressed in blue. She said "Get up, for it is the season of departure." She helped Touba up. Her placenta separated from her with a thunderous sound and fell on her children's heads. Groups of people drowned in blood. Layla said, "It is up to them to become liberated or not liberated."

She saw Prince Gil waving his naked sword in the air.
Touba asked, "Am I dead?"
Layla said, "You are dead."
Touba asked, "You too?"
The response was, "I cannot die."
Touba asked, "The prince?"
Layla answered, "He also cannot die."

Tehran
September 1987

Afterword
Touba: A Woman for All Seasons

So I said to the sage,
What is the Touba tree, and where can I find it?
He said,
The Touba tree is an enormous tree.
Whoever is marked out for Paradise, will see the tree when he goes
there.
Does it bear any fruit? I asked.
And he replied,
Any fruit you see in the world will be on that tree.
>   **—Sohrevardi, The Red Logos *(6th century C.E.)***

It is only the story that can continue beyond the war and the warrior.
It is only . . . the story that saves our progeny from blundering like
blind beggars into the spikes of the cactus fence. The story is our escort.
Without it we are blind.
>   **—Chinua Achebe, Anthills of the Savannah *(1987)***

Touba and Meaning of Night is the story of a country, a house, a legendary tree, and a woman, that all live, grow, and suffer together for
over a hundred years. The country is Iran, and the woman is named
Touba, after the tree of divine light and wisdom in Persian legend
and lore. Rooted in paradise, it is said, the Touba tree spreads its

branches over the house of the Prophet Mohammad and the homes of all the faithful. In *Touba and the Meaning of Night*, the title character is overwhelmed by the dream of reaching her legendary namesake, seeing its light, and embracing its wisdom. Her story is a spiritual quest. But at the same time, like the tree, the novel's Touba has deep roots in the soil of her native land, and her story is also the story of Iran in a turbulent century of change.

Two revolutions bookend the seemingly endless nights of Touba's life story. Her tale that begins in the last decades of the nineteenth century, with the socio-political upheavals that culminate in the Constitutional Revolution of 1906–1911, ends with the Islamic Revolution of 1979—both events with far-reaching affects on the country's social, political, and literary landscapes. Iran's Constitutional Revolution, the first of its kind in the Islamic world, converted the country from an absolute monarchy to a constitutional one, and reflected, among other things, its growing engagement with the West and modernity. The Islamic Revolution, encompassing a broad spectrum of ideas and objectives and reflecting diverse intellectual trends, social backgrounds, and political demands, put an end to the millennia-long monarchy and also represented a rejection of the Western influences and interests that had come to dominate in Iran.

As Touba lives her long life in between the two revolutions, many important things happen in her country: The Constitutional Revolution set into motion a period of social and political unrest in Iran, as the shah, with aid from Russia, sought to reclaim power from the new parliamentary government, which would operate only sporadically in the subsequent decades. The incursion of Russian, British, and Ottoman troops into Iran during World War I was an extreme expression of the ongoing encroachment of foreign powers into Iranian territory and the Iranian economy and culture. Soon afterwards, the longstanding Qajar dynasty (1796–1925) was replaced in a coup by the Pahlavi dynasty (1925–1979).

The rule of the former military leader Reza Shah Pahlavi (r. 1925–1941), saw an acceleration of Iran's assimilation into the world economy, a process begun in the closing decades of the nineteenth century. The commercialization of agriculture, a general shift from agriculture to industry, the introduction of capitalist modes of production, increased mobility across class lines and a growth in the middle class, and increasing contacts with the West, all propelled Iran's social, political, and cultural spheres away from its past at a speed unprecedented in the country's history. In tandem with these fundamental changes the struggle for women's rights, begun before the Constitutional Revolution, developed and intensified. The movement was highly influenced by social reforms in neighboring countries such as Turkey, Egypt, India, and the Transcaucasian republics (Azerbaijan, Armenia, and Georgia), as well as by European liberal ideas. The Constitutional Revolution, for which many women fought ardently, did not grant rights to women. It did, however, provide spaces within which women's advocates could fight and achieve some rights, and they went on to found health clinics, public schools, and publications. After his state visit to Turkey in the summer of 1935, Reza Shah ventured to outlaw the veil, a decision that left an indelible mark on the social fabric of Iran.

Reza Shah's quest to modernize the country, however, was accompanied by an increasingly autocratic and arbitrary style of rule, creating widespread dissatisfaction and fertile ground for growing opposition, especially on the left. With the outbreak of World War II, Iran declared its neutrality, but the Allies objected to Reza Shah's friendly relations with and economic ties to the Third Reich. British, Soviet, and U.S. forces occupied Iran in 1941, and Reza Shah was forced to abdicate in favor of his son, Mohammad Reza Pahlavi (r.1941–1979).

The young, Swiss-educated shah initially exhibited a democratic attitude. During the first decade or so of his rule, beginning with the entry of the Allied troops into Iran in 1941 and ending with a CIA-assisted military coup in 1953, Iranians enjoyed a rare and short-lived period of freedom of expression. Political and literary activities flourished. And the ascendancy of the left and the expression of radical views, culminating in the First Congress of Persian Writers in 1946, had a powerful and lasting effect on Iran's intellegentsia.

The period of freedom soon came to an end, however. On March 15, 1951 the Iranian parliament, upon the recommendation of the special oil committee headed by Mohammad Mosaddeq, voted to nationalize Iran's oil industry—until then controlled largely by the Anglo-Iranian Oil Company, with the British government as its major shareholder. On April 28, 1951 Mosaddeq was appointed prime minister. It did not take long for the Central Intelligence Agency, in collaboration with British intelligence, to foment a military coup. In 1953, in the Agency's first successful effort to bring down a foreign government, Mosaddeq was overthrown and power consolidated in the hands of the Western-backed shah.

The coup was a socio-political watershed and a defining moment in the country's history. The grip of censorship tightened, authors were imprisoned, the publication of materials hostile to the regime was banned, and dissent was kept under control by the SAVAK, the shah's notorious secret police. In 1962, in an effort to win popular and international support, the shah launched his "White Revolution," which called, among other things, for land reforms, literacy programs, and women's suffrage. Some of these reforms stirred a protest movement among the clergy, who later emerged as a major force fuelling the Islamic Revolution of 1979.

With soaring oil prices towards the end of the 1960s and early 1970s, the gap between the rich and the poor widened, and protests against social injustice and political oppression, with an ever-increasing religious bent, swelled. The turbulent years of the Islamic Revolution followed soon thereafter. Many intellectuals and writers initially embraced the revolution as a liberating force, and many took an active part in it. The departure of the shah in January of 1979, and the subsequent return of Ayatollah Khomeini (1902–1989) after a long exile opened a new chapter in Iran's history. Iran was declared an Islamic republic, with a new constitution reflecting Ayatollah Khomeni's ideas of Islamic government and law. In less than two years, women, despite their massive participation in demonstrations and social upheavals in the early revolutionary phase, were required, once again, to wear the veil. Disillusionment replaced hope.

Shahrnush Parsipur's *Touba and the Meaning of Night* meticulously captures the expansive breadth of the social and political events of this hundred-year period of Iran's history, and delicately incorporates them into the imaginary account of the different stages of Touba's life and the tale of her house. Touba's wondrous encounter with Sheikh Mohammad Khiabani (1880–1920), a political leader of the Constitutional movement, when she is carrying to the cemetery the body of a young boy who has starved to death, allows the novelist to convey the era's revolutionary sentiments and ideals, and the discontent and poverty which underpins them. The fate of Touba's husband, a Qajar prince, dramatizes the change in Iran's ruling dynasties, while her encounters with such marvels as paved roads, telephone lines, and unveiled women, marks Reza Shah Pahlavi's campaigns of modernization.

The arrival of an Azerbaijani family at Touba's house reflects the mass migration from Azerbaijan to Tehran. Ismael, the child of this new family, becomes a politically laden fictional character. His changing political philosophies, his flirtations with the Marxist Tudeh Party, and his subsequent imprisonment—apparently by the shah's secret police—all illuminate the turbulent history of Iran in the mid-twentieth century.

Less than a decade after the 1953 coup, the country would be shattered by the first waves of the religiously charged social unrest that culminated in the Islamic Revolution. Shattered, too, are the walls of Touba's house. Touba's painful submission to the illusory idea that the walls, once mended and fortified, would survive the rendered blows coincides with the arrival of another family at her house. The children of this new family—Maryam, Karim, and Kamal—are, like the period of history they represent, more absorbed by a politically charged religion than by Marxism or other political ideologies. The novel weaves the tale of these young people into the narrative of the Islamic Revolution so thoughtfully that some passages of the novel might as well be read as a socio-political document. It is interesting to note, however, that, although the characters are positioned firmly within their social and political background, they can be appreciated without precise knowledge of political or historical morphology.

Rarely is the complex relationship between the social and political structures of a country so well woven into the structure of a novel and the actions of fictional characters, and even more rarely has a novel's protagonist journeyed with a country as it painfully discards traditional cast to appear in modern attire. In other words, the narrative of Touba's house is a hall of mirrors in which the history of twentieth-century Iran appears and changes shape in all of its various incarnations. The novel laments the vanished beauty of the past, of a bygone world in which inherited ideals and adopted values had not yet clashed, and intellectual, social, and moral questions had simple, unequivocal answers. At the same time, it depicts the suffering, injustice, and oppression inherent in this pre-modern past, and sympathetically portrays the characters whose political engagements, however misguided and futile, serve their visions of Iran's future.

The impulse to modernize the concept of literature and make it reflective of social conditions also surfaced in the last decades of the nineteenth century and manifested itself in the works of a group of intellectuals and political activists who submitted various facets of Iranian culture, literary or otherwise, to unsparing criticism. They denounced, among other things, ornate styles and conventional modes of expression, prevalent in the classical tradition, and advocated the use of clear and vigorous language, the living language of the people. Poetry, as the most prominent index of Persian culture, was the first to appear in modern attire. It was soon followed by the appearance of the first modern Persian fictions. Certain historical events, most notably in education and journalism, had a direct effect on the rise of Persian modern fiction, affecting and, in a sense, creating its readers, writers, and especially the manner and the matter of its contents. The Constitutional revolution and the translation movement that had begun in mid-nineteenth century did much to change the axis of aesthetic culture from traditional concepts to one underlined by modern literary movements, in vogue in Western countries. The very popularity of translations from European languages indicate the emergence of a new reading public, mainly urban and middle class, with new tastes and preferences.

The early works of modern Persian fiction tended toward historical novels, bringing to life a distant past, real or imagined. These works, in general, convey a curious blend of nostalgia and factual information about the past, gleaned from historical chronicles and the scholarly research of the Orientalists of their time.[1]

Novels describing social conditions, despite harsh state censorship, also flourished. In most of these novels, however, the novelists' concern for the structure, and development of characters was subsumed by the desire to convey a message and to highlight social plagues within the context of the highly dramatized sensational plots. Drawing on the literary naturalism of the West, many of these novels revolved around the lives of fallen women and the tales of grim cities, both portrayed as stereotyped victims of modernity's sinister forces. The juxtaposition of the city and the village, the innocent peasant girl and her promiscuous urban counterpart, was a recurrent theme in the fictions of the period. Although this newly realized figure of the Persian woman appeared in a seemingly more realistic manner than her mythical predecessors, in the hands of her male creators she nevertheless remained far from reality. It took Persian literature several more decades to settle on a more coherent notion of history, and a more nuanced image of women as fictional characters.

In 1921, Mohammad Ali Jamalzadeh (1892–1997), traditionally known as the founder of modern Persian fiction, published his first collection of short stories, *Yeki Bud, yeki nabud* (Once upon a time). Most of the stories were colored by his vivid depiction of social "types," representing different forces in Persian society, and were subjected to his harsh unsparing criticism. In his later works, however, social types were replaced by unique and complex individuals, as in his 1942 novel Dar al-Majanin (The lunatic asylum), an intricate account of a set of characters detained in an asylum.

The realistic trend in Persian prose fiction continued through the early decades of the century, when preoccupation with story line and content was gradually replaced by concerns for formal sophistication, stylistic innovation and internal coherence. In 1937 Sadeq Hedayat (1903–1951) published his short novel *Buf-e Kur* (*The Blind Owl,* 1937), perhaps the most seminal work of modern fiction in Persian.

Both Jamalzadeh and Hedayat were to have lasting impacts on the development of Persian fiction, and its future trajectory.

The decades that followed the coup of 1953, a historical blow with profound reverberations on the nation's psyche, is generally remembered as decades of disappointments and regrets.[2] The aggressive social criticism of earlier years was replaced by self-criticism and introvert romanticism. Inspired by the drive to find the underlying causes of the plagued present, many writers whose political ideals had been betrayed, strove to dramatize recent decades of the nation's history, allegorized or otherwise.[3] The period, in which a new literary generation came of age was marked, as a whole, by two dominant and conflicting literary trends, populism and modernism. Modernist writers, discarding the confines of social realism, prominent in populist oeuvres, strove to redefine the then current concepts of commitment in literature. Persian writers also emerged as a professional class, drawing attention to their shared rights and responsibilities with the formation, in 1968, of the Association of Iranian Writers, which tried to address the problem of censorship.

This period also witnessed the rise of fiction by Iranian women. In 1947 Simin Daneshvar (1921–), the first Persian woman novelist, published her first collection of short stories, *Atash-e Khamush* (The quenched fire). The 1967 publication of her critically acclaimed and highly popular novel, *Savushun* (tr. *A Persian Requiem*, 1969) heralded the dawn of a new era in the history of modern Persian fiction. Set in a small Persian town disrupted by the British occupation during World War II, the novel chronicles the life of a perceptive woman who copes with her idealistic and uncompromising husband while struggling with her need for an individual identity.

The 1979 Islamic Revolution brought a lull in the country's literary output, but this proved to be short-lived. Many of the already established and prospective writers, voluntarily or otherwise, left the country to settle elsewhere, and many of them treated the reality of their lives in exile as the material of fiction.[4] So did those who chose to stay.[5] In the introduction to *Strange Times My Dear: The Pen Anthology of Contemporary Iranian Literature*, Nahid Mozaffari writes:

In spite of the censorship imposed by the strict religious ideology and by various organs of the state, the number of writers and poets has multiplied and literary magazines have flourished. Literature has begun to emerge from the private sphere and from the domain of the upper and upper-middle class to the public sphere, where many writers and readers from economically disadvantaged backgrounds are beginning to participate. A large body of feminist literature, written mainly but not exclusively by women, has also grown and flourished within the literary landscape.(xx)

Ironically, the institutionalized oppression seemed to invigorate women's urge to write. As bibliographies on literary production reveal, women could now claim a distinct and acclaimed space in the otherwise male dominated literary canon. Women writers experimented with different aspects of the craft of writing, the range of their work extending from weighty ideological polemics and depictions of prison, torture, and displacement to lighter genres, including detective stories. Since the seventies and eighties, Farzaneh Milani in her introduction to *Stories by the Iranian Woman Since the Revolution*, translated into English by Sorraya Sullivan, writes, "women, whether veiled or not, at home or in exile, are writing more than ever before. They are telling their stories, describing their reality, articulating the previously unarticulated. They are reappraising traditional space, literary or otherwise, and are renegotiating old sanctions and sanctuaries"(14). The passionate voice of Scheherazade, the prototypical storyteller, has indeed established itself as a contemporary literary force. The women in post-revolutionary Iran write because they feel they have to. In an interview with a Persian literary magazine, Parsipur comments on the "course of events" that pushes her to embrace this "historical imperative."

If twenty years ago, you would have asked me why I write, I would have probably answered, I write because I want to be famous; I have something to say; or I protest without even knowing why. Today, however . . . I can say I write because the course of events has suddenly pushed my generation into the crosscurrent of events. It seems as if writing now is a historical imperative. (1988, 7)

The publication of *Touba and the Meaning of Night* in 1989 won Shahrnush Parsipur instant fame. The novel was immediately celebrated as a literary landmark, and was a popular success as well, reprinted again and again. Many critics commented on the novel's setting, language, and narrative techniques. Many more—critics and readers alike—were enthralled by its protagonist, Touba, a vividly drawn and astonishingly complex woman. She is a woman deeply rooted in tradition, immersed in mysticism, absorbed by Eastern philosophy, and yet fascinated by modern Western ideas and trends; a woman with a penetrating lucidity that permits her to see the "reality" of things beyond formalism; a clairvoyant women who foresees the course of future events and communicates with the dead; a twice-married woman with an ability for empathy and a capacity for rage who does not hesitate to initiate divorce; a woman who ably supports her children and knows how to act on her own; a woman of brave judgments in response to life in all its dimensions, who could bury two corpses beneath a pomegranate tree in her house; a woman in pursuit of the age-old dream of many. Touba amazed, bewildered, and captured the nation's literary imagination.

Touba lives a long life and has a long tale to tell. The fantastic tale of her life is far from the usual fragmented, episodic, and repetitive tale of a domestic and personal.life In contrast to many fictional characters, somehow distant from perceiving their lives in terms of an ultimate goal, Touba desires to look back, to see her life as an organic whole, and to scrutinize her life in search of its meaning. Her obsessive engagement with a lifelong intellectual dream leads her to less traveled roads, and creates, in turn, a unifying linear structure in the narrative of her life. The essence of her quest and of her often conflicted personal struggle—is both mystical and worldly, religious and political, spiritual and intellectual. In this sense her deeply personal story reveals also the history of a society in the throes of modernity, with the status of women as a focal point and a touchstone.

Although Parsipur tells the story of Touba's life as a third-person omniscient narrator, the words and thoughts of various characters are almost invariably perceived from Touba's perspective. The pensive tone of Parsipur's voice is an original and refreshing addition to the expanding body of contemporary Persian fiction.

Refreshing, also is the novel's creative use of magical realism, colored by a distinctly mystical tone. "Magical realism, which exploits the often grotesque juxtaposition of the magic and the real with implied irony or even downright black humor, seemed to be the most fitting mode of expression for the incredible political 'realities' of the post-revolutionary Iran" (Yavari, 588). To reveal the mysterious elements hidden in the coexistence of two contradictory levels of reality, many novelists, notable among them Moniru Ravanipur (1954–) and Goli Taraghi (1939–), chose to weave fantastic elements into their tales and to create connections between seemingly unrelated episodes and events. As Kamran Talattof notes, these writers "found magical realism to be an accommodating genre that could convey realities that otherwise evaded expression within any satisfactory realm of rationality. Thus their texts combine realism and irrationalities resulting in a fantastic but believable portrayal of the agony of women's lives in their culture" (156).

The blend of the magical and the real in literature, as Franco Moretti posits in his description of "literature as a kind of ecosystem," is not "as much a poetics as it is a state of affairs in some parts of the world, where the seemingly fantastic is in fact a plausible representation of the daily events, and we are in daily contact with something that might be called marvelous reality." This is a world, as he further notes, "into which fiction had spread and contaminated practically everything: history, religion, poetry, science, art, speeches, journalism, and the daily habits of people. A world, in short, in which the extraordinary, the monstrous, the miracle . . . still occupies the centre of the picture" (235).

Interestingly, the *One Thousand and One Nights* and other Persian folk tales, in which flying carpets roam the skies, whales grow as large as inhabitable islands, and birds converse in many languages, are often acknowledged by critics and by novelists, including Gabriel Garcia Marquez, Jorge Luis Borges, and Italo Calvino, as the forbearers of magical realism—or rather, "marvelous reality," as the original Spanish signifies. Crossing the borders between "magic" and "real," and blending the natural environment with supernatural events, have allowed the composers of these narratives to highlight the magical wonders of Persian "reality" throughout the centuries.

In Moniru Ravanipur's *The Drowned* (1989) for example, the citizens of Jofreha, a remote village near the Persian Gulf, interact with the inhabitants of the sea through an intuitive, nonverbal mode of communication. They fully believe that the drowned continue an existence in the depth of the sea, and are repairing their vessels to return to the earth, to the realm of the living. The drowned, or submarinians, "are believed to inhabit the sea with the sea sprites and mermaids. The sprites and mermaids periodically come ashore to seek refuge from the evil spirit. To do so they rely upon the women of Jofreh who lend them their bodies and themselves undergo metamorphosis. In exchange women of Jofreh become initiated into the submarinian myths which they transmit to each other" (Rahimieh, 64).

In Parsipur's novels and short stories women grow into trees, hidden doors open and display ancient vistas, spirits cohabit houses, and some characters, archetypal in essence, live as long as several centuries and converse in many languages. In her *Women Without Men*, a novella of several distinct, and yet interrelated stories, a woman and her husband "sit on a lily together. The lily wraps them in its petals. They become smoke and rise into the sky" (131). The readers of Parsipur's fiction, much like the readers of *One Thousand and One Nights* who are accustomed to mixtures of fantasy and reality, do not hesitate to accept the simultaneous presence of the supernatural and natural events in her stories. This approach, in turn, allows for a juxtaposition of different discourses. In this sense, the magical realism of Parsipur's novels and short stories manifests itself as more than a stylistic device to lure the readers. By shuttling back and forth between past and present, between real and magic, by refusing to give either the magic or the real the upper hand, her

technique questions and subverts traditional oppositions and hierar-
chies and challenges to dissolve them.

Parsipur's literary career began before the 1979 Revolution. Her
first novel, *Shab va zemestan-e boland* (The Dog and the Long Winter), was published in 1974, when she was twenty-eight. In 1976;
while in France, she wrote her second novel, *Majera-ha-ye kuchak va
sadeh-ye ruh-e derakht* (The Small and Simple Adventures of the Tree
Spirit). In 1979, at the height of the Islamic Revolution, circumstances forced Parsipur to return to Iran, where she was jailed for
four years and seven months—a long period filled with horror and
despair, as she remembers it several year later in her article *The Executions*, published in *This Prison Where I Live: The Pen Anthology of
Imprisoned Writers*, edited by Siobhan Dowd. "There were more
than three hundred and fifty people crammed in our cells," she
writes. "Summary trials and mass executions had become routine. . .
. I was tired and disheartened. I felt the weight of all the corpses on
my shoulder" (Dowd, 31). In 1988, soon after her release, she published *Touba and the Meaning of Night* and related the story of the
days when "men, women, old, and young come and say that they
have buried a corpse under a tree, in a basement, or in a wasteland,"
(311) to the tale of corpses buried underneath a pomegranate tree in
Touba's house.

The novel delicately interweaves the highly hierarchical and
male-dominated Persian society of its times into the notion of the
sky as the husband of the earth, as maintained by Hajji Adib,
Touba's father. The novel identifies his fantasies of possessing the
passive earth in his protective embrace with the situation of women
in the end of nineteenth century Iran, when sharply drawn boundaries between private and public spheres were distinctly mirrored by
the strong solid walls that surround all houses. In *fin-de-siècle* Iran,
not only is the earth square, flat, and confined within strong walls,
but everything else, too, dwells within a wall-bound domain—above
all the women, who seem to be innately incapable of thinking.

Time and history are against walls, however. The idea of Earth as
a rotating planet penetrates through the solid walls and presents an
intellectual dilemma. For Touba's father—and, by implication, for

many like him as time goes on—envisioning the Earth as a rotating sphere represents the kind of intellectual progress that also drives men to envision women as thinking beings. And in this splendid historical moment, the destiny of Touba, and that of her female contemporaries, changes forever. This moment is immediately captured and spontaneously pronounced by Touba's father: "Unfortunately they think. Neither like the ants, nor like the minute parts of a tree, nor like the particles of the dust, but more or less as I do" (14). He is also the first to incorporate the magic of this modern notion into the realities of his traditional mind, and decides to teach his daughter all he knows. They start with the alphabet and the Qur'an and proceed to Persian literary texts. The first sentence that the girl learns remains in her memory forever: "Touba is a tree in paradise" (14). Touba follows her father as he traverses the political and intellectual landscape of the time. She learns, for instance, that "England is only a small island at the end of the world and that the English have blond hair like her but smell bad. So do the Russians. But God has created the Prussians with a good smell. The French had neither a bad smell nor a good smell" (14–15). The United States of America is still too distant to appear as an intruding "other" in Hajji's mind, and by extension, is not yet associated with a particular smell in his politically charged system of odors.

The end of the world of a sedentary Earth and non-thinking women signals the rise of another world, launched by a host of conceptual oppositions: old vs. new, traditional vs. modern, East vs. West. Parsipur employs magical imagery to bring a denser texture to these binary divisions, the tension of which keeps the history of the country and the fate of Touba's house in suspense. Touba's house, on the one hand, resembles the four-walled space that was once equated with sedentary Earth. On the other hand, like the country it represents, it undergoes a turbulent history, traversed continually by different people and their stories, by ideas and trends that originate beyond its all-enclosing walls. The traditional mix of magic and real in Persian literature acquires a modern twist in *Touba and the Meaning of Night*. The novel transposes magic, usually associated with the past and supernatural powers, to the present real world, thus uncovering the present's fantastic realities. The real magic of the novel, mysteriously empowered to penetrate a small house protected by thick, high walls, is new ideas. These are fantastic phenomena, brought on flying carpets to Persia from faraway lands. Magically woven into politics and ideologies, these are elusive enough to leave some characters with a kind of vertigo, and Touba with a fear that walls and lives will crack asunder at any moment.

Equally important is the treatment of time and space in the novel, which signifies the progression and transformation of another theme in Persian literature. In classical Persian literature, time is usually boundless and space extends far beyond frontiers. Parsipur, however, covering a time span of more than a century in the novel, shrinks the space to a small house. The house is, nevertheless, as large as the country. Time in the novel is simultaneously bound and boundless, both linear and cyclical. On the one hand, readers may follow Iranian history chronologically through the various stages of Touba's life. On the other hand, however, history is depicted as almost obsessively circular. She skillfully employs these two notions of time, to make manifest the archetypal essence of such characters, as Prince Gil' and his wife, Layla, who represents his unconscious female self. By clothing Layla in archetypal imagery, Parsipur sheds light on the dark landscape of the feminine sphere of Persian culture, offering new venues for political and cultural liberation. Layla's connection to the realm of the underworld surfaces in the final pages of the novel and the last moments of Touba's life. She illuminates Touba's passage through the Land of Darkness and the Spring of Life, which sparkles under a blaze of light. She leads her to the realm of wisdom, and is her guide in approaching her legendary namesake tree. Abbas Milani, in *Lost Wisdom: Rethinking Modernity in Iran*, describes the significance of Touba's quest:

> The leitmotif of Parsipur's fiction is the battle of self-assertive and free souls, usually women, against the conformist ethos of their time. Touba, once a tree in Paradise where the mythical bird Simorgh liked to perch, and now the indomitable heroine of an epic tale, sets out to find the meaning of the

night; the narrative of her search becomes the stuff of Parsipur's most famous novel, *Touba and the Meaning of Night*. (141)

Touba's quest, premised on the belief that humankind is innately capable of experiencing an inner self, is rarely featured in modern Iranian works of poetry or fiction, although abundant in classical Persian literature. Stretching as far back as the pre-Islamic history of Iran, the dualism of light and darkness attracted the Persian literary imagination.[6] Persian mystic poets and philosophers, as articulate interpreters of the journey toward inner spiritual harmony, have ventured through the depths of their own hearts of darkness and reemerged transformed, reborn, and illuminated by the light of wisdom. For centuries, they have spoken of the journey as a terrifying and painful voyage of contemplative solitude, borne with the promise of achieving spiritual inner wholeness and undifferentiated unification with the divine. A quintessential example of the genre is *The Conference of the Birds* by Farid al-Din Attar (ca. 1145–1221), philosopher, hagiographer, poet, and one of the most articulate advocates of Sufism in Iran. Attar's works reflect the evolution of the Islamic tradition of Sufism in its experiental, speculative, practical, and didactic expressions.[7]

Persian literature is replete with narratives of interconnected stories whose structures and content, very much like magical realist narratives, defy the conventions of time and space. Within the mystical canon, *Touba and the Meaning of Night* has borrowed much of its mystic flavor from the parables of Shahab al-Din Yahya Sohrevardi, the twelfth-century reviver of the theosophy of ancient Persia in Islamic Iran and the founder of Illuminationist philosophy. (He was put to death for his beliefs by the ruling dynasty of the time.) Sohrevardi was one of the first Persian philosophers to utilize the Platonic metaphor of light and vision. He also elaborated on an old tradition, rooted in Plato's idea of sudden inspiration: Sohrevardi contended that certain types of knowledge are immediately knowable, signifying a special intuitive mode of cognition. The legacy of Sohrevardi as an Iranian visionary executed by an oppressive and literalist establishment strikes a particularly sympathetic chord with contemporary Iranian intellectuals.[8]

Parsipur is as much indebted to Iran's tradition of mystic story telling as she is to the modern narratological techniques of magical realism. Her portrayal of Touba as a modern mystic traveler fills her narrative with moments of deep, intense, intuitive perception, to the extent that words like epiphany, illumination, or visionary, so central to the works of novelists such as Proust and Joyce, could as easily describe her novel. Visionary moments are a recurrent motif in the last pages of the narrative and the final stages of Touba's journey through darkness. Touba is left alone with the pomegranate tree in a once densely populated but now abandoned house. Beneath the tree she has buried two corpses, the slain body of a young girl, Setareh, raped by a soldier and murdered by her uncle; and the bullet-stricken body of Maryam, a political activist during the 1979 revolution. Filled with magically guarded secrets, the house resembles a graveyard, an image not far removed from the cruel realities of killing and moral amnesia that have swept Iran.

The line between past and present, dream and reality grows progressively blurred as Touba approaches her final days. Every bit of her capacity for disillusionment is exhausted, to such an extent that she no longer distinguishes hours from years, and does not know where and how to locate the boundaries of reality. She walks and thinks, as she has done for nearly a hundred years. Wandering throughout her life between the walled space of her house and a desire to traverse unbound spaces, she finds herself enclosed in a metaphysical solitude. Summing up the remembrance of things past, she realizes that she has spent her entire life in a pendulum swing between fascination and disenchantment, doubt and revelation, a yearning for the light of wisdom and a vision of herself as chained to the house.

The house was about to tumble down and she—Touba— would like to finally understand the truth and be at peace. What was the truth? Why must she care for the house? Why can't she follow her youth's desire to go after truth in the fields and mountains? Why [has she felt] forced to stay within a four-walled place? How can Touba understand the truth? (310–311)

Pacing back and forth inside the house and thinking, Touba is suddenly taken aback by the ground by the smiling mouths of numerous cracked pomegranates, sparkling in the sunshine. The pomegranate tree, as old and hollow as Touba, is yet bearing fruit. Touba immediately recognizes that the tree a graphic symbol mirroring the various stages of her spiritual quest, has borne the fruit of truth, formerly hidden in darkness, a long-forgotten reality that had existed beneath all surfaces, a truth that has always been before her, yet unnoticed by her. Touba recognizes an inner truth that becomes increasingly meaningful as exterior things, events, and relationships diminish in importance. Touba recognizes that the tree that she has guarded for so many years is pronouncing a secret, is pointing to the truth. Touba goes to the street and shares her pomegranates with people. And when she is asked, "Where is your house?" she replies, "No house. There is no returning now. I must tell the truth."

Houra Yavari
Center for Iranian Studies
Columbia University
New York City
January 2006

NOTES

1. The emergence and development of a nostalgic image of an idealized pre-Islamic Persia was a part of that process, and assumed a role radically different from earlier eras. Iran's glorified past—the illusory nature of which was to be revealed only later—had colonized the present of the period, and subsequently developed a quasi-religious status— one that carried with it the promise of redemption. In line with the mostly philologically based Orientalist

enterprises of the eighteenth and nineteenth centuries, the intellectual elites of the period were engaged in a discourse of origins and centers that gradually developed into a privileged topos in the Persian imaginary, a shimmering fantasy in the far horizon. Like all similar tales, it made use of rhetorical tropes and was determined by principles of exclusion. The pre-Islamic history of Iran, at the expense of its Islamic history, thus shaped out as the period's idealized "other," a glorified and seductive heterotopia in a virtual past that stood in opposition to a fragmented present.

2. Despite all social and political difficulties, this period is considered by some critics as the heyday of modem Persian narrative fiction. Works of form-conscious American novelists, such as Ernest Hemingway, John Steinbeck, and William Faulkner, were translated into Persian and much admired. French writers, especially Albert Camus and Jean Paul Sartre, were also influential, particularly as both wrote on the relationship between politics, philosophy, and literature, although from differing stances.

3. The Qajar era appears as a leitmotif in many novels of the period. For example, in Amir Hasan Cheheltan's (1956–) *Talar-e Aiyneh* (The Hall of Mirrors, 1991) the history of the Constitutional movement is narrated from a female perspective in five sections. Reza Jula'i (1950–) has also narrated the horrors of Iran's two disastrous wars with Russia in his novel *Shab-e Zolmani-e Yalda va Hadis-e Dordkeshan* (The Longest Night of the Year and the Tale of the Tippler, 1990). The same period furnishes the historical background to *Khaneh-ye Edrisi-ha* (The House of the Edrisis, 1992) by Ghazaleh Alizadeh (1948–1995). Immediate contemporary history, in place of the distant pasts, has been treated by many novelists of the period. Special mention should be made of Simin Daneshvar's autobiographical novel, *Jazira-ye Sargardani* (The Island of Bewilderment, 1992), which depicts the heady days before the Islamic Revolution of 1979. By creating a cast of politically confused and failure-bound characters, the novel takes a critical stand toward underpinning ideologies of the revolution.

4. The first group of Persian writers in exile, most of them former political activists, robbed of their identity and habitual environment and ill-prepared for what was to come, exclude the host country from their writings. Instead, their narratives are haunted by the revolution and transpire in the homeland. They are usually either direct autobiographical accounts or draw on the writer's personal experiences—including, more often than not, prison, torture, and war. With the slow process of adaptation, the haunting image of revolution, although never absent, is gradually relegated to the background. Memoir-like narratives of a troubled past are replaced by narratives directed to the less visible aspects of life in exile, and set against the backdrop of the host country rather than the homeland. The polar opposites of home and exile give way to the polarity of reception and rejection by the host country, and the sense of

exile is internalized. Foreign words seep into Persian narratives, and bilingual texts are produced. Persian fiction abroad has also witnessed an unprecedented surge in the number of women writers. Differing widely in their tone, content, narrative strategy, and approach to the revolution and host countries, their fictional works nevertheless share significant features. A gradual and occasionally painful move from a sheltered introspective life to one of actions and decisions features prominently in most of these narratives. The female characters of these works are highly involved in women's issues and strive to unravel the nuances of the female psyche and forge bonds with each other. The male characters are presented in contrast as emotionally barren and condemned to dysfunctional relationships.

5. As is the case with the Persian literature in exile, the first post revolutionary Persian fictions are written by the already established writers, like Esma'il Fasih (1934–), Mahmud Dowlatabadi (1940–), Houshang Golshiri (1936–2000), Jamal Mirsadeghi (1933–), Javad Mojabi (1939–), and Ja'far Modaees Sadeqi (1954–). Writers like Mohsen Makhmalbaf (1957–), Abbas Ma'rufi (1957–), Shahryar Mandanipur (1956–), and many women writers, notable among them Zoya Pirzad (1953–), Tahereh Alavi (1959–), Nahid Tabatabai (1958–), Fereshteh Molavi (1953–), Farkhondeh Aghai (1956–), and Fereshteh Sari (1955–), just to mention a few, started their literary careers chiefly after the revolution. It is interesting to note that some of the writers from both categories joined the ranks of the revolution in its very early stages. Others, however, either gradually turned against the revolution or attempted to steer clear of the ensuing debates. Some went abroad, and wrote novels and short stories colored by sentiments of exile and separation.

6. The phenomenology of darkness, as well as the extensively developed renditions of its nature and/or landscape abounds in mystical poems, tales of spiritual romance, and works of philosophy. The lore of darkness as an unknown and undecipherable vastness, and the mystical dimensions of the "Land of Darkness" have provided Persian poets and storytellers with an arsenal of archetypes. Initiation myths are embedded within the voyage through the unexplored vastness of the darkness, as dynamics between light and darkness became allegories for the conflict between the individual and his self. *The Spring of Life*, the legendary source of wisdom and immortality, and other variants of the light of wisdom lay hidden beneath its surface. It is inextricably bound with the idea of redemption and is rendered as an emblem of inner essences.

7. *The Conference of the Birds* has a frame story that encompasses the journey of birds from their terrestrial condition to their final absorption into Simorq, the legendary mystic king-bird, whose nest lies beyond Qaf, a mountain range outside the known and visible world. The birds are endowed with human characteristics and are led by a hoopoe bird.

The hoopoe, Solomon's messenger in the Qur'an, is Attar's allegory for a Sufi sheikh, or master, whose mision of leading the initiates along their path is entrusted to Geda Alishah in Parsipur's novel. Aware of the journey as perilous and arduous by nature, Geda Alishah repeatedly reminds Touba that the Truth is still too far away, and Touba, as a seeker of light, must be prepared to dedicate her entire life to the journey, the end of which is all but certain. Dick Davis, whose translation of *The Conference of the Birds* into English has won Attar an international readership, contends in his introduction to the book that Attar's style of interweaving innumerous tales and anecdotes into a frame story—a technique also employed by Parsipur—is reminiscent of some European medieval texts.

> Readers acquainted with medieval European literature will not find Attar's method unfamiliar; parallels such as *The Owl and the Nightingale* and Chaucer's *Parliament of Fowls* immediately suggest themselves . . . Like Chaucer's Canterbury Tales, it is a group of stories bound together by the convention of a pilgrimage, and as in Chaucer's work the convention allows the author to present a panorama of contemporary society. (Attar, 21)

8. Parsipur's debt to Sohrevardi's *Red Logos* is evidenced in the title of another one of her novels, *Blue Logos*, published in 1979. Sohrevardi's parable is a visionary treatise on spiritual initiation, and arguably, one of the most beautiful and intricate connections between the darkness of the mystic's quest and the light that lies at its end—or between *Touba and the Meaning of Night*. Every tale begins with the visionary in the presence of a supernatural figure of great beauty, from whom the visionary proceeds to inquire about his origins and whereabouts. The tales exemplify the experience of enlightenment as the lived history of the visionary who aspires to return home. According to Sohrevardi, the nest of Simorq sits atop the Touba tree. Night falls and darkness engulfs when Simorq leaves the tree and spreads its enormous wings across the world. In the parable, "the archangel of both knowledge and revelation," as Henry Corbin contends, "is represented in red, a symbolism connected to the mixture of night and day found in the evening. The archangel instructs its disciples about the difficulties they will have in ascending the cosmic, or rather the psycho-cosmic, mountain of Qaf . . . the mountain separating them from the spiritual world" (Corbin, 199).

WORKS CITED

Corbin, Henry. "AQL-e SORK," in *Encyclopaedia Iranica*, vol. II, edited by Ehsan Yarshater. New York and London: Routledge & Kegan Paul, 1987.

Davis, Dick. Introduction to *The Conference of the Birds by Farid un Din Attar*, translated by Afkham Darbandi and Dick Davis. London and New York: Penguin Classics, 1984.

Milani, Abbas. *Lost Wisdom: Rethinking Modernity in Iran*. Washington D.C.: Mage Publishers, 2004.

Milani, Farzaneh. Introduction to *Stories by the Iranian Women since the Revolution*. Trans. Sorraya Sullivan. Austin: Modern Middle East Literatures in Translation Series, 1991.

Moretti, Franco. *Modern Epic: the World System from Goethe to García Marquez*. London and New York: Verso, 1995.

Mozaffari, Nahid. Introduction to *Strange Times My Dear: The Pen Anthology of Contemporary Iranian Literature*, edited by Nahid Mozaffari. New York: Arcade Publishing, 2005.

Parsipur, Shahrnush. "Why Do You Write" in *Donya-e Sokhan* 17 (March 1988).

———. *Women Without Men*, translated by Kamran Talattof and Jocelyn Sharlet. New York: Feminist Press at CUNY, 1998.

———. "The Executions," in *This Prison Where I Live: The Pen Anthology of Imprisoned Writers*, edited by Siobhan Dowd. London and New York: Cassell, 1996.

Rahimieh, Nasrin. "Magical Realism in Moniru Ravanipur's *Ahl-e Gharq*," *Iranian Studies* 23:1–4 (1990): 61–75.

Talattof, Kamran. *The Politics of Writing in Iran: A History of Modern Persian Literature*. Syracuse and London: Syracuse University Press, 2000.

Yavari, Houra. "FICTION, MODERN," in *Encyclopaedia Iranica*, vol. IX, edited by Ehsan Yarshater. New York: Bibliotheca Persica, 1999.

Biography of Shahrnush Parsipur

PERSIS M. KARIM

The daughter of an attorney in the Justice Ministry, Shahrnush Parisipur was born in Tehran, Iran, in 1946. At an early age, Parsipur showed an interest in literature, and her liberal-minded parents encouraged her education and supported her interest in writing. At the age of eleven or twelve she read a translation of Fyodor Dostoyevsky's *The Insulted and Injured* and was deeply moved by the experience. She read every novel by Dostoyevsky and has said that each one of them influenced her: "Dostoyevsky is a deeply psychological writer and he understands something about the spiritual nature of human beings." As she grew into her teen years, Parsipur voraciously read literature from Russia and Europe. She was particularly taken with Charles Dickens and read *Great Expectations* a total of thirty times. Because she wrote well and received praise for her school compositions, Parsipur felt destined for a career in writing. Although there existed few models for her to emulate in Iran (very few Iranian women were actively writing and even fewer were being published), Parsipur enthusiastically pursued her love of writing. At

Originally published in Persis M. Karim's "Afterword" to *Women Without Men* by Shahrnush Parsipur, translated by Kamran Talattof and Jocelyn Sharlet (New York: Feminist Press, 2004). Reprinted by permission of the author and the publisher. All rights reserved.

the age of sixteen she published her first short story. As she developed her craft, Parsipur began to search for role models. Rather than drawing inspiration from a small and lesser-known group of women writers, Parsipur found her greatest inspiration in the modernist Iranian writer Sadeq Hedayat (1903–1951), author of the internationally acclaimed *The Blind Owl*, as well as a number of European and American writers including Charles Dickens, Franz Kafka, Mark Twain, and Ernest Hemingway.

After graduating from high school, Parsipur entered the University of Tehran among the first women to be admitted. Because the disciplinary choices available to women were limited (they were obligated to take courses in the evening), Parsipur decided to pursue her bachelor's degree in sociology because it combined her interests in social and historical issues and enabled her to continue to write. During her university years, Parsipur published several short stories including *Tupak-i qermez* (The little red ball) and *Garma dar sal-i sefr* (Heat in the year zero). A number of her short stories were published in popular Iranian literary journals, including the well-known journal *Jong-e Esfahan*. Her novella *Tajrubah'ha-yi azad* (Trial offers, 1970) was followed by her first novel, *Sag va zimistan-i buland* (The dog and the long winter, 1974). A collection of short stories called *Avizah'ha-yi bulur* (Crystal pendants) was published in 1977.

It was during her studies at the University of Tehran that Parsipur became fascinated with Chinese philosophy. After reading a book on Chinese astrology, Parsipur was introduced by an American friend to a professor at the Royal Institute of Philosophy who taught a course on *I Ching*. Sensing Parsipur's growing passion for Chinese philosophy, Professor Izutsu (originally from Japan) encouraged her to study Chinese to gain direct access to Chinese writing. While attending university, she also worked as a producer for Iranian National Television and Radio, a position from which she resigned in 1974 in protest of the execution of two poets by the shah's regime. Shortly thereafter, she was arrested by the shah's intelligence agency, SAVAK, and imprisoned for a short period. In 1976, she traveled to France to attend the Sorbonne, where she continued her studies of Chinese language and culture. During her four-year stay in Paris she completed her second book, *Majaraha-yi sadah va kuchak-i ruh-i dirakht* (The simple and small adventure adventures of the tree spirit), an erotic novel that continues the story of a character in *The Dog and the Long Winter*. The novel was published by an Iranian publisher in Sweden twenty years after she wrote it.

During the tumult of the Iranian Revolution, Parsipur interrupted her studies and decided to return to Iran. She was very interested in the role women had played in the revolution and in seeing the outcome of this popular movement against the former shah. But shortly after her return from Paris in 1980, she found herself arrested and imprisoned without ever having any formal charges made against her. Her arrest took place in 1981, a time when the new government was cracking down and specifically in response to the Mojahedin, an organization that had declared its opposition to the new regime. Parsipur describes her arrest and the arrest of her mother and brothers as the result of her brother's attempt to create an archive of political publications. Parsipur was initially held at Evin prison and then later transferred to Qazalhassar. She spent a total of four years, seven months, and seven days in prison:

> My prison term was particularly lengthy because I protested the cruelty that was inflicted on me and my fellow prisoners. They wanted to destroy the humanity of the prisoners, and they sought to do this with cruel punishment and by forcing a kind of re-education on us that was intended to break our spirits.

While Parsipur was not affiliated with any political group, she, like many of the thousands of women who were arrested and detained during this period, was made an example of due to her outspokenness and apparently nonconformist behavior. In particular, Parsipur was beaten or ostracized at times for improper *hejab*, for not praying, and for speaking her mind. In her *Khatirat-i zandan* (Prison memoirs, 1996), she recounts one incident where she was banned from speaking with anyone except her mother for having voiced concern about environmental destruction resulting from the ongo-

ing war with Iraq. Many of Parsipur's fellow inmates were a generation younger than she, and a majority of them were students. Parsipur had little opportunity to write and read in prison: "What
books we did have access to were religious books. It was only in my
last year of imprisonment that I was allowed to read anything other
than religious material."

Once Parsipur was released from prison in 1986, she faced the
problem of having no money and little chance of finding work in
the repressive climate of the mid-1980s. "I wanted to get back to
writing, and to make some money. I decided to open a bookshop,
but had to close it after six months because the Revolutionary
Guards were coming around and wanting to know who was visiting
the store," said Parsipur. Facing difficult economic circumstances,
Parsipur found piecemeal work translating books and architectural
journal articles, as well as writing an occasional book review for literary journals.

By 1989, Parsipur had found a publisher for *Tuba va ma'na-yi
shab* (Touba and the meaning of night). The novel was published to
widespread acclaim and became a national best seller. *Touba* narrates
the story of a young girl who comes of age and matures over a period
of several decades in Iran's tumultuous nineteenth- and twentieth-
century history. Like the historical figure Tahereh Qorratol'Ayn—a
woman who was executed in 1852 at the age of thirty-six for presum-
ably being a heretic and a promoter of the Babi faith—the fictional
Touba stands our because she is taught to read and write by her own
father. After her father's death, Touba assumes the responsibility of
the household, since she is the only literate member of the family. At
the age of fourteen, she proposes marriage to her father's fifty-two-
year old uncle, who has assumed the household's financial responsibilities. Her husband does not treat her respectfully and is threatened
by Touba's intelligence, beauty, and outspokenness (Nooriala 141).
The real life of Tahereh Qorratol'Ayn is surrounded by mystery and
silence, but one of the important reasons that Parsipur has claimed
her in *Touba* is because she was literate, educated, and outspoken,
"the first challenge to an age-old, male-centered, male-dominated
belief system" (Milani 98). The use of the historical figure Tahereh in

this novel contributed in part to its controversial reception. While Tahereh was considered a heretic for both her religious beliefs and for her ability to speak and write eloquently on topics and issues that were the exclusive domain of men, Parsipur portrays Touba as a woman coming to consciousness about her own oppression as a woman. The novel also portrays Touba as venturing into "orthodox religion, Sufism, nationalism, and other forms of thought only to find them futile" (Talattof 144). Even while the novel was very popular, both the depiction of Touba as a writer/critic of male discourse and her exploration into the world of religion would not sit comfortably with the Islamic Republic and would, by Parsipur's own admission, draw negative attention to the author.

In addition to *Touba's* content, Parsipur's writing style in this novel was a departure from previous prerevolutionary writing, which either deployed a straightforward social-realist style or an allegorical and often political message. Two of the main characters come from ancient times to the present, and Parsipur uses the fantastic as well as a shifting sense of narrative time. In *Women Without Men*, some of the characters of the novel die and return to life, disappear, or transform into other essences—trees, wind, smoke. While some readers and critics connect Parsipur's writing to the magical-realist tradition, Parsipur suggests that this literary phenomenon is homegrown and predates authors like Gabriel García Marquez and Isabel Allende, who have made it popular in the Latin American context. "This type of writing is not borrowed from Latin America, but is something that originates in this part of the world. If you just read *The Thousand and One Nights*, you'll see where I and other authors derive inspiration for the use of the fantastic, the unexplainable," said Parsipur. In addition to this fantastic, nonlinear narrative style that has become her trademark, Parsipur's work has consistently shown a concern with women's oppression and the limitations placed on women by patriarchal society. While Parsipur expresses some discomfort with being labeled a feminist writer, it is hard to miss a certain feminist sensibility in her writing that questions and challenges male privilege and the institutions and ideologies that reinforce it.

Despite *Touba*'s controversial depiction of women, Parsipur was able to get it published. *Women Without Men*, however, was far more radical. After the 1989 publication of *Touba* brought her some notoriety, she finally found a publisher willing to take a chance on her novella. Although the stories from *Women Without Men* were written mostly before the revolution (and several had been published as individual stories before the novella took its final form), it was while she was in Paris watching the revolution unfold that Parsipur found the thread that joined the five narratives together in the space of the garden in Karaj. *Women Without Men* proved to be far too radical in its critique of male patriarchy, and while it brought her success, it also prompted the government to arrest her two more times; on both occasions she was jailed for more than a month:

> Their chief goal was to intimidate me because they couldn't do much else. After the critical success of *Touba*, they didn't know what to do with me. So they harassed me, told me to desist from such writing and they attacked the man who published the book.

Mohammad Reza Aslani, the publisher and owner of Noghreh Publishing, was also arrested, and his publishing house was immediately closed down. The charge leveled against Parsipur was that she had written about virginity in the novella and had too forcefully broached a taboo subject. Apparently *Women Without Men* was also perceived as un-Islamic because of references to Western culture. One of the book's characters refers to *The Sound of Music* and *Gone With the Wind*; another character is compared to the actress Vivien Leigh. "After the publication of *Women Without Men*," said Parsipur, "all my books were banned and I immediately confronted the same difficult circumstances I faced after getting out of prison. I did not have the ability to make a living as a writer."

Ironically, Parispur's success and consequent condemnation in Iran allowed her to travel abroad and speak out about the difficulties of living in a repressive and censorial society. Parsipur's other publications include her novels *Aql-i abi* (Blue wisdom, 1994), *Shiva*

(1999), and *Bar bali-i bad neshastan* (Sitting on the wings of the wind, 2002). Parsipur has also published another collection of short stories, *Adab-i sarf-i chai dar huzur-i gorg* (Tea ceremony in the presence of wolfs, 1993). One of her novellas, *Tajrubah'ha-yi azad* (Trial offers) has been published in *Stories from Iran: A Chicago Anthology* (1992). In addition to her short stories and novels, Parsipur has written many articles and essays for literary journals published in Iran, the United States, and Europe.

In the early 1990s, Parsipur traveled to the United States, Canada, and Europe. After returning from a year abroad, however, Parsipur found life in Iran stressful and difficult. When she was invited back to the United States in 1994, she decided to stay and seek refugee status. She has been living in the San Francisco Bay Area since then.

WORKS CITED AND RECOMMENDED BIBLIOGRAPHY

Ahmed, Leila. *Women and Gender in Islam*. New Haven: Yale University Press, 1992.

Mernissi, Fatima. *Beyond the Veil*. Cambridge: Schenkman, 1975.

Milani, Farzaneh. *The Emerging Voices of Iranian Women Writers*. Syracuse: Syracuse University Press, 1992.

Nooriala, Partow. "Parsipur's *Touba and the Meaning of Night*: A Synopsis." In *Exiles and Explorers: Iranian Diaspora Literature Since 1980*. Ed. Ardavan Davaran. Special issue of *The Literary Review* 40:1 (fall 1996): 141–146.

Parsipur, Shahrnush. *Women Without Men*. Trans. Kamran Talattof and Jocelyn Sharlet. Syracuse: Syracuse University Press, 1998; New York: Feminist Press, 2004.

Talattof, Kamran. *The Politics of Writing in Iran: A History of Modern Persian Literature*. Syracuse: Syracuse University Press, 2000.

The Feminist Press at the City University of New York is a nonprofit literary and educational institution dedicated to publishing work by and about women. Our existence is grounded in the knowledge that women's writing has often been absent or underrepresented on bookstore and library shelves and in educational curricula—and that such absences contribute, in turn, to the exclusion of women from the literary canon, from the historical record, and from the public discourse.

The Feminist Press was founded in 1970. In its early decades, the Feminist Press launched the contemporary rediscovery of "lost" American women writers, and went on to diversify its list by publishing significant works by American women writers of color. More recently, the Press's publishing program has focused on international women writers, who remain far less likely to be translated than male writers, and on nonfiction works that explore issues affecting the lives of women around the world.

Founded in an activist spirit, the Feminist Press is currently undertaking initiatives that will bring its books and educational resources to underserved populations, including community colleges, public high schools and middle schools, literacy and ESL programs, and prison education programs. As we move forward into the twenty-first century, we continue to expand our work to respond to women's silences wherever they are found.

For a complete catalog of the Press's 250 books, please refer to our web site: www.feministpress.org.